Death of a False Physician

The second in the Hippolyta Napier series

by

Lexie Conyngham

First published in 2016 by The Kellas Cat Press, Aberdeen.

Copyright Alexandra Conyngham, 2016

ISBN: 978-1-910926-25-3

Cover illustration by Helen Braid at www.ellieillustrates.co.uk

DEDICATION

To my mother and my sister, on whom, I would emphasise, *no characters in this book are based!*

Thanks to Fiona and Rob at Deeside Water Company for showing me round the springs at Pannanich on a damp September day – I enjoyed my visit!

Dramatis Personae

Dr. Francis Gilead, a physician outstanding in his field
Mrs. Gilead, supportive consort
Peter, their son, a little less supportive

Mrs. Pumpton, a generous lady in need of support
Mr. Pumpton, her husband, when he can be seen

Mrs. Nickell, an adoring patient
Mr. Nickell, a less than adoring husband

Mrs. Dewar, an adored patient
Mr. Dewar, patiently adoring

Dr. Patrick Napier, who has proper qualifications and everything
Hippolyta Napier, his wife
Mrs. Fettes, his mother-in-law, visiting from Edinburgh
Mrs. Milton, his sister-in-law, also temporarily in Ballater
Wullie and Tam, new arrivals at the Napier house

The staff at Pannanich Wells Hotel:
Mr. Black, hotel keeper
Sim, Christy and Gelis

Mr. Durris, stalwart sheriff's officer

Sundry villagers and visitors to Ballater and Pannanich

Chapter One

Everything seemed beautifully calm.

The lilac was in serene bloom, the dense clumps of purple blossom sparkling in the sunny dew, gillyflowers glowed in borders. The first of the roses tumbled over the high garden walls, dripping petals on either side. The breeze was scented by them. Two white cats with serious faces stalked moths amongst the long grass – she hoped it was only moths – and at her feet the hens murmured appreciatively as they pecked the grain she had just strewn there. It was chilly enough to be fresh and bright enough to cheer, and the birds in the garden's trees sang incorrigibly above her. Yet she had a sense of impending dread across her shoulders.

The kitchen door was open and she could hear Mrs. Riach, the housekeeper, swearing at Ishbel, the maid, over the preparations for breakfast, but that was normal. She sighed, and stooped in to the henhouse door, feeling for and gathering the warm eggs into her little basket. The smell of dozing hens soothed her for a moment, but even its power could not last long.

She picked up the egg basket and stepped carefully up the wet granite path to the back of the house, to the little stone outhouse near the back wall of the house. The door was freshly painted, and she knocked on it. After a moment, she heard her husband's voice inside.

'Come in!'

She turned the handle, and pushed her way in, automatically blocking the doorway to any inquisitive cats or hens.

The little room was lit by a low window and a number of candles, strategically placed, and had been furnished with a well-scrubbed bench and shelves. The shelves were lined with some glass jars and wooden boxes, labelled in abbreviated Latin, and the bench was organised with presses, moulds, spoons, knives and tiny brass scales, all in their proper places. Thank goodness Patrick was tidy in his work, for he never was otherwise, she thought. She tucked her hands, still holding the eggbasket, into her skirts behind her back, training herself never to touch anything in here.

Patrick, tall and golden-haired, turned and gave her an anxious smile. The room was small enough that he had only to reach out to hold and kiss her.

'Good morning, my love!' he began. Then, 'Any news?'

'No, nothing yet, of course. Far too early.'

'Of course, of course.' He fiddled with a wooden spoon for a moment.

'What are you making this morning?' she asked.

'Oh, some powders for headaches, that is all. I like to have them made up and ready. I have to say,' he went on, growing more enthusiastic, 'that this bothy is a great addition for the practice. Being able to make up medicines quickly here, instead of waiting for supplies to come from Aberdeen, has improved treatments tremendously.'

'I suppose if Ballater had its own dispensary ...'

'It's nowhere near big enough. The nearest one is Aberdeen – unless you count any patent medicines that Mr. Strachan might choose to stock in his grocery.'

'And we don't talk about patent medicines in this house, do we, dear?' said Hippolyta, putting on the show of a submissive wife.

'No, no, no!' He shook an admonishing finger at her, and they both grinned.

'The Anti-Rheumatic Cordial Balm of Zura,' murmured Hippolyta. 'Dr. Solomon's Anti-Impetigines Drops ...Powell's Balm of Aniseed ...'

'Now, now!'

'Dr. Cullen's Highly Celebrated Abstergent Scarlet Pills ...'

'Naughty girl! Haven't you fed the hens yet?'

'I have,' she said, and brought the egg basket out from behind her back. 'See? Ten eggs today, clever ladies.'

'Then let us go and show our appreciation in the traditional way, and eat them.' He washed his hands in a basin of water, poured it outside the door, and wiped his hands very thoroughly dry on a towel. Then he shooed Hippolyta out, blew out the candles and locked the door carefully behind him, with a key attached to his watch chain. Hippolyta watched him, pleased at his caution. He may use them to heal people, but there were some unpleasant substances in that little shed for anyone less benevolent. She shivered, and then told herself off. Whatever she was expecting, it couldn't be that bad, could it? It would be fine.

The Royal Highlander coach was due to arrive at the inn by the river at one in the afternoon, the quicker coach on the route. It was usually prompt, and rarely early, but Hippolyta and Patrick were there waiting at half past twelve with the pony and its little trap. Hippolyta was wearing her best dark red walking dress, the sleeves each nearly as wide as the rest of her, and hoped that Edinburgh fashion had not changed dramatically in the time – almost a year! – she had been away. Patrick propped himself against the wall of the inn and chatted with several passersby, while Hippolyta absently kept the pony on a tight rein: its interest in passersby tended to be more to do with nipping.

She turned when the pony skipped a little in the shafts and gave a jerk of its head. A small white dog was playing recklessly about its hooves, more likely to suffer damage than inflict it, and she tried to call it out while at the same time glancing around to see to whom it might belong.

A few yards away was a man so striking she was surprised she had not noticed him before.

He was at least six feet tall, hatless, with hair so white it seemed to glisten like a cloud, overlong and tied at the nape of his neck with a black satin ribbon. His nose was aquiline, his skin fine, his lips full over very white teeth, and his eyes crystalline blue. His clothes were so exquisite he could have walked out of a fashion plate, and he stood as if showing them off to the best advantage, one shiningly slippered toe pointed out to the side, a dove-grey gloved hand caressing the silver knob of an ebony cane. He was handsome, no doubt, and yet Hippolyta instinctively glanced away. There was something about him that looked so good, she automatically did not trust it.

She leaned over to Patrick.

'Who's that man? Don't look at him!'

'What man? And how can I tell if you won't let me look at him? Oh – he's a bit of a picture, isn't he? I have no idea who he is.' Patrick watched discreetly for a moment, while Hippolyta busied herself pulling the little dog – a terrier of a more than usually determined disposition - out from under the trap without being kicked. 'He seems popular, though, doesn't he?'

'Does he?' She threw a quick look in the stranger's direction. It was true: she had not noticed, but around him were several people, two women of a certain age, a young man, and a thin girl with protruding eyes, all eagerly attending to his every word. Not that he seemed to speak much, she realised: there was a good deal of pausing with his eyes half-closed, while they all waited, breathless.

Then suddenly he glanced in their direction.

'Ah, my dog!'

'Yours? Good: I was afraid he would cause himself some damage amongst our pony's legs,' said Hippolyta, but he was already talking over her.

'Enchanting! This village improves by the moment. Dear lady,' he said, bending low and seizing Hippolyta's hand as she released the dog in his direction, 'allow me to introduce myself. My name is Francis Gilead, doctor of medicine. I am but newly arrived in this charming spa, to bring the very latest in medical science to the people of the Highlands and the many visitors who flock to the healing waters of Pannanich.'

'How do you do?' said Hippolyta, feeling her teeth clench. His very voice was oiled to perfection. 'May I present my husband, Dr. Patrick Napier? You may find, Dr. Gilead, that the very latest in medical science has arrived in the Highlands before you.'

Patrick managed to bow with a bland look, not committing himself to any rivalry. Hippolyta felt mildly ashamed of herself.

'Ah, a fellow professional!' Dr. Gilead exclaimed after only the least pause. 'No doubt you have heard of me.'

'Ahm, I'm not sure …' But again Dr. Gilead had no need of replies.

'I am resident for the summer at the Pannanich Wells Hotel, where I shall be available for any consultations you wish to bring me: no doubt there are some difficult cases here where you will be anxious for a second opinion. Now, ladies, if we wish to return in time for dinner, we must finish our business in the village. You must excuse me, Mrs. Napier, Dr. Napier.' He bowed like a dancer, and stalked off up the main street to the green, followed by the women, the young man, and at a rather more reserved distance, the small white terrier.

'My,' said Hippolyta.

'I haven't heard of him at all,' said Patrick. 'But I don't suppose that matters much to him.'

'I don't suppose so. Well, my dearest, I think you may retire: there is a doctor of medicine in Ballater now!'

'Hm.' Patrick looked more worried than Hippolyta had expected. 'I hope he doesn't steal my patients, you know.'

'I should need to be quite desperate for medical attention before I went anywhere near him,' said Hippolyta with emphasis.

'Yes, dear, but you're my wife: others might not be quite so loyal!' The pony turned and nipped his arm, and he laughed. 'See? Your wretched beast is making my case for me!'

'He's not a wretched beast!' Hippolyta stroked the pony's nose to console it for such harsh words. 'He's a dear old thing: he's just easily upset.'

'Did you know there are chicken feathers all over the cushions?' Patrick asked mildly.

'Oh! Oh, no! I brushed the whole trap out only yesterday! Here: hold this.' She handed the reins to a very reluctant Patrick, and hurried round to flap at the cushions. Chicken feathers flew up and mostly landed back on the same cushions, though others attached to her dress.

Just then, the Royal Highlander could at last be heard from some distance approaching Ballater along the flat road from the last turnpike. Not every vehicle had four heavy horses and a superstructure comprising quite so much luggage and quite so many people. Patrick and Hippolyta, she still brushing her dress, stood amongst the sudden business at the gateway to the inn yard, watching its approach, and surreptitiously gripping each other's hands in the depths of Hippolyta's wide skirts. The horses trotted on to the cobbled surface, slowed to a walk and guided by the coachman took a wide turn into the yard of the inn, while the pony tried to back the trap into the wall. All was activity: the horses were swiftly unharnessed and led off, the postilion jumped down

13

and opened the door, luggage was tossed from the top and back of the coach, and passengers squeezed out one by one, stretching stiff limbs and looking about them, straightening their backs and identifying their luggage and helping each other adjust cloaks and hats. Anyone who had started with the coach from Aberdeen had had a six hour journey, but the coachman and postilion were not wasting time lingering with them: they had an hour and three quarters before they set off back to the city again, and there was a hot meal waiting for them indoors.

Two women, as tall as Hippolyta, were amongst the first out, and were efficiently cutting their own trunks out from amongst the general heap with a series of short directions to the inn staff. Hippolyta risked leaving the pony for a moment – no local would approach it anyway – and hurried over with a wide grin to greet them.

'Mother! Galatea! We're here!'

The two women turned and watched her as she skipped amongst the other travellers, Patrick following her to direct the luggage. The younger had a close-eyed, headachey look, squinting at her. The older surveyed her, bonnet, walking dress, chicken feathers and all, with an analytical expression.

'Hippolyta. No babies yet, I see.'

Hippolyta's grin froze only for half a second.

'Not yet, no, Mother. How was your journey? We have a trap over here to take you to the house, if you do not wish to stretch your legs with the walk. It is only five minutes.'

'We will ride, thank you.'

'Galatea? How are you?'

'I shall walk, I think, Mother,' said Hippolyta's sister.

'The trap is just here. Don't go near the pony, though,' Hippolyta added quickly. She grabbed the reins just as the pony lunged for the boy bringing the trunks. He skipped out of the way from long habit: the pony was usually stabled at the inn and the boy knew it well. He loaded the trunks expertly around the trap, and Patrick handed his mother-in-law in to the seat, surreptitiously removing a last chicken feather as he did so.

'Are you quite comfortable, Mrs. Fettes?' he asked.

'Yes, Patrick, I thank you.' She did not look very comfortable: she sat with a doorpost-straight back, and now Hippolyta looked at her her face was a little washed-out. But six hours in a coach could do that to the strongest constitution. Hippolyta turned the trap in the street, and they set off.

'Don't you have a man to see to the pony?' Galatea asked sourly. Her headaches Hippolyta knew of old, and made allowances.

'We couldn't pay any man enough to see to this pony! Everyone is far too well acquainted with it,' said Hippolyta with a smile. 'But no: there is little need for a manservant here. We have a housekeeper and a maid: she is a general maid but she is learning the business of a lady's maid very quickly.'

'The simple life, then,' Galatea remarked.

'And a very pleasant one,' Hippolyta agreed.

She continued to chatter nervously, indicating a few things of interest. Galatea did not look around her much as they marched up the hill with the pony pacing behind. Patrick walked alongside Mrs. Fettes, who did at least take an interest in the village, noting, Hippolyta hoped, the fact that the houses had no middens in front of them as happened in other villages, that the cottages were slate-roofed, that the streets were laid out in a neat grid, that the green was well kept and even the ditches by the roadside were relatively clean, and that the great centrical parish church was a really very impressive building, even if none of them belonged to it. It was true that some of the fresh paint and new building was a result of the clearing up after the severe flood – the Muckle Spate, many were calling it – that had swept through the town from two parts of the River Dee last summer, caught in a low-lying loop of the river as they were, but the people, too, looked healthy and well cared-for, as well they might in the fresh Deeside air.

'That great rock is Craigendarroch,' she pointed it out to Galatea, who frowned up at the crag standing guard over the town. 'I've made several studies of it: there's always some new detail to see!'

'Oh, yes?' Galatea stared at it more intently, then looked away. 'It's all more modern than I expected.'

'Well, the village was mostly built by the old laird about thirty years ago, to give more accommodation for people visiting the spa. Did you know there was a spa? It's over the river – but of course you did. That's why Patrick is able to set up his practice here, for the number of visitors is extraordinary, and seems to grow all the time!'

'Yes, very good,' said Galatea distantly.

'Patrick makes some very good powders for headaches, by the way.'

'Does he? I have some with me from my own physician.'

'Well, should you run out at any time and need more … And here we are,' said Hippolyta with relief. 'This is our little cottage here.'

'Well,' said Galatea, surveying the granite face with its neat dormers and pretty front garden, 'it's convenient, I suppose.'

Hippolyta smiled. At least her sister had found something positive to say about her beloved house. The pony stopped abruptly beside her and Patrick handed Mrs. Fettes down. A boy they had hired for the purpose emerged from the lane and helped to carry the luggage indoors, the idea being that he would then be brave enough to take the pony and trap round to the back of the house to their summer shelter. Hippolyta told herself that she would check that in an hour or so: the boy did not look particularly confident, and that pony could sense weakness a mile off.

Indoors she was pleased to see Mrs. Riach in all her grey state appear to take her mother's cloak and bonnet, while Ishbel, at her smartest, whisked off with Galatea's spencer and bonnet and Hippolyta's own outdoor things. Hippolyta nodded to Mrs. Riach for tea, and ushered her relations into the parlour. She and Patrick exchanged a quick rise of the eyebrows behind their backs: all well so far.

But inside the parlour Mrs. Fettes had stopped abruptly.

'Hippolyta, there is a cat on your table.'

'Is there? Oh, Polar, you naughty cat: you know you're not allowed there!'

Polar, who knew no such thing, stretched outrageously across the pleasantly soft tablecover and looked astonished when Hippolyta picked her up and set her gently on the floor. She cast a quick glance around for any dead birds or mice that might have appeared in their absence, but saw none. The parlour was dusted and polished to within an inch of its interesting life. Mrs. Fettes, with a look at Polar that might have worked on anything but a cat, stepped past and seated herself on a sofa. Galatea selected an armchair at some distance from her mother. Hippolyta sat at the table and Patrick, after diplomatically escorting Polar to the door, sat beside her.

'And how was your journey? How was the voyage?'

'Very smooth,' said her mother, in tones of mild surprise. 'I remember you had some complaints about it, but we travelled direct by steam to Aberdeen and had a cabin to ourselves and no concerns. We stayed a night in Aberdeen at Dempster's, and of course the coach set off from there this morning. You could almost be in Haddingtonshire or somewhere much nearer Edinburgh: it was all very efficiently done.'

'I'm delighted to hear it, Mrs. Fettes,' said Patrick. 'It can be a very long journey, particularly in the winter.'

'I have no intention of making it in the winter,' said Mrs. Fettes.

'Well, I'm delighted you have come now. And how is Papa?' said Hippolyta quickly.

'Busy, as ever,' said Mrs. Fettes with satisfaction. As far as Hippolyta had ever been able to judge, for her mother being busy was as close as one could come to perfection on earth: her father, though, had not often shared this opinion.

'I'm sorry he could not accompany you,' she said truthfully.

'He – he sends his compliments to you both,' said her mother.

'And a letter?'

'No, no letter,' said her mother more smoothly. 'He said he would write imminently.'

'He must be very busy then.' Not to take the opportunity of a convenient and safe carrier was an odd thing indeed. Hippolyta eyed her mother as discreetly as she could. If it had been anyone else she would almost have said that the woman looked shifty. Could she be hiding something? Was her father really all right? A spasm of anxiety passed through her. She had not seen her father since her wedding, and missed him.

The tea arrived, and Hippolyta noted with satisfaction that Mrs. Riach had indeed done as instructed and made her nicest biscuits for a light post-journey nourishment. Galatea evidently approved, and ate two, but Hippolyta noticed that her mother took only tea, and that with no milk or sugar. Had she decided that she was too fat? Surely not: she looked, if anything, thinner than she remembered.

'And how is your family, Galatea?' she pulled herself back to the conversation. 'How is Mr. Milton?'

'My husband is quite well, thank you.'

'As busy as our father, no doubt!'

'As busy … no. No, not quite so busy.' Her lips sealed themselves in a thin line, and Hippolyta bounced off to another subject.

'And the children? All well?'

'Quite well, thank you,' Galatea Milton repeated. 'They are spending some time with Claudia and her family at Haddington.'

'Oh, that will be lovely for them, all the children there together!' said Hippolyta. Her sister Claudia was strict, but there would be horses and dogs and country walks, unlike Galatea's Edinburgh house.

'They will be quite wild when they return, I have no doubt,' said Galatea. Hippolyta had been about to offer hospitality to the children herself, but the thought of what Galatea might think of Ballater's wildness stopped her in her tracks. Perhaps later.

'We'll have dinner at five,' she tried a more amenable subject. 'We keep Edinburgh hours, you see, as do the better part of society in the village. Before then, I wondered if you might like to go for a short walk and see the village? The views are very pretty.'

'I feel we have seen most of it already, have we not?' asked Galatea. 'It is, after all, only a village.'

'I shall lie down for an hour or so, Hippolyta,' said her mother. 'The journey may have been smooth but it was still very tiring.'

'Oh, of course. Your rooms are ready for you at any moment, and as I was saying to Galatea, Ishbel the maid is becoming very proficient at the tasks of a lady's maid.' She wondered why neither of them had brought a maid with them, but it would be good practice for Ishbel. Then she took in what her mother had said. Tired? Her mother was never tired.

'Galatea will help me to undress,' said Mrs. Fettes. Hippolyta looked with surprise at Galatea. Galatea was gazing at the floor with a rather bored distaste. Hippolyta reached for Patrick's hand under the table: she felt she needed support. Why could not her father have come instead?

'And,' she said, drawing breath, 'how long are you both able to stay?'

Galatea shot a look at Mrs. Fettes. It was a look of challenge.

'I am not yet sure,' said their mother.

'Oh! then you could be here for some time?' asked Hippolyta, trying to sound delighted. 'That is very good – I had assumed that your various duties in Edinburgh would mean you would have to return very soon.'

'Even I am not indispensable,' said Mrs. Fettes, with the slightest smile. 'No doubt like Galatea's children they will all have run wild in my absence, but I feel that it is good for the various committees in which I participate to find their own way for a few months.'

'A few months!' Hippolyta could hear her voice squeak. She was not sure if it was shock at her mother's apparent abandonment of all those good causes that had kept her busy for as long as Hippolyta could remember, or horror at the idea of her mother and sister staying with them for so long. She cleared her throat quickly. 'Well, you will be able to meet all the society of Ballater and if the weather holds we can have some lovely excursions into the hills. It is so picturesque around here that I am sure you will find walks and drives to charm you into staying all summer!'

'All summer may be what it requires,' her mother nodded.

'All summer will be more than I can take,' muttered Galatea.

Patrick squeezed Hippolyta's hand hard under the table. She squeezed back desperately, then freed herself to pour more tea.

'Now,' said her mother, with a return almost to her usual briskness, 'how does one go to Pannanich Wells from here?'

Chapter Two

'Time to get up, dearest!'

Hippolyta rolled over towards her husband and pulled the blankets tight over her head, only showing her face like a wary mouse in a hole.

'Must I?'

'They would think it strange if you did not.'

'You could tell them I'm ill. You're a physician, you can think of something.'

'Then they might want to come in and nurse you.'

'Oh, horrors!' Hippolyta sat up, and pushed the bedclothes off her legs. 'It's all very well for you, you'll only see them at dinner time and supper. I'll have to stay with them all day!'

'I thought you were looking forward to seeing them.' Patrick glanced round at her as he tucked his shirt tails into his breeches. 'And I thought that your sister Galatea was always your mother's right hand man.'

Hippolyta frowned.

'Yes, I noticed that. I have never known them on bad terms before, but some of the looks Galatea was shooting Mother yesterday! I wonder what on earth has happened?'

'Perhaps they'll explain. Perhaps they were just tired after the journey. You know what some people are like when they travel together – the least little aggravation of the journey becomes a bone of contention for them.'

'Mother certainly was tired. I have never seen her look so pale – or volunteer to go and lie down in the middle of the day. It can't have been as smooth as they claim.'

Patrick said nothing, and buttoned his waistcoat. Hippolyta contemplated his back: it sat very nicely in a waistcoat, she thought, broad shouldered and trim waisted. She sighed, and pulled her shift over on to the bed to put on.

'What if they do stay months?' she mumbled from within the folds of linen.

'Well, if you want them gone you'll need to get the constable to help you. I'm not tackling your sister on my own, let alone your mother as well,' said Patrick plainly.

'The constable? We'd need the night watchman, too, and probably a company of dragoons.' Hippolyta's mouth turned down dramatically at the corners.

'We'll manage. You'll manage. Everyone will manage. Mrs. Riach will love having something new to complain about.'

Hippolyta pursed her lips, sure Patrick was only trying to comfort her but at the same time unwilling to turn such comfort away. Then the worst thought, the one that had been in her mind since yesterday afternoon, came to her lips at last.

'And why didn't Papa send me a letter? That's very odd.'

Patrick tied his neckcloth and sat to pull on his boots.

'Yes, it's a strange thing to pass up the opportunity to send something. But perhaps they are quite right and he was very busy. After all, he sent you his love, didn't he?'

'So they said ... Patrick, what if he is ill, and they won't tell me?'

'Why on earth would they not tell you?'

'They know I'm his favourite – they might not want to upset me, or maybe they don't want him upset if I go to see him – because I would, you know. If they said he was ill I'd be on the next coach to Aberdeen for the boat.'

'Of course you would, and I can't see any reason why your mother and sister would hide such a thing from you. I'm sure he's perfectly well, and very busy, and he'll write as soon as he can and send it by the usual way.' He leaned back over the bed and kissed the top of her head, followed, distractingly, by both her shoulders. 'Now, dress yourself and be ready to face the day, and I'm sure it won't be anywhere near as bad as you think. You'll enjoy showing Ballater off to them, no doubt, and the day seems set fine, so it will look its best!'

He went to the bedroom door.

'I'll be in my dispensary till breakfast. I'm not sure I shall ever grow tired of saying that! "I'll be in my dispensary" … I bet the famous Dr. Gilead doesn't have such a place!'

He strode out with a cheerful whistle, and she heard him tap down the stairs. Bah, she thought – and I have to face Mrs. Riach before breakfast.

She went slowly through the complexities of stockings and stays, skirts and sleeves, and arranged her hair in its usual side bunches of ringlets, made a face at herself in the mirror, and trotted down the stairs in her husband's wake.

She heard her sister's voice in the kitchen before she even opened the door to the servants' quarters.

'I don't know what you think you're doing but I can tell you, it would never be allowed in my house so it won't be here, either!'

Shocked, Hippolyta hurried down the passage to the kitchen door. Galatea was standing angular in the middle of the room and Ishbel was frozen in place with a broken eggshell in one hand and the bowl into which she had broken the contents in the other. The look on her face was an odd mixture of wishing to be almost anywhere else and not wishing to miss a second of this extraordinary event. Mrs. Riach was in her usual chair by the fireplace, but unaccustomedly uncomfortable looking. She was perched on the edge of it, one hand leaning on her footstool, the other braced in her lap, breathing heavily and glaring wild-eyed at Galatea.

'Mrs. Napier!' she gasped.

'And stand up when you address me – or Mrs. Napier!' Galatea snapped.

'Ah'm trying to,' said Mrs. Riach, 'if ye'd ever give a body a minty to catch its breath in its lichts…'

'What is going on here?' Hippolyta demanded, and Galatea cast her the briefest of glances.

'I'm sorting out your housekeeper, if this is she.'

'Aye, well,' said Mrs. Riach, 'see, the reet and the rise o' it is this –'

'Does she speak English at all?' Galatea asked, waving at her.

'No that yon feel can unnersteed,' Mrs. Riach responded, chin out.

'Sitting with her feet up by the fire reading the newspaper, if you please! And the breakfast wanted imminently!'

'"Imminently", is it? She's in richt bone, yon quine. Mind, ah've snite mair fantoosh nor her.'

Hippolyta drew breath and dived in.

'Galatea, would you mind? I need to have a private meeting with Mrs. Riach now.'

'I'll stay and help,' said Galatea, folding her arms.

'Is Mother up yet?' Hippolyta asked quickly. The shadow of a scowl passed swiftly over Galatea's face.

'Not yet. She's not sleeping very well these days, and lies a little late. Yesterday the coach left Aberdeen at seven in the morning, so today she needs a little longer.'

'Perhaps we could have a word, then? I'd like you to see the garden. Come this way. Mrs. Riach, we'll have our meeting later.'

'Aye, mirra hine!' Mrs. Riach added obscurely.

Hippolyta led Galatea out through the back door and into the garden too quickly for her to object: as far as Hippolyta knew her sister had no particular interest in gardens at all.

'Look,' she said, 'I hope you don't mind, but I'd be very grateful if you didn't upset Mrs. Riach. She's a – an unusual person, but she's a very good cook and devoted to the household,' she said, crossing her fingers behind her back. She had to release them again to unfasten the hen house, but she hoped it had been enough to cover the lie. Something certainly seemed to keep Mrs. Riach working for them, but she was fairly sure it was not devotion.

'Poll, dear, you don't understand. You need to train them: it's like keeping a dog. You can't let them get away with things and then expect them to behave well.'

'Mrs. Riach is certainly not a dog,' said Hippolyta shortly. She hated being called Poll. It made her feel as if she were seven again. The hens came cooing out of the henhouse, and she reached into the slithering comfort of the mealbin to feed them. She had forgotten the egg basket in her haste. 'And anyway, I think Mrs. Riach is too old and set in her ways to train.'

'Do you understand a word she is saying?'

'Of course,' said Hippolyta, fingers crossed again. It was true she understood a good deal more than she had done: what she principally understood was that Mrs. Riach's Deeside accent grew significantly stronger the crosser she was, and it mattered less that one understood individual words than the general sense.

'Then what was she saying in there?'

'Ah.' Hippolyta thought fast. She did not feel that the relationship between Galatea and Mrs. Riach would be improved by a word-for-word translation. 'She was explaining that she has a good deal of pain in her hip, and often has to take a seat in a warm place, but that she is able to supervise Ishbel quite well from there.'

'I see.' Galatea sounded dubious, as well she might. 'You've looked into replacing her, of course.'

'Not at all: as I say, she is devoted to the household, and you have to admit the food has been good, hasn't it?'

'That's true,' Galatea admitted reluctantly. The food had indeed been very good, though Mrs. Fettes had not eaten much of it.

'Galatea,' Hippolyta said suddenly, 'is Papa ill?'

Galatea stopped and stared at her in surprise.

'Papa? No, not at all! Papa is perfectly well. He was out playing golf when – when we left.'

There was a sudden squawk and Hippolyta spun round, to see one of the cats ambitiously attempting the life of a black hen. She shooed it off and reassured the hen, but the cat came curling around her legs in imitation of an apology.

'Silly animal,' said Hippolyta fondly, picking it up and cradling it. It climbed on to her shoulder and surveyed Galatea with clinical interest. 'They know it's not going to work. I need the egg basket if I'm going to bring in the night's harvest.'

'I hope you wash them,' said Galatea with a little shudder, and preceded her into the house.

Hippolyta sighed, and bent to gather the eggs into one place, at least, leaving the egg basket until Galatea was clear of the kitchen. Galatea and Claudia always did treat her like a child. She supposed it was understandable: Galatea had been twenty and married when Hippolyta was born, and Claudia eighteen. Then there were a couple of brothers, who wisely kept their thoughts to themselves, then Hippolyta as an afterthought, very much in her mother's eyes an impediment to her longed-for freedom from motherhood. Mrs. Fettes had never been prepared to offer much time to her youngest child, but Mr. Fettes, kindly lawyer, had more than made up for it.

Nine eggs today. Why had her father not written? Why, indeed, was he not here himself? It was near the end of the legal term and he would soon be free to travel up as far as Ballater to see her. She was completely astonished to receive the letter from Galatea announcing that she and their mother were on their way. Had they come up in person to break the awful news of her father's illness? They were denying it until they could find a suitable moment, perhaps. Whatever it was, she was convinced that something was not right.

She decided, daringly, to cradle the eggs in her apron, and made a reasonable job of it, tiptoeing past Patrick's dispensary with a longing glance, and gliding as best she could up the steps to the back door. In the kitchen was peace, if a rather tense one. She found the egg basket and carefully decanted the eggs into it one by one. Mrs. Riach was at the table slicing beef with a sharp knife and a surly expression. She looked up and watched Hippolyta as if waiting for disaster to strike. When the eggs were all secure, she demanded,

'Fa long is yon quine biding here?'

'I'm afraid I'm not sure. I'll try to keep her out of the kitchen, though,' said Hippolyta. There was not much point in hiding the fact that she and Galatea did not see eye to eye: if she wanted Mrs. Riach on her side at all she needed to show some sympathy, not automatically side with family against staff. 'Ishbel, will you be at hand, please, to help Mrs. Fettes or Mrs. Milton if they need anything? I've told them you're doing very well as a lady's maid. Mrs. Riach, if you feel you need more help, then tell me and we'll see if we can find someone.'

Ishbel blushed, and Mrs. Riach muttered something, possibly a spell, at the beef. She did not answer back, though, which Hippolyta thought was probably as good a sign as she was going to get.

Ishbel was called upon sooner than expected, for Mrs. Fettes asked for her breakfast to be brought to her room. Ishbel took her a lightly boiled egg and a small piece of toasted bread with no butter, and a pot of weak tea. Hippolyta, hearing the instructions, wondered again. Her mother's breakfasts usually consisted of several eggs and bacon, and a large pot of chocolate, which sustained her through her work until dinner time, however late. A lightly boiled egg and a piece of plain toast would hardly sustain her half an hour after breakfast.

Galatea, by contrast, seemed now full of energy. She interrogated Hippolyta and Patrick over breakfast on the subjects of Ballater and Patrick's medical practice. How many patients had he? He could not tell, for many were visitors to the Wells or travellers to the area, and did not stay. Who had built the town? Why was there no bridge over the river? The fine bridge built by Thomas Telford for the old laird had been swept away the previous summer in the flood. How did the visitors to the Wells travel there, then? There were a number of boatmen who competed for business. How well was the centrical church attended? How many Episcopalians were there, and when would the next service be? Was there a school, and was it any good? Hippolyta was able to tell her there were two, the parish school, which sent pupils with bursaries to King's College or Marischal College, the universities in Aberdeen, and a school for girls run by the old minister's widow, which taught needlework, reading, writing, and for more advanced girls French, Italian and whatever else the erudite Mrs. Kynoch could muster. Was there a poorhouse? A hospital? A post office? Well, no – or not yet. Ballater seemed to be expanding all the time. Perhaps it was only a matter of time.

'If our mother is well enough,' Hippolyta began a little tentatively. Galatea did not respond, though she gave Hippolyta an odd look. 'If she is well enough Mrs. Strachan, whose husband owns the warehouse up the hill, has invited us to visit her. She is a little shy, but comes from a good family.'

'I'm sure Mother will be quite well enough,' said Galatea precisely. 'No doubt she will want to be out and about and see things.'

'What is her interest in Pannanich?' Patrick asked.

Galatea took on the expression of someone who had bitten into a honey cake only to find the bee still in there.

'I daresay she wants to find out if it is worth sending some of her charitable cases to the wells for the water.'

'Her charities still keep her busy, then?' Patrick asked with polite interest.

'I should be anxious about her if they did not,' said Galatea shortly. 'But our mother does a great deal of good work in Edinburgh. She is more than competent in all her roles. If she is here considering the uses of Pannanich Wells for sickly mothers of the poor or imbecilic lunatics, then I am quite sure she is well able to judge their usefulness.'

She finished rather sharply, and Hippolyta and Patrick exchanged puzzled looks.

'What?' demanded Galatea. 'What is it?'

'I should be delighted to hear if the waters were useful in either case,' said Patrick mildly. 'Neither use has yet been recorded, but there is always room for the business there to expand.'

'Perhaps you might be able to make a study of it. It might help you in your career,' said Galatea kindly. Hippolyta's mouth opened but Patrick caught her eye and shook his head slightly, unwilling, it seemed, to mention the papers he had already published.

'It's a very busy practice,' he said instead. 'There isn't much time. And recently I have taken to dispensing my own mixtures more efficiently from my little dispensary, which is better in general but of course requires concentration.'

'You have a proper dispensary? I should like to see that!' said Galatea. 'I have visited several physicians in Edinburgh who have well-organised dispensaries: I should be happy to offer you any advice you might require.'

'That would be most kind,' said Patrick without emphasis. 'Perhaps tomorrow? I have patients to visit just now.'

He rose and bowed, and Hippolyta followed him out into the hall while he collected his case from his study, and a few packages from the hall table for his patients. Hippolyta went to close the study door as he found his coat and gloves, but he stopped her quickly.

'Leave it open,' he whispered. 'That hen is under the desk again.'

'How did it get in this time?' Hippolyta sighed. She set the door slightly ajar, and hoped that when the hen did leave it did not encounter either her mother or her sister in the hallway. She said goodbye to Patrick at the door, and turned to find her mother descending the narrow stairway, a little sideways to make room for her sleeves and skirts, adjusting a scarf about her throat as she came.

'Good morning, Mother! I hope you slept well.'

'Quite well, I thank you, Hippolyta.' She pulled herself straight and allowed Hippolyta to peck her on the cheek. She smelled of her usual lavender water but that scent was almost completely masked by something else: something mint-like, Hippolyta thought, but not quite so nice. 'I notice that your maid has not yet learned to write.'

'Well …'

'It is an invaluable skill in a servant, Hippolyta. If there is not some local woman who is in a position to teach her, you must teach her yourself.'

'Of course, Mother.' She had tried, but Ishbel found it hard to form her letters, and Hippolyta was not a patient teacher, and always found more interesting things to do. She resolved to try harder.

'Now, what have you planned for today? What works are you involved in?'

'Um … Well, Mrs. Strachan has invited us to tea this morning.'

'And what is she? The minister's wife?'

'No, no, a merchant's wife, but a gentlewoman.'

'And what does she do?'

'Do? Well … she is quite shy. And a bit sickly. I'm not sure …'

'Does she visit the sick? Organise food and blankets for the poor?'

'Not really …'

'Then what about the minister's wife? I take it you haven't found yourselves an Episcopalian incumbent yet.'

'No, not yet. The Bishop said …'

'Then it must be the established church. It is not impossible to work together.'

'Not at all, but …'

'Is Galatea in the parlour?' Mrs. Fettes marched past Hippolyta, who only then noticed that her mother had been supporting herself on the end of the banisters. She followed her into the parlour, where Galatea was finishing her tea.

'I gather we have a visit to make,' said Mrs. Fettes.

'Apparently so,' said Galatea, rising from her chair.

'Then we had best get on!'

It was a positive procession when they left the house, and Hippolyta felt as if she were suddenly back in her childhood. Her mother swept out through the front gate into the street like a ship in full sail, followed by Galatea, the well-trimmed jollyboat, followed at a respectful distance, feeling like a toy yacht in a duck pond, by Hippolyta. Hippolyta had vaguely described the Strachans' house as being 'up the hill', and Mrs. Fettes had needed no further direction, confidently striding out around the green and up towards the top of the town. There were already enough spring visitors in the town that nobody stood and stared at a stranger, to Hippolyta's relief. She was allowing herself to pretend that she had no connexion at all with the two ladies in front of her, and gazing about to see what the day might bring, when she walked into Galatea's back, and earned a hard look.

'I beg your pardon!' she murmured. Mother, in front of Mr. Strachan's shop, had found a charitable case. A small boy in bare feet was playing in the ditch with a dog, blissfully unaware of the irresistible force for good that was about to sweep around him.

'Boy! What is your name?'

The boy looked about him, assuming that the grand lady must be addressing some worthier subject. Then he jumped visibly when he realised he was the focus of the piercing gaze.

'Wullie, ma'am,' he mumbled.

'Do you go to school, Willie?' asked Mrs. Fettes, with what she considered kindness.

'I bin,' Wullie qualified thoughtfully. 'I dinna gae the noo.'

'Then what work have you?'

'I've no work the noo,' Wullie explained. 'It's no hairst yet, so I'm helping Al.'

'Who is Al?' asked Mrs. Fettes.

'Al's Mr. Strachan's second shop boy. He's ma big brother.'

'And do you get paid?' Mrs. Fettes was relentless.

'Well, see, if I help Al he'll no soosh me when he comes hame.'

'Soosh you?'

'Aye, ma'am. So it's a kind of payment.'

'It's not ideal, though, is it?'

Wullie admitted that there were perhaps more promising careers. The dog lost interest in the conversation and went to identify cat smells from Hippolyta's skirts. Galatea, who had no doubt seen small boys being dealt with like this a hundred times, also looked away. Hippolyta bent down to talk to the dog, a shapeless grey creature with a mild manner, her mother's strange bilingual conversation wafting over her until she heard the words,

'The doctor's house, you know it? Go to the back door there tomorrow morning at eight precisely.'

'What did you say, Mother?' Hippolyta asked, alarmed, just as Galatea exclaimed,

'Good heavens, that's – isn't that - ?'

Mrs. Fettes turned to look, and grasped Hippolyta's arm hard, making her cry out. The dog jumped away, and Wullie called it and ran off, seeing his chance. Galatea's face was a picture, but Mrs. Fettes' expression was pure annoyance.

'Mrs. Fettes!' came a shrill English voice. 'What a delight to see you here! Such a surprise!'

Hippolyta pulled herself gently away from her mother's claw-like grip, and Mrs. Fettes, realising what she was doing, snatched her hand away. Advancing on them with all the subtlety of a coach and four was an enormous woman in eau de Tiber floral silk, her steel grey hair curled ferociously and her bonnet at least two feet wide. The overall impression was of a cheese press under a curtain, Hippolyta thought, slightly nervously. She glanced at her mother. Mrs. Fettes had retrieved a smile from somewhere, and was standing her ground in the path of the monster.

'Mrs. Pumpton! An unexpected pleasure, so far north! What brings you here?'

Hippolyta thought she heard an odd noise from Galatea, as if she were being choked. She looked but her sister was also wearing something that might have gone down as a smile.

'Well, I'm sure you can guess!' said the vision. 'No doubt you are on the same path, eh?' She gave an arch little giggle, and poked Mrs. Fettes with her fan. Hippolyta winced. She had never seen anyone poke her mother, and retribution seemed inevitable. She half-closed her eyes, but nothing seemed to happen.

'I have no idea what you mean!' Mrs. Fettes was saying, in an unnaturally playful tone. 'I am here to visit my youngest daughter, who is married to a – a gentleman in this town. Here,' she prodded Hippolyta forward. 'You won't have met her. Hippolyta – I mean Mrs. Napier – this is Mrs. Pumpton, with whom we are acquainted in Bath.'

'Acquainted with!' Mrs. Pumpton emitted another shrill giggle. 'Best of friends, that's what we are! Well, except in our little rivalry, eh?' She poked Mrs. Fettes again.

'Where are you staying?' asked Mrs. Fettes, doing her best to ignore the fan.

'Oh, at the Hotel at the Wells, of course. Much more convenient, though it's lovely to have a little trip into the village each day for the air and the sights! There's a boat, you know – such hilarity! I declare I have had three gowns ruined already! Mr. Pumpton will never forgive me. Oh, this is Mr. Pumpton – Mrs. Nailor, was it?'

'Napier,' Hippolyta was saying, when to her surprise a small man appeared from behind Mrs. Pumpton as if he had been hiding in her reticule.

'Good day to you, Mrs. Napier,' he said, with a polite bow.

'Good day, Mr. Pumpton,' she replied.

'Well, we must be going. A social engagement,' said Mrs. Fettes with a small air of triumph Hippolyta did not quite understand.

'I'm sure we shall see each other again soon!' chortled Mrs. Pumpton happily. 'You cannot resist for long! Good day to you, Mrs. Fettes, Mrs. Milton, Mrs. Nailor!'

She sailed into Mr. Strachan's shop, followed by her husband. Hippolyta was an observant woman, but even she, the moment he had vanished, could not have said what Mr. Pumpton looked like.

Chapter Three

Hippolyta's mother did not mention Pannanich for the rest of the morning, and neither she nor Galatea would say much about Mrs. Pumpton. Hippolyta guided them up to the Strachans' modern house on the upper edge of the village and was pleased to see them both nod with approval. Mrs. Strachan greeted them with her usual shy charm, and Mrs. Kynoch was there too. The widow of the previous minister of the three parishes was outlandish in her dress but otherwise a sensible and kind person, and Mrs. Fettes seemed pleased with the answers she gave about the little dame school she ran for some of the village girls. Hippolyta felt that 'dame school' was a dismissive term for Mrs. Kynoch's ambitious education programme, but Mrs. Kynoch herself submitted to the interrogation with a calm smile, and apparently no offence. Neither she nor Mrs. Strachan had any reason to question why a devoted mother and sister would travel all the way from Edinburgh to visit Mrs. Napier in her new marital home: it was only Hippolyta who found it strange.

They returned to the cottage on the green in good time for dinner, and Mrs. Fettes took the opportunity to inspect the parts of the cottage she had not yet seen. Her inspection was a thorough one, and not, Hippolyta thought, particularly helpful: she examined the linen presses in the side passage, sniffed at the contents of the pantry, and discussed the dressing of salmon with Mrs. Riach, but did not give Hippolyta any hints as to how she might improve her housekeeping. Mrs. Fettes had trained her older daughters at the appropriate age: whether she had forgotten to bother with Hippolyta, or simply been too busy by the time she needed to learn, it had never been clear. She herself now had a housekeeper who ran everything with independent efficiency and a spirit of employer-employee co-operation that was entirely alien to Mrs. Riach, and Hippolyta would have cheerfully swapped her best bonnet for the secret of achieving such a miracle. No such offer was forthcoming, though, and in any case, Mrs. Riach developed a painful limp as Mrs. Fettes walked her about the kitchen, which Hippolyta knew was one of her indicators of non-co-operation just a level below dropping into broad dialect.

By dinner time, with the hens checked for disease and the cats for fleas, Hippolyta was exhausted, and Pannanich had still not been mentioned. Only after dinner, while Patrick was trying to play the flute to Galatea's heavy accompaniment, did her mother say briskly,

'I wish to visit the Wells tomorrow, Hippolyta. Please make whatever arrangements are necessary for an early start.'

The arrangements, such as they were, could be made as they went along the next day. They had all taken heed of Mrs. Pumpton's experience and not worn their best clothes, and Mrs. Fettes and her daughters, escorted by Patrick who had to go there anyway, assembled on the bank of the river next morning before breakfast, just below the inn. The great spike of masonry which was all that was left of Thomas Telford's strong stone bridge still stood in the middle of a fast-flowing stream, a stream so shallow it was hard to imagine, if one had not seen it, how it could have swollen and risen so ferociously last summer, wreaking so much destruction.

'I am surprised that work has not begun on another bridge,' said Mrs. Fettes, who if she had lived locally would no doubt have set about it while the waters were still going down.

'Public subscriptions are being collected. It took a while for everyone to recover and make plans,' Hippolyta explained, a little defensively. 'Ah, here's the boat.'

Jamesie, one of the more experienced boatmen, hopped into the shallow shore of the river and hauled his bows over the pebbles. He had little need to assist his disembarking passengers, for they were a couple of boys from Strachan's shop, returning from the morning's deliveries, and no sooner had the boat stilled than they were out and away. It took rather longer to settle their own party in the boat: Patrick was by now well used to the little voyage, and tried to help as best he could, but neither Galatea nor their mother was well disposed to allow any vagaries on the part of the boat and sat as stiff as the old masonry pillar themselves, making everyone else work around them. Jamesie, who was training himself to be the trusted boatman of the grandest visitors to the Wells, said nothing but smiled and bowed excessively before shoving the boat back out into the current, and hopping in after it.

The crossing was not long, though Hippolyta could feel the way the little boat was dragged and tugged down to their left by the stream. She could not quite suppress a shiver, thinking back to the flood. When they reached the opposite bank she was first out on to dry land, ostensibly to help the others, but really for her own peace of mind.

'It's less than two miles up the hill,' she said brightly. Galatea, whose boot had just found a soft spot in the pebbles and been submerged, gave her a sour look, but their mother seemed to have woken again with her usual energy and merely nodded, taking Patrick's arm as she surveyed the birch woodlands above them.

'I suppose you have been spending your time in painting views like this,' she remarked.

'Yes, Mother,' Hippolyta replied dutifully, knowing it was a telling-off.

'Huh,' grunted Galatea. 'That explains the housekeeper, I suppose.'

Hippolyta chose to ignore this. She had not been this side of the river for a while, and the birch woods were as always a delight. The sun picked out the pale trunks, many only a handspan wide, and between them the earth was soft with blaeberry and foxglove … while the high ditch frilled the roadside with ferns. The purple shades of March were edging into bright, fresh green, like a society lady first with a new fashion. Her fingers itched for pencils and paints so that she could add to her collection of birch wood studies.

Instead she helped her sister up on to the roadway, and the four of them walked at a gentle but steady pace up the sloping path.

'Is that the hotel?' her mother asked after a few minutes.

Hippolyta surveyed the low-lying, square set building by the riverbank.

'No, Mother, that's Pannanich Lodge. The hotel is further up,

I'm afraid, but it is much nearer the wells themselves.'

'The air is quite invigorating,' Mrs. Fettes remarked with only a hint of surprise.

'That alone seems to help many people,' said Patrick. 'I have heard many remark that when they have accompanied a relative to the wells, they have felt much better themselves, even if they have not taken the waters.'

'A fortunate village, indeed,' said Mrs. Fettes. She seemed a little breathless and said nothing more, holding her scarf close to her throat.

'The Lodge was built to accommodate the visitors which the hotel could not take,' Patrick explained, allowing her to catch her breath. 'Then the bridge was built and the village begun, for the whole business of the spa attracted more people than there was room for on this side of the river!'

'But are the wells really any good?' asked Galatea.

'Well, there are three, and they are all different,' Patrick said. 'They are chalybeate, like the one at Tunbridge Wells in Kent, or one I think in Brighton. They don't seem to do much good for consumptives, but they are a tonic for most people. Ladies, in particular, find them strengthening.'

'If they are good for you, no doubt they taste vile,' Galatea observed.

'Not at all! These ones are very pleasant. I have no difficulty in persuading my patients to take them regularly,' said Patrick. 'Perhaps you have been to Pitkeathly? The water there tastes much worse.'

'Pitkeathly?' Galatea echoed uncertainly.

'Yes, in Perthshire. You must have heard of it. Have you not been? I gather it is very fashionable.'

'Ah, yes,' said Galatea, at exactly the same time as her mother said,

'No.'

'I went with … my husband,' Galatea explained after a moment.

'Did you, dear?' asked Mrs. Fettes. 'And what was it like?'

'Miserable,' said Galatea with feeling. Hippolyta thought she saw her mother's mouth twitch.

'I hope Mr. Milton is not unwell,' said Hippolyta. 'Or perhaps it was for your own benefit?'

'Mr. Milton is perfectly well,' Galatea snapped. 'As am I.'

'I'm delighted to hear it,' said Hippolyta politely.

They progressed in silence for a few minutes, making some pretence at the effort required to climb the hill. Less than forty-eight hours, Hippolyta thought: they've been here for less than two whole days and already I'd pay a moderate amount to see them leave. What a dreadful daughter and sister I must be!

Below them to the left the valley of the Dee was opening out, showing between the trees glimpses of the grid of Ballater village on the flat plain over the water. The hills in the distance emerged tentatively from the morning mist, the sunlight that already shone in their faces easing off the moisture from the air. Hippolyta let the sights ease off her worries in a similar way, and enjoyed the rest of the climb up to the long, elegantly plain bath house that loomed over the road at the top of the hill.

'Is this it?' asked her mother, stopping to gaze up at it.

'It's not exactly Bath, is it?' said Galatea.

'It doesn't need to be,' said Patrick quickly, seeing Hippolyta open her mouth to object. 'Every facility is here. We go up the path beyond the building, and in through the back.'

He led the way, and from the angle of his gait Hippolyta could see that her mother was leaning on him quite heavily. The steep curl of the path up from the road led between the bathhouse and the equally long and narrow hotel behind it, an odd construction demanded by the steep slope on which the buildings had been established. Little in the way of ornament had been included on the exteriors except for the handsome angular bay to the front of the bath house, and so nothing seemed out of fashion though the whole thing was eighty years old. Hippolyta found it rather pleasing, if a little industrial. She had appreciated the shelter of its shell-pink granite walls before.

Patrick showed them into the bath house.

'This central part,' he indicated a doorway into what must have been the back of the angular bay, 'is for the gentry's bathing.' Indeed by the doorway stood several smart attendants, male and female, ready for their first bathers of the morning. 'That way are the hot baths for the lesser sorts, and this way their cold baths. Priced accordingly, of course: you'll be interested in what your

Edinburgh – um, people might have to pay.'

'Of course.' Mrs. Fettes examined the price list. 'It's cheaper than Peterhead, I believe,' she said, apparently pleased. After her declaration of intent the night before, she had outlined her plans for organised spa visits for the poor of her parish.

'And the air is much more salubrious,' said Patrick quickly. 'Herring has a fine smell, but on the whole it does not gladden the heart in quite the same way as birch woods and pine trees. Anyone who is suffering from the smoky atmosphere of a busy city will find much benefit here – and the sea journey as far as Aberdeen will give them as much herring as they could wish for.'

'And your practice might also benefit,' said Galatea astutely. Patrick grinned.

'It might indeed – though as I told you, I'm already very busy! I must, in fact, abandon you now and go to visit some of my patients here.'

Hippolyta shot him a look of despair, but he bowed politely to his mother and sister in law and squeezed her hand in support.

'His little dispensary is very good,' said Galatea kindly. 'In its way.'

'Oh, you saw it?'

'He showed it to me briefly this morning. You need to make sure he works hard, Poll: he might be inclined to spend too much time in there perfecting mixtures when he could manage perfectly well with much simpler treatments.'

'I'm sure he knows what he is doing,' Hippolyta said, tucking her nails into her palms. She could feel their bite even through her gloves.

'Well, shall we bathe?' said Mrs. Fettes suddenly.

'What?' Hippolyta almost jumped.

'We might as well sample the waters while we are here, might we not? Have you tasted them before? Have you bathed here?'

'Well, no, not yet …' Hippolyta glanced at Galatea. Her sister had a look of sulky resignation on her face.

'Come on,' said Galatea, 'we'd better just get on with it.'

'But I don't want …'

'It will do you good, no doubt!' said her mother, who was already making her way towards the smart attendants, her reticule at the ready to make her modest payment. 'You heard what your husband said: ladies find them strengthening. It must do you some good.' She made it sound as if something would have to, some time. Hippolyta opened her mouth to protest, then caught Galatea's eye. She was grinning.

'Well, why not?' said Hippolyta. 'If it's as pleasant as Patrick says.'

Strangely, it sort of was, though very odd indeed.

Hippolyta had never been to a bathing place, whatever Galatea's experiences at Pitkeathly. Her mother seemed entirely familiar with the whole procedure, too. Hippolyta was guided into a wooden cubicle by her attendant, who took her bonnet, reticule and gloves, helped her out of her gown and stays, and waited in polite silence while she removed her boots and stockings. Then she was provided with a linen cap, which looked clean enough, to cover her hair, and an equally clean shift with which to replace her own. Clad only in these, Hippolyta was led out of the cubicle, feeling with a kind of thrilled horror the cool air around her legs, to a room where there was a small pool in the floor, designed to accommodate perhaps six people sitting in the water. Galatea was already there, eyes closed, her head propped against the side of the pool, apparently completely at ease. In a moment her mother appeared from another cubicle, straight-backed in her shift, her scarf still about her throat.

'Draughts,' she remarked, as she descended into the pool. Her shift rose about her and she calmly pushed it down until it sank, soaked. Hippolyta followed her. The water was bitingly cold, and made her dizzy, until she warmed against it and allowed it to rise all the way up to her ears. She felt light, wobbly, not sure how to keep her balance in this element. It was entirely unlike a raging flood-torrent: it felt kindly, but a little threatening, as if it would lull you before sucking you in.

They must have been there for twenty minutes, she supposed: there was no clock, but every five minutes or so attendants brought trays with glasses of spa water, the glasses differently labelled depending on which spring they had been filled at. The water was refreshing, milder than the bath, and made Hippolyta feel her blood tingle from her head to her toes. It was delicious.

At last the attendants came with great white towels, and

assisted them from the pool. Hippolyta expected to be taken back to her cubicle but instead they were led through to another room, where the air was heavy with steam. They coughed as they entered, feeling the damp across their faces, legs sweating straightaway where their wet shifts were not plastered to them. Here there was another pool, and the attendants allowed them to lower themselves slowly into it. At first it felt burning hot, then comfortably warm, better than any bath Hippolyta had ever had. They relaxed, heads propped against the sides again, wordless in the luxury of the sustaining water. More glasses were brought and emptied, until eventually they were drawn reluctantly again from their warm pool and returned with a shock to the cold one. This time they did not have it to themselves.

'Mrs. Fettes! There, I knew you could not long resist!'

It was Mrs. Pumpton, wallowing in the cold water like a pig in mud. With her was a much younger, thinner woman, her borrowed cap sitting oversized on her head like an autumn mushroom.

'Well, even when one is visiting relatives,' said Mrs. Fettes with some emphasis, 'one is obliged to sample the local attractions. Oh, Mrs. Nickell, is that you?'

The thin woman nodded excitedly.

'Mrs. Pumpton said she had seen you!' she cried. 'How lovely to find you have followed us all here!'

'I am visiting my daughter,' said Mrs. Fettes again, very clearly. 'You remember Mrs. Milton, my eldest daughter? This is Mrs. Napier, my youngest. Her husband is a native of Ballater.'

Patrick was not, but Hippolyta decided not to say so. Mrs. Nickell looked quite jumpy: her eyes were already protruding as if in shock. They were a kind of green that reminded Hippolyta of the scum on a pond: she did not see much sign of intelligence there, but conceded she had been wrong before in her first assessments of people. And what was one to do if one were introduced to someone in a pool of water? Curtseying would seem ridiculous. She contented herself with a nod and a smile.

'I take it you have just started bathing for the day?' Mrs. Fettes asked crisply.

'Oh, yes! It's such lovely water,' said Mrs. Nickell. 'Much nicer than Pitkeathly, don't you think?'

'I think so,' said Galatea quickly.

'And cheaper than Bath,' Mrs. Fettes put in. 'Even cheaper than Peterhead.'

'Nowhere near as elegant as Bath, of course,' said Mrs. Pumpton, with a wriggle that sent quite significant waves over the pool. One of the attendants, approaching with a tray of glasses, jumped back.

'Of course not: one would not expect it.' Mrs. Fettes was gracious.

'So,' said Mrs. Nickell, 'have you seen him yet?'

'Seen ... I am not here to see anyone,' said Mrs. Fettes. 'I am here to sample the local bathing, that is all.'

'It must be time to get out now,' Galatea muttered, swallowing down another glass of spring water. 'We've been through the hot room already,' she explained more clearly. 'It's time we went back.'

'I believe you must be right,' said Mrs. Fettes. She summoned an attendant, and allowed herself to be helped out of the pool. Galatea and Hippolyta followed with as much grace as could be managed in sopping wet shifts and the sudden envelopment of towels. They retreated to their separate cubicles, and were helped to dry and dress. Hippolyta was silent, thinking about Mrs. Pumpton and Mrs. Nickell, and their conversation with her mother. She seemed to have met them before at a spa, or perhaps at several. What was her mother up to? Was she carrying out a survey of all the spas in the country, just to decide where to send her sickly poor? Knowing her mother's efficiency, that did not seem entirely unlikely. But why was Galatea so reluctant to help her, as she seemed to be? If only they did not think she was still a child, they might tell her what was going on. A sudden awful thought struck her: were they trying to find a spa suitable for her father's treatment? Oh, why would they not admit that he was ill?

Dressed again, and feeling not quite at ease in her clothes over slightly damp skin, she tied her bonnet strings and pulled on her gloves as she emerged, just after Galatea, who seemed well practised at changing in these little wooden cubicles, and a little before their mother, who sailed out of her cubicle as serene as if her own maid had just dressed her for church.

'Now,' said Mrs. Fettes, 'I feel the need of a cup of tea before that walk back down to the river. Did you say that the other building was a hotel? Is it respectable?'

'Perfectly respectable, Mother. And the tea is very good.'

'Very well.' Mrs. Fettes left the bath house, pressing coins into the palms of their attendants, and crossed the cobbled yard to the main door of the hotel. Its low-ceilinged hallway was very familiar to Hippolyta, and she was able to guide her mother to the main parlour before the hotel servant appeared to ask their will. Mrs. Fettes ordered tea and bread and butter, and they found a table close to, but not too near, the fire. Hippolyta's skin felt as if it had been taken off and put on again very slightly differently, but she was still invigorated and she wondered how long it would take the effect to wear off. She felt she could run all the way to the river crossing, skip home and paint for a week – and probably eat several dinners at one sitting.

'What on earth is that wretched woman doing here?' Mrs. Fettes was murmuring to Galatea.

'Who, the Nickell creature? Well, the same as – as Mrs. Pumpton, presumably.'

'Making themselves ridiculous,' said Mrs. Fettes waspishly. 'Mrs. Pumpton? Pump room, I should have said. She's the same size.'

'Mother!' Galatea complained, but she did not seem very shocked. Hippolyta was.

'Why don't you like her, Mother?' she asked. Mrs. Fettes jumped, as if she had forgotten Hippolyta was there.

'She's a dreadful woman,' she said shortly. 'And Mrs. Nickell is a foolish child.'

'It sounded as if you had met them at a number of watering places,' said Hippolyta carefully, but her mother was not going to rise to it.

'Did it?' she asked, not expecting Hippolyta to risk an answer.

'There are people,' said Galatea in a voice that sounded terribly weary, 'who travel from spa to spa like – like, oh, I don't know! They have nothing better to do with their time, and so they become appreciators of spas.'

'Are they perhaps unwell?'

'Some of them,' Galatea conceded acidly. 'Not as many as you might think.'

Their mother pursed her lips.

'Ah, the tea,' she said, and they were silent until the servant had arranged the pot, cups and saucers, sugar, milk and bread and butter like a hand of cards on the table. Mrs. Fettes lifted the teapot lid and peered inside, tutted, and replaced it, swirling the heavy pot slowly for a moment. Then she poured it for all of them and offered the bread and butter around. Hippolyta, snatching a slice hungrily, noticed that she took none herself.

'So where did you meet them last?' she asked casually.

'Pitkeathly,' said Galatea, without thinking.

'Bath,' said her mother.

'You went to Bath? That's – that's a long way,' said Hippolyta. They had been once when she was a child, but it had been to visit relatives, not to indulge in lazing around in dirty old Roman bathing pools, as her mother had told them at the time. Hippolyta remembered a beautiful city in a stuffy valley in the hills, so crowded it was impossible to breathe: no, she would rather have Ballater, she thought.

'Yes: you remember I have a cousin there,' said Mrs. Fettes as if to a slow child.

'Of course, but you ventured into the baths?'

'As I said earlier, just because one is visiting relatives does not mean that one should not sample the local attractions.'

'Of course not,' said Hippolyta, but it was certainly a change of opinion.

'Mrs. Nickell was in Harrogate,' said Galatea. Her tone, puzzlingly, was rather sly.

'You were in Harrogate?'

'Mrs. Nickell is from Harrogate, or thereabouts,' said Mrs. Fettes precisely, ignoring Hippolyta's question.

'She is indeed,' came a familiar voice, as someone entered the parlour behind Hippolyta. 'And you are from Edinburgh, Mrs. Fettes: could it be that you have travelled all this way just to see me?'

Hippolyta turned, and to her astonishment saw the famous Dr. Gilead approach, bend, and kiss her mother's willingly outstretched hand.

Chapter Four

The parlour, which had been tranquil and cool, suddenly seemed rather full and hot. Hippolyta pushed her chair back quietly to take in the newcomers. Apart from the tall, graceful figure of Dr. Gilead, and the very short but assertive one of his devoted terrier, there were three others, all strangers to Hippolyta – or so she thought, until with an effort she recognised Mrs. Pumpton's quiet little husband. He had only advanced a few paces into the room and looked as if only the constraints of good manners prevented him from bolting away to somewhere much more congenial, perhaps solitary with a good book. He nodded to Hippolyta with a pleasant smile, though uncertainly, as though he were used to being forgotten very quickly.

The woman who accompanied Dr. Gilead left almost as little impression as Mr. Pumpton, if that were possible. She had a whey-coloured face with unremarkable eyes and grey hair under a neat cap, and a gown of stiff grey wool like a carpet. If she were there to bathe, Hippolyta thought inconsequentially, her gown would probably stand in one place upright waiting for her return. Her hands, in lace fingerless gloves like a governess, met neatly in front of her as though she was wary of what each might do on its own. She observed Dr. Gilead's warm greeting with no apparent emotion. Hippolyta was not quite sure how she fitted into the group: she was too old, surely, to be the wife of the last newcomer.

He was of all of them, with the obvious exception of the famous physician, the most likely to be noticed in a crowd. He stood out a little to one side, one leg akimbo, hand on his hip and the other at his chin, observing the meeting with amusement. He was young and slim enough but was developing a little paunch, rather larger than his years would normally allow. Hair stood high on his head but was combed back proudly, reminding Hippolyta of the cockerel that had fathered her hens. He allowed his face to crinkle a little in a knowing smile, which only broadened when he caught Hippolyta's eye and realised she had been watching him. She looked away immediately.

But the most extraordinary appearance in the room, she suddenly realised, was her mother's.

Mrs. Fettes, her hand still being held lightly by Dr. Gilead, was beaming like a girl asked for her first dance. There was colour in her cheeks which, Hippolyta realised, she had not seen for some years, let alone since her arrival in Ballater, and her eyes shone with the kind of smile that simply belonged on someone else entirely. Hippolyta looked over at Galatea, hoping for some kind of reassurance, but Galatea had sat back very upright, an echo of her mother's more usual disapproving stance, with a face that could sour cream at twenty paces. When Dr. Gilead turned his attention to her, Hippolyta was amused to watch the way her sister had to wrench her mouth into some kind of smile.

'Mrs. Milton, a pleasure as always.' He nodded, then turned to Hippolyta. 'But who is this charming young lady? No – wait, I believe we have already met!'

'Not at all,' said Mrs. Fettes quickly.

'But I must disagree with you for once, Mrs. Fettes. I have indeed met this lady. How could I forget such a face - and the very image of you! now I come to look at it. Mrs. Napier, is it not?'

'My daughter, Mrs. Napier,' agreed her mother, darting a sharp look at Hippolyta.

'Your husband ... is a gentleman with some interest in medicine, I seem to remember?' There seemed to be no malice in his dismissal of Patrick, but Hippolyta was not slow to correct him.

'He is a physician, Dr. Gilead.'

'Of course: my colleague, Dr. Napier. No doubt we shall share many a yarn about our miraculous cures!' He smiled at her, and despite herself she found herself smiling back. The moment he turned away, however, her smile slid off, as if an enchantment had only glanced in her direction. 'This gentleman is Mr. Nickell – you ladies will have met him, of course, but for the benefit of Mrs. Napier who no doubt is eager to make herself familiar with our society.' He waved at the younger man, who drew in his angled leg and bowed expressively.

'Delighted, Mrs. Napier. We have travelled all the way from Yorkshire – we're from Yorkshire, the wife and I - to visit Ballater, and I can only say it is as grand a place as any other we have visited since leaving Harrogate.'

Hippolyta inclined her head, quite aware that he had paid Ballater very little compliment at all with his careful words, charming though they might have sounded. He caught her eye again and she saw that he was checking to see that she had seen through him: there was amusement in his face but not at her expense, she thought. This, then, was the husband presumably of the thin woman in the bath with Mrs. Pumpton.

'This gentleman is Mr. Pumpton, from Somersetshire,' Dr. Gilead waved again, only glancing to see that Mr. Pumpton had not left altogether.

'We have met, sir,' she smiled, and he returned the smile rather sweetly. He was of middle years, and had a rosy face with a button nose, on which perched a pair of round glasses which amplified his gentle gaze, altogether pleasant if only one noticed it.

'Oh, and here is my wife,' Dr. Gilead added as an afterthought. Taken by surprise, Hippolyta rose and curtseyed to the woman in grey, who completely failed to look at her as she curtseyed stiffly back.

'Will you join us for tea, Dr. Gilead? Hippolyta, ring the bell for some more tea,' said Mrs. Fettes.

'We'd be delighted,' said Dr. Gilead without reference to the others, and seated himself with a magnificent swoop on the chair between Hippolyta and her mother. The table was fortunately large, and the others came to join them. Hippolyta found herself between Dr. Gilead and Mr. Nickell, and when the tea arrived she passed Mr. Nickell his cup.

'So what do you think of the great man, then?' Mr. Nickell asked quite quietly, the general conversation enough to cover his words – or rather, Dr. Gilead's conversation, for he had a splendid voice.

'Is he a great man? I had never heard of him before I met him the other day,' said Hippolyta, with an effort not to sound acidic.

'Ah, so you haven't fallen under his spell, yet?' asked Mr. Nickell, with a little chuckle. 'You and Mrs. Milton both, I note.'

Indeed, Galatea was deliberately avoiding conversation with Dr. Gilead, having trapped Mr. Pumpton beside her. 'Well, I wonder about him myself, but there you are: the wife's convinced she'd be at death's door without his ministrations, so here we are in Ballater. She's followed him up the country, one spa at a time.'

'I'm sorry to hear she is ill,' said Hippolyta, curious. His wife had seemed very energetic, if a little nervy.

'Oh, ill enough, I suppose! You can't fatten her,' he confided, 'and she doesn't sleep well, and then she gets herself worked up and I get the butt end of it,' he added obliquely, with a sharply indrawn breath in emphasis. 'But whatever he gives her doesn't help much, I reckon. Smearing her with all kinds of concoctions, feeding her who knows what pills and powders made from orange peel and dead slaters, no doubt. See this?' He drew from his pocket first a round, red tin, with a label, and then a red paper package. 'Let me make you acquainted with the famous cordial balm and the infallible scarlet powders, a bargain at six shillings the set! And she gets through four of each a week. I'm fed up with her smelling like an alchemist's midden, quite honestly, Mrs. Napier. I'm telling you, I'll doctor her myself soon and have nothing more to do with him. I didn't make my money to pay it over to a fancy medical man when I could do just as well myself.'

'Do you have some medical training, then, Mr. Nickell?' Hippolyta asked, trying not to sound too dubious.

'Medical training? I've lived this long: I have some idea of how things work. If brandy and water don't fix it, then soda powders and strong ale will, and a feed of beef, just nicely done. Cure anything, that would.' He surveyed her over his tea cup, and his eyes twinkled again, but she was not sure that it was entirely a joke.

She glanced around the table to see if anyone else had been paying any attention to their conversation. Dr. Gilead was speaking mostly to her mother, but with the assumption, from his tone of voice, that everyone was attending to their conversation. Galatea was questioning Mr. Pumpton about, apparently, his legal business: as the wife of a lawyer and the daughter of another one she had enough information to make their exchange an intelligent one, though she seemed to be doing most of the talking. Mrs. Gilead, on the other hand, had fallen sideways out of the company

– she sat with her teacup already empty in front of her, working industriously at a piece of bread and butter, and staring at the table, saying nothing.

Hippolyta was about to lean over and ask her how she was finding Ballater, for want of anything better to say, when there was a loud voice at the parlour door demanding tea and cakes. Everyone turned at the sound except for little Mr. Pumpton, who shrank into himself as if he had suddenly been dried. The doorway was filled with red satin and nodding feathers on an enormous winged bonnet. Mrs. Pumpton had arrived.

'Here we all are!' she exclaimed when she saw them. 'How marvellous! Room for a little one?' she joked, pushing a spare chair towards the table like a costermonger with a particularly prominent barrow. Mrs. Nickell followed and stood beside Hippolyta, smiling brightly, as if expecting her to give up her seat beside Dr. Gilead. Instead Mr. Nickell quickly rose to offer his seat to his wife, and fetched himself another chair, sitting a little behind her and Hippolyta to leave room for Mrs. Pumpton's excessive girth. 'I've called for more tea, and cake, too,' Mrs. Pumpton explained, as if half the parish had not already heard her. 'Bathing always leaves me starving! Don't you find that, Mrs. Fettes? Absolutely ravenous!'

'Oh, me too!' cried Mrs. Nickell. 'Dr. Gilead, I am ravenous! May I have some bread and butter, please? Would that be all right?'

'Of course, dear,' said Mr. Nickell, passing her the plate. She took two slices. Hippolyta looked away hastily: Mrs. Nickell was so thin even in her gown that Hippolyta was half-afraid she might see the bread going down.

'Dear Dr. Gilead,' breathed Mrs. Pumpton across the table, her voluminous bosom billowing, 'is it quite right that bathing should improve my appetite so much? I feel – quite primitive, I assure you!' Her eyes widened dramatically. Mr. Pumpton by contrast closed his eyes.

'Bathing enlivens us, particularly in these invigorating chalybeate waters,' said Dr. Gilead with warm assurance. 'It is quite natural that your appetites should be stimulated, dear lady. Our modern society, misguided as it is, may frown on something so at one with creation, but it is wrong to do so.'

'I thought so,' said Mrs. Pumpton in satisfaction. 'And dear Dr. Gilead, the waters here are so delicious! It seems almost wrong to enjoy them so much – but now that you have explained about nature I know they are doing me so much good! I feel a new energy coursing through me!'

Mr. Pumpton, eyes still closed, gave a little involuntary shudder. Hippolyta was consumed by an urge to laugh, and had to dig her fingernails into the back of her hand this time. There was an air of unreality about the whole table: who were all these people who seemed so well acquainted with her mother and sister, and of whom she had never heard? Her mother had never mentioned a trip to Bath in her regular but scarce letters, nor to Harrogate, nor had Galatea talked before of Pitkeathly. And how were they so knowledgeable about bathing costs in Peterhead? And how her mother gazed up at Dr. Gilead's heavy lidded, piercing glances, as if she actually thought his grandiose utterances worthwhile. And Mr. Pumpton was such a nonentity, and Mrs. Gilead seemed far away, too. Hippolyta examined her more closely out of the corner of her eye. In the presence of Mrs. Pumpton she was even less communicative. She seemed a mousy creature, even her lips colourless, her only distinguishing features a mole on her chin sprouting a few faint hairs, and the bridge of her nose, which looked as if it had been stung by several bees. There was no dip between brow and nose, as was conventional.

Mrs. Pumpton was holding court now, very loud and confident. Rather than resenting the diversion of attention from him, Dr. Gilead seemed a little abstracted: any slight sound made him turn towards the parlour door. Was he expecting someone? Surely the courtiers he had gathered here were enough for him? For it was plain that Mrs. Nickell and Mrs. Pumpton would hang on his every word, and more alarmingly, so would her own mother. Was he as great a physician as he claimed? She could not imagine her mother falling for the blandishments of a charlatan, but if it were not so, and Dr. Gilead were really a great doctor, what harm would that do Patrick's practice? She felt a little less like laughing at the thought.

'Well, no doubt we'll see you all at the ball!' Mrs. Pumpton's generous voice issued forth over everyone else.

'What ball?' asked Galatea, suddenly wary.

'Why, the one on Friday night! I'm sure the whole village is talking about it!'

'No,' said Hippolyta, 'I don't think we are.'

'But everyone's invited. Here, in the hotel. There'll be fifty couples there, I'm sure, from the hotel and the lodge down the road and the village. It's the social occasion of the year around here!'

Mrs. Strachan had not mentioned it yesterday, and as far as Hippolyta was concerned Mrs. Strachan was the leader of Ballater society – the society of the village proper, not of the summer visitors. But a ball would be lovely, she thought wistfully. She had not danced with Patrick since they were married, except on silly evenings when they sang and danced around the parlour on their own, to amuse the cats. It would be delightful to stand up with him again in company. But no doubt her mother would consider it a waste of time, and Galatea would regard it as a tedious business.

'Of course we shall be there,' she heard her mother saying. 'Galatea is particularly eager to dance, are you not, dear?'

Hippolyta stared at them both. She could not remember ever in her life seeing her mother dance, and only recalled Galatea walloping about like a reluctant stook of corn at some charitable affair in the Assembly Rooms in Edinburgh, when provoked into it by their middle sister.

'Oh, yes,' said Galatea, with a mouth made to suck lemons. 'I'm looking forward to it.'

'Oh, it will be wonderful!' cried Mrs. Nickell, eyes alarmingly wide. 'I love to dance. I hope to dance with every man in the room!'

'Including me, I hope,' put in her husband with just the slightest edge to his voice.

'Of course, dear!' Mrs. Nickell frowned at him.

'I assume that dancing is beneficial exercise, dear Dr. Gilead,' Mrs. Pumpton boomed. 'I have always found it so.'

'In moderation, dear lady, it is a great benefit to the whole body.'

'Perhaps you will be able to demonstrate on the evening, as you have done so ably before, Dr. Gilead?' She surged over the table again. Hippolyta wondered that she managed not to knock over cups and saucers as she went.

'I shall be delighted to dance with all you ladies!' said Dr.

Gilead with benevolence, nodding at each of them with what Hippolyta felt was undue significance. Galatea responded only with a discontented sigh. Their mother smiled a little tightly.

'Such a shame Mr. and Mrs. Dewar cannot be with us, isn't it?' Mrs. Pumpton said, with just a hint of slyness.

'Mrs. Dewar cannot be here?' asked Mrs. Fettes in surprise.

'She has been delayed!' Mrs. Nickell assumed a tragic expression, but it looked artificial to Hippolyta.

'Has she?' Dr. Gilead's query was unusually quiet, and for once his wife lifted her dull gaze to stare at him. He did not appear to notice. 'I hope her health has not prevented her from travelling.'

'No, it was some family business,' said Mrs. Pumpton, without expression. She, too, glanced at Dr. Gilead before looking away and meeting Mrs. Nickell's eye briefly. Mrs. Fettes pursed her lips.

More tea and a plate of cake arrived, which did not long survive its appearance: Mrs. Pumpton and Mrs. Nickell demolished most of it, and Mr. Nickell managed to save a small slice for himself: no one else was able to get near it, though it looked good. Mrs. Pumpton wiped crumbs extravagantly from around her generous lips while Dr. Gilead expatiated upon a variety of current medical topics. Hippolyta tried to remember some of the names in order to ask Patrick about them later, though in the end each subject seemed to come back to the efficacy of the application of Dr. Gilead's famous cordial balm, or Dr. Gilead's celebrated infallible scarlet powders, neither of which Hippolyta ever remembered Patrick even mentioning, let alone recommending. She began to find Dr. Gilead rather boring, with his sonorous, dreamy voice, and felt embarrassed to catch his glittering gaze, so she found herself staring at the table cloth and letting her thoughts meander, the meaningless words rolling over her like a warm fog.

There was general coming and going in the parlour, but it took the hotel keeper approaching their table to rouse Hippolyta from her dwam, discreet though he was. He handed Mrs. Gilead a letter, murmuring inaudibly in her ear, but instead of slipping it into her reticule to read later, she rose and stood away from the table and opened it, scanning the contents swiftly. Then she stopped, and reread it, and took two steps after the hotel keeper, stopping him and asking some urgent question. The hotel keeper shrugged apologetically, and she frowned, folding the paper in her hands with great exactitude. This time she did place it in her reticule, and returned to the table, where the conversation had continued quite as if nothing had happened. She paused and caught her husband's eye. Whatever was there, he broke off at once.

'But no doubt I shall see you all again later. I must for the moment retire and rest a little from my labours, as must we all!' He stepped out gracefully from his seat and followed his wife from the room. Mrs. Nickell and Mrs. Pumpton sighed heavily, and Mr. Nickell stretched extravagantly.

'I could do with a little rest myself,' he said with a yawn, 'though damned if I know what I've been doing with my time. What about you, my dear? Time to catch up on some sleep?'

'I might go for another bathe,' said Mrs. Nickell. 'Mrs. Pumpton, what about you?'

'No, no, a nap first, I think,' said Mrs. Pumpton, rising from her seat like flood waters. 'Mrs. Fettes, are you going to sample the waters again today?'

'We shall go home, I think,' said Hippolyta's mother. She did look tired: Hippolyta hoped she would manage the walk back down the hill. Galatea helped her to gather up her things while Hippolyta waited.

'Delighted to have met you, Mrs. Nailor,' said Mrs. Nickell.

'Indeed, Mrs. Napier,' her husband said clearly. 'I hope we shall meet again soon – if not before, then at the ball?'

'If my mother wishes it, and my husband agrees, then certainly at the ball,' said Hippolyta politely. 'I hope it is well attended: I'm not sure that anyone in the village knows about it.'

'Oh, we'll make it a grand evening, whoever is here!' said Nickell cheerfully. 'If nothing else, watching old Mrs. Pumpton smothering Dr. Gilead is well worth the admission!'

'Hm,' said Hippolyta, trying not to smile.

'How ridiculous,' said Mrs. Fettes, as they set off down the hill. 'Imagine following Dr. Gilead all the way from Harrogate. And Bath!'

'Whereas following him from Edinburgh is perfectly reasonable,' Galatea muttered.

'What was that?' her mother demanded.

'Nothing, Mother: I was wondering what might have delayed the Dewars coming from Edinburgh, that is all.'

'Another hanger-on. How can the poor gentleman work when he is pursued by such a crowd of silly women?'

This time Galatea managed to say nothing. Hippolyta was silent, too, listening in bewilderment. What, she wondered again, was her mother up to? Whatever it was, Galatea clearly did not approve.

They arrived home without incident, though the last climb up the hill from the river had been a slow one. Mrs. Riach met them in the hall, and stopped Hippolyta before she could ask for tea.

'Mrs. Napier, could I have a word, ma'am?' Mrs. Riach's greeting was enough to turn Hippolyta's heart. She followed the housekeeper back to the kitchen in alarm.

'Fit's thon loon?' Mrs. Riach flung out a hand at a small boy sitting by the back door with a dog. The dog, soft, grey and inoffensive, recognised Hippolyta and trotted over, panting happily.

'Oh!' It was the boy that Mrs. Fettes had interrogated outside Strachan's shop the previous day. Hippolyta approached, and the boy, who had been looking thoroughly bored, pushed himself to his feet and brushed down the front of his coat. He was more neatly dressed than he had been: he had acquired a large pair of boots and some stockings, and at some point today his hair had been brushed.

'When did he arrive?' she asked.

'Eight o'clock this morn. He's been here ever since,' said Mrs. Riach sourly.

'Wullie, isn't it?' asked Hippolyta.

'Aye, ma'am.' The boy smiled, then seemed to remember some instructions not to. He scowled instead.

'What did my mother – what did Mrs. Fettes tell you would happen if you came here this morning?'

'She said there was work needing doing, ma'am. And I'd be paid, and not have to be sooshed by Al every night.'

'Hm.' Hippolyta did not appreciate her mother's attempts to change her household staff, nor her assumption that her welfare projects could be accommodated here. Nevertheless the boy had been clean and prompt, and it was not his fault that no one had mentioned his coming to Mrs. Riach. And with Ishbel busy upstairs, surely Mrs. Riach would appreciate a hand with heavy things in the kitchen?

'Mrs. Riach,' she said, hoping she was right, 'this is Wullie. Wullie will help you with kitchen things and such outdoor work as Ishbel has been doing, for two weeks, for bed and board and – and let me know what you think he is worth for his pay. At the end of two weeks we'll see how he has done. How does that sound, Wullie?'

'That sounds very fair, ma'am,' said Wullie, generously.

'Mrs. Riach?'

'Aye, I suppose.' But she did not look unhappy.

'You'll have to find him somewhere to sleep,' said Hippolyta.

'Under the kitchen table would do him grand. We've spare blankets,' said Mrs. Riach.

'There's just one thing, ma'am,' added Wullie.

'What's that?'

'It's my dog, ma'am. If I leave it at hame on its ainsome, Al'll kick it.'

'Will he indeed?' Hippolyta looked down at the little dog. It was difficult to say with any degree of accuracy what form its parents might have taken, but it was an endearing little thing.

'Does it chase cats or hens?'

Wullie contemplated the dog with pursed lips.

'I dinna ken that he would, ma'am.'

'Better tie him outside for now, while you're working, but make sure he has a bowl of water.'

'Aye, ma'am. Thank you, ma'am,' said Wullie, with a half-formed bow he had borrowed from someone bigger.

'You'd better get yon coat off and get started, then,' said Mrs. Riach, as Hippolyta left the room, wondering how to break it to Patrick that they had acquired a serving boy and, indeed, a dog.

Chapter Five

'I'm just not sure we can afford a manservant.' Patrick looked worried.

'He's not a manservant,' said Hippolyta quickly. 'He's just a boy. I'm sure he won't expect much. In his last job his payment was not being beaten by his big brother.'

'Who is his big brother?'

'Al, at Strachan's shop.'

'Oh, yes.' Patrick's eyes widened in recognition. He thought. 'And how was it again that you came to employ him?'

'Well, it was Mother, actually. She stopped to ask him why he wasn't in school, and it turned out he had left ... and then I missed a bit, and the next thing was that I overheard her telling him to turn up here yesterday morning. Which she presumably then forgot – which isn't like her,' she added, puzzled.

'So you have no idea what use he might be? Can he read? Write?'

'He looks clean and fit and healthy. He can do all kinds of heavy work inside and out for Mrs. Riach. I'm sure she's going to test him very thoroughly. And because my mother and Galatea haven't brought a maid with them – for some reason I have yet to fathom - Ishbel is having to do much more for them.'

'Has Mrs. Riach complained?' Patrick asked sharply.

'Well, no ...' Hippolyta had to be honest. 'But she has been limping again.'

Patrick looked more worried.

'What's the boy's name again?' he asked at last.

'Wullie.'

'Wullie.'

Hippolyta watched him, waiting to see if she would have to go and send Wullie home. Not that Patrick had yet sent home anything she had adopted, not even the hens which had arrived rather unexpectedly, but there might be a first time.

'He's willing to sleep under the kitchen table, just to avoid going home to his brother,' she said softly. Patrick met her eye, raising one eyebrow.

'So we're feeding him, too?'

'He can hardly eat much!'

'How many ten year old boys do you know?' Patrick asked with a laugh. 'Well, I hope he makes himself useful. If he doesn't, I'm afraid he will have to go home, Al or no Al.'

'Thank you, Patrick! I'm sure he'll be more than useful!' She kissed her husband emphatically, and went to her morning meeting with Mrs. Riach. Her feelings were mixed: she had managed not to mention the dog.

It might have been less than twelve hours in to Wullie's employment in the Napier household, but the effect on Mrs. Riach's mood had been marvellously beneficial. Hippolyta found her by the fire with Wullie's dog cradled comfortably on her lap, calmly observing breakfast being prepared by Ishbel. Wullie appeared cheerfully with the first buckets of water for the day, and asked what he was to do next. Ishbel had taken on an air of slight superiority, which was understandable, but Wullie caught on fast and had the wisdom to treat her with the respect her extra two years' seniority deserved. He bowed at Hippolyta's appearance in the kitchen, remembering not to grin. Hippolyta was impressed.

On her way back to the front of the house, though, she noticed movement out of the corner of her eye and found her sister Galatea inspecting the contents of the presses along the side passage, where Ishbel and Mrs. Riach had their rooms. The presses contained the linen, for the most part.

'Can I help?' Hippolyta asked, pointedly. 'Do you need a fresh towel?'

Galatea scowled, though as it was becoming her habitual expression it was hard to know if she was dissatisfied or not.

'I'm seeing if that housekeeper of yours is keeping your linen properly.'

'I'm certain she is,' said Hippolyta. She was not very sure how to keep linen properly, but nothing seemed to have gone amiss so far.

'I'm not sure I like the smell of her moth powders.'

'She mixes them herself. I rather like the smell,' said Hippolyta. 'Galatea, what is Mother doing?'

Galatea surveyed her little sister with apparent distaste.

'As far as I know she is still sleeping. Why?'

'That's not what I meant. I mean, what is she doing with all this bathing and talking with Dr. Gilead? He seems – he seems a bit odd to me.'

'Odd?' Galatea challenged her.

'Mother seems very fond of him. It's not like her,' she hedged. She was not sure she should repeat what Patrick had said last night when she had described Dr. Gilead's persuasive descriptions of his own patent cures. It had not been flattering. 'And you don't seem very happy. You don't seem to trust him, either. And where did she meet all these people?'

Galatea closed the door of the press.

'She met them in Bath – most of them. And it's none of your business what she's doing with them, or what I might think for or against them.'

'But you're staying in my house ...' Hippolyta began uncertainly. She was not used to speaking back to her sisters.

'We could move to the hotel if you'd prefer,' Galatea snapped.

'Oh no! No, please stay here.'

'Then concentrate on keeping your servants under control, and not on what Mother might or might not be doing. Now, do you imagine that woman will have any breakfast ready?'

She stalked past Hippolyta and through the door to the main hallway. Hippolyta stayed for a moment where she was. When would any of her family acknowledge that she was a grown woman now, with a household of her own – of her own, not one for Galatea to poke about in? She thought back over the conversation. Perhaps she should have told Galatea to go and stay in the hotel. It would have meant much less trouble for her and Patrick, not to mention the rest of the household. But it would have been very embarrassing to have to admit that her mother and sister were staying in Ballater but not at her own house. How could she explain that to people? Then another thought came to her, and she hurried after Galatea. Her sister had already gone into the parlour, and was seated at the breakfast table, waiting.

'Are you really going to go to the ball on Friday?' she asked.

'If Mother says so, then yes.'

Hippolyta studied her closely: she was sure that Galatea was less than thrilled to be going to the ball, but she was trying hard to hide it now.

'Do you think she'll say so?'

'Oh, yes. She'll want to go, no doubt.'

'Right.' Hippolyta left the room and went thoughtfully back through the kitchen – where breakfast was not yet ready – and out to the dispensary in the garden. She knocked on the door, and Patrick let her in.

'Good,' he said at once, 'I was afraid it was your sister again.'

'Did you know about the ball at Pannanich Wells Hotel on Friday night?' she asked, leaning against the door to avoid touching anything she should not.

'A ball? That sounds fun. Who is invited?'

'We all are, apparently: well, the society of the village.'

'Well, it's tempting, but I suppose we cannot very well go while your mother is here.'

'My mother intends to go.'

'What?' Patrick's hand slipped and he almost dropped a tray of lozenges. 'Your mother wants to go to a ball?'

'And Galatea is pretending that she wants to go too, but it's only because she doesn't want to explain to me what Mother is up to. What is she up to, Patrick? Is Papa ill? Is she assessing spas for her Edinburgh poor? Is something wrong with her? And what does she see in Dr. Gilead?'

'That's the real question: if nothing else your mother has always been a sensible woman – to the point of ...' He broke off with a grin. 'To the point of insensitivity, surely?'

Hippolyta nodded, distracted.

'It's a whole little circle up there, the Pumptons, the Nickells, the Gileads and Mother and Galatea. It's a club. It's not like Mother at all.'

'No, it isn't, you're right.' He set the lozenges safely on the bench and stepped over to take her hands. 'But no doubt we'll find out all in good time. Meanwhile, would you like to go to the ball?'

'Of course I would!'

'And if we go will you spend the whole evening worrying about your mother and your sister?'

'Not if you dance with me enough,' she said, looking up at him with a smile.

'Then let us go, and enjoy ourselves, and whatever happens will happen. Now, surely breakfast is ready? I'm starving!'

During breakfast Mrs. Fettes, who was contained in a cloud of medicinal scent that quite put Hippolyta off her eggs, confirmed that indeed, she had every intention of going to the ball on Friday, and also of bathing again that very morning. Hippolyta was not entirely surprised, and not reluctant to savour the strange, floating sensation again. Her mother had imperiously paid for yesterday's baths, so she did not even have to feel guilty about wasting money.

They travelled over in the boat again with Patrick. Mrs. Fettes seemed to feel that he was there to attend to them, rather than to see his patients, but as this pleased her no particular comment was made. At the other side of the crossing a couple of lads waited, ready to carry bags or run to fetch a chair from the hotel or the lodge: along with the boatmen they had been earning a healthy income since the bridge had been swept away. It was indeed an ill wind, Hippolyta thought.

Her mother seemed to have more of her usual energy today, and though she held Patrick's arm she did not seem to lean so heavily on it until they were almost at the top of the hill.

With the strength, Mrs. Fettes' ability to face her acquaintances equably, if not amicably, had also returned. Mrs. Pumpton was already taking up most of the hot bath when they reached it, and Mrs. Nickell slid in shortly afterwards, apparently more shift than flesh, but Mrs. Fettes was courteous and surprisingly tolerant even of Mrs. Pumpton's endless talk of what Dr. Gilead had said at dinner the previous evening, and how beautifully he had played the box piano for her own singing afterwards. Hippolyta blinked, and hoped Patrick would not have to listen to them. He had a very musical ear.

Whether the other ladies had procrastinated in their cold bath and dressing to allow them to catch up, or not, they all seemed to be ready at the same time to cross the cobbled space between the baths and the hotel, and Mrs. Pumpton was hardly in the doorway before she called out heartily for tea and cake, and plenty of both. The large table in the corner of the parlour was free – or rather, one nervous-looking man vacated it rapidly when he saw Mrs. Pumpton and Mrs. Fettes approach – and they established themselves around it as if they had been doing so every day for weeks. The tea appeared very rapidly: Hippolyta supposed that they made the trays ready when they saw guests go off to the bathhouse, so as to be prompt on their return. After a moment, she realised that someone else had anticipated their return very aptly: in another corner of the parlour, where the spring sunlight poured reverently over the glistening crown of his white hair, sat Dr. Gilead. Though he was frowning down at a notebook, the pen poised above the page and his other hand touching his brow and cheek so lightly they would leave no unsightly blotch, Hippolyta was quite sure he knew exactly who had just arrived and probably just how long it would take them to discover him. Not long, it appeared.

'Dear Dr. Gilead!' Mrs. Pumpton exclaimed, and if he had really been concentrating he would have jumped in astonishment. Instead he affected a drawing-back in surprise, then rose at once and came over to them. 'You'll join us for tea, of course?'

'I should be delighted,' Dr. Gilead murmured, kissing first her hand, then giggling Mrs. Nickell's, and last, with a kind of agonised grace, Mrs. Fettes. 'You ladies have been bathing?'

'Of course,' said Mrs. Pumpton. Dr. Gilead moved on smoothly to bow to Galatea and Hippolyta, though she noted that he did not waste his hand-kissing on them. 'Come here, dear Dr. Gilead, I insist you sit beside me!'

'Then who am I to refuse such an honour?' He swept out his coat tails and seated himself by her. Hippolyta was sure he was angling his legs beneath the table like an old-fashioned gallant in a French tapestry.

'Hippolyta, call for another cup and saucer,' said her mother, and Hippolyta obediently rose and went to find a hotel servant. When she returned, the conversation was already circling around Dr. Gilead's famous cures.

'The balm, of course,' said Dr. Gilead, his unctuous tones somewhere between physician and flirt, 'is for external application only. Indeed I am sure it would be most unpleasant were one to consume it!' The ladies, except for Galatea and Hippolyta, tittered: Hippolyta found it very uncomfortable to acknowledge that her mother was capable of tittering. Galatea merely looked as if an idea had struck her. 'But no doubt you ladies are all expert in the use of both the balm and the powders.' He had drawn breath to continue with his sermon, when Mrs. Fettes, who was facing the parlour door, suddenly exclaimed,

'Mrs. Dewar! You have arrived!'

Several things happened at once. Mrs. Pumpton squawked in delight, surging back from the table for a better view. Mrs. Nickell choked on her biscuit, and Galatea thumped her back a little too harshly. Dr. Gilead sprang from his seat so fast that it toppled over backwards, and was at the door in a moment to greet the newcomer. Hippolyta, surprised at all this fuss, looked on with interest.

For a moment she could not see Mrs. Dewar, for Dr. Gilead entirely concealed her from view. Instead all Hippolyta could see around him was a fine-looking man, a face marred only by a weak chin and a forehead creased with anxiety, standing in the doorway, entirely impeded by the meeting between his wife and Dr. Gilead. For a moment no words were spoken, then Dr. Gilead bowed and led Mrs. Dewar to the table, followed by her silent husband.

Mrs. Dewar was beautiful, Hippolyta saw at once. The second thing she saw was that Mrs. Dewar had been more beautiful, but that her beauty was fading, not so much through age as through illness. Her hair, which was thick, had almost certainly been more glossy and without that sprinkle of grey. Her face, formed in loveliness, was lined with pain, and her eyes, still a deep brown, were tired. Yet she smiled, not only at Dr. Gilead, but around the table generally, with a pleasure more genuine than that of all the other ladies there. Dr. Gilead gave her his own seat, and she sank into it gratefully. Mr. Dewar bowed to the company and sat beside her, while Dr. Gilead, his movements for once unplanned, looked about him in confusion and eventually moved to the seat between Mrs. Pumpton and Mrs. Fettes.

'How lovely to see you all again!' said Mrs. Dewar in a voice that was clear, but seemed to have some effort behind it. 'I had hoped to be here earlier, but we were delayed a little.'

'Business matters in Edinburgh,' her husband added apologetically. He reached out a hand to his wife's, concerned eyes on her face. 'Otherwise we should have come directly.'

'Well, you are here in good time for a ball on Friday night!' cried Mrs. Pumpton heartily.

'A ball? How lovely!' said Mrs. Dewar, though she did not look strong enough to dance. 'We'll look forward to that, won't we, dear?'

'Of course.' Mr. Dewar looked about the table. 'Would you like some refreshment? You mentioned tea, I think.'

'Of course!' Mrs. Pumpton waved a broad hand about the table. 'There's plenty!'

'Hippolyta, fetch more cups and saucers,' her mother commanded.

'Yes, mother.' Hippolyta reluctantly tore herself away from her perusal of the new arrivals, and was about to hurry out to the hall again when Mr. Dewar rose beside her.

'Madam, forgive me: we have not been introduced?'

'My daughter, Mrs. Napier,' said Mrs. Fettes shortly. Hippolyta curtseyed with a smile to both of them.

'Frederick Dewar,' said the man, 'and my wife.'

'How do you do?' said Hippolyta.

'Poll, cups and saucers.'

'Yes, Mother.' Wondering if she should then go and play in the nursery like a good little girl, Hippolyta contented herself with rolling her eyes at the wall, and went to find a hotel servant.

In the hallway, there was no one, and she ventured further into the hotel to see whom she could find. Along the passageway, a door opened, and a stocky man perhaps in his early thirties emerged directly into her path.

'I beg your pardon,' he said gruffly, looking displeased. He had a rough face and a small, ungenerous mouth, his upper teeth slightly protruding as though he would like to bite something. His eyes were tiny and somehow flat.

'Not at all,' she replied. The door of the room he had left stood open, and inside it she glimpsed Mrs. Gilead, talking with a man who had his back to her. There was no sign of a servant, and so she continued, glancing back, while the man who had walked into her strode out through the front door and into the cobbled yard outside.

She found a door across the passageway and pushed through, ending up as she had expected in the staff quarters. This attracted the attention of the hotel servants much faster than ringing a bell, and a young man sped up to her very promptly. She gave her instructions, and made him feel better by returning to the correct side of the door at once.

Further up the passageway she could see Mrs. Gilead emerging from the room she had seen her in, and heading towards the parlour. Hippolyta lingered a little, not particularly wanting to catch up with the famous physician's mousy wife, and instead collided with yet another person emerging from the same room. It was the man she had glimpsed speaking with Mrs. Gilead, and one she knew well.

'Mr. Durris!'

'Mrs. Napier! I did not expect to see you here.'

The sheriff's man, well-built and dark haired, bowed respectfully. His grey eyes blinked behind his round glasses.

'Nor I you! Has something happened?' She dropped her voice, aware of the proximity of the open parlour door.

'Well ...' he said slowly. 'May I ask what you are doing here, first?'

Hippolyta hesitated, not quite sure how to explain, then decided that the simple facts would be sufficient for now. As usual with Durris, she felt that odd ambiguity: was he a gentleman or a servant? No one seemed quite to know where he stood, though he appeared completely comfortable wherever he was encountered.

'I'm here with my mother and sister: they have come to stay with us. My mother wanted to bathe, and while in the baths she met some acquaintances of hers. They include,' she added, wanting to make a connexion with whatever he was up to, 'Dr. and Mrs. Gilead.'

Durris' eyebrows rose politely.

'I should not have thought,' he said slowly, 'that Dr. Napier would have found Dr. Gilead particularly congenial.'

'My husband has only met him once,' Hippolyta explained. 'Dr. Gilead was very ... kindly towards him. As a colleague.' They met one another's eye.

'But you find him more persuasive, perhaps?' Durris

suggested gently. Hippolyta was shocked.

'Not at all! Nor does my sister, I believe!'

'And your mother? Forgive me, I do not know her name.'

'Mrs. Fettes.'

There was a pause, during which Hippolyta did not answer Durris' question. He nodded, and she was forced to respond.

'No, you don't understand! She would never normally … She's not in the least an impressionable woman, I promise you!'

'I never said she was.'

They stared at each other in silence, before Durris cleared his throat pointedly.

'Have you by any chance – or has Mrs. Fettes – come across a Mrs. Dewar?'

'Mrs. Dewar? Oh, she is in the parlour now: I believe she and her husband have only just arrived.'

'Oh!' Durris thought for a moment. 'Mrs. Napier, would you consider it quite proper to step into this room with me for a moment? We can leave the door open, but here in the passageway – I am not comfortable that we might not be overheard.'

'Of course.' She led the way into the room where he had been speaking with Mrs. Gilead. It was a pleasantly furnished little private parlour, where a few ladies might without distress sit and attend to their correspondence of a morning. The fire was not lit, but it was not chilly. Hippolyta sat in a chair which was clearly visible from the door, and Durris placed himself opposite her – just as he had been seated with Mrs. Gilead.

'Mrs. Napier, you say that Mrs. Dewar has just arrived, and that you are acquainted with Dr. Gilead. Have you any idea of Dr. Gilead's estimation of Mrs. Dewar?'

'He was there just now when she arrived with her husband.' Something made her want to keep stressing the presence of Mr. Dewar: if nothing else, it implied Mrs. Dewar's respectability.

'May I ask what you thought when you saw them meeting?'

'Have you met Dr. Gilead?'

'Yes, briefly.'

'Were there ladies present?'

His eyebrows rose.

'Only Mrs. Gilead, when I met him.'

'Mm. Well, to give you a fair impression, I should tell you

what he is like when there are ladies around. He is attentive to the point of nausea, Mr. Durris: he kisses hands and gazes and flatters, but all the time he is completely in control of himself and the situation, as far as I have seen, and once everything is in place it is merely a stage for his performance, and that is an advertisement for his blessed cordial balm and efficacious powders, or whatever they are.'

'He's that obvious?'

'He is: but he seems to have chosen his audience well, and they lap it up. Even my mother … Anyway, never mind her.'

'So he has an entourage, perhaps?'

'That is the very word! There are three ladies in there, Mrs. Pumpton, Mrs. Nickell and my mother, and they hang on his every word. Mr. Pumpton is almost invisible, and Mr. Nickell doesn't take things seriously, and my father is not here, and Dr. Gilead simply holds court.'

'And Mrs. Dewar?'

'Mrs. Dewar … yes. Well, when she came in – with her husband – it was as if Dr. Gilead lost all that control. He knocked his chair over, and seemed confused.'

'Perhaps a coincidence.'

'Perhaps. I have not known him for long, certainly.'

'And what was Mrs. Dewar's reaction?'

'Mrs. Dewar – well, I did not have much chance to see that. Mother sent me out – that is, I went to order more cups and saucers for the new arrivals.' She frowned, not so willing to let Mr. Durris see how easily her mother could order her about.

'But your first impression?'

'She was not so bowled over by Dr. Gilead as the others, I thought. It was a moment's impression, I grant you, but my thought was that I liked her: that she was a sensible woman. But very beautiful,' she added, her artist's eye demanding she be fair.

'Just a first impression,' said Durris, thoughtfully. 'Have you met Mrs. Gilead?'

'Yes, though one would hardly know it. I am not sure I have heard her say a word. She seems a mouse, beside Dr. Gilead.'

'I see. She called me here today,' Mr. Durris explained, 'because her husband has been receiving anonymous letters. Perhaps it would do no harm – I know it will go no further, unless you discuss it with Dr. Napier – if you were to see this.'

He handed her a sheet of letter paper, thin and folded in the conventional way. She undid it and skimmed the neat hand that covered the page within.

'I know,' it said, 'that you and Mrs. Dewar are up to no good. Cease at once, or both your marriage and your honour will be in ruins, and your business destroyed. Cordially yours: RETRIBUTION.'

'Good gracious!' said Hippolyta.

Chapter Six

'A ball? Michty me!' exclaimed Miss Strong, stocky, stern, and sixty if she was a day, surely. She glanced about her where she stood at the top of the village green, looking for other people to tell.

'Aye,' said her sister Ada with an extravagant nudge of the elbow, 'Borrow one of Mrs. Napier's fashionable gowns and we'll maybe get you married off at last!'

'Ada!' said Miss Strong in her usual admonitory tone. 'And anyway, you're no more married off than I am!'

'Aye, but I have to wait for my elder to go first,' said Ada solemnly. She was maybe all of a couple of years the younger. 'And besides, never mind borrowing Mrs. Napier's fashionable gowns – I'll make do with borrowing Dr. Napier himself!' She widened her faded brown eyes suggestively at Hippolyta, who managed to be less shocked than she used to be at the idea that this old maid might pounce on her beloved husband. She laughed.

She was simply enjoying escaping for what the locals called a news, without her mother or Galatea listening in disapprovingly. Mrs. Fettes that morning was tired after two days bathing, and Galatea, grim as ever, had elected to stay at home and write letters. The phrase made Hippolyta remember her conversation with Mr. Durris, the sheriff's man, the previous day at the hotel, and the anonymous letter he had shown her. They had discussed briefly whether it was warning or threatening, and neither could decide entirely. When Galatea had emerged from the parlour like a dissatisfied fog to see what had become of her, Mr. Durris had mysteriously faded away before he could be introduced, and Hippolyta had chosen to follow his example by not mentioning either him or the letters to anyone else.

'I'm sure my husband would love to dance with you, Miss Strong,' she said to Ada with a grin. 'I gather the ball is principally for the people staying at the hotel and the lodge, but they seemed to feel that the village had been invited, too.'

'Well, it will take us out of ourselves, no doubt,' said Miss Strong, resignedly. She gave the impression she would far rather be left peacefully inside herself.

'What'll take me out of myself,' said Ada, 'after the prospect of that dance with Dr. Napier, of course, is watching all the dancers trying to keep their gowns out of the water on the boat across to Pannanich! That'll be the divert of the evening!'

'Oh.' Hippolyta had not gone as far as thinking of that. She mentally crossed off her best evening dress, and moved down to the second best. Miss Ada's eyes twinkled.

'Do you ken any of the high heidyins up at the hotel, then, that you're up to the minute with all this enterteenment?' she asked, poking Hippolyta in the arm not too gently. It was part of her habitual provoking of her sister that she spoke when she remembered to in Scots.

'Ada!' said her sister automatically.

'My mother Mrs. Fettes has been bathing up there for two days and she has some acquaintance amongst some of the other bathers – from Bath, I believe. The acquaintance, not the people. Well, two of them are from Somersetshire, but the rest are from other places.'

'And what like are they?' Ada was ready for any gossip.

'There's a Mrs. Pumpton, who is generously built and lively, with a quiet husband. They're from near Bath. Then there's a couple called Nickell, who are from Yorkshire: they're younger, and seem eager to enjoy themselves - in a respectable way, of course,' she added.

'Of course,' said Miss Strong, gripping her sister's arm to stop her saying anything.

'Then there are the Dewars, from down Edinburgh direction – I've only just met them. She doesn't seem very well: she's perhaps not fit to dance. She's very lovely, though in a faded way. Then there are the Gileads.'

'Heavens, you know the whole boorachie!' cried Ada in delight.

'Ada!'

'What like are the Gileads, then?' She nudged Hippolyta again. 'Is he *balmy*?' She chortled at her own joke.

'Well, he sells balm,' said Hippolyta when Ada had calmed down again. Miss Strong frowned heavily, presumably in righteous disapproval of a Biblical pun.

'Does he, though?' she asked, curious despite herself.

'He's a – well, he's Dr. Gilead,' Hippolyta amended, mindful of Patrick's reservations She hoped to keep the Strongs amongst Patrick's patients, not have them wandering off to the newcomer, but Miss Ada was always susceptible to a handsome man. 'He seems to have a small coterie of patients who use various spas about the country, and they have all just arrived here.'

'Oh,' said Miss Strong, still frowning. 'And is Mrs. Fettes one of the coterie? For that would be some recommendation of his skills, I should think: not that we should wish to go to anyone but dear Dr. Napier, of course,' she added, sensitive enough to realise that Hippolyta might be anxious. 'And it would be useful to know what Dr. Napier thinks of the balm.'

'I'm not sure if my mother is of the coterie or not,' said Hippolyta honestly, but skipping the question of Patrick's professional opinions. 'I have never known my mother be ill.'

'She is not ill now, either, surely!'

'No, she is not. I think,' she added, but she did wonder. It was not like her mother to be tired so often, either.

'Mrs. Strachan!' exclaimed Miss Ada. 'Mrs. Kynoch!'

The beautiful Mrs. Strachan was approaching carrying a little basket of elegant design. Mrs. Kynoch, not much more than half her height and decidedly unaffected by any elegance, trotted along beside her.

'Mrs. Strachan, you'll know all about the ball at Pannanich Wells Hotel!' cried Miss Ada by way of greeting.

'Yes, indeed.' Mrs. Strachan smiled. 'Mr. Strachan hopes to take our daughters and me, if the weather is not unfavourable. The tickets are to be sold to raise money for the new bridge.'

'A worthy cause as well, then,' said Miss Strong, as if there were no further point in resistance. She sighed. 'I suppose we may go, if our brother will rouse himself from his papers and escort us.' Mr. Strong was the village's law agent.

71

'How exciting!' said Mrs. Kynoch. 'I shall look forward to that!'

'Now, Mrs. Kynoch,' said Miss Ada sternly, 'you've had your chance with a husband, so I want none of your competition if we can get my sister a good partner in the first two dances. Do you agree to let her go before you if a worthy man presents himself? I'm not saying a gentleman, mind,' she added, to the accompaniment of her sister's sharp 'Ada!'. 'She's beyond the age where she can afford to be perjink. A comfortably off tradesman with a few years left in him would do very well. And it would be best if he were not too perjink, either.'

'Dear Miss Ada!' Mrs. Kynoch laughed. 'I shan't stand in the way of either of you!'

'Then away we go!' cried Miss Ada. 'There'll be wedding bells before midsummer, I can tell you!' Even Miss Strong had to allow a smile at her sister's silliness, before dragging her off home, leaving the other ladies still laughing.

'I doubt there are too many eligible husbands up at the Pannanich Wells Hotel,' squeaked Mrs. Kynoch as the Strongs went. 'It seems to me that more ladies than gentlemen visit the wells, and most of the visiting males are married.'

'Of the ones I have met, yes, that is certainly the case,' said Hippolyta. She repeated what she had told the Strongs about the couples she had met at Pannanich. Mrs. Strachan nodded quickly.

'Is Dr. Gilead tall, with white hair in a tail, like a rather fine wig?' she asked. 'I believe I may have seen him about the village.'

'That's quite possible: Dr. Napier and I met him just outside the inn on Monday.'

'An extraordinary looking man,' said Mrs. Strachan. Hippolyta could not quite make out if she meant it as a compliment or not.

'Extraordinarily struck by his own good looks, I thought,' murmured Mrs. Kynoch discreetly, but Mrs. Strachan did not appear to hear. Hippolyta nodded to herself: Mrs. Kynoch's good sense confirmed that her own instincts were correct. It looked as if Patrick were in no danger of losing Mrs. Kynoch as a patient – though she had never, to Hippolyta's knowledge, asked for his help. 'And is Mrs. Fettes enjoying her stay? And your sister Mrs. Milton?' Mrs. Kynoch went on.

'My mother is deriving some benefit from bathing at the wells,' said Hippolyta. She was not quite sure what the benefit was, but no doubt her mother was deriving something useful. 'She has not done much else since she arrived, but I think the freshness of the air impresses her greatly. Indeed, she would have to be quite insensitive not to notice it, would she not?'

'Well, we all think so!' Mrs. Kynoch agreed. 'And after a smoky city it is particularly noticeable, certainly. And Mrs. Milton is occupying her time usefully?'

That was perceptive of Mrs. Kynoch, Hippolyta thought. Useful employment, or what she thought was useful employment, was much more likely to keep her sister happy than leisure to read or to paint. She reflected on Galatea's examination of Mrs. Riach's work.

'Um, yes,' she said after a moment. 'Up to a point, certainly. But if you had any practical thing that might need doing over the next few weeks, I am sure she would be only too happy to take command – er, to help. She is a good and quick seamstress, for example, if something needed to be sewn. Or she is well used to visiting the sick … should you happen to know of any sick person in need of such a visit? A – a more robust sick person, that is. Perhaps in one of the farther hamlets? She has great energy,' she added quickly, lest Mrs. Kynoch think she wanted her sister out of the house for as long as possible. Perish the thought that Mrs. Kynoch should think any such thing.

'I'll have a word with the minister's wife,' said Mrs. Kynoch – everyone knew that the present minister's wife was a timid, nervy thing and that Mrs. Kynoch had very much kept on with the parish work she had done when her own husband, the late minister, had been alive. 'We'll see if we can come up with something useful. No doubt we'll be very grateful.'

'Oh, I too!' said Hippolyta slightly too enthusiastically. 'I mean, I should like her to feel that her stay is of some practical value.'

'Of course: it is always lovely to be wanted.'

She returned home mid-morning to find that Galatea had cleaned out the pantry, including the last four jars of Mrs. Riach's remarkable strawberry conserve, rendering Mrs. Riach prone to violence; Wullie's dog had been pursued by three of the cats and was hiding under the henhouse, refusing to emerge; one of the hens had succeeded in gaining the seclusion of Patrick's study again and shown her gratitude by laying a stray egg in the coal scuttle; and her mother had risen refreshed and re-energised, and wished to go to Pannanich to bathe before dinner. Hippolyta's wary suggestion that she and Galatea knew the way now and could easily go without her (while she dealt with the various minor crises about the house which she chose not to describe to her mother) was met with a look of cold disbelief, and she found herself tying her bonnet back on in front of the hall mirror, aware of Mrs. Riach's presence in the kitchen, of Ishbel clearing up the mess in the study, and of several smug cats washing innocently in the parlour. She sighed, and followed her mother and Galatea off to cross the river and climb the hill again to the wells.

Bathing at a slightly different time of day meant that they met strangers from the lodge in the baths rather than their acquaintances, and for once Hippolyta was grateful. The company of the ebullient Mrs. Pumpton and Mrs. Nickell with her nervous energy was tiring, and though she would have liked to have seen more of Mrs. Dewar, her frailness made Hippolyta, healthy as she was, nervous. Her mother seemed reluctant to converse much in the company of strangers, and Hippolyta was able just to float and relax, enjoying the buoyant sensation and the luxurious lapping of water against her skin. The attendant was a particularly good one, who rubbed her dry with a pleasant rough efficiency, and it was with some regret that she left the baths at last and joined her mother and sister for the inevitable tea in the hotel. She hoped that as with the bath itself, changing the time of arrival might mean that they did not have to sit and have tea with the usual people, either.

Mrs. Pumpton was not going to allow such a deviation from the routine. She flung herself back from the usual large table in the parlour, arms spread, welcoming them the moment they arrived. Her husband was as usual somewhat obscured in her voluminous shadow, and Mr. Nickell was attendant upon his springy, pop-eyed wife. Hippolyta expected to see Mr. and Mrs. Dewar completing the table, or Dr. Gilead holding court, but instead Mr. Dewar was in attendance without his wife, Mrs. Gilead without her husband, and the flat-eyed young man she had met in the hall the day before had joined their table. He seemed not to remember Hippolyta, and scowled up equally at all three of them as they came in. Mrs. Fettes gave him a brusque nod, of the kind she was accustomed to reserving for tradesmen who persistently failed to donate what she felt they could afford to her good causes. Galatea for once seemed less hostile.

Mrs. Gilead nodded to them all, then indicated the young man.

'My son, Peter,' she murmured, so low that Hippolyta wondered whether she would have preferred to hide the fact. Peter rose ungraciously, and bowed.

'My daughter, Mrs. Napier,' Mrs. Fettes responded without emphasis. Chairs were fetched, and they joined the party, with Mr. Nickell playing humorous reluctance to go and order more tea. Peter Gilead watched him go with an expression of distaste. Hippolyta tried to observe him without being seen. He had certainly inherited none of his father's striking looks, and along with his generally unappealing appearance he had his mother's odd thick bridge to the nose. In his case it gave the impression of someone who had lost one or two fights too many in the boxing ring. Hippolyta wondered if his resentment at the ill fortune dealt to him made him appear so hostile. She felt she would like to draw him, though on the whole she was better at animals and landscapes. Did he look more like an animal – or perhaps a rocky headland? He could easily have been either, for all he joined in the conversation. In fact, an animal would have been more communicative. She remembered poor Wullie's dog, and hoped it had dared to come out from under the henhouse. The cats would have to be taught that it was not a plaything. And that poor hen would have to be discouraged from regarding the study as her nest box: why was she doing that? Were the other hens persecuting her in some way? She must remember to close the study door on the night of the dance, for they might be away for some hours and who knew what havoc the hen might wreak, particularly if the cats followed her in – or followed the dog in. And she must remember to wear her second best evening gown for the dance, because of the boat. She had found a ribbon in Strachan's shop that was the perfect colour for her hair, but she had so imagined herself in her best gown that she was having difficulty in rearranging her plans. The best gown had such a beautiful heavy skirt, with lilies

embroidered on it in swags of thick stitching, and it sat so well
through the figures of a quadrille, particularly La Pastourelle.
Could she remember how to dance a quadrille? It had been so long
since she had last danced properly. Patrick would know, though: he
would guide her through it. And what other partners might she
have? There were not so many men of dancing age in the village.
Mr. Nickell? Poor little Mr. Pumpton? Please not Dr. Gilead, or
she would have to refuse and then she would not be able to dance
with anyone else. His surly son? Even that might be better.

'Poll!'

She came back to the tea table with a jump.

'Yes, Mother?'

'Go and see if there is any of that shortbread. Mr. Dewar was
just saying how little Mrs. Dewar is eating, but she might just
manage a little of that. The hotel cook's shortbread is quite
delicious, Mr. Dewar.'

'I fear it might be a little rich for her stomach,' said Mr.
Dewar.

'Nonsense. Anyone can manage a morsel of excellent
shortbread. I heard Dr. Gilead say she was growing much better.
Poll!'

'Yes, Mother.'

Hippolyta rose, digging her fingernails into her palms, and left
to find a hotel servant.

In the hallway, near a door that led to a little lodge for the
porter, she found a maid who was prepared to go and interrogate
the cook about shortbread. She watched the girl go, but stayed
there, just out of sight of the occupants of the parlour, drawing
breath before she should go back in. Would she ever be even
remotely grown up in her mother's eyes? Probably not: she
pictured herself at ninety, impossibly hooped and wrinkled, sharing
a grim house of widows with her mother and sisters, and still being
treated as the baby. On the other hand, her mother would then be
around a hundred and thirty … Suddenly that seemed like a terrible
possibility.

'Mrs. Napier!'

She jumped so violently she had to clutch at the wall for
support. Looking about her for the source of the sudden whisper,
she poked her head around the door of the porter's lodge and found

Mr. Durris, just risen from a stool, looking apologetic.

'Mr. Durris! What on earth are you doing here?'

'Oh, quietly, please, Mrs. Napier! Forgive me,' he added with his usual steady decorum. 'I had not intended you to share this tiny space in such a position of intimacy.'

'But why are you here? Is this to do with the anonymous letter?' she said in a low voice, knowing that the very sound of a whisper can attract attention in exactly the way the whisperer does not want.

'Yes, it is. I'm waiting to see if another letter is delivered. That was not the only one, you see: only one in a series.'

'And have you seen any more arrive?'

'No.' He looked unhappy for a moment. 'Did you by any chance mention your meeting with me to anyone else yesterday?'

'No, not at all. Well, I told my husband in the evening that I had seen you here, but not what you were doing. You did ask me not to,' she went on, with an edge of reproach in her voice. He nodded, acknowledging it.

'Yes, I am sorry to doubt you. Perhaps Mrs. Gilead ... You see, the only people who should know who I am or why I am here amongst that circle are Mrs. Gilead, her husband and her son. Yet this morning a letter did arrive for Dr. Gilead, just as previously, and worded very much like the one I showed you.'

'Well, presumably the writer did not know that you would be keeping watch ...'

'But that is just it, Mrs. Napier,' Durris interrupted, pushing his glasses up his nose. 'I have been here since half-past five this morning, with the exception of five minutes when I left – for the usual reasons. And in that five minutes, today's letter was delivered.'

'But ... but that means that the person who sent it knows exactly who you are and why you are here, does it not?'

'It seems that way,' agreed Durris.

'And that means ... well, did you say that they had been receiving letters for some time?'

'Since they arrived here.'

'Then the person sending them is perhaps not of that party at all, but a local inhabitant? Would you not agree?'

'It looks very like it, I'm afraid.'

'I feel slightly ashamed. As if I were somehow responsible for the behaviour of all the people in Ballater.'

'I know what you mean,' he said in a low voice, staring at the floor. 'But you are not: I am not, though perhaps I come closer to it, in a way.' He looked dejected, and she grinned at him, trying to cheer him up.

'No, neither of us is. The difference between us is, though, that you will no doubt discover the perpetrator and see to his punishment, whereas I, I'm afraid, will do nothing so useful.'

'Mrs. Napier?'

A voice from near the parlour door made her turn round. Durris slipped silently back into the porter's lodge and pushed the door against her gently. She stepped out properly into the hallway. Mr. Nickell was propped against the hall wall, watching her with an amused expression that dropped her into mild confusion.

'I came to see if you were managing to find a supply of that marvellous shortbread,' he said, drawling out his north country vowels. 'Though Mr. Dewar is convinced Mrs. Dewar doesn't have a hope of eating any of it. No doubt we'd find a use for it, somewhere amongst us.' He smiled at her.

'Yes, I sent a maid to see if there was any,' Hippolyta confirmed. 'She shouldn't be long now.'

'But you thought it might be a good idea to see if there were any in the porter's lodge?' he asked, still smiling. There was something conspiratorial about that smile, Hippolyta decided.

'Now that would be a silly idea, wouldn't it, Mr. Nickell?' she tried. 'If we want to trace the shortbread – and I am sure we would all appreciate having some with our tea – then we need to pursue the maid in the other direction.'

'I should hate to think of you risking all kinds of perils alone in the staff quarters on our behalf, Mrs. Napier,' said Mr. Nickell. 'If you must pursue this quest, please at least allow me to be your knight errant, and escort you?'

He gave a bow which would have been more elegant before he developed his well-fed stomach.

'I believe,' said Hippolyta, frowning studiously, 'that a knight errant went on the quest instead of the lady, rather than alongside her. We ladies are not noted for questing, you know!'

'Nevertheless, madam,' Mr. Nickell began, but at that moment the maid appeared in the passageway, bearing a large ashet of fresh shortbread. From the scent, it had only just been liberated from the oven. It would have been enough to distract the boldest knight errant with any degree of a sweet tooth, and Mr. Nickell, still grinning, followed it and the maid back into the parlour, pausing only in the doorway to wave Hippolyta after him.

'Come along, Mrs. Napier, for not even a knight errant could guarantee the safety of that little plateful!' he cried cheerfully, and vanished. Hippolyta glanced back at the half-closed door of the porter's lodge.

'A bit of a character, then?' came the low voice of Mr. Durris. 'That was Mr. Nickell, did I hear you say?'

'That's right. I'd better go, or I suspect he will tease me endlessly about porter's lodges. He's that kind of man. Good day to you, ah, porter.'

'Good day, Mrs. Napier, ma'am.'

By the time she had returned to her seat in the parlour, half the shortbread had already disappeared, and there seemed to be little hope of Mrs. Dewar on her sickbed receiving any of it.

Chapter Seven

There was to be no bathing at the Wells on the Friday, not even the earliest session, for the hotel was preparing for the ball in the evening. It was quite possible that only the most sickly of the guests missed it, for all those for whom bathing was simply a distraction from the ennui of their existence had plenty to think about. Hippolyta, whose life was already quite busy, woke in the morning with her head so full of what she would wear and how she would arrange her hair and what the hotel might look like laid out for such a gala occasion that the thought of bobbing around in a pool of hot water in her shift never even crossed her mind.

Dressing began after an early and informal dinner, with a fresh shift, silk stockings, and stays (drawn tight by Ishbel, who was almost as excited as Hippolyta). Reluctantly Hippolyta then stepped into her best thick quilted petticoat: it would lend the perfect shape to her gown, but it meant that the least exertion and she would be ready to try the cold bath again. The laces were secured, and then Ishbel turned to lift the great heap of silk that was her best evening gown. Well, she thought, how could she only wear her second best one when there was not likely to be another ball on this scale in a twelvemonth? No, she was going to risk it, boat or no boat.

Patrick had made her a present of the gown for her birthday, listening to her lively accounts of each fitting as attentively as a good husband should, and she remembered finally trying it on to show him. The result had been very gratifying for both of them, she remembered with a smile, as Ishbel fastened the tapes at her waist. She stroked the steep slopes of deep pink silk that flowed down to just above her ankles, ornamented with the lush embroidered roses in darker pink and white, matching the little rosebuds on her pink slippers. Above her slim waist her sleeves swept out to each side, emphasised with rows of frills, finishing with a final white ribboned edge at her elbow. The setting drew attention to her ivory shoulders and throat, and Ishbel helped her to fasten a pretty collar of seed pearls around her neck. Warily, trying not to knock the stool over with her weighty skirts, she sat at the dressing table, and watched with satisfaction as Ishbel with newly-acquired skill drew her fair hair up into the practised arrangement, a high elaborate knot at the back of her head, with pink and white silk flowers inserted about it and just the right quantity of curls teased out to rest on either side of her central parting, against her forehead. Hippolyta drew on her white evening gloves and stood, turning and twisting to check all the details, while Ishbel watched with her mouth open at the finished effect.

'Well done, Ishbel!' cried Hippolyta at last. 'My mother's maid in Edinburgh could not have done it better. Now, I must sit still and not move a muscle while you help Mrs. Milton and Mrs. Fettes to dress.'

She was nearly as good as her word: when Ishbel had gone she did tug her gloves off again and sat by the window with a little mirror and her drawing pad, trying to record Ishbel's success with her hair. It was a shame it was so unremarkably fair, she thought: dark hair was what appeared in all the fashion plates just now, and if it had to be fair it should be truly golden, rather than just – well, not dark. On the other hand, tall and thin as she was, she was lucky that fashions had developed into wide skirts and sleeves: in the old Empire style, still favoured by old ladies and Mrs. Riach, she would have looked ridiculous, as if she had been stretched.

It seemed an age before everyone was as ready as they wanted to be, and Ishbel helped them into their cloaks at the door. Patrick was laughing and cheerful in his smart black coat, Galatea looked determined in a gown of gold silk with green embroidery, and their mother was monumental and serene in dark blue with a thick lacy scarf about her neck and shoulders. Hippolyta, noting that she had seen neither gown before in their week's stay, realised that they must have brought them expecting there to be a ball of some kind: again, things were going on of which she seemed to know nothing. It was disconcerting, though increasingly familiar.

The evening was mild with a hint of summer to come, and

only a suspicion of damp in the air. A few of the local people came to their doors to watch them as the four of them paraded past towards the bridge, joined in a moment by the Strongs, the Strachans with their two daughters, and Mrs. Kynoch in her accustomed but regrettable yellow evening gown, just the wrong shade particularly if she stood beside Galatea's gold dress. Mrs. Strachan and the girls, a couple of giggling children with promise of their mother's beauty, were all in new gowns in the very height of fashion, busy with lace and embroidery but in perfect taste, nevertheless. The walk down to the boat was like a gala day as they waved at acquaintances and exchanged good evenings along the way.

The Strachans went in the first boat, the Strongs in the second and the Napiers and family in the third, carrying on their conversations as best they could across the noisy water. Even the boatman seemed excited, dressed in his best, and the boys at the Pannanich end were scrubbed bright and full of enthusiasm, offering to carry the tails of the ladies' cloaks out of the mud on the way up the hill. One took Patrick's medical bag as usual: he had been anxious lest one of the invalids should overdo things at the ball. They went at an easy pace, not wishing to tire themselves out before they started their evening, despite the Strachan girls who would have run up the hill in their eagerness had it not been for their mother's warning glare restraining them.

They climbed the last steep curl of pathway to the courtyard between the bathhouse and the hotel, and found it transformed. For want of a ballroom inside, the hotel staff had laid boards across the cassies to form a dancing floor, and rigged up a pale canvas roof above them – no doubt the hotel keeper had been praying for such a calm evening for weeks. It was already lit with dozens of candles against the dusk, and decorated with as many late spring flowers as could be squeezed in, and everyone gasped in delight at the combination of scent, light and colour. The boards were satisfyingly springy as they crossed them to the hotel's usual entrance, where the attendants from the bathhouse were taking coats and cloaks and hats and canes from the visitors from the village and from Pannanich Lodge down on the river. Though there were closer to a score of couples than fifty, guests who were staying at the hotel itself mingled with the incomers, half proprietorial, half wide eyed at the transformation to their temporary home. The parlour where they had had tea was now laid out for supper later, smaller parlours were set aside for cards, and seats had been set around the dancefloor, too. Invalids in chairs, who had no intention of dancing, were already eagerly arranged around the floor, awaiting the evening's spectacles. A band of musicians brought for the night specially from Kincardine O'Neil (much to the disgust of the local fiddler and his friends) was tuning up on a painted wooden stage at the far end, and Hippolyta could see Patrick's feet tapping in anticipation. Her heart gave a little skip, and she turned to take his hand as they waited in the cloak queue. He smiled at her, his eyes shining. It was going to be a wonderful evening.

Mrs. Fettes was looking about her, now she had shed her cloak, and in a moment she had inevitably spotted Dr. Gilead's circle at a small side table in the midst of the courtyard. It was a prime position, tucked against the doorway into the bathhouse which was of course not in use, but with a good view of anything happening under the canvas ceiling. Mrs. Pumpton was firmly established in place, with Mrs. Nickell jiggling, shivering with excitement, beside her, and Mr. Pumpton somewhere at the back. Mr. Nickell rose at once when he saw Mrs. Fettes and her party approach. Patrick exchanged glances with Hippolyta: he had not yet met these people, but she had talked of little else for the last three days, and he had an expression of bland politeness on his handsome face which she was sure covered a deep curiosity.

'You've found us! That is good!' called Mrs. Pumpton at her usual volume, causing most of the other ball guests to turn and see who had found whom. Mr. Nickell bowed, as did Mr. Pumpton, Hippolyta thought, though he was half-concealed in the shadows of the doorway.

Mrs. Fettes introduced Patrick to the company. Hippolyta thought she noticed Mr. Nickell retreat, just a little, and was pleased. Mrs. Pumpton subjected Patrick to considerable scrutiny, then summoned him over to her side. Hippolyta could hear some of her interrogation.

'A doctor, are you? You'll know Dr. Gilead, then, by reputation, if nothing else. I daresay you'll be eager for the chance to consult him. Aberdeen and Edinburgh, was it? Well. I believe

Dr. Gilead attended several European universities, you know. And how long have you been in practice? I see. That's not very long, is it?' Patrick's amiable smile was becoming rather fixed, and he extracted himself as soon as he could within the bounds of politeness. He made his way back to Hippolyta and took her hand firmly, managing for the moment not to pass any comment.

Mrs. Fettes moved aside a little behind them, and they turned to find that Mrs. Gilead had arrived, along with her son. Mrs. Fettes carried out the introductions again, and Mrs. Gilead nodded, murmuring a greeting. Peter, the son, had a belligerent look, but it must have applied to something they had been talking about, for when he surveyed the table of acquaintances he seated himself beside Mrs. Nickell and looked about him with a more generally pleasant expression on his face. It must be hard, Hippolyta thought, to be endowed with a face like his, that spoke of hostility before ever he had opened his mouth. Yet his eyes still had a calculating, unhappy glint to them that seemed to say that the hostility was not entirely accidental.

Mr. Dewar was the next to arrive, an anxious expression on his face.

'I'm not sure if my wife will be able to attend or not,' he explained, hovering near the table as if he could not quite commit himself to the evening. 'She longs to be here, at least to see all the gaiety, but she is so frail today. The journey was not at all good for her. Dr. Gilead is with her now,' he added, with a frown.

Hippolyta's mind sprang back to the letter Durris had shown her. She supposed that a physician, particularly one with a personality like Dr. Gilead's, was susceptible to charges of becoming overfond of his patients: she hoped that Patrick would never lay himself open to such an accusation. Obviously women found Patrick attractive – he was a very handsome man with his golden hair and fine shoulders - but she thought that apart from Miss Ada's lascivious comments he did not have the kind of following that Dr. Gilead cultivated. She hoped he never would, however beneficial it might be to his practice.

The band gave a skirl, drawing everyone's attention. There was a last hurried scramble for partners: Hippolyta clutched Patrick's hand tightly, happy that they were newly-enough married to be allowed the first two dances together without question. They made their way on to the floor, lining up with the gentlemen on one side and the ladies poised like a nervous flower garden on the other, making the most of their appearances before the night's exertions rendered them damp and wilted. The Nickells took their places beside Patrick and Hippolyta, Mrs. Nickell unable to stand still for even a moment. Mrs. Pumpton, still watching the door for a better offer, stood up with Peter Gilead, who looked as eager as if his mother had pushed him into it. Mrs. Gilead and Mr. Pumpton, a mouselike couple altogether, found a space at the very end of the line, almost on the cobbles. Mrs. Strachan found partners for her daughters and almost belatedly hurried on to the floor with her husband, while Mrs. Kynoch stood up with Mr. Strong, the lawyer. Mrs. Fettes and Galatea spread their skirts out about their chairs and stayed at the table with the superior expressions of those who know they will not be asked to dance. Mr. Dewar, still not quite sure what to do, perched on the edge of an adjacent chair and gazed woefully at the assembly, his mind clearly upstairs with his ailing wife.

Another little skirl brought them to order, and with a grand downbeat the dance began. With such a mixed company they had chosen to start with something well known, and they made a fine picture together, swirling and bowing and skipping in time like a well ordered pattern in lace, woven with ribbons and jewels. They kept their partners for the next dance, a round one, and retreated to their tables afterwards all laughingly breathless and calling for cold drinks. The hotel staff scurried from table to table taking orders, and ran into the hotel building to bring back jugs of sweet cordials and ice.

The band struck up for the next set, then paused. At the hotel door a couple appeared, so striking that everyone stopped to look. Stepping down on to the scrubbed wooden floor like Oberon and Titania arriving on a cloud, were Dr. Gilead and, her hand on his arm for support, Mrs. Dewar.

The candlelight played on his silver hair and her fine complexion, disguising the webbed lines that her illness had cast there. He was gently attentive, bearing her, it almost seemed, across the floor under everyone's gaze, to float to rest at the little table in the doorway. Hippolyta heard Patrick take in a little sharp breath, and knew that she had done the same herself. Dr. Gilead bowed in one smooth movement as he settled Mrs. Dewar at the table and poured a glass of cordial for her as if the jug had been brought for the convenience of no one but her.

'Susan, my dear, are you sure?' Mr. Dewar was at her side in a moment. 'Are you quite well enough?' He took her hand gently in his own.

Mrs. Dewar smiled at him.

'Dr. Gilead thinks I will derive some amusement from the spectacle here, and I decided I must make the effort. I long to see all of you dancing!' Her eyes laughed, though her face looked weary. Hippolyta noticed that she was exquisitely dressed, in a soft green that would have upset the more superstitious locals, but here seemed like the epitome of a spring evening with fresh white lace about her shoulders and yellow flowers around the hem. She must have decided earlier in the evening that she was going to attend the ball, for this was not the kind of gown in which one would relax, feeling ill, in one's hotel room alone. She bent her head to her husband's and seemed to whisper him some soothing words, for he sat back a little, looking less anxious. 'I shall not dance,' she added more loudly, for the company to hear, 'but dear, you must find partners and enjoy the evening: you know how much you love dancing, and there are rarely enough men to go round!'

'But my dear – without you ...' Mr. Dewar was distraught, more distraught, perhaps, than missing a mere evening's dancing with his wife might warrant. His receding chin almost trembled. Hippolyta looked away, wondering if Mrs. Dewar did not seem a little stifled by his attention. She smiled fondly at her husband, but her eyes were tired.

Recovering from the general interest in Dr. Gilead's arrival, the band tried another chord and again a mass of couples formed on the floor. Here was the complex quadrille that Hippolyta had been anticipating with equal measures of dread and delight, and she was not entirely reassured when Mr. Strachan offered her his arm and led her to a place at the head of one of the squares. Mrs. Pumpton secured Dr. Gilead through sheer force of bodily presence, leaving Mrs. Nickell scowling on the sidelines, while Patrick kindly invited one of the Misses Strachan to the floor, neatly evading Miss Ada's approach. Miss Ada, nothing deterred, scooped up Mr. Nickell and swept him off. The floor was an awkward shape for squares, being long and narrow, but the company fitted into it with a will, pacing out the five movements with good humoured dignity. *L'été* followed *Le Pantaloon*, *La Pastourelle* followed *La Poule* before the splendid finale, and they ended all very pleased with themselves and to a sustained round of applause from those not dancing.

Dr. Gilead broke away from Mrs. Pumpton as soon as he could and summoned, with a click of his white fingers, a hotel servant to fetch some hot negus for Mrs. Dewar. He assumed an elegant position in the chair beside her, one knee almost on the floor, taking her hand gently and apparently noting her pulse. Hippolyta caught Patrick's expression, as he eyed Dr. Gilead with mild disgust.

'The next dance, Mrs. Napier?' Mr. Nickell was assured, grinning as he asked her. Hippolyta glanced quickly around the ball room.

'We will need a third: it is a Dashing White Sergeant, I believe.'

'That is a dance I do not know,' said Mr. Nickell, not at all abashed. 'I am glad to have secured your guidance in it.'

'Perhaps Mrs. Nickell?' Hippolyta suggested.

'Oh, that would be no use,' said her husband quickly. 'She won't know it either.' But a quick survey showed both of them that Mrs. Nickell was standing close to Dr. Gilead, ready to accept the second he might ask her to dance. The doctor's attention, however, was still closely focussed on Mrs. Dewar. 'What about Mrs. Milton?'

'Well, she'll know the dance,' said Hippolyta uncertainly, but Mr. Nickell had already seized her hand and was tugging her off to where Galatea sat with all the eagerness to dance of a doorstop. To Hippolyta's surprise she accepted the invitation, and the three of them stood up together while the other threes formed. Patrick had been trapped, to his evident amusement, by both the Misses Strong, and the Strachan girls had managed, with their mother's help, to draw Mr. Dewar reluctantly on to the floor. Once he had gone it seemed that Mrs. Dewar sent Dr. Gilead off, too, and he resigned himself to Mrs. Nickell. Looking around for a third they were unexpectedly joined by Peter Gilead, and Mrs. Nickell looked inordinately pleased with herself, though it was quickly clear that none of the three knew the dance at all. It was not a difficult one to pick up after a turn or two, and Dr. Gilead certainly, Hippolyta thought, as her sister took her turn to set to Mr. Nickell, was as graceful a dancer as one might expect. Patrick, grinning, was besieged by the two little Strong sisters, and Mrs. Pumpton swung her husband and Mrs. Kynoch through the figures of eight with ferocious enthusiasm.

More cordial arrived in icy cold jugs, and then great bowls of punch, steaming hot, amongst arrangements of cups and ladles. Sweating but still energetic, the hotel servants filled cup after cup. Faces grew pink, eyes glittered, and the band began to play again. The evening grew less distinct: Hippolyta recalled afterwards odd little glimpses about the ball room. Her mother danced a stately square with Dr. Gilead, who treated her with as much punctilious gallantry as if she were a royal princess. Galatea danced with Peter Gilead, neither looking pleased at the experience. Peter moved back to join Mrs. Nickell in a frantic Strip the Willow, laughing uncharacteristically as they galloped the length of the floor. Mr. Nickell snared Hippolyta once again before Patrick claimed her back. Mr. Pumpton and Mrs. Kynoch danced more than once, she thought, noting that he was a neat little dancer with a kindly air towards his partners. Mrs. Pumpton never sat out a single dance, walloping about the floor with the energy of a young steer, refuelling with alternate hot punch and cold cordial every time she returned to the table, and panting so loudly it seemed to make the canvas ceiling flap. Slippers lost their ornaments, lace was snatched and torn, drinks were spilled and hotel servants raced to wipe them up before a dancer should lose their footing in a pool of sticky cordial. Invalids in their chairs clapped and cheered at every dance, as eager with the punch as any dancer. Several men slunk off, including Mr. Strachan, to a card room for a few reviving hands, and returned grinning or frowning, depending on how their luck had been. Fans agitated the air and bosoms heaved in constraining stays, and the smell of powder and sweat overcame the scent of wax candles and spring flowers so completely the air was like a thick broth.

'If I dance one more dance without a rest, I shall expire on the spot,' Hippolyta gasped to Patrick. 'Is there somewhere cool we could go to catch our breath?'

'There's a whole hillside,' Patrick yelled into her ear, taking her arm. 'Come on: I'm not fond of this next dance anyway. And,' he added, with a grin, 'that Mr. Nickell is heading your way again. I'm not sure I like the way he has succumbed to your charms, my dear!'

Hippolyta laughed.

'I'm not so keen on it myself!' she agreed, and let Patrick lead her out past the end of the dance floor to where the path up from the road was lit by lamps, the damp air from earlier had cleared, and they were not the only couple hand in hand, gazing past the pools of light to the stars beyond. It gave Hippolyta a little thrill to be amongst them, like a courting couple again.

'Well, I see what you mean about your new acquaintances,' Patrick said quietly, when they had found a place a little apart from the other couples. 'They are an extraordinary gathering, and the ladies at least are very much devoted to my, ah, colleague, Dr. Gilead.'

'It's quite alarming, isn't it?' Hippolyta said. 'I thought Mrs. Pumpton and Mrs. Nickell would come to blows over that last dance with him.'

'And I should not like to have to guess who would have won that particular battle,' Patrick put in. She laughed.

'Then Mother shot them such a look they should both have shrivelled on the spot!'

'Yet your sister does not seem so susceptible to his obvious charms,' said Patrick.

'No, I don't believe she is. In fact, the impression I have is that she disapproves of him deeply. She seems so unhappy: I wish she would tell me why.'

Patrick rubbed her hand gently in its white evening glove, and she leaned against his broad shoulder.

'What about the Dewars?' he asked after a moment. 'She seems less smitten, too.'

'They only arrived yesterday, though everyone had met them before, of course. She is quite lovely, isn't she?'

'She must have been. But she is not at all well.'

'No ... even I can see that. I wonder what the matter is?'

'Hard to say,' said Patrick discreetly.

'Of course. Patrick,' she began tentatively.

'Yes, dearest?'

'Do you think Mother is quite well?'

'Why do you ask?'

'Well, I thought she was checking on the Wells just for her impoverished Edinburgh mothers, but she has been travelling the country, it appears, with Dr. Gilead, and I have never known her grow so tired so quickly. Do you think perhaps there is something wrong?'

'I'm sure she would tell you if anything was the matter,' said Patrick, considering.

'Are you? I'm not at all sure she would.'

'Would you like me to ask her?'

'No! No, leave it for now.' The impression she had was that Mrs. Fettes regarded Patrick as as much of an infant as Hippolyta, and she did not want her mother to offend her husband.

'Ladies and gentlemen!' came a cry from the hotel, cracking in an effort to be heard over the crowd. 'Supper is served!'

'Shall we go in?' Patrick asked. She took his arm, and they plunged back into the hot mob to fight for their supper.

Chapter Eight

The parlour dressed for supper was another thing of wonder. No doubt someone amongst the hotel staff had come across grand French methods for serving food on such occasions, and the long table (made up, if one looked closely, by laying a board across a number of small tables) was covered first in a fair linen cloth, then made tiered by the addition of several boxes of diminishing sizes, all covered again in sparkling white linen. The dishes were arranged on these tiers, with the meats already carved and everything as easy to serve as possible, and as pretty as could be, with swags of flowers and fruit amongst the pastries and pancakes. The cook, thought Hippolyta, would be exhausted: there would be no shortbread for a day or two.

Hotel servants scooped servings on to ready plates, and their colleagues helped carry the laden plates back to tables in the ball room or in the side parlours. The invalids were quickly attended to, and one or two took the opportunity to retire for the night taking their supper with them, exhausted simply by watching the entertainment. Mr. Dewar took a plate of the lightest food to his wife who remained at the table, and joined the party who were all served and sampling the delicious dishes already. So far almost everyone seemed more than delighted with the evening: Mrs. Pumpton bellowed her comments on the dances across the table to Dr. Gilead, and Mrs. Nickell exchanged remarks with Galatea, who was remarkably composed after dancing several reels in her usual plodding manner. At the next table, the Misses Strong debated the practicality of modern fashions with Mrs. Kynoch and declared that the dresses of their young day were altogether easier to move in, though the skirts did not swirl out in so pleasing a pattern.

'I declare this beef is the best I have ever tasted!' exclaimed Mr. Nickell generally.

'And the chatnee with it is perfect,' Mrs. Pumpton agreed, waving her fork in demonstration. A little of the chatnee dribbled down her chin, and she swallowed a large mouthful of punch as if to dilute it.

'Altogether this is a splendid place to stay, if one has to leave Harrogate,' Mr. Nickell declared generously. 'My wife is finding it quite beneficial to her health. Aren't you, dear?' he asked a little sharply. Mrs. Nickell looked up in surprise.

'Oh, yes, yes indeed. My appetite has never been so good.'

Hippolyta caught a sour look passing swiftly over Mr. Nickell's face. Was she eating him out of house and home? she wondered. Yet there was very little of her.

'I never see much in the way of appetite in Mr. Pumpton,' said Mrs. Pumpton carelessly. Mr. Pumpton, who was leaning away from their table to join in Mrs. Kynoch's conversation, jumped.

'Ah – well, dear,' he began, but she talked over him as if he had not opened his mouth.

'I think a good appetite is a fine thing in a man. You there, Mr. Napier,' she addressed Patrick without troubling to interrupt her own chewing. 'That's a healthy plateful you have there. Fond of ham, are you?'

'Very much so, yes,' said Patrick genially.

'And Dr. Gilead. I suppose your wife keeps you well fed?'

'She does,' said Dr. Gilead, darting a glance at Mrs. Gilead. She did not look up from her plate. 'I am very well provided for, of course. But this is a sumptuous supper,' he added, returning to his normal self-assured manner. 'One must be careful only to eat food that agrees with one, but if one is constrained to eat the more damaging foods – spicy, over-heated meats, or underboiled vegetables, for example, or that chatnee, dear Mrs. Pumpton - then only a few spoonfuls of my infallible scarlet powders will instantly realign the ducts of the digestive system, allowing the difficult foodstuffs to pass along them and through the body without lingering to ill effect.' He gestured beautifully with his white hands to show this beneficial realignment. Hippolyta heard an odd little noise from Patrick beside her, and he put his napkin quickly to his lips, his gaze firmly on the table. Hippolyta tried not to giggle with him. Her mother, pinning her with a look, raised a disapproving eyebrow, but the punch seemed to have been strong enough to render even Mrs. Fettes relaxed.

'Well, I'm going for seconds,' said Mr. Nickell, rising abruptly but clutching the table just a little. 'Coming, Peter?' he added. Peter Gilead looked up at him in surprise, but rose to join him.

'I suppose so,' he muttered.

The Strachans with their giggling daughters rose to return to the supper table at the same moment, and Peter seemed happy enough to attend them all into the hotel building.

Ices followed not long after the hungry had satisfied themselves with the remains of the first course: the hotel must have borrowed moulds from near and far, for every shape of ice was present in different colours and flavours, and there were further delights in the shape of moulds and jellies and fools.

'I hope there's something left from the ticket money to go towards the new bridge,' said Patrick cynically, examining the tiered table once again.

'It's an extraordinary display, isn't it?' Mrs. Kynoch agreed. 'But perhaps it is more economical than it looks.'

'I doubt that,' said Miss Strong. 'But I suppose it's bonny enough.'

'I didna see you holding back from the first course, sister!' said Miss Ada. 'Nor from the dancing, when you had the chance! Now, that long-faced apothecary fae Peebles: he would do you very nicely, would he not?'

'He has a wife already, you silly goose,' snapped Miss Strong, glancing quickly about to see that the apothecary in question was not within hearing.

'Aye, but he's here without her – and no doubt but an apothecary is in a better position than most to remove a wife that's surplus to requirements, wouldn't you say, Dr. Napier?'

'Ada!'

'Now, who are you dancing the next with, Dr. Napier?' Miss Ada went on with a relentless smirk, 'for I'm not taken, ye ken!'

'I'm dancing the next with my wife, if she'll have me, Miss Ada,' said Patrick, laughing. 'She's one wife who is definitely not surplus to requirements!'

'I'm glad to hear it!' said Hippolyta.

As supper drew to an end at different speeds for different tables, the guests took the opportunity if they had finished to wander about the rooms and gossip, as the band were then allowed their own supper. The hotel staff were carrying out a few running repairs to the floorboards, which had seen hard wear in their short time in place, while others cleared away abandoned plates and cutlery. Mrs. Dewar announced that she was going to go and lie down for half an hour, and declined assistance from either her husband or Dr. Gilead. Mrs. Gilead watched her go anxiously – presumably she had a vested interest in her husband's medical success, Hippolyta thought. A moment later, as though a thought had suddenly struck her, Mrs. Gilead herself rose, muttered some excuse, and went out. Mr. Nickell offered an arm to his wife and suggested they might get some air: they went towards the open end of the ball room and disappeared into the darkness where Patrick and Hippolyta had stood before supper.

'Galatea,' announced their mother, 'I should like to find a fire to sit beside for a little.'

'Yes, Mother,' said Galatea. It amused Hippolyta – and appalled her – to see that Galatea, so much older than she was, still responded like that to their mother. Galatea, a little pink after the punch, rose and helped her mother arrange her shawl around her shoulders, over the lacy scarf. They paced across the ball room, very straight and dignified, very alike, it struck her. Did she look much the same? Surely not quite so dignified, not unless she tried very hard, which she usually forgot to do.

She would have to leave the table soon herself: Patrick had gone to help one of his patients, resident at the hotel, to bed, and she was there with Dr. Gilead and Mrs. Pumpton, and Peter Gilead, whose head was slumped on his hands, though his eyes were alert. Dr. Gilead and Mrs. Pumpton were competing with each other to dominate their conversation, so Hippolyta out of politeness turned to Peter.

'And are you enjoying your stay here in Pannanich, Mr. Gilead?' she asked.

'It's not Mr. Gilead,' he snapped, suddenly sitting up. 'It's Snark. Peter Snark.' Every consonant of the word, his London accent acute, seemed to echo about the table. Dr. Gilead must have heard – and presumably also felt the stabbing glare with which Mr. Snark accompanied his words – but he carried smoothly on in his conversation with Mrs. Pumpton. Peter Snark rose clumsily and left the table, and after a suitable moment of stunned silence, so did Hippolyta.

Mrs. Gilead's son, then, and not Dr. Gilead's? If so, that look implied that the second marriage had not been very acceptable to the son of the first. Or could it be – Hippolyta remembered Miss Ada's Old Testament joke about the balm of Gilead – could it be that the elegant gentleman with the silver hair was not, in real life, Dr. Gilead at all, but a mere Mr. Snark senior?

She had to press her lips together to avoid a giggle, and by some chance discovered she was standing next to the Strachan girls. There would be no better way to hide an ill-mannered giggle than to keep them company for a few minutes, so she asked them how they were enjoying themselves, smiled at their eager replies, speculated with them as to the marital status of a couple of fairly handsome young men, and felt much older than her twenty years.

There was a limit to how much conversation she felt she could have with them, and after a few moments she moved on, drifting through the crowds, wondering when Patrick would be free. In the distance she saw Mrs. Strachan and Mrs. Kynoch talking with Mr. Pumpton, who seemed to have been taken under their wings. She was pleased, and was about to go over to them when she noticed Mr. Nickell standing beside them, watching her keenly. Confused, and a little cross, she turned and went to find her sister instead.

A few minutes later Hippolyta found herself with Galatea near the entrance, taking another reviving breath of the night air. Through the spring-clad trees, dark beyond the road below, she could just see the starlight twinkle on the running Dee.

'Have you enjoyed the evening so far?' she asked Galatea.

Her sister snorted quietly.

'Yes, well enough, I suppose. The food was very good, and the band are accomplished, for a country ensemble. But too many people crammed into one place, as usual with these entertainments. All over hot and over attentive and over familiar. I suppose you enjoy it,' she finished in a tone somewhere between disapproval and regret.

'I enjoy dancing – with Patrick, anyway. Don't you enjoy

dancing with Mr. Milton?'

'Maybe. Once upon a time.' Galatea seemed no more disposed to chat than usual, and after a moment she excused herself and left Hippolyta there, admiring the starlight. Tucked half behind a floral arrangement as she was, she was not immediately visible to the rest of the room, and though she turned around at the sound of her husband's voice he did not see her and carried on what seemed to be a new conversation. It took a moment for Hippolyta to recognised the voice.

'So you're a physician, Dr. Napier?' the man asked.

'That's right: my practice extends around the village and the three parishes, and many of my patients are visitors to the Wells.'

'You can't have liked it much when Dr. Gilead arrived, I suppose.'

Patrick did not reply at once.

'It's often useful to meet a colleague,' he said at last. 'I gather you have consulted him for some time, so you must be happy with him.'

It was not a question: Patrick would not like to be seen to discuss even someone like Dr. Gilead with one of his patients.

'My wife is,' said the man in a tone full of meaning. Again there was a pause. 'Tell me honestly, Dr. Napier, what do you think of him? Of Gilead?'

'I don't like to –'

'Please. For this is what it is, Dr. Napier. I've spent a fortune on that man and his powders and his balm. A fortune. And I wouldn't mind, I wouldn't count it a farthing too much if I had any idea that my wife was getting better. But I don't believe she is.'

Somewhere further back in the room there was a small cheer, and a voice announced,

'Miss Teasle will now delight us with her rendition of 'Those Endearing Young Charms'.' Applause surged briefly, and a reedy soprano began, almost immediately floundering on the low notes.

'What does he say is the matter with her?' Patrick asked at last, with resignation.

'He says it's a dietary disorder,' said the man. 'She cannot eat properly, is sick if she has the wrong things.'

'It sounds as if he might be right,' said Patrick cautiously. 'Mr. Dewar, I cannot make a diagnosis without examining Mrs.

Dewar, and I need to be sure that you really want to have her consult me before I am willing to offend Dr. Gilead, whatever – whatever I might think of him as a doctor.'

'Oh, Gilead won't let her go,' said Dewar in despair. 'Not now he's got her in his clutches. You've seen them all flocking around him. Mrs. Napier's own mother, even! She seemed a sensible woman when I first met her, and now look at her! Following him round the country like sheep, the lot of them! And not one of them any healthier now than when I first set eyes on them: only their husbands poorer.'

'Look ...' Hippolyta knew Patrick could never resist someone injured or ill. 'Why don't I come to see her tomorrow morning? But Mrs. Dewar has to be willing to be seen: if you can persuade her to accept a second opinion on her condition, say, then I shall be happy to examine her.'

'But she's my wife!'

'It's no use treating someone who does not want to be treated,' said Patrick firmly. 'That puts one off to a very bad start.'

Mr. Dewar thought for a moment, then sighed loudly.

'Very well, I'll talk to her. But if I can get her to agree, you'll come, won't you?'

'I will. Here's my hand on it.'

Hippolyta heard them moving away, and slid out from her unintended hiding place to return to the table. A man pushed past her suddenly out of the darkness, and stalked back across the ball room as though he saw no one in his way. It was Peter Gilead. A moment later Mrs. Nickell sprang past her.

'Oh, Mrs. Napier!' she said quickly, her voice as breathless as ever. 'What a lovely evening! Isn't it?'

'It has been very interesting so far,' agreed Hippolyta. 'You enjoy dancing, then?'

Mrs. Nickell nodded.

'I sleep much better after exercise than otherwise,' she explained, 'and what fun dancing is as an exercise!' Indeed she had been skipping about the dance floor with obvious delight earlier, with a variety of partners including Dr. Gilead. 'Do you think the band will start again soon? For I must just ... And I should hate to miss anything.'

'I think a few people want to perform first,' said Hippolyta. 'It allows us to rest after our supper.'

'Of course, of course,' she said, 'but I'll hurry, nonetheless.' She bounced urgently away in the direction of the hotel building. Hippolyta watched her go, then saw her husband move out from under the doorway and bar her way: he must not have moved much since she had seen him near the Strachans a little while before. She hoped he would regard his wife with the same fascinated stare he had been using on her, and looked on, but instead of a loving greeting it seemed that Mr. and Mrs. Nickell exchanged a few less than friendly words in the doorway. Hippolyta could hear nothing of the conversation, and from the people around and their lack of reaction their voices could not have been very loud: nevertheless Mr. Nickell took his wife firmly by her scrawny elbow and marched her, fixedly, back to their table. Mrs. Nickell looked furious. Mrs. Gilead, who was sitting at the table already on her own, marked their arrival with a nervous expression. She did not look at all comfortable, and Hippolyta did not blame her. For anyone, let alone such a self-effacing person as Mrs. Gilead, to be forced to share a table with some kind of marital scuffle would not be pleasant. She wondered where everyone else had gone.

Just as she was turning around on her heel, looking for familiar faces, Mr. Dewar brushed past her, anxiety exuding from him.

'I beg your pardon, Mrs. Napier. I wonder – have you seen my wife?'

'I haven't seen her since she went to lie down,' said Hippolyta. 'Have you looked in your rooms?'

'She's not there,' he said, 'and if she lay down anywhere since that bed was made up it wasn't there, I'd swear.' His face was black. Hippolyta did not like his implication.

'Perhaps she was on her way there and took a little turn, and someone else let her lie down – or,' she added hastily, for this did not seem to help, 'perhaps she is resting in one of the parlours. Or she went out for a breath of fresh air.'

'She hates the evening air: she feels it does her harm,' he almost wailed, frustrated, as if Hippolyta should have known that.

'Well, shall we check the parlours, then, Mr. Dewar? Come along: I perhaps know the hotel better than you do, and I'll help you.' She sent up a quick prayer that they would indeed find Mrs.

Dewar innocently resting, for Mr. Dewar seemed to be strung on thin wire and now she had rashly taken responsibility for him. She led him back towards the hotel building, where they had last seen Mrs. Dewar vanish into the hallway.

There were three parlours, including the large one where the supper had been laid out. Though it had fewer chairs in it than usual, to make way for the grand supper table, they looked in. Mrs. Dewar was not amongst the half dozen gossips still there. The next parlour on that side, set up as a small card room, held two gentlemen, snoring fit to bring on a thunderstorm. One clutched his dancing pumps to his heart, as though they were his dearest possession.

'This is more of a ladies' parlour,' Hippolyta explained when they reached the third one which faced the rear of the building. It was where she had seen Mrs. Gilead – or was it Snark? – speaking with Mr. Durris about the anonymous letter. She had expected that it was where her mother had gone to sit beside a fire for a little, though she had already seen her in the supper room, and she tried the door handle with confidence. She almost walked into the door when she discovered that it was locked. 'That's strange,' she said.

'Locked?' Mr. Dewar nearly shoved her aside, seizing the handle himself. He rattled it as if it had insulted him personally. 'Locked!' he cried again.

'I wonder what ...' Hippolyta tailed off, already coming up with one or two possibilities in her head.

'So do I!' shouted Mr. Dewar. 'You there!' he yelled at a passing hotel servant. 'Have you the key for this door?'

'No, sir,' said the man shakily. 'That would be the hotel keeper has that, sir.'

'Then find him!' He turned back to the parlour door, the servant dismissed. He rattled the handle again. 'You in there! Open this door at once!'

As far as Hippolyta could hear against the background noise of the ball guests, there was no sound from inside the parlour. Mr. Dewar rattled the handle once more, so hard that it broke off in his hand with a muffled crack. He looked at it in disbelief for a ridiculous moment, then flung it down in disgust, and applied his eye to the keyhole.

'Covered on the other side,' he muttered. He was quite

101

breathless.

'Against the draught, you know,' said Hippolyta in a vain effort to calm or distract him. She picked up the handle, thinking that someone might trip up on it, but her ball gown had no pocket beneath it and she ended up tossing it from hand to hand. She almost dropped it when a heavy hand slapped on to her bare shoulder.

'Mrs. Napier! Oh, Mr. Dewar, thank the Lord I've found you!'

Mrs. Pumpton stood gasping for breath, one hand clutching at her enormous décolletage. Inconsequentially Hippolyta noticed droplets of chatnee still in the expensive lace on her bodice.

'What is it?' Mr. Dewar barely cast her a glance, and seemed to be assessing whether or not he could knock the parlour door in with his shoulder.

'It's your wife, Mr. Dewar. She's upstairs. She's collapsed!'

'My wife?' For a moment the words did not quite seem to make sense to him. Then he spun and ran for the stairs.

'In our room, Mr. Dewar!' Mrs. Pumpton called after him. He made no acknowledgement. 'I found her at the top of the back stairs, Mrs. Napier, you know. White as a sheet – no, grey, I should say. But where's Dr. Gilead? She must have Dr. Gilead!'

'Or Patrick,' said Hippolyta, and ran to the stairs herself. She had not seen Dr. Gilead for a while, and besides, she would not trust him to apply a plaister to a bruise. Up on the long, narrow landing she found Mr. Dewar darting about, confused.

'In Mrs. Pumpton's room, she said, Mr. Dewar,' she reminded him. He looked blank, then ran to the first door on his left. The instant he vanished inside, he let out a howl. Hippolyta hurried after him.

Mrs. Dewar was lying across the bed where Mrs. Pumpton had presumably managed to carry her. She looked as if she had been dumped there, and did not move at their arrival. Her face was indeed grey in the light of a single candle by the bedside, the shadows around her eyes deep and heavy. Hippolyta stepped back to the doorway.

'Loosen her stays,' she said quickly, 'and try to turn her on her side, but gently. Do it!' she added, this time using her mother's most imperious voice. 'I'm going to look for Patrick.'

In the passage outside, all the doors to the bedchambers were shut. There was nothing for it, even if it were not quite decorous.

'Patrick!' she cried at the top of her voice. 'Patrick! Quickly!'

A door shot open.

'What is it?' Patrick stuck his head out into the passage. 'No, it's all right, Mr. Brown: just swallow that down. Hippolyta?'

'It's Mrs. Dewar – she has collapsed. She's in a faint, and quite grey – in here,' she added, as he reached back for his medical bag and then ran after her. He took one look at Mrs. Dewar.

'Hippolyta, can you fetch hot water, please? As hot as they can make it in as quick a time. And clean towels would be good, too. Quickly, my love.'

She shot back out of the room and down the stairs to where the staff quarters were, seizing the first sensible-looking servant she could find. She explained what she needed, where, and how fast, and waited to help carry them, standing in the doorway between the hall and the servants' passageway. Somewhere in the ball room a tenor voice was performing *Tom Bowling* with gusto and a vigorous piano accompaniment. From where she waited, she could see that a small crowd had gathered around the locked parlour door. Well, it was not Mrs. Dewar in there, anyway.

'Has anyone seen my husband?' came an almost familiar voice from the back of the crowd.

'Who's your husband, then, madam?' asked a man who had been trying, it seemed, to look under the door.

'Dr. Gilead,' said the woman. It was indeed the mousy Mrs. Gilead, now Hippolyta could see her. It seemed to be night for missing spouses. She glanced back down towards the kitchens. Where was that water? The maid, Christy, reappeared with an armful of towels and Hippolyta snatched them from her.

'Water's near ready, ma'am,' the maid murmured.

'Very good,' said Hippolyta urgently.

'The key should be in the door,' said the hotel keeper, puzzled. 'But I have a spare one … now, where's the spare set?'

'We could go round and smash the window,' suggested a keen young fellow.

'I'd rather you didna, sir, if it can be helped,' said the hotel keeper mildly. 'Ah, I mind now.' He stepped away to the porter's lodge, and came back with a large bunch of keys. It seemed the obvious place to look for them. 'Now, here we are – soon find out what the matter is.' He applied the spare key to the parlour door, fiddled with the broken end of the handle, and swung it wide.

The crowd struggled to look inside.

There was a scream, like nothing Hippolyta had heard before, and the hotel keeper was sick on the floor.

Chapter Nine

Within a few seconds the hotel keeper had pulled himself together and shut the door of the parlour with a kind of respectful haste. He drew out a large handkerchief, and wiped his face slowly. The crowd behind him had surged forward but the closed door caused them to stop and shuffle, slightly ashamed of their curiosity. What on earth had they seen? Hippolyta wondered. She had found that her own curiosity was only distantly acquainted with shame.

'You, there,' said the hotel keeper, and the crowd fell silent. He pointed to one of the servants. 'Yon fellow Mr. Durris, that's been in the kitchen this night – fetch him.' The servant jogged away.

'Who's he?' asked one of the less restrained characters in the crowd – it might have been the young man who had suggested breaking the window. 'Durris, I mean.'

'He's the sheriff's man,' the hotel keeper explained, then raised his voice again with terrific solemnity. 'There's been an accident. Away yez all go out the road – er, ladies and gentlemen, please,' he amended.

'An accident?' Mrs. Pumpton was at the back of the crowd and must not have had an adequate view through the parlour door. 'You'll need a physician, then. Where is Dr. Gilead?'

That was a good question, thought Hippolyta. Where was the graceful doctor? And why was he not attending to his patient upstairs?

At that the maid Christy appeared, wide-eyed at the crowd and the scream, and carrying two heavy jugs of hot water. Steam curled from it. The hotel keeper noticed it and it occurred to Hippolyta that he might commandeer the water to slop away his own vomit from the stone hall floor. She adjusted her grip on the heap of towels, and chivvied the maid quickly up the stairs.

In Mrs. Pumpton's room Patrick and Mr. Dewar had managed to shift Mrs. Dewar into what looked a more comfortable position, and loosened her elaborate clothing. Her evening gown had been tugged off completely, her stays had been flung on to a chair like a dead bird, and she lay on top of the covers in her shift, breathing harshly.

'There are combs in her hair,' Hippolyta murmured. 'They might be sticking into her head.'

'Can you find them, dearest?' Patrick had lifted the shift and was gently probing Mrs. Dewar's stomach with his long fingers. Hippolyta squeezed past Mr. Dewar and felt through Mrs. Dewar's thick hair, slipping three tortoiseshell combs out and on to the bedside table. She undid the more complex loops of hair, and laid Mrs. Dewar's head down softly again on the pillow. The woman did not even blink. Hippolyta dismissed the maid, and stepped back out of the way.

'There has been a lump here for some time,' Patrick said in a low voice to Mr. Dewar, indicating a swelling in the pale flesh. Mr. Dewar nodded, swallowing hard.

'That's right. Dr. Gilead told us it was a knot in the tendrils of her stomach.'

'A knot in the what?' Patrick's voice faded in disbelief. He stared at Mr. Dewar for a moment. 'And how was Dr. Gilead treating this knot?'

'With his scarlet powders,' said Mr. Dewar. He was on the verge of tears. 'Twice daily, and more if it was painful. And massaging with his balm, too: he said it would draw out any poisons that had caught inside the knot, and might result in infection.'

'I wonder what is in these blessed infallible scarlet powders?' Patrick muttered in Hippolyta's general direction. He glanced up at her suddenly. 'Did I hear a scream downstairs?'

'Ah, yes,' said Hippolyta.

'Am I wanted down there? For this is very serious.'

'I don't know. They can't find Dr. Gilead, but they were looking for him, so it must be something bad. The hotel keeper said there had been an accident – and he was sick when he saw it.'

'Felt sick, he told you?'

'No, he was sick. I saw it happen.'

'Right,' said Patrick, already dismissing it from his mind. 'Mr. Dewar, there is no knot in the tendrils of the stomach. There never was. This is a tumour, and I fear that something has happened to it to cause this sudden collapse in Mrs. Dewar's condition. She is, I must tell you, very seriously ill.'

'And all his treatment?' demanded Mr. Dewar, his voice trembling. It sounded as if he was trying to summon anger to cope with his fear.

'Now is not the time to discuss that. It will not help us. I have to tell you, Mr. Dewar that I can see only one possible course of action at this moment, and it is not something for which I can guarantee any kind of success. There is the remotest possibility that if I cut open your wife's stomach and removed what I can of the tumour, that it will relieve the pressure on the internal organs and she may live.'

'Cut open?' repeated Mr. Dewar unsteadily.

'That's right. You will know that there are all kinds of risks attached to that. I studied surgery in Edinburgh and I have carried out something similar before – though not around the stomach,' he added honestly. 'The patient lived for several more years. But infections can occur, or the tumour may have spread too far to be cut out completely. The only other thing I can tell you is that your wife is dying. If I do not do this – or if some other chirurgeon of your choosing does not – then she will die within, I should say, the next few hours.'

He leaned over Mrs. Dewar again and took her pulse, frowning. Then he stepped away from her, allowing Dewar to consider the matter for as long as was available. Patrick stepped across to Hippolyta and murmured,

'I have no laudanum with me for her pain. Do you think you could find Dr. Gilead – or even Mrs. Gilead – and see if you can borrow some?'

'Of course.' Hippolyta darted out of the room. If she could find Dr. Gilead, would he stop Patrick from cutting open that poor woman? Patrick had talked about having Mrs. Dewar's consent to examine her, but matters had gone far beyond that, now. Dr.

Gilead could concern himself with whatever had happened in the accident downstairs, instead. Or perhaps Patrick could deal with both, for downstairs had not seemed so urgent, to judge by the hotel keeper's demand for Mr. Durris rather than Dr. Gilead or Patrick. This might be the chance for Patrick to prove himself in the eyes of the hotel guests against Dr. Gilead's extravagant claims and hollow charms. In the eyes of the hotel guests, and perhaps even in the eyes of her mother and sister? But what if Mrs. Dewar died? What then?

Down in the hallway, the hotel keeper's firm guardianship of the parlour door had not allowed the crowd to experience any further sensations, and so they had pretty much dispersed, even Mrs. Pumpton. By the noises from the ball room beyond the front door, the band had begun to play again, though whether the guests were dancing or not Hippolyta could not see. Durris, by contrast, had just arrived, and the hotel keeper was reaching out his hand as Hippolyta descended the stairs, preparatory to explaining himself.

'Mr. Durris, I felt this matter might be best dealt with by you, sir.'

'I don't understand.'

Hippolyta glanced across the hall. Peter Gilead – no, Peter Snark – was standing as if on guard by a chair against the wall. Hippolyta had not noticed him.

'Mr. Snark,' she said quickly, 'do you know if Dr. Gilead would have any laudanum we could borrow? My husband has – has a patient in some need. Urgently,' she added, for Mr. Snark was gazing past her at the parlour door and Mr. Durris. In the chair he was guarding, she suddenly realised, was Mrs. Gilead, looking even smaller and less significant than usual. 'Mrs. Gilead, would you know? Laudanum?' she asked, but Mrs. Gilead was not listening to her, either. She turned in despair to Mr. Durris. 'It's really urgent, Mr. Durris!'

'Mrs. Napier, will you step back a moment, please?' said Mr. Durris.

'You don't want to see it, Mrs. Napier, truly,' added the hotel keeper. There was a sudden sob, and she turned to see it had emerged from Mrs. Gilead. It was the loudest noise she had ever heard her make. Distracted, Mr. Durris unlocked the door and pushed it open. Hippolyta, without thinking, looked inside – then stared, her jaw dropping.

In the centre of the room, where Hippolyta remembered there had been a space amidst the furniture, stood a hard chair with plain wooden arms. On the chair, his head flung back and his silver-white hair hanging loose from its usual ribbon, was Dr. Gilead.

He was dead, she knew that very quickly. If there had not been a certain laxity to the body, one had only, she thought with a portion of her mind, to look at the face. The blue eyes bulged, the mouth was open and curiously – lumpy – and the skin around it was reddened, as if it had been rubbed. The rest of his long face had a bluish tinge. She managed to look away. Two distinctive red pots lay empty on the floor, and there was a very strong smell of Dr. Gilead's famous cordial balm. She blinked. That was what the problem was with his mouth: it was full, stuffed, with the balm.

'Oh, my goodness,' she breathed.

'Mrs. Napier, I have a bitty laudanum locked in a press in the kitchen, against my bad back,' said the hotel keeper. 'Would that do you?'

'Anything would help,' Hippolyta said, though she was still staring into the parlour. Mr. Durris glanced at her, then closed the door softly behind him, shutting off the awful vision. The hotel keeper dashed away, and returned in a moment to find her still stuck in the same place, her back to Mrs. Gilead and her son, staring at the closed door.

'Here: that's all I have,' said the hotel keeper, abruptly returned. He handed Hippolyta a bottle wrapped in brown paper. As if it opened a curtain in her mind, Hippolyta suddenly came back to life.

'Thank you.' She seized the bottle, and with a last look at the closed parlour door, she raced back upstairs.

Dewar was standing at the window, staring out at the night. Patrick, by contrast, was a flurry of activity. Every candle in the room had been lit and brought to shed light on the bed. He had laid the thickest of the clean towels around and under Mrs. Dewar's body, and had drawn from his medical bag his set of scalpels, laying them out on the bedside table which he had drawn over to a better position for the purpose. Mrs. Dewar's tortoiseshell combs had been tossed over to lie on the extravagant spread of her evening gown. Hippolyta handed him the laudanum, and went to tidy the gown over the chair to stop the wrinkles from setting in.

'I'll need your help, dearest, if you can bear it,' said Patrick. They were the words she had been dreading, but she knew that Mr. Dewar would not be much use. She finished arranging the gown.

'Of course.'

'I just want you to hold her hands, to keep her quiet,' he explained, giving her a reassuring grin. 'Didn't the famous doctor have any more laudanum than this?'

'Ah, that's from the hotel keeper. Dr. Gilead was – unavailable.'

He glanced up at her as he bent over the bed, but his curiosity could wait. He was obviously already focussed on his task.

'Difficult to administer,' he commented, 'but with luck she's too far under just now to feel too much.' He squinted down at her. 'If you want to help, Mr. Dewar, and you are not already doing so, prayers would definitely not go amiss at this stage.'

Mr. Dewar shuddered, unable even to look round at them.

'I'm praying,' he said in a choked voice.

'Well then,' said Patrick, in a voice calmer than seemed remotely possible in the circumstances, 'we'd better begin.'

Hippolyta had never seen her husband move so quickly. Hands pink from the hot water and a brisk rub on the clean towels, he set to work: from the moment the laudanum drops touched Mrs. Dewar's lips, his fingers were like lightning and yet at the same time so controlled that it was as if he were following a pattern drawn out in front of him. Only occasionally as he pushed his glasses back up his nose with the heel of his thumb did he even seem to breathe. Hippolyta held towels to the edge of the wound he made, as he directed, for there was an extraordinary quantity of blood. She did not wince: she had already seen worse that evening. Even when Patrick withdrew from the wound a soft, bloody mass and dropped it with a horrid noise into the basin she held ready, she managed not to be sick. She set it aside, and handed him what he needed as he stitched the various layers of the wound with remarkable neatness. At last he stood back, letting out a great sigh of relief, and dipped his hands into the other jug of hot water, sluicing blood from his arms. Then he turned to check once again on Mrs. Dewar's pulse and temperature. The wound was covered, the towels removed and heaped by the door, and he delicately pulled her shift back down over her stomach.

'The pressure is off her other organs now,' he said, 'though who knows what damage has been done by the prolonged cramping of them.' He picked up the basin and held it near a candlestand, examining the lump inside it. 'It's huge. I hope I found all of it.' He slipped a towel over it as Mr. Dewar turned from his sentry post at the window, his face asking all manner of questions.

'She is breathing more easily now,' Patrick told him, 'and her vital signs are not bad, considering. She must lie flat and move as little as possible, and there should be someone here with her when she wakens. I'll send a maid up to bear you company, and to bring you some boiled water. A little on her lips now and again to ease her will be necessary. I'll leave the laudanum – do you know what to do with it?'

Dewar shook his head, bewildered. He would not have known what to do with a cup of tea, Hippolyta thought. Patrick scribbled a few directions on a piece of paper from his medical bag and laid them on the bedside table, now back in its proper place.

'She will need a great deal of care,' he said gently and clearly. 'I shall come back in an hour or so and see how she is doing.'

Dewar nodded, but his eyes were only on his wife's face as he sat by her side.

Patrick and Hippolyta gathered towels, jugs and his belongings and left the room quietly. Outside on the landing, he stopped to pull his coat back on: Hippolyta saw that he was shivering.

'You need a brandy,' she told him.

'A cup of tea, too,' he said. 'I don't want to be full of drink when I go back to see her.'

'What chance has she?' Hippolyta asked softly, one eye on the door of the room.

Patrick blew out sharply.

'A slim one,' he admitted. 'It should never have been left so long. I need to talk to Dr. Gilead, though I must admit that if I never see him again it would please me no end.'

'I fear,' said Hippolyta, 'that you may have to see him at least once more. But let us fetch that maid, and some tea.'

Downstairs she found Christy, the maid who had helped with the hot water, and sent her back upstairs with tea and shortbread for Mr. Dewar.

'And make sure he drinks it, please,' she added, 'for he is not entirely in his right mind.'

The maid curtseyed, looking interested.

The hotel keeper was still in the hallway, leaning against the wall by the closed parlour door. Mrs. Gilead and her son were still at the other side. It was as if Hippolyta had only been upstairs for a moment. Patrick blinked at Mrs. Gilead, unwilling to tackle her for her husband's shortcomings, but clearly tempted.

'Ah, Dr. Napier!' said the hotel keeper, who had been in a bit of a dwam. Hippolyta did not blame him: it had been an eventful evening, and the band were still playing. 'Would you mind, sir – Mr. Durris asked if you would go in?'

'Could he have a cup of tea and some brandy first, please?' Hippolyta put in. Knowing Patrick, he would forget in the face of more medical work.

'Of course, ma'am. There is tea and brandy where the supper was laid out.'

The main parlour was only along the passage: Hippolyta hurried off and returned with a hot cup and a cold glass. Patrick downed the glass gratefully, then held the cup close in his hands for a moment before swallowing the contents down, too.

'Thank you, my dear,' he said, smiling at her. 'Now, what's happened?'

The hotel keeper peeked round him at Mrs. Gilead and Peter Snark. Patrick frowned.

'There's been a – a kind of an accident, Dr. Napier,' said the hotel keeper in a low voice. 'It's Dr. Gilead, sir. He's – well, he's dead. Mr. Durris is in there now with him.'

'Dr. Gilead?' Patrick fell silent for a moment. He would not have his reckoning with the egregious doctor now, though whether this was a matter for regret or relief it was hard to tell. But if Durris was there – Hippolyta could see the thoughts passing across Patrick's suddenly exhausted face – if Durris was present there must be some question about the death. He turned to give

Hippolyta a long look and then nodded, put out a hand to the remains of the broken door handle, and slipped into the room, not opening the door quite far enough for Mrs. Gilead and Peter Snark to see properly inside again. The door closed, but Hippolyta could still hear her husband's little cry of shock. The hotel keeper just avoided meeting her eye.

There was another of those disturbing groans from Mrs. Gilead, and with a little self-reproof Hippolyta knelt quickly beside her chair.

'Has anyone fetched you a brandy, Mrs. Gilead? Would you like one? I think you probably need one.' She looked up at Peter Snark but he was still focussed on the closed parlour door. Who knew how long he might stay there if nobody moved him? She wondered if he were suffering from the aftereffects of shock, or felt he needed to monitor closely any investigation into his father's death – if Dr. Gilead was his father. Down at chair level Mrs. Gilead was clutching the wooden edges of the seat, her evening gloves taut across her knuckles.

'Brandy, Mrs. Gilead?'

Mrs. Gilead nodded without looking at her, little nods in a desperate pecking motion, as if she were afraid her head might tumble off if she bent her neck too far. Hippolyta rose in a rustle of skirts and went again to the main parlour for the brandy and another glass. This time she allowed herself a small one, too, and a cup of tea, before returning with both for Mrs. Gilead. She held the glass to the woman's grey lips, and was eventually rewarded by seeing a little colour come back to her cheeks.

'Mrs. Gilead, I think you should probably go and lie down. There's nothing you can do here just now. Mr. Durris will no doubt want to ask you some questions later, but he will not expect you to wait here on a hard chair when you are so distressed.' There was no reaction. She handed Mrs. Gilead the tea cup, and was pleased to see how she automatically lifted it to her lips. After a moment, Mrs. Gilead finally looked up at her.

'Yes,' she said, so softly Hippolyta would have missed it if she had not been watching her face. 'Yes, I'd like to go to bed now.' She pushed herself up from the chair with an effort, and lurched to clutch Hippolyta's arm. Hippolyta had not particularly wished to abandon the hallway while Patrick was still in the little parlour with Durris, but she found herself inevitably supporting Mrs. Gilead up the stairs again – Peter watched them go but did nothing to assist - and under her whispered direction Hippolyta took her slowly to a room at the back of the hotel. It was a small place, even poky, and Hippolyta surveyed it in some surprise when she had lit the only candle she could find. The white terrier came to meet them, stretching, interested, but looking beyond them for his master. The room smelled of stale dog. She would have expected Dr. Gilead to be staying in some state, as befitted at least his own good opinion, but this was almost the kind of room a servant would stay in. Yet there were some medical texts, and a trunk against the wall was open to reveal a half-full stock of the crimson packets that contained the celebrated infallible scarlet powders, and a number of the red tins that held the famous cordial balm. Dr. Gilead's name was writ large on each of them, like some kind of memorial: the smell was very distinct, and for a second Hippolyta was back at the parlour door, with the two empty tins on the floor and Dr. Gilead's mouth ... She swallowed hard.

'Have you a maid I could call?' she asked Mrs. Gilead, but she had slumped on to the side of the bed and knotted her gloved hands together. She just about pulled herself upright.

'No, no, I'll manage,' she murmured. 'Thank you, Mrs. Napier. It's been a dreadful shock.'

'I'm sure it has. It is quite natural for you to be upset. Have you ...' She wondered if she should go on, but did not seem able quite to stop herself. 'Have you any idea who could have done such terrible thing?'

'Done ...?' Mrs. Gilead looked vaguely at her.

'Done – that – to Dr. Gilead.'

'Oh.' Surely she did not believe the hotel keeper's kindly line that it had been an accident? The famous cordial balm did not smell that appetising. She noticed, now she had heard Mrs. Gilead speak, that her voice was like her appearance much less cultivated than her husband's: as she thought of the word she suddenly saw Dr. Gilead as a hot house lily, and Mrs. Gilead as a mundane kale plant. She shook herself, trying to pay attention to the kale plant. 'I suppose ... could it have been Mr. Dewar?' She did not look at Hippolyta, but then she would not have known that Hippolyta had seen the anonymous letter Mrs. Gilead had given Durris. 'I wonder where Mrs. Dewar is? I thought … I thought perhaps they … I couldn't find him, you see.' A dry sob issued from her, heaving her shoulders in their drab evening gown.

'Now, then, don't distress yourself, Mrs. Gilead.' She should probably not have raised the subject, she thought, a little shamed. Yet the idea would surely have occurred to Mrs. Gilead sooner or later anyway, without Hippolyta's help – interference, she corrected herself for once. She would have thought about the anonymous letters and put two and two together.

But surely Mr. Dewar had not written the anonymous letters: they seemed to threaten, but there was no sense that Hippolyta remembered in them that a friendship with Mrs. Dewar specifically was the problem for the writer. He seemed rather to feel that Dr. Gilead had brought his own reputation into disrepute - and who would murder him for that? Patrick? She smiled. She was not going to go down that road.

Mrs. Gilead was still sitting slumped on the edge of the bed, though she was a healthier colour now. Hippolyta was eager to return downstairs, away from the poky little miserable room.

'Will you be all right if I leave you now?' she asked. Mrs. Gilead nodded: she seemed ready to cry, but holding it back. Hippolyta was sure it was a good time to leave.

She returned to the long landing, and the top of the stairs, pausing to listen at Mrs. Pumpton's door for any sound of the Dewars within.

What had Mr. Dewar been doing this evening anyway? Could he have found the time to go and murder Dr. Gilead – and had he wanted to?

Chapter Ten

'Oh, it's all right, it's only my wife.' The smile that Patrick sent her up the stairs took away any possible dismissive sting in his words. She had paused because her feet, in their thin slippers, were tired, and she could feel each step in detail. She continued down to the hallway, where Durris and the hotel keeper stood at the parlour door – once again closed – and Peter Snark kept his station at the other side, his expression distrustful.

'Mrs. Gilead says she's all right,' she reported.

'Good,' said Patrick. 'One fewer to worry about for now – I must go up again shortly, though.'

The hotel keeper looked more concerned than Durris did: a sick guest was his problem, not the sheriff's, and Patrick had not yet said which guest he had been attending upstairs. His medical bag sat exhausted beside him on the hall's stone-flagged floor. Who knew what would have happened had he not chosen to bring it?

'Mr. – ah, Snark, isn't it?' Mr. Durris asked.

'That's right.'

'Would you like to step a little closer, sir? I'm sure you have no particular wish for these details to spread far and wide.'

Peter Snark snorted.

'That was the way my father liked to live,' he said.

'He was your father, then, sir? Not your stepfather? Just to keep the records straight, if you don't mind.'

'He was my father. He chose that stupid name, and my mother had to go with it. I didn't.' He stepped closer to them all the same, perhaps afraid they might try to hide something from him otherwise.

'Very good.' Durris had his notebook out and appeared to make a minute dot on one page. Hippolyta edged a little sideways to see if she could see what he had written, but though he seemed not to have noticed he adjusted the angle of his hand to turn the page away. She looked away, and caught Patrick making an admonishing wiggle of his eyebrows at her. She almost stuck her tongue out at him, then remembered that Peter Snark had been bereaved, and deserved some respect. 'Now, can you think of anyone, Mr. Snark, who might have wished your father harm?'

Peter Stark's eyes narrowed.

'I think I should be told first what kind of harm he has come to, don't you? You with your closed doors.'

'I beg your pardon, Mr. Snark, I thought you had seen.' Durris cleared his throat. 'It is not pleasant. Please stop me if at any point -'

'Just get on with it.'

'Very well.' Durris glanced down at his notebook. 'Dr. Gilead – or Mr. Snark – was found dead in a chair in that room, on his own. His head had been pushed back and his mouth filled with – with a sticky substance.' He looked at Patrick. 'Dr. Napier, perhaps you would provide the medical details?'

'Of course,' said Patrick. 'Mr. Snark's mouth and nose had been filled with the contents of two jars – probably full – of his own cordial balm. As you'll no doubt know, it is a calorificient: it induces heat in the skin in the way certain spices do. That would no doubt have caused extreme and sudden inflammation in the throat and mouth, though whether he died of that, or of suffocation because the substance itself blocked his airways, or whether the substance poisoned him, is difficult to say. I can't imagine that it would be at all good to ingest, but his face had a bluish tinge, which would point to asphyxiation.'

Hippolyta must have moved slightly, for all three men suddenly remembered she was there.

'You don't find your wife is too delicate to hear these descriptions, then, Dr Napier?' Snark asked in a mocking tone.

'No,' said Patrick, stalwart. 'She has just been assisting me in a delicate medical procedure upstairs: she is quite capable of dealing with such things.'

Hippolyta hoped he was right: there was no possibility that she could be sick or faint now. To prove it to herself, she asked,

'Is there no chance that it could have been accident or self-harm?'

'You didn't see his hands, Mrs. Napier, did you?' asked Durris.

'I may have seen them,' she admitted. 'I didn't notice them.'

'For one thing, they are completely clean,' said Durris. 'He did not force the substance into his own mouth, by intention or accident, even if one could imagine such a thing. For another, his hands are tied with his hair ribbons to the arms of the chair.'

'Oh.'

'So,' said Snark, ignoring her again, 'the old man was stuffed with his disgusting balm pots. Serve him right.'

'I was about to revert to my former question, Mr. Snark, and ask if you knew of anyone who wished your father harm, but perhaps first you would like to tell me something about your own connexion with your father?'

Snark's eyes glinted with his unpleasant smile.

'He was my father. It's easy seen you can't choose your parents, or I'd have sent him back and got a real man, who could earn a living without beguiling old women and their blind husbands. If I had the choice I wouldn't even touch his stinking money. Every coin of it smells of famous cordial balm, like the rest of us. That foul stench has followed me round my whole life: I doubt I'll ever rid my nostrils of it.'

'Do you know what the ingredients are?' Patrick asked, curious. Snark tried to look down his flat nose at him, but he was not quite tall enough.

'Another quack, are you, *Dr.* Napier? No doubt if I tell you what's in it, you'll be filling your own little tins at three shillings a time. 'Napier's Famous Cordial Balm' – got a nice ring to it, that!'

Patrick drew breath to reply, a little pink in the face, but Durris stepped in smoothly.

'Apart from you, then, sir, can you think of others who might have wished him harm?'

'I could give you a list,' said Snark. 'Let me think. Of those I know who are here, and not left behind at Harrogate, or Bath, or Brighton, or whatever other damp, nasty, overcrowded extravagances that pass for fashionable watering holes where he plied his trade, I daresay Mr. Pumpton had no time for him, though it would need to be a small goose for him to say boo to it; Mr. Nickell thought he was a waste of money and time, and didn't like the way my father looked at his wife. Thought to be fair she was nothing special: my father looked that way at anything in a skirt, especially if they agreed with his views. His views being chiefly that there was nothing greater than Dr. Francis Gilead.'

'So, Mr. Pumpton and Mr. Nickell,' Durris repeated solemnly. 'Anyone else strike you?'

'Maybe the good doctor here didn't fancy the competition?' said Snark slyly.

That time, Patrick managed to keep still.

'Oh, and Mr. Dewar, I suppose,' Snark added, for once sounding more serious. 'My mother showed you the letter the other day. If he was rangling with Mr. Dewar's good lady, no doubt he would be the first in line to shove balm up his stuck up nose.'

'Your mother, presumably, would also have some reason to show her distress,' said Durris quietly. Snark jerked back as if he had been slapped. The thought had clearly not occurred to him.

'I don't think so.'

'And it is another reason why you yourself might have felt some hostility to your father, perhaps enough to drive your former dislike to a wish to destroy him?' asked Durris, still in the most polite of tones. 'I cannot imagine any man seeing his mother so insulted would not wish to take some kind of revenge.'

Snark sneered.

'Oh, yes, that's right,' he said. 'Blame it on me, just because I'm honest. I tell you, if I had thought of ramming his mouth full of his vile concoctions and killing him that way, I would have, and I'd have danced around his corpse singing Fa-la-la. And I tell you that because I'm honest. My father never spoke a true word in his life. And what's the result? Every job I've ever had I've lost, and he's making three shillings a tin on his damned balm and more on the infallible scarlet powders, and I have to live with him and follow him round the country like a damned royal court with all his drooping women, when he's a scoundrel and I'm honest!' His voice had risen: several of the hotel servants had emerged from various doorways to see what was going on. He saw them, but did not care. 'So arrest me now if you're going to. Go on, then!'

Durris did not move.

'Right, then, I'm off to bed. It quite takes it out of you, finding your father's been murdered in just the right way!'

He stamped up the stairs. If he was expecting a surge of action on the part of Durris to seize him, he was disappointed.

'What was that about a letter?' Patrick asked. Durris cast a glance at Hippolyta, evidently surprised that she had not mentioned it to her husband. He told Patrick the gist of the anonymous letter and its predecessors.

'So somebody thought that Dr. Gilead – I can't help thinking of him by that name,' said Patrick apologetically. 'It suited him so: just as Snark suits his son. Somebody thought that Dr. Gilead was enjoying some kind of association with Mrs. Dewar, under the noses of their respective spouses.'

'That's right. And Peter Snark seems to have thought it credible. Would you have said that Dr. Gilead was inclined to enter into intimacies with his female patients?' he asked carefully.

'I've hardly met the man,' said Patrick, but Hippolyta was quicker.

'No! I'm sure not. Not all of them.'

Both men stopped and stared at her for a moment.

'Hippolyta, dearest, I'm sure Mr. Durris had no intention –'

'My mother is one of his patients,' she explained coldly.

'I apologise,' said Durris at once. 'Of course I would never have included her in such a summary. Nevertheless, just because she is obviously innocent of any harm in this, it does not mean that Dr. Gilead might not have tried to approach her.'

Hippolyta swallowed.

'True,' she said. 'I'm sorry: I'm very tired. What time is it, does anyone know?'

Durris pulled out his watch.

'One in the morning,' he said, with surprise. 'I had no idea.'

'The dancing seems to be running down a little.' Patrick cocked an ear towards the courtyard dance floor. Durris shook himself.

'I need to speak to some of his patients as soon as possible,' he said, 'before the news flies around, as it will. I wonder,' he turned to the hotel keeper, 'Mr. Black, could I use another small room to talk to them, two at a time?'

'Aye, sir. I think the card room is free now – just over here.'

'Dr. Napier, Mrs. Napier – do you think you could do something for me? It might cause some suspicion if I or if Mr. Black were to summon guests out here. Do you think you could go, one or other or both of you, and bring here ... let me see ... Mrs. Pumpton and her husband?'

'Of course,' said Hippolyta, still repenting her outburst.

'Just say that someone wants to meet them. I shan't keep any of them long, at this stage. I'll be in there.' He pointed to the card room, and Hippolyta nodded.

'I'd better go and check on my patient,' said Patrick. 'Will you be all right, dearest?'

'Of course.'

She walked steadily despite her painful feet back to the dance floor. Mrs. Nickell was being flung round the room by a large man with a bald pate, and Mr. Nickell, absently watching her, greeted Hippolyta like the entertainment he had been hoping for for the last hour. Hippolyta skipped about him, but he stopped her.

'Have you heard the scandal?' he asked, mock horror on his face. 'Dr. Gilead has been found in a locked parlour – *in flagrante* with Mrs. Dewar!'

'Really?' asked Hippolyta, as though it were of little importance. She smiled and pulled away, heading for the table where her mother was seated with the Pumptons. Galatea was fanning herself and looked half asleep.

'Mrs. Napier! Mrs. Napier! Over here!' Mrs. Pumpton was still wide awake, anyway. 'Such dreadful news! The hotel keeper has been found in the parlour, locked in with Mrs. Gilead! Did you ever?'

'Never, Mrs. Pumpton. But it was you I was looking for – you and Mr. Pumpton. Somebody wants to meet you. May I take you?'

'Somebody? Who? Who?' Mrs. Pumpton, curiosity piqued, rose up unsteadily from the table, propped from behind by her husband. He rounded the broad coastline of her, and offered her his arm.

'Of course, Mrs. Napier. Lead on,' he said in good enough humour.

'Mr. and Mrs. Pumpton,' she announced at the door of the card room.

'Please come in, madam, sir,' said Durris, rising smoothly from a chair at the card table. 'I represent the sheriff for Aberdeenshire. I'm afraid I have some bad news for you. Please be seated.'

They established themselves in two separate chairs, Mrs. Pumpton's groaning ominously, as Hippolyta made for the door.

'Now, I believe you were both acquainted with a Francis Gilead or Snark?'

'That's Doctor Gilead to you, young man!' Mrs. Pumpton waved her fan imperiously at Durris. 'Yes, I've known him a couple of years. What of it?' she asked, suddenly alert.

'I'm afraid Dr. Gilead has met with an accident, Mrs. Pumpton.'

'What!'

Hippolyta retreated rapidly. By Mrs. Pumpton's hectoring cries as she stood some distance away, you would have thought that Durris himself was entirely responsible for anything that had happened to her precious Dr. Gilead, and she was going to see to it that he was dealt with accordingly – or possibly more so. Hippolyta wondered what Durris was making of it all. Would he conclude that this was the first either Pumpton had known of Gilead's death? Hippolyta was not sure.

After ten minutes or so, during which the shouting became more sporadic, though undiminished in volume, the card room door shot open, and Mrs. Pumpton left, stately as the Bass Rock, with Mr. Pumpton thoughtful behind her. Without a glance at Hippolyta, she ascended the stairs. Hippolyta was glad to remember that Patrick was up with Mrs. Dewar: Mrs. Pumpton seemed likely to have forgotten completely that their bedchamber was now a sickroom. Durris popped his head out from the card room.

'Ears still ringing?' Hippolyta asked him. He gave the briefest of nods.

'Could you please fetch the Nickells? Thank you, Mrs. Napier.' He rubbed his temples, and disappeared back into the room.

Hippolyta returned to the ball room and the table.

'Where is Mrs. Pumpton?' demanded her mother. 'Whom did she meet?'

'I need to find the Nickells,' said Hippolyta. 'The Pumptons have retired for the night.'

'We should be going soon, too,' said Galatea, who looked beyond bored.

'We need to say good night to Dr. Gilead first,' said her mother. Mr. Nickell, who never seemed to be far away, sidled up to Hippolyta.

'Want to hear the latest rumour?' he asked, with a glance at Mrs. Fettes. 'The locked parlour: Dr. Gilead *and your sister*,' he said in a whisper.

'Where is Mrs. Nickell?' Hippolyta asked him.

'Over there – unless she's found some other fancy man,' he added acidly. Hippolyta looked over, to where Mrs. Nickell had just finished dancing with the balding man.

'Someone wants to see you both, if you wouldn't mind coming with me,' she said hurriedly.

'Ooh, yes,' he said 'I'll come with you.' With a wink at Hippolyta that was entirely improper, he caught his wife's arm and led them both back into the hotel building. 'Where is this mysterious person, then?'

'Just in here.' Hippolyta pushed the half-open card room door. 'Mr. and Mrs. Nickell,' she announced.

Durris rose again and went through the same procedure as he had with the Pumptons. The result was just as noisy, though of a different style: Mrs. Nickell fell into hysterics, while Mr. Nickell laughed heartily then slapped her into silence. Hippolyta once again fled into the hallway.

Sobbing continued to issue from the room. This time Hippolyta felt fairly sure Mrs. Nickell at least had no prior knowledge of Dr. Gilead's death. Mr. Nickell, however, seemed to be positively cheerful in the face of the news. They emerged eventually, Mrs. Nickell still in tears and Mr. Nickell with another cheery wink at Hippolyta, and like the Pumptons they made straight for the stairs and their room. Hippolyta went to the card room door.

'Next?' she asked, nervously. Durris looked up, his expression understanding.

'Would you mind very much? I'd like to see Mrs. Fettes and Mrs. Milton, if that is all right.'

'Of course,' she said, but her stomach filled with butterflies instantly. She pattered along tenderly – heavens, would this evening never end for her poor feet? The thought of the walk back down to the boat was something she longed for, and dreaded. Her mother and Galatea were still seated at the table.

'Our turn?' asked her mother, who was not stupid. Hippolyta nodded. Her mother rose, in the usual waft of cordial balm, but turned back to her. 'What is going on, Poll?'

'I can't say just yet. Please come into the hotel, Mother. Galatea, come on, you too.'

Refusing to be led by her daughter, Mrs. Fettes stalked across the ball room. Galatea hauled herself up and with a scowl at Hippolyta followed her. Hippolyta waved her hand in gracious if silent sarcasm, and went after them both in as dignified a fashion as she could muster.

This time after Durris had seated Mrs. Fettes and Galatea Hippolyta hovered at the open door. Mrs. Fettes was studying Durris curiously, clearly wondering where to put him. Good luck to her, Hippolyta thought: she would be interested to hear her conclusions, if she reached any. Durris, however, was watching Hippolyta expectantly, waiting for her to leave. Hippolyta pretended to misunderstand, closed the door from the inside, and sat on a hard chair by the wall. Durris sighed, and turned back to Mrs. Fettes.

'Thank you so much for coming here, Mrs. Fettes,' said Durris without any misplaced humility. 'I'm sure when you hear what the matter is, you will understand the need for some discretion in the case. This is not something to be mooted about the ball room.'

'Go on,' said Mrs. Fettes. Her analysis of Durris had evidently not been satisfactorily completed, and a little frown remained on her face.

'I regret to have to inform you that an accident, of sorts, has befallen a person of your acquaintance. Dr. Gilead, to be precise.'

'I see,' said Mrs. Fettes. She was staring straight ahead: from the angle of Hippolyta's seat it was hard to tell whether she was gazing at Durris or past him. 'I had suspected something of the sort. I take it that the matter is not straightforward.'

'Not at all, Mrs. Fettes.'

'He was – he met a violent death?' she found the words, the

first time in the conversation she had sound less than sure of herself.

'He did. And the identity of the perpetrator is not clear.'

'I understand.'

Silence landed on the room for a moment. Hippolyta looked away from her mother's intelligent, expressionless face to Galatea. She, too, seemed to be trying to show no emotion, but she was not as practised as their mother at such things. There was the least glint of a nasty little smile on her face. Unable to resist, Hippolyta looked down at Galatea's hands, twisting on her lap: they were, of course, gloved.

'Mrs. Fettes, you are clearly a woman with a mind of her own. I should value your opinion in this matter,' said Durris, seriously. 'Can you think of any reason anyone here would have to want Dr. Gilead dead?'

'Anyone here? I suppose that makes sense,' Mrs. Fettes conceded. 'Let me give that a little thought.' She applied her mind, gaze now on the floor, concentrating. 'You too seem a sensible man, and I think you will not take anything I say and use it without further investigation. These, then, are impressions and perhaps deductions from observations I have made of those acquainted with Dr. Gilead in this circle. I have seen no signs of professional jealousy displayed, despite the fact that Dr. Gilead was of course a leader in his field.' Hippolyta glanced quickly at her: was she thinking of Patrick? 'Presumably he was altogether too exalted for any emotion but admiration. His son Peter was resentful of his success, and is, I think, of an ill-tempered disposition: if someone were to strike Dr. Gilead down I should think that Peter is a likely candidate. Other motives ... Mr. Dewar, of course, is a devoted husband, and Dr. Gilead was more than attentive to his wife. He may have taken Dr. Gilead's natural gallantry seriously. The same might apply to Mr. Nickell, though I am not sure that he would necessarily bother. His wife is a universal flirt and it does not usually seem to concern him: he is a lazy oaf, more given to flirting himself than considering what might be respectable behaviour.' At this she turned her head on her long neck and gave Hippolyta a hard look. Durris followed it in surprise, and made a tiny mark in his notebook. Then Mrs. Fettes frowned suddenly. 'Although ...' she added, surprised by something that had just occurred to her '... I wonder if perhaps Mrs. Nickell had changed her feelings for Dr. Gilead.'

'In what way?'

Mrs. Fettes was still frowning.

'I'm not sure I'm right ... Let me consider that at more length.'

'Very well. Can you think of anyone else who might wish Dr. Gilead dead?'

Mrs. Fettes paused.

'Mrs. Gilead might be pleased enough to see him dead,' said Galatea abruptly. 'How did he die, anyway?'

Durris adjusted his glasses and regarded her directly for a moment.

'He was smothered with his own cordial balm.'

'Good gracious!' cried Mrs. Fettes, turning white. Galatea slapped her gloved hand to her mouth, eyes wide. It took a second before Hippolyta realised she was laughing.

'Galatea!' Mrs. Fettes turned on her. 'Stop that at once.'

Galatea hiccoughed, and for a wonder stopped. Mr. Durris made another tiny shape in his notebook. Hippolyta wondered if the marks formed part of a larger pattern, like stitches in an embroidery, or if they were minuscule letters in a code only he could later interpret. She longed to see.

'Do you need us for anything further this evening?' Mrs. Fettes was asking, 'or may we go? I fear both my daughters are quite exhausted by the excitements of the evening.'

There was nothing like a statement of that sort to make Hippolyta feel she could dance for at least another hour, but the grown up part of her knew it was true: the only wonder was that her mother seemed quite fresh.

'Patrick is seeing to a patient. He may have to stay here,' she put in.

'I am sure that three of us together will be quite safe going back to the village unescorted,' said her mother. 'It is not Leith.'

'I'm afraid I must stay here too, or it would be my pleasure to escort you,' said Durris politely.

'I suppose you will be talking to everyone, even if they did not know him,' said Hippolyta sympathetically as she rose.

'Everyone,' said Durris with a smile. 'I hope that someone

may have seen him entering that room. Perhaps even that someone saw who went in with him.'

'I wish you luck, Mr. Durris,' said Mrs. Fettes briskly. 'Come along, Galatea.'

'I must go and see Patrick,' said Hippolyta, but when she opened the door she found he was waiting for them in the passageway outside.

'All well?' he asked, glancing behind her with a nod to Durris.

'Quite well. My mother would like to go home now,' she said. 'How is – your patient?'

He made a face.

'Stable, I think. Will you be all right?'

'We'll manage: as long as there is still a boat. If not we'll be back!'

'The boatman was to stay there all night. You might have to wake him, but you should get across.' He touched her arms, then took her hands. 'Take care, my love.'

'You, too. Don't provoke any murderers, will you?'

'I'll do my best not to!'

'And I hope – I hope she's all right.'

He could not reply to that in any useful way, and pulled her to him to kiss her forehead. Then her mother was in the passage, too, and they had to recover their cloaks and find their way down to the boat and home.

Chapter Eleven

Saturday morning dawned clear, fresh and chilly. The shutters had been left open, and the window was propped wide, letting in a cool breeze that flicked at the curtains and made the pillow deliciously cold. Hippolyta reluctantly opened her eyes when one of the cats came pointedly to miaow in her ear, felt across the bed and discovered only two more cats. Patrick had evidently been constrained to stay all night at the hotel, as they had feared. She sent up a quick prayer for Mrs. Dewar and for her husband, and as a second thought for Mrs. Gilead and her son in their bereavement. She stretched carefully so as not to dislodge her feline friends, sat up and pushed her hair back, and looked about the room. Her grand evening gown was half-upright on the floor, resting on its heavy hem and petticoats, cast aside as quickly as she could last night, and her hair was all in a tangle from going to bed without brushing out her elaborate arrangement. There were silk flowers scattered about the floor, to her shame, and it seemed like the kind of simple task she could face straightaway to pick them up and lay them back on the dressing table. Then she sat down wearily on the stool, and considered her reflection, and reluctantly took up her hair brush and set to work.

It was a while before she was even ready to ring for Ishbel to bring up some hot water, with the church clock striking nine across the green.

'Are Mrs. Fettes or Mrs. Milton up yet?' she asked Ishbel, as she sluiced off the weariness in hot suds.

'No, ma'am, they're no.'

Galatea must indeed have been tired not to be up early and interfering in something, Hippolyta thought ungraciously.

'The blue walking dress today, I think, Ishbel. And I'll keep my hair quite simple. Even it feels tired after last night.'

'Is it true what they're saying, ma'am? That Dr. Gilead is dead?'

'That's right – had you met him, Ishbel?' She pulled on a clean shift, luxuriating in its crisp chill.

'Oh, no, ma'am, but I had seen him in the village. He was very handsome, was he no?'

'Well, someone was evidently less than impressed with him.'

'I heard,' said Ishbel cautiously, 'that a gentleman found Dr. Gilead about to run off with his wife, and ran him through with his sword on the spot! And then the lady collapsed and is near to death with a broken heart!'

'Hm,' said Hippolyta. 'It was not quite like that, I'm afraid. No one knows yet who murdered him, but I don't know of anyone suffering a broken heart up at the hotel.'

Ishbel shrugged resignedly, starting to do up the lacings of her gown.

'Aye, well, stories are always better than the truth, it seems. And a bit of romance brightens up a dull day, ma'am!'

'That's true. Any more problems with Wullie's dog?'

'No, ma'am, not today. He slept in Mrs. Riach's room last night – '

'Wullie did?'

'No, no, ma'am, the dog. Just on the floor. He seems to have taken to her, ken.'

'And how does Wullie feel about that?'

'I think he missed the company in the kitchen at night.'

'I'm sure he did.' Hippolyta had mixed feelings about Mrs. Riach's new admirer. She did not want Wullie upset: the boy seemed to have had a rough enough life up to now, and to be abandoned by his dog for a grumpy housekeeper was harsh. On the other hand, something that kept Mrs. Riach happy was not to be dismissed out of hand, either. She would have to consider the matter. Ishbel finished the laces, and began on her hair. It was already well enough brushed that a plain arrangement took only a moment or two, and Hippolyta tied on an apron, helped Ishbel carry the hot water back downstairs, and went to feed the hens.

After a solitary breakfast, she packed some clean linen for Patrick and his everyday clothes and boots, and hung up her apron, and went to take a boat across to Pannanich. She was beginning to feel like a regular traveller on the route: would she have to come back again later with her mother for the baths, or would the appeal of bathing be lessened now that Dr. Gilead was no longer there to consult? Her mother had been very sharp last night, despite the lateness of the hour: Mr. Durris would soon see how clever she was. Yet how could such a clever woman fall for an awful man like Dr. Gilead?

A very young lad was waiting at the other side of the bridge to help anyone that needed it: all his older brothers and their friends had seen the night through for the guests at the ball, and were evidently sleeping it off, and he had been sent out to cover the business for the morning. He seemed too small under his great woollen bonnet to carry Hippolyta's basket, but he looked close to tears when she said she could manage, so she handed it to him and then had to pace slowly up the hill so that he was not left too far behind. When he set the basket down at last at the hotel gate – not the first time he had had to set it down on the walk – she paid him a penny and he solemnly bowed and placed it in a tiny pocket, before skipping back down the hill for the next boat. She grinned after him.

The canvas was still over the cobbled courtyard that had formed last night's ball room, but the tables and chairs were gone, the flowers had been heaped up on the midden round the corner, the stage and the floor had been taken up and stacked against the wall, some parts still with spilt food stuck to them, and two men on ladders were consulting with another man at an upstairs window about the best way to roll up the canvas. Hippolyta was impressed at their industry: one at least of the men on ladders she had seen serving tea as she was leaving last night, and here he was fresh as perhaps yesterday's daisy.

The same could not be said for the hotel keeper, whom she chanced upon in the hall.

'Ah, Mrs. Napier,' he said blearily. His eyes were three-quarters closed, though he was upright and moving. 'You'll find Dr. Napier in the card room there, with Mr. Durris. I'd, ah –' he considered for a moment, trying to remember what he had been saying. 'I'd knock, if I was you.'

Curious, Hippolyta rapped sharply on the card room door,

where Durris had at some time last night carried out his interviews. There was a dull thud inside, and a small cry of pain or surprise, it was hard to tell. After a moment, the door opened: the room inside was dark, with the shutters still closed. At the door was Patrick, his collar missing and his coat gone, in his stocking soles. He blinked and recognised her, then glanced back into the room.

'Hush,' he said. 'Durris is sleeping.'

A soft snore issued from the darkness.

'Could they not find you a bedchamber, either of you?'

'All full,' Patrick mumbled. 'And it was past four? Five, maybe? Dawn, I think.' He stopped and yawned excessively. 'Is that clean clothes?'

'Yes.' She handed him the basket.

'I knew you were an angel. Just a minute.'

He closed the door in her face, and she could hear inside the minute sounds that he usually made when he was back late from seeing a patient, and thought he could undress and come to bed without waking her. She hoped Durris was a heavier sleeper. In a few moments, Patrick was back at the door, changed, with his boots in his hand. He shut the door softly behind him.

'All well at home?' he asked quietly, leaning against the wall to haul on his boots.

'Yes – well, Mother and Galatea had not surfaced when I left. Otherwise I think all is well. What about here? What about – your patient?'

'I'll have to go up again and see in a minute. She came round for a few minutes about half past three, I should say it was, and seemed confused. But not overly so: I should not have expected anything else. The pain was quite bad, of course, so she has had some more laudanum. Forgive me talking endlessly about it like this: I'm tired, and Mr. Dewar is not someone capable of a normal conversation at present. He just sits and stares. Did you by any chance bring any more laudanum?'

'I'm sorry, I didn't think.'

'That's all right: I'll come home with you when you're going and take my evening things back, and restock my medical bag. Oh, blow.'

He opened the card room door again quietly, reached in, and pulled out his medical bag, but fumbled it or knocked it, Hippolyta couldn't see. It landed solidly on the floor, and she could hear Durris grunt.

'What's that?'

'Nothing, Durris, just me,' said Patrick, pulling the bag out of the room.

'Dr. Napier?'

'That's right. My wife's here, and I have to go up and see my patient shortly anyway. You go back to sleep.'

There was the sound of someone rearranging themselves heavily in blankets.

'What time is it?' Durris' voice was a little clearer. Patrick looked about and found the long case clock in the hallway. He squinted at it, pulled out his glasses and tried again.

'It's near eleven,' he said. 'Good gracious, eleven!'

'Eleven?' Stockinged feet hit the stone floor. There was a certain amount of crashing about, then the shutters were opened, one at a time. The room was revealed: two low armchairs had been set each side of the fire, the card tables folded against the walls, and two upright chairs sat in front of the armchairs, forming very uncomfortable looking beds. The situation had been improved as much as possible with mountains of blankets and a couple of decent pillows. Now that he could see, Patrick darted back into the room to recover his discarded evening clothes, and Durris straightened his waistcoat before turning, hand out for his neckcloth, to see that Hippolyta was there.

'I beg your pardon, Mrs. Napier: I had no idea you were present.'

'My fault, Mr. Durris,' she said, turning away. She could feel her face a little pink, and was annoyed at herself.

'Shall we see if there's anything like breakfast around?' Patrick asked, taking her arm. 'Durris, do you want something to eat?'

'Very much so, Dr. Napier. If you want to go and see your patient, I'll talk to Mr. Black.'

'Perfect, thank you.'

Patrick headed for the stairs, and Hippolyta, a little embarrassed at being left behind with Mr. Durris, followed quickly behind him. In the Pumptons' room, Mr. Dewar was slumped in his chair and a different maid was seeing to the fire with neat efficiency. Dewar stirred a little as they came in, and Mrs. Dewar, whose hand he clutched as if afraid she would disappear if he closed his eyes, moved her head very slightly on the pillow. Patrick went to the other side of the bed.

'Mrs. Dewar, how are you feeling?' he asked, already touching her forehead and reaching for her other hand for her pulse.

'A little better, I believe,' she said, though it seemed a struggle.

'You are a healthier colour than I have seen you,' said Patrick encouragingly. 'I'm afraid, though, you will have to stay where you are for some time yet.'

She gave a little sigh, though it might have been effort more than resignation. Her gaze flickered around the room.

'This was not our room, I think,' she said slowly.

'No, this was the room which the Pumptons had. Mrs. Pumpton found you and carried you here. I believe they are in your room.'

Another little sigh this time stood for a chuckle.

'She is a strong woman, Mrs. Pumpton,' she whispered. 'I hope I was somewhere near by.'

'You were at the top of the servants' stairs, apparently,' said Patrick lightly. 'Perhaps you had felt ill and tried to find someone to help.'

There was a long pause, and Hippolyta thought she might have fallen asleep again, before she said,

'Yes, that was it. I felt ill – very ill. I rang the bell but …' She tailed off uncertainly.

'You are lucky Mrs. Pumpton was passing the top of the servants' stairs,' said Patrick, glancing at Hippolyta. Why would Mrs. Pumpton have been passing there, she wondered. It was not on a direct line between her room and the top of the main stairs. In fact, she was not quite sure where it was: she would go and look, she thought, as soon as possible.

Patrick settled Mrs. Dewar back and gave her a little more water and laudanum. Mr. Dewar grunted and shifted in his chair, but did not waken. Assuring the maid that he would return some time after breakfast, Patrick opened the door for Hippolyta and followed her out on to the landing.

'I wonder,' he said quietly, 'though I have not mentioned it to Durris yet, if that was really the reason Mrs. Dewar was at the top of the servants' stairs?'

'Where are they?' asked Hippolyta, seizing the opportunity.

'Along here: I looked last night.' He led the way along the narrow corridor that crossed the top of the stairs and went from one end of the hotel to the other. Just past the door to the poky room where she had left Mrs. Gilead last night, Patrick pushed open a door in the end wall, and showed her the dark little staircase and two doorways beyond, evidently the servants' rooms.

'How did she even know it was here?' Hippolyta asked. 'Where was their room anyway?'

'Almost the other end of the building,' said Patrick. 'I found out when I had to redirect the Pumptons from their old room last night: they had no idea Mrs. Dewar was still in their bed.'

'Then she would normally have no reason to be down this end of the passage at all – normally,' said Hippolyta. She met his eye. 'The Gileads' room – complete with a trunk full of balm and scarlet powders – is just here.'

'Is it, indeed?' He bit his lip. 'Then do you think the anonymous letter writer was right? That Dr. Gilead and Mrs. Dewar were intending to elope?'

'I have no idea,' said Hippolyta, 'but I do wonder.'

They had the parlour to themselves for breakfast, with Mr. Durris, who had ordered eggs and bread and butter enough for all three of them. Hippolyta sipped some tea and despite having had breakfast earlier at home, tackled a plateful of bread and butter with a good appetite. Nudged by Patrick, she described the layout upstairs.

'Your patient, then, is Mrs. Dewar? You did not say,' said Durris to Patrick, but not with hostility.

'I wanted to wait for a good moment – when we were both fully awake, for one thing. I knew you were interested in her from the perspective of that letter.'

'Yes: and the temptation is to think that the letter has something to do with the murder. It might not, of course.'

'But if that were to be the motive for the murder,' said Patrick, 'an affair between them, it still does not tell us who might have done the murder.'

'The obvious suspects would be, I suppose, Mrs. Gilead, Mr. Dewar, and perhaps for his mother's sake Peter Snark.'

'Oh, surely it must be Peter Snark!' cried Hippolyta, then swept the room belatedly for any possible eavesdroppers. Fortunately there were none. 'I mean, if one were to look for someone who looks like a violent thug ... I know, I know,' she said to Patrick before he could say anything. 'There is no art to find the mind's construction in the face, and all that. But it would be such a waste if he were not the murderer!' She grinned at them both: she had no intention that they should take her seriously.

'Well, we have no way of knowing yet,' said Durris, solemnly, though there was a twinkle in his eye. 'You may get your wish, Mrs. Napier. I take it Mr. Dewar is attending his wife's sickbed?'

'He is: and if you were thinking of questioning him about anything even slightly complicated,' said Patrick, 'I'd wait until he has had a little more sleep.'

'He has my sympathy,' said Durris, hunching and dropping his shoulders stiffly. 'I appreciate Mr. Black's hospitality, but I hope his paying guests have more comfortable beds than ours were last night.' He sighed, and took his glasses off to clean them on his handkerchief. 'Well, the carpenter has been sent for and will arrived with the coffin some time this morning,' he said, failing to focus until the glasses were replaced. 'Have you seen all you want to see of the body, Dr. Napier?'

'After our more extensive examination last night? I believe so,' said Patrick. 'There was nothing on the body to make me think that there was any other cause of death. My only thought is that it is possible that laudanum was administered to him before he was killed: even though his wrists were tied to the chair, quite tightly, he would surely have tossed his head from side to side to avoid the balm if he could, and there is no sign of that. Someone took handfuls of it and simply smeared it into his mouth and nose: the skin around his face was red from it, but not bruised.'

'Anyone who used their bare hands to administer it would have been red too, would they not?' Durris asked.

'Yes, for a while,' said Patrick. 'And they would smell of the stuff. But as Peter Snark pointed out, it's a lingering smell, and as far as I can see all Gilead's patients used both the balm and the scarlet powders: they and their spouses would easily have smelled of it, as would, no doubt, Mrs. Gilead and Mr. Snark.'

Durris considered for a moment. Hippolyta was thinking, too.

'If he was dosed with laudanum,' she said tentatively, 'would that not mean that even someone quite slight could administer the balm?'

'Yes, I believe it does mean that,' said Patrick.

'Even, say, Mr. Pumpton? Or a woman?'

'In the case of Mrs. Pumpton I think no laudanum would have been necessary,' said Durris with feeling. 'She could have felled him with one hand, had she so chosen.'

'But she was devoted to him!' Hippolyta protested.

'What if she discovered that he really was intending to elope with Mrs. Dewar, though?' said Durris. 'Would she have been as devoted to him then?'

'But to kill him!'

'If you had to choose a woman who could kill a man,' Patrick put in, 'Mrs. Pumpton would be high on my list. Though I would have expected instead the felling with one hand, as Mr. Durris suggests.'

'I thought she was going to fell me with one hand last night,' Durris admitted. 'She was ferocious! And I only asked her where she had been in the course of the evening. What she might do to someone who actually accused her of murder I dread to think: should it come to that, I shall need to ask the sheriff for more men.'

'Here's a thought,' said Hippolyta, 'if we are looking for reasons beyond the possible elopement. What if someone, one of his patients or one of their spouses, found out that Gilead was a complete quack?'

'Are we sure that he was?' Durris asked, turning to Patrick.

'There is certainly some evidence that he was not entirely sound,' said Patrick delicately. 'I should like to take a closer look at some of the balm and the powders. Something he told Mrs. Dewar about her condition implied that he had at least very little medical knowledge, and even when it came to someone he apparently cared for, in her case, he either bluffed or told complete lies, and simply resorted to his usual treatment.'

'Mr. Snark said he told lies the whole time,' said Hippolyta.

'He said his father had based his whole fortune on deceit, didn't he?'

'I wonder if he was any kind of doctor at all, at any stage?' Durris said, pressing his pencil on to the paper of his notebook eloquently. 'What was his background? Did he start off in the profession, make some useful general medicines and think it was easier to sell those, or did he wake up one morning and decide to become Dr. Gilead, seller of famous balm and infallible scarlet powders?'

Patrick shrugged.

'I could write to some colleagues in Edinburgh, and some I know in London. He seems to have practised, if that's the word, in Pitkeathly, Harrogate, Bath and perhaps Brighton, too.'

'And maybe Tunbridge and Leamington? Those are spas, aren't they?' added Hippolyta helpfully. 'I have a distant cousin in Bath, but she has no connexion with the medical profession.'

'It would be useful, I think, to find out more about him – and I'll talk to Mrs. Gilead, too, and see what she knows. She's such a wee mouse she was probably just dragged along on the great man's coat tails.'

'But in the meantime,' said Hippolyta firmly, 'we're wondering if it's jealousy, revenge, or gain – is that it?'

'Or some madman who happened to wander past the hotel at midnight,' added Durris with a little smile. 'Unless we can find a political motive, I think we've covered everything, Mrs. Napier.'

'I'm afraid it's very hard to keep my wife out of anything that interests her,' said Patrick apologetically.

'Of that I am well aware, Dr. Napier. Now, tell me: is Mrs. Dewar like to live?'

Patrick grew more solemn.

'I should not like to promise anything just now. She is quiet and there is at the moment no sign of infection, but I shall be keeping a careful eye on her.'

'I understand. You say that she collapsed when something, ah, went wrong with a tumour in her stomach?'

'That's right. I don't know what, exactly. The tumour was very large and had spread – I pray I removed it all, but one can never be entirely sure.'

Durris' mouth turned down a little at the corners.

'This had been misdiagnosed by Dr. Gilead, you say?'

'That's right, from what Mr. Dewar said.'

'And she was found – by Mrs. Pumpton – at the top of the servants' stair?'

'Well, not the top, exactly,' Hippolyta explained. 'At the door to the servants' stair on the first floor. It leads through to the funny little extension at the end of the building, where the servants have their rooms, presumably.'

'Inside the door or out?'

'I beg your pardon?'

'Was she in the corridor, or on the stair? Are we sure that was where she was going, or did she just happen to be passing it?'

Patrick and Hippolyta exchanged looks.

'Mrs. Pumpton would know,' Patrick said, sounding more confident than he looked.

'And Mrs. Pumpton carried her back to her own room, laying her on the bed, unconscious. Is that right?'

Hippolyta nodded, thinking back. Mrs. Dewar had certainly been in a dead faint.

'So the first either of you saw her, she was on Mrs. Pumpton's bed?'

'I could quite believe Mrs. Pumpton had carried her in,' said Hippolyta. 'It looked as if she had only just reached the bed before dropping her, you know? Her feet were almost on the floor, and her arms were flung out to one side.'

'I see,' said Durris. Another little shape was added to the notebook page. 'What bothers me,' he said at last, contemplating what he had drawn, or written, 'is this. How sure are we that what caused her collapse was natural? I mean, did someone try to murder her, too?'

Chapter Twelve

A knock on the parlour door startled them from their contemplations. One of the servants opened it from outside, and with a look to them for approval ushered in Mrs. Gilead. The widow was dressed in mottled black with her bonnet, gloves and shawl in place, her dull complexion even more lifeless against her reddish eyes. On a lead behind her came the little white terrier, looking even more subdued, half-hidden in her skirts. The men stood, flinging down their napkins, and Mrs. Gilead advanced to about halfway across the room, stopping uncertainly.

'Please, ma'am, come in and be seated,' said Durris, pulling out a chair. 'Can we offer you some tea or chocolate? Perhaps some food?'

'I thank you, no. I have eaten – a little.'

They all had to pause to hear her, she was so quiet.

'Well, then,' said Durris, and his own steady voice was loud by contrast, 'what can we do to help you?'

'Er, I wanted to know if you knew anything more about – about what happened last night.' She barely met their eyes with her own faded brown ones, a sludgy brown, Hippolyta thought, like puddles in the dregs of winter. 'I could hardly sleep,' she added, almost inaudibly. Durris considered for a moment.

'We need to work out,' he began, 'why someone should want to do what they did, and we need to work out when they did it. I've been talking to the hotel servants, and it was so busy last night it is hard to tell what happened when. But after some work – and I have yet to talk to many of the guests so we might eventually manage to pin things down more closely – after some work I have established that the parlour door was locked at some time between half past eleven and half past midnight.' He regarded her for a moment, but she said nothing, chewing her lower lip. 'Are you able to help us? Where were you yourself between half past eleven and half past midnight?'

She flicked a glance up at him and as quickly down again. Her hands smoothed and resmoothed the folds of her skirt, pinching the fabric between her gloved fingers.

'I think,' she began softly, 'I think I was mostly looking for him.'

'For your husband? For Dr. Gilead?'

She nodded, and blinked. Durris' voice was kind, but Hippolyta hoped that the widow was not going to cry. Durris carried on.

'When did you notice that he was not about? Or that he was not where you expected him to be, perhaps?'

'After supper,' she whispered.

'So you went to look for him? Where did you look?'

'I looked all around the ball room first, and then in the card room, and then in the supper room, and then in the small parlour.' She enumerated the rooms on her fingers, and at the last one her head jerked very slightly in the direction of the room where the body had been found.

'And he was not there then?'

She shook her head quickly, her eyes closed.

'But it was unlocked?'

She nodded.

'What time would that have been?'

That took a little thought.

'Perhaps eleven o'clock? I wasn't really looking at the time.'

Durris nodded, and placed the tip of his pencil on a page of his notebook, applying just a little pressure. He examined the effect, then looked back at Mrs. Gilead.

'Did you look anywhere else?'

'I went outside,' she breathed, 'but it was too dark to see who was who.'

'Did you think to call out to see if your husband would answer?' asked Durris, curious. She gave a little gasp.

'No, no! Not that.' Durris stayed silent, and after a long moment she explained, 'I wanted to see … who he was with.'

'I see.'

'I thought, you know, he might be with … Mrs. Dewar.'

'I understand,' said Durris, speaking almost as softly as she did.

'That letter, and the ones before it – they made me very unhappy.' She drew in a deep breath. 'He has always been a flirt – well, he's so handsome, no woman can resist him.' She stopped, and breathed deeply again. Hippolyta, desperately wanting to say that she herself had been perfectly capable of resisting him, wondered suddenly what the handsome but unappealing quack had seen in this little mouse. 'But he would never have left me, never. Not until she came along. And then …'

'Then?'

'Then he might.'

Durris left the sad little words hanging in the air for a moment.

'When you couldn't find him outside, did you look elsewhere inside?' he asked.

'I went up to our room. I was – I was scared he might already have packed his belongings.'

'Was there a reason you thought they might elope last night?'

'I thought – I suppose I thought with all the fuss of the ball … but no, I don't think I really had a reason. I was just afraid.'

As well she might be, Hippolyta thought. She had heard of abandoned wives who had much more apparent chance of survival alone than this little creature – though presumably her son Peter would stand by her.

'And had he packed anything?'

'No.' She sniffed then, but did not seem on the brink of tears. 'I went to their room, then, and knocked on the door. I think I thought perhaps I could reason with her. She had gone up to lie down, you see, and she had told her husband and – and my husband – that she didn't want their help. But there was no reply. I told myself that she was asleep.' The words came out contorted, a little desperate: Hippolyta considered how she might have been picturing what might be going on inside the Dewars' bedroom, when she could find her husband nowhere else, and how firmly she must have told herself that Mrs. Dewar was asleep. Did that make her strong or weak? she wondered. Determined that things were all right, or denying the possibility of disaster? Too frightened to face the truth? Yet she had searched all through the hotel for her husband, despite what she feared she might find.

'When did you find out about the parlour door being locked?'

'When I came downstairs again,' she said. 'Already there were several people there, and my heart sank. I knew, somehow, even though I had looked in there earlier and he was not there, I knew he was now. I knew something terrible had happened. And then I'm afraid I don't know much after that. It all seems blurry. I think I sat down somewhere. I hope,' she added miserably, 'I hope I wasn't any trouble.'

'Not at all,' Durris replied automatically. 'Well, Mrs. Gilead, I know this has all been a terrible shock, but you'll want to know about arrangements. A woman from the village came this morning and has made him tidy, and there's a carpenter on his way to kist him.'

'To what?' she asked blankly.

'To see to his coffin,' he explained.

'Oh.' Her eyes were bleak. 'Perhaps I should have ...'

'But then you and your son will need to sort out a minister or – well, there's a minister in the English church – sorry,' he added to Patrick and Hippolyta, 'the Episcopal church, that visits sometimes. You've maybe met him.'

She frowned, not sure.

'I'll talk things over with Peter,' she said. 'I don't know ... we went to the village church once.'

'The minister's a very kind man,' said Patrick, professionally reassuring. She blinked, perhaps having forgotten that anyone was there but Durris. 'I'm sure he would come and visit you and help you make some decisions, with your son, of course.'

She nodded, her face blank now at the enormity of the decisions to be made. How was she going to cope? Hippolyta felt sorry for her: for a woman so far tucked into her husband's shadow, the world must seem suddenly horridly bright and sharp.

'Do – do you need me any more just now?' she asked. Durris shook his head.

'I'm sure Dr. Napier here would suggest that it's best for you to rest for now.'

'I would indeed,' Patrick agreed. She rose, plucking at the dog's lead absently.

'I'll go and sit with him,' she said.

'He's still across in the small parlour.'

'Thank you, sir.'

The men stood, and waited until she and the terrier, each as dejected as the other, left the parlour and shut the door silently behind them. A moment later they heard a small howl of anguish from the terrier, encountering his dead master for the first time.

Durris, instead of sitting down again at the table, stepped over to the parlour window and eased it open a few inches. A snatch of chilly air slid in.

'I'm sorry,' he said. 'I had a sudden urge for fresh air. Everything here seems to smell of that cordial balm.' He leaned on it to close it again.

'Oh, leave it open!' cried Hippolyta. 'Please: it's such a lovely fresh day.' Patrick grinned at her, shivering. He always needed more warmth than she did. 'There's a trunk full of balm and scarlet powders in their room,' she added, suddenly remembering. 'She couldn't help but smell of it.'

'The same seems to apply to all his patients,' said Patrick. 'I should hate to cast aspersions on a lady, but Mrs. Dewar reeked of it.'

'And Mother ...'

'All of them, I should think,' said Durris calmly. 'It won't help us to wonder who would have conveniently had two tins of cordial balm. Amongst those of interest to us so far the patients had the balm and the husbands had access to their wives' tins. We don't know of anyone else who knew him before he came to Ballater, and they had only been here a week.'

'The two cures seem to have been his full arsenal,' Patrick remarked. 'I wonder if he mixed it up himself or had it made?'

'We need to take a look at his things,' said Durris, 'or rather I do.' He considered, still standing by the window, watching the descent of the canvas in the courtyard. 'And I'll take out some balm and powders for you to examine, Dr. Napier. I'd better go up and do the job now while Mrs. Gilead is occupied – I suppose she's Mrs. Snark really, but we'll leave that for now, unless she tells us otherwise. I don't want to disturb her.' He rubbed his forehead, and readjusted his glasses.

'Well, I'll be back up here later,' said Patrick, 'but I'd like to go home for a little now and fetch some more laudanum for Mrs.

Dewar: we're all right for a few hours yet but the time will come. Hippolyta, dearest, are you ready to go back home?'

Hippolyta nodded, opening her mouth to reply but at that second there came an awful crash from the courtyard. Durris flung the window fully open, and stuck his head out.

'Man's fallen off a ladder,' he snapped. Patrick was out of the parlour in a flash and in the yard, Durris and Hippolyta just after him. Peter Snark was outside the hotel door, blinking with shock.

'It just missed me!' he muttered, as affronted as if it had been personally intended. The ladder, one of those being used to remove the canvas roof from the erstwhile ball room, had tumbled on the cobbles, and a young hotel servant was sprawled on the ground, gasping tearfully. Patrick was already beside him. He glanced back at Hippolyta.

'Can you call for some ice, please, dearest, and bandages? And then I'm afraid we may be delayed!'

Hippolyta stepped back into the hotel and called Christy the maid, who scuttled away in delighted shock. When she returned to the courtyard Durris was crouching down beside Patrick. He rose when he saw her, and came back to the door.

'Dr. Napier says he'll be a little while,' he confirmed. 'I wonder, Mrs. Napier, if you would mind coming up to the Gileads' room with me? I fear that Mrs. Gilead might return suddenly while I look about, and be upset, and I should prefer to have a lady with me in that case. Dr. Napier says he does not mind.' He glanced back at Patrick, who waved a hand. The hotel servant clutched his elbow as if afraid his arm would fall off, but his ankle was at an odd angle, too.

'If Patrick's sure he can manage ...'

The maid had run back with the requisite bandages and a bucket full of greenish ice, and Patrick nodded.

'Go ahead,' he said. 'Next time you can help me!'

Hippolyta grinned, and followed Durris back into the hotel.

The Gileads' room was just as pokey and dark as she remembered. The bed was small: she had a sudden vision of Dr. Gilead's feet sticking splendidly out of the end of it, while Mrs. Gilead would have been squashed up in a corner. There was not much else in the room: a few decent coats of his, two gowns of hers – both of them dark-coloured and far from new, and from the marks carefully refashioned - clean linen and some grubby pieces, a flurry of silk handkerchiefs and black satin ribbons, the trunk of balm and powders, an old blanket on the floor for the dog. Durris seemed most interested in the trunk, and started lifting out the tins and packages two at a time. She knelt beside him to help him. In a moment the cures were all heaped neatly against the outside of the trunk, and they could see what had been beneath them. There were several bundles of papers, and a leatherbound ledger, all arranged for organised use. Durris lifted out the ledger with delicate fingers, and opened it.

'Sales of balm and powders, of course,' he murmured. 'Just this year, I note – I wonder if they leave older ones in some permanent home they have? - but the balance carried over is substantial.' He showed Hippolyta. Her eyebrows rose.

'Two hands, wouldn't you say?'

'Oh, yes.'

The column headings were in a black, flamboyant hand that immediately made one think of Dr. Gilead. It seemed to be written in black satin ribbon. All the entries, though, were in a dull brown ink, in economical letters, quick to read.

'Too grand to fill in his own accounts?' Hippolyta asked, smiling.

'You think he dictated them to her?' He frowned.

'Perhaps. Or perhaps Peter helped him with them.'

'Reluctantly, presumably. I wonder how reluctantly? He might not be free to do as he wishes, but he looks well funded.' He flicked through the pages. 'Dewar, Pumpton, Nickell – Fettes,' he listed, hesitating slightly on the last name. 'And plenty of others. Addresses in Brighton ... then in Bath ... then in Harrogate ... I wonder if there was a reason he moved so often? Pitkeathly, Peterhead, then Pannanich. Six spas in five months?'

'Running from his creditors?' Hippolyta suggested. 'Though if that's the money he was making, then surely he could have paid them off.'

'We don't know that he had any financial problems,' said Durris, 'and this certainly doesn't indicate any.'

'He didn't spend much on his wife's wardrobe, anyway, or his room here.' She thought for a moment, remembering not only the Dewars, but all Gilead's other hand-kissing and attentive gazes.

'Could he have been running from angry husbands?'

'Ah. Well, yes, perhaps.'

He did not look at her, but looked where the ledger had been in the trunk. Beneath it there was a clay morter and pestle, a large and worn knife, many times sharpened, and a wooden board, presumably all equipment for mixing cures. He laid the ledger back on top of them carefully, and picked up one of the bundles of letters.

'Orders for balm and powders,' he read from the label. He pulled out one or two. 'All marked "Sent" with the date in that brown ink again, followed by "Paid" in the same hand, with a date.'

'This is blank receipts – you know, printed ones that a tradesman fills in. Not used yet, I mean. This one is copy outgoing letters,' said Hippolyta, trying to be as tidy with the bundles as Durris had been. 'And they're in the brown ink, too. Listen: "Dear Sirs, Please be so kind as to send at your earliest convenience two stone of chalk, quality as you delivered before, to the above address. Also a pound of cochineal powder and a quarter pound of dried red chilli if it is the price and quality you were able to supply in December, otherwise two ounces only. An early delivery to the above address will oblige. Yours faithfully, Ada Snark." Her writing, then, not Peter's?'

'Interesting.'

'And here's another – it's to a lodging house keeper, I think, in Harrogate – wait, what was that?'

'What?'

'I thought I heard someone outside in the passage.'

Durris, who was nearer the door, leaned back, then turned on to his knees to peer round the doorpost.

'Nobody there now, anyway. The passage is empty. It may have been a servant on the back stairs: they're just through there.' They both listened, but heard nothing else. He nodded to her. 'Go on.'

'If you're sure. "Dear Mrs. Ogden, We shall require the usual accommodation beginning on the 12th. February, including a small room for Mr. Snark. As we shall be bringing a good deal of business into your lodging and public rooms, I trust you will be able to offer us a very good price on our own accommodation during our stay. I suggest a reduction to three quarters of your usual price for this time of the year. I expect to hear from you at your earliest convenience. Yours faithfully, Ada Snark." A brisk businesswoman, then.'

'It sounds like it – and in her own name, too.' Dewar was quiet for a moment, thoughtfully touching with the tip of his finger the tape on the letters he was holding. 'Here's a question: I don't know what you think, but until now I have thought of Mrs. Gilead as a wee bit of a nobody, and Dr. Gilead as the high heidyin in the household – possibly followed by Peter. Now, though: what do you say to the idea that she is the businesswoman, and he only the advertisement?'

'Like a performing monkey?' Hippolyta gave a little smile as she considered it. Somehow the letters did not read like ones that had been dictated by a third party. There was ordered authority in the dull brown hand. She thought back to the day she had first met Mrs. Gilead. At the tea table she had received a letter – perhaps one of the anonymous letters? And at her least glance, it seemed, Dr. Gilead had excused himself and left the room with her. She had forgotten, but now she could see it clearly in her mind's eye.

'I think it's possible,' she said. 'But if that is so, and she was not just a passive associate of her husband's business, how does Peter feel about her, when he seems to have despised his father and his way of life so much?'

Durris looked up at her.

'A very fair question.' They watched each other, lost in thought, until the bedchamber door, already ajar, was pushed wide open behind them. Both of them jumped. It was Patrick.

'That's me done: broken ankle and broken elbow, poor fellow,' he announced cheerfully. 'I've packed him in ice and bandages, and I think I've found a counterirritant to that balm.' He held out a hand to each of them. 'Apples,' he explained with a grin. 'It was the only ice left after last night. The poor man is packed up in pudding.'

'That sounds lovely!' said Hippolyta. 'And it smells good, too.'

'I'm already growing tired of it,' Patrick admitted. 'Well, he's in a bed in the kitchen, and I'm ready to go home – and perhaps have some early dinner, after a late breakfast. Shall I take a couple of those tins?'

'Oh, yes,' said Durris, handing him the nearest two. 'And the infallible scarlet powders.' His face twisted in a slight smile.

'Anything interesting?'

'I think we've finished here,' Durris said, packing the rest of the powders and tins back into the trunk on top of the papers. When he had finished, it was impossible to see that they had been disturbed at all. He peeped under the bed, but apparently saw nothing to their advantage. 'Come on: I'll tell you about it downstairs.'

In fact downstairs they walked outside a little to be away from any prying ears as Durris explained to Patrick what they had found and their guesswork. Patrick frowned.

'She certainly doesn't look like a tough businesswoman,' he admitted. 'But I agree that that's what the letters sound like.' He stepped absently down the steep slope to the road and paused, thinking. Durris and Hippolyta followed, and as Patrick had his coat and medical bag, Durris was politely carrying her basket once again filled with Patrick's evening clothes and slippers. Patrick took his glasses off and slipped them into his pocket, smiling at Hippolyta. 'So perhaps we can say that she's not as helpless as she looks?'

'What?' Durris snapped. In a moment the basket was on the ground and Durris was springing off the far side of the road. Patrick and Hippolyta stared, shocked. Durris plunged behind a thick tangle of brown bracken and last year's bramble arches. There was a cry of surprise, then what seemed to be a struggle of some kind. The crisp bracken shook, and there was a grunt of pain. Patrick dropped his medical bag – gently – and ran down the steep little slope, following Durris, but just as he reached the tangle of dried vegetation Durris emerged, panting and uncharacteristically tousled. He dragged a hunching figure by one arm turned up behind his back. It was Peter Snark, flecked with bracken and smudged with mud, his hands bare and grubby. In Durris' other hand, he was holding something black, a small bundle of some soft material.

'Here, take these,' he said to Patrick, handing him the black bundle. He pushed Peter Snark up on to the road ahead of him: Snark's eyes were narrow slits, and his mouth was sealed shut in a sour little smile. Up on the road, Durris adjusted his hold on Snark.

'Right,' he said, in a tone Hippolyta had not heard him use before. 'Mr. Snark, would you care to explain what you were doing there?'

'No,' said Snark. 'Work it out for yourself, since you're so interested.' He snapped his mouth shut again.

'What was he doing?' Hippolyta's curiosity was too much for her.

'He was trying to bury these.' Durris pointed at the soft bundle in Patrick's grasp. Patrick opened his hands wide, carefully.

'It's a pair of gloves,' she said in surprise.

'That's right: black leather gloves. Men's gloves,' Durris added. 'He was digging a hole with a bit of a board – not very expertly, mind,' he added critically, 'and these were lying by, ready to go in.'

'Maybe I just took them off to dig,' said Snark, never losing the knowing little smile.

'Maybe you did,' said Durris, unmoved, 'though even a worse digger than you, supposing there was one, wouldn't leave his gloves where they were going to be covered in glour. Let's take a closer look,' he added, angling Snark so that he could step over more closely to Patrick and the gloves. Hippolyta took a step closer, too. The smell from the gloves was strong, and when Patrick straightened out the fingers she could see why. The palms and inside surface of the fingers was coated in a pinkish, chalky substance, ground into the black leather and smeared across it in different places. By the smell, it was unmistakeable. It was a generous quantity of Dr. Gilead's famous cordial balm.

Chapter Thirteen

On the evidence, Durris decided that it was worth locking Snark up at least for the time being: he explained that there was a cell beneath the church he was allowed to use in an emergency. Not trusting Snark, even though he seemed smugly passive at his situation, Durris locked him in a press in the hotel until he could fetch a set of manacles from his room to impede any chance of escape on the way, and so at last Patrick and Hippolyta walked down the road with Durris and his prisoner, and the gloves fragrant in a sack, heading back to the village. Having a legally captive man on the boat provided the boatman – and the lads at the river – with their best thrill since the news of the murder had come down the hill to them, and the boatman generously declined payment from the party in celebration. At the village green they went their separate ways, and Patrick sighed happily as he pushed open their own front door.

'I was beginning to think I was in a nightmare, and would never be allowed to leave the hotel!' he said. 'Thank goodness to be home.'

At the sound of their voices, the parlour door swung open fast, and Galatea peered out.

'Where on earth have you been?' she asked Hippolyta. 'You've been out for hours, and no word. What did you think you were doing?'

Hippolyta felt guilty.

'I'm sorry,' she said at once. 'I wanted to take some fresh clothes up to the hotel for Patrick, and then I just waited for him to finish what he was doing.'

'He must have been doing something very slowly,' said Galatea suspiciously.

'We were just about to leave when a man fell off a ladder and broke his ankle,' said Patrick, not willing to go into details about Mrs. Dewar. 'I had to use apple ice pudding to take down the bruising! I must wash my hands again: I wonder if the smell will ever leave me?' He slipped down the hall and through to the kitchen quarters where he was most likely to find water.

'He could have rung for water,' said Galatea sourly. 'There's no need for a man to go near his kitchen. If it's properly run.'

'He's just in a hurry,' said Hippolyta, trying to be soothing but sounding, in her own ears anyway, defensive instead. The scent of apple wafted away, to be replaced by the persistent odour of famous cordial balm. Hippolyta sniffed suspiciously. 'Is Mother in there with you?'

'Of course she is: where else would she be?' Galatea demanded, and ungraciously allowed Hippolyta to pass into the room. Her mother sat bolt upright on one of the sofas, but Hippolyta had an uneasy impression that before they had arrived home, she had been reclining on it: one side of her face was rosier than the other, and her lace cap was the tiniest degree askew. She looked tired and drawn, but both she and Galatea were already dressed for dinner. Hippolyta felt shabby at once.

'Mother, are you all right?' she asked.

'Of course I am – or as well as anyone could be, when they are taken to an exhausting ball, informed that a valued acquaintance has died violently, been questioned by a sheriff's officer like a common criminal, then brought to her bed in the middle of the night. How well did you think I should be?'

'I'm sure Mr. Durris did not question you like a common criminal, Mother,' Hippolyta daringly objected – she could have mentioned, too, that it had been her mother's idea to attend the ball in the first place, but that seemed like bravery verging on foolhardiness.

'Mr. Durris, is it?' said Mrs. Fettes, in a tone that implied it was no more than she expected. Hippolyta chose not to respond. 'Well, is there any news from the hotel, or are we to wait all day to know anything?'

'Well … I hardly know. Mrs. Gilead is up and about, Mrs. Dewar keeps to her bed, I did not see either the Nickells or the Pumptons. The man who fell off the ladder was one of the hotel's servants – you'll have seen him last night, Sim, a boy with ginger hair –'

'I do not remotely care about the hotel's servants and their accidents,' said her mother in a voice like a hat pin.

'In that case I don't believe I can help you,' said Hippolyta, her voice a small echo of her mother's. Mrs. Fettes, slightly surprised, sat back. Hippolyta immediately felt guilty at not telling her about Peter Snark's imprisonment, when half the village would know by now, but she knew that Mr. Durris often mentioned things to Patrick, and by extension to her, that he did not wish to go further, and a lack of discretion on her part with one detail might make her more careless over the other details. She bit her lip, and stroked Ella, the monumental mother cat.

'Mrs. Dewar keeps to her bed, does she?' Her mother was evidently reviewing what information she had managed to glean. 'I wonder how ill she really is?'

Hippolyta shrugged slightly.

'If Dr. Gilead believed she was ill …'

'Oh, Dr. Gilead was very susceptible to scheming women. He was kindness to a fault. But you're right: if he had told her she was ill, then she was, obviously.'

Galatea shot Hippolyta a filthy look from her seat at the table.

'I think I'll go and get changed,' said Hippolyta.

'Probably best,' her mother agreed, and closed her mouth like a trap.

Dinner was a stiff meal, in which Patrick did his level best to keep a cheerful conversation alive with the slightly desperate air of a man hovering over the last flame in a damp fire. Galatea, to be fair, passed a few comments, but Mrs. Fettes said almost nothing, and Hippolyta, not used as Patrick was to a high level of professional discretion, kept finding her mind bouncing back to the events of the last twenty-four hours and words she should not speak springing to her lips. Both Patrick and Hippolyta were aware of the fragrance of balm about the room. Mrs. Fettes seemed to be the principal source, and Hippolyta noticed a particular wave of it when Mrs. Fettes adjusted the scarf about her throat. It quite spoiled her enjoyment of Mrs. Riach's delicately flavoured beef: she hoped there would be some left so that she could go back to it later, balm-free.

They had retreated into the parlour where at least Patrick's violin could keep the silence away, when there came a knock on the front door. After a moment, Ishbel appeared at the parlour door with a practised curtsey.

'Mr. Durris to see Dr. Napier, please, sir.'

'Oh!' said Patrick, setting down his violin. 'Very good.' He disappeared and Hippolyta heard both men going into the study across the hall. She longed to go, too, but managed, just, to stay in her seat, valiantly making another attempt at conversation.

'I thought Mrs. Strachan and her daughters were all prodigiously pretty last night, didn't you?' she asked.

'She dresses very young for a woman who has two daughters out in society,' said Galatea sniffily.

'Perhaps, but she's very fashionable. I'm sure you did not think to see such Edinburgh fashions this far north!'

'I know little of Edinburgh fashions these days,' said Galatea. 'You'll find, when you take on responsibilities of your own, that there are more important things than the tilt of a bonnet, or the depth of ornament on your skirt hem.'

Hippolyta had rather thought that she had taken on responsibilities of her own, but Galatea probably thought she had not taken them on thoroughly enough. She sighed. She probably meant children, but then she was sure she remembered Galatea still dressing fashionably after her children were born. She wondered if she would be allowed to be grown up by her family when she herself had children: she imagined not.

The silence must at last have overcome even Mrs. Fettes' stoicism, and she announced that she would retire for the night. Galatea quickly agreed that she would do so, too. Hippolyta waited until they had gone upstairs, then went and tapped on the study door.

'Come in!' Patrick called.

'I'm sorry to interrupt,' said Hippolyta disingenuously, 'but I thought I ought to tell you that Mother and Galatea have retired for the night.'

'Oh good!' said Patrick. 'I mean: they both looked tired. I'm glad they have gone to rest early.'

She met his eye with a raised eyebrow, and he had the grace to pinken just a little. Durris cleared his throat, and Patrick straightened, gesturing to them both to sit down. He returned to his chair at the desk, and set his glasses on his nose.

'Mr. Durris was just telling me about Mr. Snark.'

'He won't admit to anything,' said Durris, clearly frustrated. 'He won't even say that the gloves are his, though his name is stitched inside them. He just sits there with that wee smile on his face.'

Hippolyta wondered if that was why Snark looked as if his nose had been broken a few times. If she had been a man she would have found it difficult to resist.

'But it's definitely the balm on his gloves?'

'Oh, aye, not a doubt of that. It looks as if someone put the gloves on, took a great handful of the balm and just squashed it hard, then rubbed as if it was a bar of soap.'

'Or rubbed it into a person's mouth and nose?'

Durris sighed.

'It's hard to tell.'

Patrick shrugged, too.

'It wasn't something they taught us in medical jurisprudence, patterns of famous cordial balm on leather gloves.'

'If he were going to hide them,' said Hippolyta slowly, 'why would he do it so close to the road and the hotel, and in broad daylight, too?'

'Well, he wouldn't know the area well,' said Durris.

'No, but he would know that the woods are extensive, and that there are lonelier parts of the road. Why go to a place just opposite the hotel?'

Durris looked at her.

'Perhaps he was in a hurry?'

'Then why go to the trouble of trying to dig a hole, when he could have thrust them into a bramble patch? Or into a ditch? Or into the midden, under all those flowers from the ball?'

'You have an idea, don't you, Mrs. Napier?'

'Well … maybe. I can't understand why a man who has been imprisoned by the sheriff's officer and questioned over his part in a murder should look so smug. It makes me think that however it appears to us, matters are under his control, going the way he intends. So that makes me think that he wanted you to suspect him, which makes me think that he meant to be caught trying to bury the gloves. I mean, using a bit of wood to try to dig a hole! Even he could not be that stupid, when there are plenty of other hiding places around.'

'Unless he panicked?' suggested Patrick.

'Did he look like a man who was panicking?' asked Hippolyta.

Both men shook their heads.

'Well, then, what is his notion?' asked Durris.

'If he wants you to suspect him, then presumably he also wants you not to suspect someone else. And as he's being smug about it, I think he probably has a good witness up his sleeve who will come out and say, at the appropriate time, that he could not have murdered his father at all.'

Durris and Patrick exchanged looks, and Durris nodded thoughtfully.

'It makes a degree of sense. But who is he protecting, then? His mother?'

'Maybe. Does he know she did it or does he think she did it?' asked Patrick, rubbing his nose under his glasses.

'No, wait,' said Hippolyta. 'Here's what we've been thinking so far. Mrs. Gilead is the businesswoman, but she could not run the business that she does without Dr. Gilead, so she wasn't likely to kill him. In addition, Peter Snark hated what his father did, and therefore, by extension, what his mother did: he must have disapproved of both of his parents, so even if he thought she killed him, and it seems unlikely that she did, he is unlikely to want to protect her.'

She breathed again after this gallop, and looked to both of them for their reaction.

'Right,' said Durris slowly. 'But if not Mrs. Gilead, then who?'

'That I don't know.' She flopped back in her chair. 'One thing at a time, though?'

'I think I'll keep him in the cell just for now,' said Durris. 'Maybe something will surface.'

Sunday passed with little to be said for it: it was not one of the Sabbaths when an Episcopalian minister rode in from Banchory or

Aboyne to take a service, so the Napiers and their guests said
Morning Prayer together and sang a few hymns which Patrick
accompanied on the piano. Fortunately the day was fine and they
could spend some time in the garden, taking the air: Mrs. Fettes
declined the opportunity of a longer walk outside the property,
even though she might have gleaned some gossip that way,
perhaps because she did not wish to be interrogated for any gossip
herself. They dined early, as soon as Mrs. Riach could manage it
after her own return from church. On her return she had reported
that Wullie's parents were taken aback to see him there with the
doctor's servants, having thought he had taken himself away
somewhere to hide. Wullie graciously agreed to go home for the
afternoon for a news, but left his dog with Mrs. Riach for
safekeeping, still not trusting his brother Al not to kick it. After
dinner Patrick took a quick trip up to the hotel to check on Mrs.
Dewar and on the lad with the broken ankle, but he was soon back
to report that they were both making reasonable progress.

The restful day seemed to do Mrs. Fettes some good, for on
Monday morning she surprised Hippolyta by rising bright and
early and announcing that they would once again go up to the
Wells for a bathe. Hippolyta had intended to oversee the laundry as
best she could, and hoped that her mother would be happy just
taking Galatea, but apparently the presence of both her daughters
was mandatory and she changed into her walking dress and
followed her mother and sister to the boat, wondering if anything
had developed up at the hotel in her single day of absence.

The main difference, she thought at once, was the atmosphere
in the bathing pools. Mrs. Pumpton and Mrs. Nickell were both
bobbing about as before, but Mrs. Pumpton was mercifully
subdued, while Mrs. Nickell was touchy, snapping at anyone
whose shift seemed close to tangling with hers, shouting at the
attendant who could not seem to find a happy medium between too
fast and too slow, twitching with dissatisfaction at her gown when
she was dressed again. In the hallway of the bathing house she and
Hippolyta waited for the others to finish dressing, and she was in
such an edgy mood that Hippolyta's heart sank when Mrs. Nickell
came over closer to her and beckoned her into a position of
confidence.

'Tell me, Mrs. Napier,' she whispered, 'is it true that Mrs.

Dewar is dangerously ill?'

'Well, you know she was ill,' said Hippolyta, 'for it was common knowledge that Dr. Gilead was treating her.'

A kind of shiver ran through Mrs. Nickell from top to bottom. Hippolyta noticed that her face was flushed, and beyond the omnipresent odour of balm there was something else, a warmer scent. Could it be brandy?

'Yes, we all knew he was *treating* her,' she retorted. 'But I heard she had been attacked and left for dead.'

'I don't think that's true,' said Hippolyta, not quite sure how far she could deny erroneous rumours with regard to Patrick's patient. 'She was taken ill and has received some further treatment, and is recovering, so I believe.'

'Recovering?' Mrs. Nickell stared into her face, sharp and angry. 'I heard she was close to death!'

Hippolyta paused.

'She is my husband's patient. I'm sorry, I can't really say any more.'

'Oh, of course, your husband is some kind of apothecary.' She considered for a moment. 'Perhaps you can't say any more because if she's not getting well it looks bad for him, is that right?' She did not wait for Hippolyta to answer. 'I heard she was dangerously ill, close to death,' she repeated, as if she had learned a lesson. 'She hasn't been seen since the night of the ball, and nor has her husband. If she isn't ill, she's dead: that seems most likely to me. Dead and gone, and good riddance to her!' She finished on a spiky little cackle, and Hippolyta felt her jaw drop.

'What on earth do you mean, Mrs. Nickell? What harm had she done to you?'

'Harm? To me? She was a conniving seductress, that's all. Oh, she looked grand, with her bonny face and her nice manners, but she took one look at my fine Dr. Gilead and just decided to take him for her own. I mean, before she came along there was no question: he only had eyes for me. That fat Pumpton woman thought he fancied her, but how daft is that? One look at her and you could see – I mean, Dr. Gilead could take his pick of the ladies, he didn't have to stoop so low as to allow a prize sow like that anywhere near him! And Mrs. Fettes, well, obviously she's far too old. No, I had a clear field, until that cow came along, with her low voice and her shiny eyes and her "Oh, Dr. Gilead, I feel so faint!".'

'Mrs. Nickell,' said Hippolyta at the first opportunity, 'I'm sure you would benefit from a cup of nice hot tea.' The indiscretions had washed over her like a wave, and while she knew something here was bound to be of use to Mr. Durris, she was not sure she could take much more of Mrs. Nickell's spiteful whisperings.

'And the worst of it was, he fell for it! My fine Dr. Gilead!' She gestured wildly with one hand, and unbalanced herself, sitting heavily on a fortuitously placed chair. Hippolyta crouched quickly beside her.

'Are you all right, Mrs. Nickell?'

'Fine Dr. Gilead,' Mrs. Nickell repeated, her eyes slightly glazed. 'Fine, he was. But where is he now, eh? Where is he: lying in his coffin with his mouth full of his bloody balm. He's dead, she's dead, and where does that leave me? Where does that leave poor little me?' And to Hippolyta's horror, Mrs. Nickell began to sob, great wracking sobs that seemed likely to break her thin ribcage. She had to be moved or silenced before the other ladies came out, or who knew what might ensue? She stood up and wrapped one arm tightly around Mrs. Nickell, catching her under the arms. She lifted her quite easily, and marched her out of the bath house and down the hill to the road, which was fortunately deserted. Mrs. Nickell seemed to rediscover the use of her own feet, anyway, and Hippolyta let go of her, standing her upright gently. With a few last gasps, Mrs. Nickell stopped crying, and dug in her reticule for a handkerchief to wipe her face.

'I feel a bit unsteady,' she observed. 'Maybe – I have some brandy in here, I think.'

She plunged a hand into her reticule again.

'I'm not sure you should drink any more of it,' said Hippolyta, putting a hand over hers. 'You've had some already, haven't you?'

'Have I?' Mrs. Nickell looked vaguely surprised. 'Is that why I'm all wobbly like?'

'I believe so,' said Hippolyta, smiling.

'Oh.' Mrs. Nickell considered the idea. 'What was I saying?'

'Er … you were talking about Dr. Gilead, and how sorry you were that he had died,' Hippolyta suggested.

'Was I? But I'm not really sorry he's died,' she said, regaining some of her energy. 'He told me he loved me, and then he told me he didn't. That's not gentlemanly behaviour, is it?'

'No, certainly not. But Mrs. Nickell, you have a husband of your own, and Dr. Gilead was married, too.'

'What does that have to do with it?' Mrs. Nickell demanded, shockingly. 'If a gentleman tells a lady he loves her, he has no right to go back on that just because some Scotch beauty with her – her hair and her eyes and her skin drapes herself over a chair and says she feels faint!'

'No, you're right, it seems very unfair,' said Hippolyta. 'And I can see you might be glad that he's no longer able to insult you in that way.'

'Aye. That's right. He can't insult me anymore.'

Hippolyta wondered if there was any further she could push this, while Mrs. Nickell was in such a confiding mood, or if she would even remember what she had said when she was sober. Would what she said be reliable? Was she imagining things? Had Dr. Gilead really told her he loved her, or was it all in Mrs. Nickell's imagination?

'It would have been quite reasonable if you had been very angry with him,' she tried.

'Aye, I was, and all. I was furious.'

'And if you had decided to – to punish him in some way, that would have been perfectly understandable, wouldn't it?'

'Aye, it would. I should have punished him.'

'You mean you didn't?' Hippolyta floundered for a moment. 'There he was at the ball, with you all beautifully dressed in your nicest evening gown' – for the life of her she could not immediately call to mind what Mrs. Nickell had been wearing to the ball, but she felt safe enough with this description – 'and all Dr. Gilead had eyes for was Mrs. Dewar, isn't that right?'

'That's it exactly. That's it, exactly. All round her, he was, like – like sauce on a plate of meat.'

Hippolyta managed to stifle a giggle. Mrs. Nickell was deadly serious.

'So what did you do?' Hippolyta asked as levelly as she could.

'What did I do?' Mrs. Nickell looked suddenly blank.

'Yes: you had every reason to punish him. Did you do it?'

'Punish him? Punish Dr. Gilead? My Dr. Gilead was too beautiful to punish, Mrs. Nailor. How could anyone punish him?' Her voice died wistfully away. She seemed to be sobering up: Hippolyta was fairly sure she would make no more progress with her now. She sighed, and just thought she caught behind her own sigh Mrs. Nickell's soft words: 'Her, on the other hand ...'

'What was that?' Hippolyta asked.

Mrs. Nickell looked back at her, her face already sharper and her eyes more alert.

'It's been a nice little walk, hasn't it, Mrs. Nailor? Thank you for helping me: I think I overheated just a little in that last bath. Shall we see if the others are ready for their cup of tea? Mrs. Pumpton, at any rate, is always ready for a cup of tea, in my experience. Did you ever see a woman so enormous? I wonder she can find Mr. Pumpton at all, he's so tiny beside her. And is your Mamma keeping well? Enjoying the benefits of the Wells? It's right handy for her to have you staying nearby, where she can have all the comforts of home instead of staying in another spa hotel, and cheaper, too, of course. All this gadding about the country doesn't come cheap, does it? Mr. Nickell's always complaining about the amount he has to spend to stay in all these places, but I say to him, you can't put a price on your health, can you? Or your wife's health, either. But he doesn't see it that way: always giving off about more tins of balm and more packets of powders. Oh!' She stopped suddenly at the door of the hotel. 'Where will I get my balm and powders from now?'

Chapter Fourteen

'I almost thought I had her!' Hippolyta groaned.

Patrick had appeared at the hotel during their tea after visiting his patients, and not much later Durris had appeared from the kitchen quarters. The three of them walked outside: the birchwoods bobbed purple below them down to the innocent Dee, and Ballater's neat grid lay upstream on the other side, on the loop of flat land where the river had swept so ferociously the previous summer. She prayed it would never happen again.

'You truly think she was about to confess to his murder?' asked Durris, frowning.

'You said yourself that if he had had laudanum even a woman could have done it.'

'I know, but ...'

'She had been drinking brandy,' Hippolyta reminded him. 'And why does one drink brandy at that time of the morning?'

'Boredom,' Patrick suggested.

'Anxiety,' said Durris.

'Guilt,' added Hippolyta firmly. The men did not look entirely convinced.

'How did she persuade him into the parlour?' Durris asked.

'Oh, the gallant Dr. Gilead would follow a woman anywhere if she asked him, I think,' said Hippolyta. 'Anyway, how many people know that his mouth was stuffed with the balm? She mentioned it specifically.'

Durris looked thoughtful.

'She could have been outside the parlour window,' said Patrick.

'And seen the murder happen? Surely she would have cried out, or told someone,' said Durris.

'No, I mean afterwards. The murderer left two candles burning: anyone looking in could probably have seen Gilead's body, couldn't they? The shutters weren't closed.'

'Still, wouldn't she have said?'

'Not if she wanted to see him punished,' Hippolyta put in, 'and she talked a good deal about punishment. But I still think she's a good suspect for doing it herself. She was wearing evening gloves, of course, and that would have hidden any reddening on her hands.'

Durris sighed.

'Does either of you remember seeing her at any time after supper?'

Patrick and Hippolyta were silent, thinking back. Durris added,

'I wish I had attended the ball myself, after all. There I was, sitting in the kitchens hoping for an anonymous letter, and all the time I could have been watching to see who was doing what at the front of the place.'

'Do you dance, Mr. Durris?' asked Hippolyta with a grin.

'When duty demands it,' he replied, fairly straightfaced.

'I'm not sure I saw her at all,' said Patrick. 'I was talking with Mr. Dewar for a little while, and then - no, before that I helped old Mrs. Cordon to her bed, for her maid said she was more confused than usual with all the noise and crowds. I'm not sure she was, really, but her maid finds her a bit of a handful. I saw to her, then I came back down and I was heading over to you, my dear, when Mr. Dewar caught me.'

'Oh, yes, I was talking with Galatea at the edge of the dance floor,' Hippolyta remembered. 'At some point I think I saw Mr. and Mrs. Nickell go outside together, but I believe that was earlier, maybe just after supper. Then he was back, on his own: I didn't see her. She may have been dancing. She certainly danced a great deal.' She stopped walking and closed her eyes, trying to picture the ball room and the dancers, and her view from the corner by the floral arrangement, after Galatea had gone. One or two people had walked past … 'Oh, no! I did see her! She came back into the ball room on her own, from outside somewhere. She stopped and talked to me for a moment. She seemed very excited, but then she often does. She was talking about how much she was enjoying the evening, that was all.'

'And she was on her own?' Durris repeated. 'Mr. Nickell came in first?'

'That's right. I'm sure I saw him before that, near the hotel door.'

'I wonder what she was doing, staying out on her own?'

'Where would Dr. Gilead have been at that point?' Patrick asked.

'I think by then he was probably already in the parlour, dead,' said Durris.

Hippolyta shivered.

'We were all enjoying ourselves in the ball room, while in there, so close by, something like that was happening. It's almost – I don't know. It's hard to imagine someone struggling for breath and dying while we were outside, but it's almost worse to imagine what the murderer was feeling. Because whoever it was, to do a thing like that, with the balm: they must have really hated him, mustn't they?'

'I'm afraid so,' said Durris. Patrick reached out a hand and took Hippolyta's, warming it in both of his.

'Jealousy, or love turned to hate: those seem most likely,' he said softly. 'Wouldn't you say?'

'The answer is somewhere amongst these ladies that followed him about the country, I'm sure of it,' said Durris, more forcefully than usual. 'Either they know something, or one of them is the murderer.'

'And what about Mrs. Dewar?' Hippolyta asked.

'What about her?'

'It sounded to me as if Mrs. Nickell, for one, would happily have pushed Mrs. Dewar down the stairs, too.'

'But she wasn't pushed down the stairs, dear,' said Patrick. 'There was a crisis with her condition.'

'Could something have brought that on, though? An attack? A punch in the stomach, perhaps?'

Patrick frowned.

'I'm not sure. I would be cautious, but on the other hand I wouldn't rule it out. There was a great deal of damage inside her.'

They walked on in silence for a moment, thinking about that.

'Have you had the chance to look at the balm yet? Or the

powders?' Durris asked.

'Oh, yes,' said Patrick, on firmer ground. 'I examined them both in my dispensary this morning. The powders are simply saleratus with, I think, some sugar and flour, dyed with cochineal.'

'Mrs. Gilead was ordering cochineal,' Hippolyta remembered.

'The best that can be said for them is that they would do little harm,' said Patrick. 'The balm was a bit more complicated. It seems to be made from chalk and some kind of fat – maybe lard – with a number of things mixed in. Mint, certainly, and garlic, and something hot.'

'Chilli, perhaps?' asked Hippolyta eagerly. 'She ordered that, too.'

Patrick nodded.

'That's likely. They were indeed mixing their own cures, then: one has to give him some credit for industry, I suppose. And there was something crunchy in it: I can't be sure, but I think it's crab shells, ground fairly fine.'

'And what would all that do?' asked Durris with mild scepticism.

'Well, again, not much harm, though you wouldn't want to put it on an open wound, for example, though, or into your eye.' Patrick adjusted his glasses thoughtfully. 'On tired limbs, it might be found comforting: the heat of the chilli and the cooling effect of the mint would stimulate the blood, and the crab shells would smooth the skin. After bathing there would certainly be a pleasant enough tingle. But as to what he told his patients either of these things did, that's another matter. Straightening the digestive system? Untangling the tendrils of the stomach? Drawing out poisons?' He listed bitterly the claims he had heard so far. 'Neither of them would be of the least use in the case of a cancer, or in the goitrous condition that Mrs. Nickell seems to suffer, or whatever might be wrong with Mrs. Pumpton. I should by no means have wished death on the man,' he went on, 'let alone a death like that, but I am glad that he is out of harm's way, nevertheless.'

'Well, then, I go back to my earlier conclusion,' said Durris, nodding at this. 'Someone in his circle of followers knows something. Mrs. Pumpton, Mrs. Nickell and Mrs. Dewar were his ardent admirers, let us say.'

'And my mother,' Hippolyta added with a shiver. 'That, if

nothing else, is a sign of the power of his charms. My mother admires very few people, Mr. Durris.'

'Hm. Mrs. Fettes, then.'

'I'm not so sure about Mrs. Dewar,' said Patrick unexpectedly. 'I only saw them together a little, but it struck me that she was not so charmed by Dr. Gilead as Mrs. Pumpton and Mrs. Nickell – I set aside your mother, dearest, because she at least was not drooling over him like a puppy. Nor was Mrs. Dewar. And while he was attentive to all the women, his attentions to her, I thought, were less those of an accomplished flirt and more like a man who is not sure he has made his conquest, or that he will. Having been in that position myself,' he added lightly, with a sideways look at Hippolyta, 'I can readily recognise it in others.'

Hippolyta thought back. She had, she remembered, noticed more attention paid by Dr. Gilead to Mrs. Dewar, but had assumed that it reflected the severity of her illness and his eagerness to look like a concerned physician. Perhaps Patrick was right.

'So in that case, if we take that to be the case, Dr. Napier,' said Durris tidily, 'we have his three admirers, Mrs. Fettes, Mrs. Nickell and Mrs. Pumpton. We have at any rate an interested party, Mrs. Dewar. We have three jealous husbands, Mr. Nickell, Mr. Pumpton and Mr. Dewar. We have a jealous wife, Mrs. Gilead, and an angry son, Peter Snark, who may or may not be willing to defend her if he thinks she is guilty of murder. We have –'

'Wait,' said Hippolyta breathlessly. 'Just a minute: maybe it isn't his mother that Peter Snark is trying to protect. I've just remembered. You know I said that Mrs. Nickell came in past me on her own, all chatty, and we wondered what she had been doing outside on her own when her husband had already come in some time before? Well, the person who walked back into the ball room just in front of her was Peter Snark.'

Durris and Patrick looked at her.

'You mean you think they had been together outside?'

'I feel now that they had been. I'm not sure if I thought it at the time,' she said honestly.

Durris and Patrick exchanged glances.

'Did you notice anything between him and Mrs. Nickell?' Durris asked.

'I can't say I did,' said Patrick.

'I think maybe Mr. Nickell did,' said Hippolyta. 'Do you remember, when he left the table to fetch more supper, and pretty much ordered Peter Snark to accompany him? Maybe he wanted a stern word, or maybe he didn't want to leave Mr. Snark at the table with Mrs. Nickell.'

'I think I'd need something more than that,' said Durris kindly. Hippolyta scowled.

'They stood up together twice,' she said, trying not to sound waspish about it.

'What does Mrs. Milton think about it all?' asked Durris suddenly.

'Galatea? Why do you ask?'

'She was not as enamoured of Dr. Gilead as the rest, was she?' Durris said. 'I saw her face when I told Mrs. Fettes and her that Gilead was dead: she seemed more pleased than anything.'

'I wish I could tell you,' said Hippolyta frankly. 'She tells me nothing. But I do not think that she is happy to be here, and part of that unhappiness seems to stem from my mother's activities and the company she is keeping. Perhaps she only thinks they'll be able to go home now.'

'I'd ask them not to go just yet, anyway,' said Durris drily. 'I still want to talk to everyone again.'

'Well, you know where they're staying,' said Patrick, with a grin.

They turned and began to walk back up the hill towards the hotel, pacing slowly together.

'Do you want to speak to them today?' Hippolyta asked.

'Maybe later,' said Durris. 'I think I'll go back down to the village and tell Peter Snark we're going to charge him with murder. If he has an interesting witness to prove his innocence, let him name him – or her.'

'I have some patients to see at the Lodge down the hill,' said Patrick. 'I'll need to pick up my bag from the hotel.'

'I'll see if my mother and Galatea are ready to go home,' said Hippolyta with a sigh. 'And then I think I might issue some invitations to tea.'

On Tuesday morning Patrick fled the house early, and Mrs. Fettes was deterred from a bathe. Mrs. Pumpton and Mrs. Nickell were coming to tea.

They arrived in a flurry of black at the door together, a little later than expected.

'We've been doing some marketing in your little village,' said Mrs. Pumpton grandly. 'Your Mr. Strachan runs an extraordinary store, doesn't he? I found the most beautiful black silk to have made up for the funeral.'

'And there was a black satin reticule I've just had to buy,' added Mrs. Nickell. 'I'd show you, but we've had the things sent up to the hotel, of course. What will you be wearing, Mrs. Fettes?' she asked.

Mrs. Fettes, stately and stark in flat black bombazine, raised an eyebrow.

'I am in mourning already,' she stated.

Galatea was not, any more than Hippolyta was.

'He was no relative of mine,' Galatea said. 'I suppose we ought to go to the funeral, but that's the extent of any black I'm going to wear.'

'Oh, but Mrs. Milton! Out of respect for such a great man!' cried Mrs. Pumpton, slamming down into the sofa in shock. A cat fled.

'Oh, cats!' cried Mrs. Nickell. 'That's adorable. But they make me sneeze dreadfully.'

'Hippolyta, put the cats out,' said Mrs. Fettes, just as Hippolyta had stooped to catch the other cat in the room. 'My daughter indulges herself with these creatures,' she added to Mrs. Nickell. Mrs. Pumpton nodded.

'I like cats, myself.' She smiled at Hippolyta. 'We have a couple at home. Not that we've seen them for a while, of course: my daughter's looking after them in Bristol.'

'Have you been away from home for so long?' Hippolyta asked, nodding to Mrs. Riach to bring the tea.

'Oh, over a year now, I should think! We found Dr. Gilead in Bath at the beginning of the season in – let me think, what is it now? 1830? 1828, it would have been. Such an impressive man: I knew straightaway he was the only one that could help me with my complaints. Not that I ever complain!'

Honestly, Hippolyta thought, she had never heard Mrs. Pumpton complain – to such an extent she had wondered why she had attached herself to Dr. Gilead at all.

'And you and Mr. Pumpton have travelled from spa to spa with him ever since?'

Mrs. Pumpton laughed loudly. Mrs. Riach, coming in with the tea tray, jumped and the cups rattled.

'My husband? Mr. Pumpton? No, not him! He goes home every now and again to see to his business. He's in stationery, you know,' she added dismissively, as if Mr. Pumpton had been popped in a letter wrapper and folded down. 'He says we can't afford all this travelling about, otherwise.'

'That's what Jack says, too!' said Mrs. Nickell in surprise. 'He keeps telling me how expensive it all is, staying in hotels when, he says, we have a perfectly good home of our own in Yorkshire. I tell him he shouldn't grudge the money when it's for my health, but then he says I don't ever seem to get any better …' She drew to a stop, frowning a little, and Hippolyta handed her a cup of tea. Mrs. Nickell looked up and smiled automatically. Hippolyta thought she caught another waft of brandy on her breath.

'So where did you go with Dr. Gilead after Bath? I find your peregrinations fascinating! What you must have seen along the way!'

'Like a travelling circus,' muttered Galatea. Hippolyta offered her a large piece of sticky cake, and hoped it would keep her mouth shut.

'Well, dear, we went from Bath to Leamington – such a pretty town – then to Harrogate, where we met you for the first time, didn't we, Mrs. Nickell?'

'That's right,' said Mrs. Nickell. 'I saw Dr. Gilead in the parlour at the Crown in Low Harrogate, and the way the candlelight caught his hair it looked like a halo! I knew at once he was a good man, and a good physician. Of course I had seen some of his advertisements in the newspapers.'

'Had you?' asked Hippolyta. Mrs. Nickell searched quickly through her reticule – Hippolyta wondered if she had brought her brandy again – and produced a piece of folded writing paper. From within the folds she took, with reverence, a neatly cut oblong of thick newspaper.

'This one's from up here in North Britain,' she explained. 'I have a collection.'

Hippolyta accepted the cutting with care.

'Dr. Gilead's Celebrated Infallible Scarlet Powders,' it read, 'are highly esteemed for nourishing and invigorating the Nervous System and acting as a general Restorative to Debilitated Constitutions ...' She scanned it quickly. 'Females and the studious, as well as the sedentary part of the community, should not be without the Infallible Scarlet Powders Which, in happy conjunction with Dr. Gilead's Famous Cordial Balm, remove diseases in the head, invigorate the mind, improve the memory, and enliven the imagination, revive and exhilarate the languid drooping spirits, promote digestion and brace the nerves ...' It continued for another couple of hundred words at least, listing ailments and extolling the cures' efficacy in every case. Hippolyta had seen advertisements like it for dozens of patent cures in the newspapers. 'Solely Available,' it finished sternly, 'from Francis Gilead, M.D. Vienna, Bologna and Paris, himself. Apply at Gracechurch Street, in London, for prices. No wholesalers need apply.'

'He's very exclusive,' she remarked, not quite trusting herself with voicing any other opinion. She handed the paper back and it disappeared at once into its secure folder.

'Of course: otherwise he would have collapsed from exhaustion,' said her mother. 'When one is as successful as he was, one has to ration oneself. He was a perfectionist, poor man: he could not have allowed anyone else to take responsibility for his cures. What if they had been contaminated, and sold under his name, and done some harm to a patient who had faith in him? It would have been devastating.'

'I can see that,' said Hippolyta humbly. 'And after Harrogate – did both of you continue together with him, then?'

'I think we did,' said Mrs. Nickell, favouring Mrs. Pumpton with a slightly sour look. Mrs. Pumpton did not notice.

'Oh, yes, we became quite the jolly party! Down to Tunbridge for Christmas – what a fine time we had there! Do you remember Mr. Nickell singing *Rule Britannia* at the dinner? Then on to Brighton for the New Year. Then up to Bath and start again!'

'So was this his first visit to Scotland?' asked Hippolyta.

'Well, that was your mother's idea, wasn't it, Mrs. Fettes?'

Mrs. Fettes grimaced.

'It was, you know,' added Mrs. Nickell. 'We met your mother in Bath, and while she didn't have much time to stay just then, she told Dr. Gilead about Pitkeathly and Peterhead, and then she met us when we went back to Harrogate again. You stayed with us there, didn't you, Mrs. Fettes?'

'Yes,' said Galatea, without emphasis. 'We did.'

'We left for Scotland a little sooner than I'd expected,' Mrs. Nickell went on. 'Dr. Gilead was so keen to move on.'

'He was excited,' said Mrs. Pumpton. 'It was the thought of meeting more patients, being able to help more people, wasn't it? The man was a saint.'

'A beautiful saint,' Mrs. Nickell agreed, wistfully.

'And at Pitkeathly, then, we met the Dewars.'

'Oh, was that the first you had seen of them?' asked Hippolyta.

'Yes, I think so,' said Mrs Pumpton, with a frown.

'I thought perhaps Dr. Gilead had met them somewhere before?' said Mrs. Nickell.

'Yes, maybe. But we hadn't,' Mrs. Pumpton confirmed.

'Pitkeathly was nice,' said Mrs. Nickell. 'Quiet. We stayed in Bridge of Earn.'

'In that nice hotel,' added Mrs. Pumpton.

'That's right,' said Mrs. Nickell with a smile.

'It was damp,' said Galatea.

'The waters were excellent,' remarked Mrs. Fettes.

'Then Peterhead,' Mrs. Pumpton went on. 'Not so much of a spa town, that, though it was bracing to walk along the shore.'

'The whole town smelled of fish,' said Galatea.

'Very bracing,' Mrs. Pumpton repeated, giving her a look. 'And you went back to Edinburgh early. Then you sent word that there was a spa here at Ballater – well, we'd never heard of such a place. But what a lark! Dr. Gilead said yes, he knew about the chalybeate waters and that they were very beneficial, which is quite right, of course. We wrote back and said we'd meet you here, and we sent word to the Dewars. And here we all are!'

'Except of course it wasn't such a lark for Dr. Gilead,' said Galatea, slyly. 'I doubt he's too happy about it – wherever he is.'

'Galatea!' her mother reproached her.

'Not a happy occasion for Mrs. Gilead and their son, either,'

Hippolyta hurried on. 'Poor Peter – is it Gilead or Snark?' she asked innocently.

'He claims it's Snark,' said Mrs. Pumpton, 'but it's my belief he made it up. Who has ever met anyone called Snark?'

'Has he been with your party from the start?'

'Yes, I think so,' said Mrs. Pumpton. 'He's not a very happy soul, poor thing. I know Dr. Gilead had tried several cures on him, but when one has no desire to improve, treatment must always be unrewarded.'

'A shame,' said Hippolyta. 'Has he no household of his own? No prospect of marriage?' She looked at Mrs. Nickell.

'I don't think – ' she began, then cleared her throat. 'I don't want to cast aspersions on poor Mrs. Gilead, but I wonder if he was ever really Dr. Gilead's son at all? Perhaps they adopted him.'

'He looks like his mother,' said Mrs. Pumpton grimly.

'Then … a previous marriage, perhaps? I've often wondered, but I've never liked to ask. Someone so completely graceless, to be the son of – of the beautiful angel …'

'At least,' said Hippolyta quickly, feeling nauseous, 'he and his mother have each other for support.'

'Oh, I'm not sure they're that close,' said Mrs. Pumpton dismissively. 'He only hangs around for the money, you know.'

'That's a little harsh,' said Mrs. Fettes, surprisingly. 'I suspect he feels a little overwhelmed by his father's character and handsome appearance. It would be a hard thing for any son to live up to.'

'If he is his son,' Mrs. Nickell said darkly again.

'Does anyone know when the funeral is to be?' Hippolyta asked.

'On Friday,' said Mrs. Pumpton at once. 'I only hope my gown will be ready.'

'From the hotel?'

'Well, there's nowhere else, really, is there? Do you know the seamstress across the green? I'm told she's very good, but is she fast, too?'

Talk turned to seamstresses and gowns and fashions in Edinburgh, Bath and Harrogate, and Hippolyta relaxed just a little. Her mind was seething with information and thoughts – and still a question that echoed behind all her more recent concerns. Why was her mother following Dr. Gilead around the country, and was her father well?

Patrick returned warily for his dinner.

'Have they all gone?' he asked, pretending fear. Hippolyta followed him into the study.

'Yes, yes, you are quite safe. And Mother and Galatea are upstairs changing.'

'How did it go? Did you find anything out?'

Hippolyta frowned.

'I think I'm going to have to talk to the men, too,' she said.

'And how do you plan to do that?' Patrick set his medical bag down by his desk and looked at her suspiciously.

'Well, obviously I can't just go and visit them,' she said. 'I think we must invite them all to dinner.'

'To dinner? Oh, Hippolyta! When?'

'The funeral is to be on Friday. I think it must be Friday evening.'

'A week to the day. Oh, very well: but once and no more!'

Chapter Fifteen

'They all just follow him around the country, from spa to spa, then? Buying his cures, taking his powders, rubbing in his balm?'

'That seems to be the sum of it,' said Hippolyta. 'The Gileads were based in London – that address we saw on some of the letters. Gracechurch Street, I think it was.'

Durris rubbed his forehead.

'It seems an odd way to live,' he said.

'Neither Mrs. Pumpton nor Mrs. Nickell seem to like Peter very much. In fact, they wondered if he was not Dr. Gilead's own son. He certainly looks like Mrs. Gilead, but there's not much of his father in him, in his appearance, at least.'

'And very little fatherly affection in him, either. He told me today that he had no respect for his father at all. If you will excuse the language, Mrs. Napier, he confided that he would have been prouder to have a piss prophet for a father, for at least then he would have been doing something for his patients, lowering himself to inspect something that might lead to a proper diagnosis. But he said his father was too lazy even to touch his patients: his powders and his balm cured everything, so there was no need for diagnosis.'

'Perhaps that's a fair point,' said Patrick, who had just returned from draining two Scotch pints from a dropsical patient at Tullich, and had admitted to feeling a little jaded.

'He's talking to you, then?' Hippolyta asked.

'Nothing much to the point, then. But as I said, then I told him we would have to charge him with murder. That opened his eyes a wee bitty: that smile vanished just for a moment. Then he said that was all right by him, because I was the one that was going to look a fool at the trial, if not before.'

'Why would that be?'

'I asked him, but he just started smiling again.' Durris sighed. 'I left before he tempted me further to do him some damage.'

'Do you want to come to dinner on Friday?' Hippolyta asked him. Patrick groaned.

'I wish you would!'

In the end, Durris politely declined the invitation to dinner. The funeral had been a quiet affair, despite the constant sobbing of Mrs. Nickell and the heaving sighs of Mrs. Pumpton: the hotel had hosted it with the discretion of those who feel death is bad for business, but ignoring death is worse. The widow sat like a lump of washed out clay, speaking to no one and staring at the floor. The minister came up from the kirk to say a few prayers over the coffin at the kisting, and the wailing women were left behind while the men escorted the coffin down the hill, across on the boat and up through the edge of the village for the burial at Tullich kirkyard. Durris brought Peter Snark to meet the cortege and accompany it: his eyes flickered like a lizard's at the coffin and the mourners.

The minister stayed with the ladies for more prayers and a news, then left. Mrs. Gilead followed him to the door and when she did not reappear, Hippolyta went outside to look for her. She found the widow perched on the other side of the road, near where they had found Peter Snark burying the gloves. She was gazing out over the broad valley of the Dee, and at the other side of the river, where Hippolyta realised she was just able to see the ruined kirk of Tullich and the graveyard where Dr. Gilead was being buried. She stood a little distance from her, in case she was needed, and when Mrs. Gilead's shoulders sank and she turned to go back into the hotel, Hippolyta offered her an arm to lean on. Mrs. Gilead said nothing throughout.

When Mr. Nickell and Mr. Pumpton reappeared in the hotel, Hippolyta, Galatea and Mrs. Fettes, along with a few of the village women, returned across the Dee and home. Preparations in the kitchen were well under way: if nothing else Mrs. Riach could be trusted to cook a fine dinner and Hippolyta did nothing more than check that she was happy, and encourage her to lock the kitchen door against any possible interruption – by which she meant interference from Galatea, but chose not to say so. Ishbel was polishing cutlery at one end of the table and Wullie was chopping vegetables, while Mrs. Riach was making a neat job of boning a shoulder of mutton with a very sharp knife, Wullie's dog and three cats present as interested observers. Hippolyta smiled at the pleasant domestic scene, and went to change out of her black mourning walking gown into her second best evening gown, reckoning to manage without Ishbel at least for now. Later the maid would have to be released from the kitchen to help Galatea and their mother.

Back downstairs she popped her head into the study to see if Patrick was there. He sat at the desk, and did not rise as she came in.

'You're looking pretty. All all right?' he asked, turning a little stiffly to greet her.

'I think so. Did the interment go well?'

'I suppose so. Peter Snark looked daggers at everybody till Durris took him back to the cell under the church. I think we were all glad to see him go. If he's not the murderer he's doing a very fair impression of one.'

'I know: he's very convincing. I wonder what trick he hopes to pull to make Mr. Durris look a fool, though?'

'Hm.' Patrick shifted very slightly in his chair. 'It would be good to know before Durris is forced to take the whole business to trial, don't you think?'

'Definitely. I wish he were coming this evening, don't you?'

'But you can see why he chose not to. He thought that everyone would speak more freely without him there.'

'That will mostly fall on you, my dear,' she reminded him. 'I've talked with the women. You have to find out more about the men.'

'I suppose.' Patrick shifted again, and peered under the desk.

'Cat on your feet?' Hippolyta asked sympathetically.

'Hen,' said Patrick.

'Ah. Cup of tea?'

'No, I'll be fine, thank you.'

Mr. Durris' attendance would at least have made them even numbers for dinner, but they had to manage with nine at the table. Mrs. Kynoch, the late minister's widow, was the odd one out but perhaps the most welcome guest, despite her squeaky voice and slightly silly face. Hippolyta knew her now for a woman of both information and good sense, and she was her consolation for the evening. She arrived first, and was cosily established chatting to Galatea and their mother before the Pumptons and Nickells appeared together, in one boatload, so to speak.

They did not come entirely unescorted.

'I hope you don't mind,' said Mr. Nickell, grinning at Hippolyta as if assured of her good opinion. Behind him Dr. Gilead's white terrier trailed on a lead, head down and humble. 'Mrs. Gilead can't deal with him, and with Peter Snark ... wherever that sheriff's officer is keeping him, I offered to look after him.'

'Well, as long as he doesn't chase the cats,' said Hippolyta, but inevitably the moment the terrier arrived in the parlour by the door, two cats left in a marked manner by the window. Hippolyta closed it. The terrier sat by Mr. Nickell's feet, with an expression perhaps intended to convey all the misery of his life along with a kind of undeserving innocence. Patrick, who was kind-hearted, fell for it, and knelt beside the dog, making much of it. Hippolyta asked Mrs. Riach to bring a bowl of water and some scraps when she was fetching the negus.

'You're no adopting another ain?' asked Mrs. Riach in alarm, but Hippolyta shook her head.

'This one is only visiting.'

The dog took the scraps delicately, and settled down to sleep, so that when they went in to dinner they considered it safe to leave it closed in the parlour while they ate.

After the funeral had been talked over and examined with the benefit of hindsight, Hippolyta asked generally,

'What will you all do now? After all, weren't you mostly here to consult Dr. Gilead, Mrs. Pumpton? And you, too, Mrs. Nickell.' She did not address the question to her own mother, though she did wonder.

'Go home,' said Mr. Nickell promptly. Mrs. Nickell shot him a look.

'It seems disrespectful to hurry off when the poor dear man is only just laid in his grave!' cried Mrs. Pumpton. 'And still no one with the least idea who might have wished him any harm! I believe,' she said, laying a hand across her mighty bosom, 'that it was some jealous colleague, following him here to steal the secrets of his cures.'

'The secrets of his business success, more likely,' drawled Mr. Nickell. 'I know I'll have my head bitten off for saying it, but the only cures Dr. Gilead ever made were lightening over-fat purses.'

'How can you say that?' Mrs. Nickell demanded at once. 'You know how much better I am since the moment I met Dr. Gilead!'

'Aye, your heart beats faster and you have a good colour, but that never came from taking powders and rubbing in that stinking balm, did it?' he asked, in a voice oiled with meaning.

'Mrs. Pumpton,' said Mrs. Kynoch hurriedly, 'did you see any stranger about the hotel that you thought might be such a professional rival?'

Mrs. Pumpton drew in a great breath, then admitted,

'No, I didn't.'

'What about the sheriff's officer arresting Mr. Snark?' asked Mr. Pumpton quietly, when it seemed certain no one else was going to speak. 'Indeed, is he really arrested?'

'I'm not sure what the technical words might be,' said Patrick. 'Mr. Durris certainly hopes that Mr. Snark might have more information for him: information that Mr. Snark seems reluctant to give him.'

'But do you think he's the murderer?' asked Mr. Nickell, at last distracted from his domestic spat.

'He seems very sure that he is not, yet he is taking little trouble to defend himself, I believe,' Patrick explained.

'That's a strange way to go about things,' said Mr. Pumpton, taking courage from his wife's silence. 'You would think he would be eager to defend himself, if he's really innocent. I would,' he added thoughtfully.

'Maybe,' said Mrs. Pumpton at last, 'he knows who committed the dreadful deed, but he wishes to protect the killer!'

'Why would he do that?' asked Mrs. Kynoch, sounding shocked.

'Perhaps it is someone for whom he has, let us say,' said Mrs. Pumpton dramatically, 'a romantic attachment!'

'Oh, aye?' asked Mr. Nickell, interested. He no more than glanced at his wife, though she was blushing just a little. 'I can't think who that might be.'

'What about the Dewars?' Mrs. Nickell demanded suddenly. 'No one has mentioned the Dewars. What's going on there, then? She's attacked and left for dead, dear Dr. Gilead's murdered, and no one has even mentioned arresting Mr. Dewar! Surely it's obvious he's the killer!'

'He was certainly near that parlour door,' said her husband, a little surprised at himself at agreeing with her. 'He said he was looking for his wife.'

'What time was that, then?' asked Hippolyta, helping Mrs. Kynoch to some more of the spinach she knew she liked.

'It would have been near enough half past eleven, I think,' said Mr. Nickell after some thought. 'I was in the hallway about then, and after that I went back outside for a bit – I mean, into the courtyard where the dancing was. The band was still off having their supper – remember they played while we were eating, then went off for theirs? I felt like doing a bit of a song, so I was up that end seeing who to talk to and if there was anyone ready to accompany me at all. I didn't see Mr. Dewar after that.' His eyes glazed as if he were trying to remember exactly what he saw and when, and his cutlery paused on his plate. Then with a clank he dropped his knife. Everyone jumped.

'I beg pardon, Mrs. Napier,' he said quickly, 'my hand slipped.'

'He could have been upstairs attacking his wife and then come down pretending to be looking for her,' Mrs. Nickell continued. 'And as soon as he could, he slipped into the parlour and locked the door.'

'How did he know dear Dr. Gilead was in there? And alone?' asked Mrs. Pumpton breathlessly. 'Oh! I know! He sent him a message, purporting to be from Mrs. Dewar, knowing that Mrs. Dewar was left for dead upstairs, and dear Dr. Gilead was bound to answer the call and go to meet her!'

Mr. Pumpton muttered something behind his wine glass. Hippolyta was sitting beside him, or she might never have heard the words:

'Too many novels by far!'

'I think Mrs. Gilead feared they were meeting,' she said seriously. 'Poor Mrs. Gilead: how dreadful to fear finding – that, but finding instead something so much worse!'

'If it was worse,' murmured Mr. Nickell. He felt the look straightaway of his wife and Mrs. Pumpton. 'Well, maybe she's a bit happier now that she's not having to worry what he's up to all the time? It can't have been an easy life for her, can it? Trailing around the country, no home of her own, while her husband flirts with every woman he comes across?'

'Mr. Nickell.' Hippolyta's mother had not spoken more than please and thank you up to this point. Everyone fell silent and turned to her. 'You will not speak like that of Dr. Gilead at this table. Cease at once, or I shall have to request you to leave.'

Hippolyta and Patrick exchanged a quick, angry glare: it was not her table or her place, but neither of them dared say anything. Only Galatea, who had also been more of an ornament than entertainment so far, spoke up.

'I think you're confusing Dr. Gilead and God, Mother. I've noticed you do that recently. Maybe you should reconsider your priorities.'

Mrs. Fettes' was not the only jaw that dropped. Hippolyta, appalled, still felt the tickle of a thrill up her spine.

'Galatea!' Mrs. Fettes spoke in a voice like cold iron.

'Oh, you needn't bother sending me off to my bed without any supper. I'm off,' Galatea announced, standing up. The men, surprised, pushed untidily to their feet clutching napkins. 'I don't care who killed the old quack, I'm just glad that somebody did and saved me the trouble of pushing him into a mineral well somewhere. I've had enough of being your secret nurse. I'm off home to Edinburgh tomorrow: see to it that my bags are packed, Poll.'

She marched out of the dining room, leaving the party behind in silence. Then, just as the men were about to take their seats again, Mrs. Fettes stood, an unsteady hand on the edge of the table.

'I fear I must retire. I beg you will continue your little party without me.'

'Mother!' said Hippolyta.

'We shall speak in the morning, Poll,' said Mrs. Fettes, as stately as she could manage, and followed in Galatea's path out of the room.

This time the men sat quickly while they had the chance.

'I apologise for that interruption,' said Hippolyta, trying her best to sound calm. 'More fish, anyone?'

'Oh, yes, please,' said Mrs. Nickell at once, spooning fish and sauce on to her cleared plate.

'You have an excellent cook, Mrs. Napier,' said Mrs. Pumpton enthusiastically. 'Is she a local woman?'

'It helps, too,' Mrs. Kynoch put in, 'that so much of the food is so very local and fresh – much fresher than one finds in the city, I believe. What food is best in Harrogate, Mr. Nickell?'

'Oh, well ...' Mr. Nickell considered his list of Yorkshire delicacies, and the company breathed again. Hippolyta tried not to think about her mother and sister. Would Galatea really leave tomorrow? And what had she meant by "secret nurse"? What was her mother going to say in the morning? But she needed to concentrate on her guests.

Mrs. Kynoch had led the conversation into encouraging Mr. Pumpton to talk a little of his business in the West Country: she seemed capable of interested questions on almost any subject, a skill Hippolyta imagined was developed as a minister's wife. Mrs. Kynoch steered his wife gently away and allowed Mr. Pumpton to talk of qualities of paper and ink and the prices wholesale and retail about the country, before Mr. Nickell, who preferred not just to be a spectator in conversations, chipped in.

'And I bet you didn't like seeing all that hard earned cash draining away on balm and powders, did you, Pumpton?'

'Well ...' Mr. Pumpton cast a look at his wife in which terror was a major constituent. 'I couldn't say ...'

'Jack! Constantly you insist on putting a price on good health!' snapped Mrs. Nickell. 'Dr. Gilead always said that the price was immaterial.'

'That's right,' agreed Mrs. Pumpton at once. 'One's good health was priceless, he always said. And of course he was right, for what is money without good health?'

'And what's good health without money, eh, Pumpton?' asked Mr. Nickell. 'I'm sure we'd find others to agree: not Dr. Napier here perhaps, in his line of business, but Mr. Dewar, no doubt?'

Mrs. Nickell gave a sharp sigh, but managed not to say anything while Mrs. Riach and Ishbel cleared the dishes from the main course, and nimbly distributed the puddings. Mrs. Riach assigned a pointed look to the two empty chairs, but said nothing.

'Oh, good gracious, what delights!' cried Mrs. Pumpton as the dining room door closed once again.

'What if Mrs. Dewar killed him?' Mrs. Nickell asked across her, helping herself to a large slice of creamy pie before Hippolyta had the chance to offer. 'What if they had a quarrel?'

'I believe Mrs. Dewar was almost certainly too weak to do anything of the sort,' said Patrick.

'Did she charm you, too, then?' asked Mrs. Nickell sourly.

Patrick looked at Hippolyta. They both knew that Mrs. Dewar had not had much chance to charm anyone in the last few days, being mostly asleep. He was about to say something when there came a sharp bark from the parlour across the hall.

'Oh! Duty calls,' said Mr. Nickell. 'Will you excuse me, please, Mrs. Napier? I'd better take the terrier outside.'

'Would you mind if I join you, Nickell?' asked Mr. Pumpton. 'With your permission, Mrs. Napier. I'm afraid I'm feeling a little over heated.'

'Of course,' said Hippolyta, as the two men left the room. They heard the parlour door open, then the front door open and shut.

'Always going on about a waste of money, aren't they?' complained Mrs. Pumpton as soon as they had gone. 'It's not as if they don't have plenty.'

'I suppose they worry about keeping you comfortable when your health is restored,' said Mrs. Kynoch diplomatically. Mrs. Pumpton sniffed.

'He only wants an excuse to run off and play with his inkpots,' she said. 'You would think he didn't enjoy staying at spas. I like to see a bit of life!'

'Well, this time it was a bit of death,' said Mrs. Nickell, pleased with her clever remark. Mrs. Pumpton's broad face fell.

'I know. What are we going to do?'

'And where are we going to get our balm and powders?' countered Mrs. Nickell. Both ladies sighed heavily.

The emotional moment was broken by a burst of noise from outside the window. The dining room faced the side of the house and a small strip of garden and path. A ferocious flurry of barking rose, echoing off the walls of the cottage next door. Hippolyta hurried to the window and opened one shutter.

'Is everything all right?' she asked.

Outside it was growing dusky, but she could easily make out Mr. Nickell, Mr. Pumpton and the small white terrier. Two other shapes were there, too, though: Wullie was trying to drag his dog away from the terrier's grasp. Hippolyta excused herself and hurried out of the house.

The two men stood helpless as Hippolyta, skirts dragged on the muddy path, crouched down to calm the two dogs. The terrier turned to her as if to plead its innocence, but Wullie's poor dog was bleeding and bewildered. Hippolyta restored the end of the lead to Mr. Nickell, who took it in shock, and bundled up Wullie's dog to hand to him.

'Take him into the kitchen quickly before this fellow changes his mind,' she said briskly. 'Mrs. Riach will see to his injuries, no doubt, but if she needs help ask her to ring for Dr. Napier.'

'Yes, ma'am,' said Wullie, a bit white about the face.

'Are you all finished out here? I'm a little worried about that terrier's enthusiasm for armed combat,' said Hippolyta brightly to Mr. Nickell.

'Oh, yes, of course,' said Mr. Nickell humbly. 'I'll take him back inside.'

'Ma'am,' said Wullie quickly, watching the men go. 'Please, ma'am, can I say something?'

His dog seemed happy just to have the warmth of his arms around it, so she allowed him to pause.

'What's the matter?'

'I dinna ken those men – those gentlemen,' said Wullie quietly, 'but I think one of them's going to rob something!'

'What do you mean?' Hippolyta stopped brushing down her skirts and stared at him.

'I was out here with Tam – this is Tam, ma'am,' he said, then was struck by how awkward that had sounded, and floundered. 'They didna see me, for we was over behind the bushes. Then that terrier must have smelled him, and he just flew at Tam, ma'am!'

'Yes, I understand. But you said something about robbery?'

'Aye, ma'am. Well,' he said, and she could see a glint of delight in his eyes at a story to tell, 'the wee man with the rosy nose, he was saying that he was sorry that Dr. Gilead – that's the mannie that was killt, was it no?'

'It was.'

'The wee man was sorry that Dr. Gilead didn't just take his wife off his hands and away, ken. But then the thin man with the fat wame, he said that the other man was lucky enough, for his wife – the wee man's wife, that would be – was no as smitten as his ain wife, and so he was glad that Dr. Gilead was gone. "Job done", that's what he said, and he looked that pleased wi' himself, ma'am, you'd have thought he had the hairst in and was dancing in the barn. Then the wee mannie, he says "It's a right pity we couldna win back some of our wasted money, an' all," and the tall mannie, he says he has a plan to win it back, or a good sum of it, if all goes well. And I thought, ma'am, that mebbe he had a plan to rob the widow wumman up at the hotel, mebbe as she gangs hame? If he set yon dog on her he could bumbazle her and rob her and she'd never ken a'thin' till they'd gone.'

'Well, it's her dog.'

'So he's started already!' whispered Wullie in wonderment.

'No, he's looking after it for her. But he said he had a plan to win back his money? That's very interesting. Was that all?'

'Aye, ma'am. The dogs began their shangie and that was that for conversation,' he finished grandly.

'Then take Tam in and see to his wounds, and thank you.'

'Thank you, ma'am.'

Hippolyta, frowning, walked slowly back to the front door. What was Mr. Nickell up to? And could it be that he had killed Dr. Gilead in the first place?

Chapter Sixteen

'What a very unhappy set of people,' said Mrs. Kynoch.

'I suppose they are: it's the thing they have in common,' said Hippolyta, mentally adding her mother and sister to the list. 'Mrs. Nickell and Mrs. Pumpton are mourning Dr. Gilead, and Mr. Pumpton is frightened of his wife, and Mr. Nickell does not trust his.' And Galatea and Mother are at odds, and not used to it, she added again silently.

'Do you think you learned anything?' Mrs. Kynoch asked. Patrick and Hippolyta were walking her home across the green: the others had taken the complacent terrier and gone down to waken the boatman to take them back across the river. They had all stayed very late. Hippolyta stifled a yawn.

'I learned they would rather stay in our house and quarrel than go home to their beds,' Patrick groaned. 'But of the murder, very little.'

'We learned that Mr. Pumpton wanted Dr. Gilead alive,' said Hippolyta. She told them what Wullie had overheard outside in the garden.

'Maybe,' Patrick conceded.

'Only if he and Mrs. Pumpton eloped and caused him no more expense. It must be very worrying for him,' said Mrs. Kynoch, who had rather taken Mr. Pumpton under her wing at the ball. 'He told me he fears his business faces ruin if he does not spend more time there, and it would not surprise me. Yet if he does not stay with his wife, she will be even more extravagant.'

'He must stop meeting her bills,' said Hippolyta firmly.

'He's too frightened of her,' said Mrs. Kynoch with simple force. 'She will drive him to bankruptcy, then no doubt blame him. It is a great shame, for he is a pleasant little soul.'

'You would not say, then, that he would have taken matters into his own hands by killing Dr. Gilead?' asked Patrick, as they reached her cottage.

'I should not say so at all – by no means. Mr. Nickell I thought a much more likely killer. He thinks a great deal of himself, that one, and I should imagine a degree of self-assurance is useful if one is to lure one's victim into a secluded room, feed them laudanum and murder them, wouldn't you?'

'And what do you think of his plans, as Wullie sees them, to rob Mrs. Gilead?'

'He's greedy, no doubt,' said Mrs. Kynoch after a moment's thought, 'but I cannot see how he might do it. He strikes me as too lazy to go in for highway robbery, and she might recognise him and accuse him, and he cannot want to risk that, surely?'

'It's all very perplexing,' said Hippolyta, and they bade Mrs. Kynoch goodnight, making sure she was in with a candle lit before they set off back across the green.

'And then, my dearest,' said Patrick once they were clear, 'there is the matter of your mother.'

'I don't even want to contemplate that problem,' said Hippolyta. But that was more easily said than done: she passed a restless night, wondering what questions she should be asking, before even allowing herself to contemplate what the answers might be.

In the morning she heard Galatea stamping around the house and giving orders before she herself even wanted to leave her bed. Patrick had already gone to work in his dispensary, safely locked in. Hippolyta turned over, listening, trying to think of excuses to let her sister be and please herself, but in the end she pushed back the covers and sat up, rubbing her eyes. Her wrapper was over the end of the bed and she pulled it on, and went to see what was happening.

Galatea was in the hall, shoving at her trunk and keeping up a sustained grumble of complaint against Mrs. Riach, who stood lips pursed, fists on her hips, watching her.

'Galatea,' said Hippolyta, doing her best to sound as much like her mother as possible. 'Into the parlour, now, and sit down.'

To her surprise, Galatea did exactly as she was told: it was only when she sat down that she looked up at Hippolyta and almost growled at her.

'That won't do,' she said. 'I've had that tone of voice used to me all my life, and I won't take it anymore, not from Mother, and certainly not from you.'

'But you did, didn't you?' Hippolyta could not help saying, her little moment of triumph. 'It's the voice that has to be obeyed!'

'I don't know how you would know. We never paid much attention to you. She never wanted you, you know,' Galatea added nastily.

'I know that,' said Hippolyta. No one had ever told her explicitly, but she had always suspected it.

'You just got in the way. We were old enough to be useful,' she added, with almost as much bitterness.

'Why have you fallen out with Mother?' Hippolyta sat in a hard chair opposite her sister. She wanted to take Galatea's hands, remembering what Mrs. Kynoch had said about unhappiness, but Galatea was so prickly it was hard even to touch her without fearing some kind of attack. Instead she tried to make her voice soothing.

'It's none of your business.'

'It is my business,' Hippolyta insisted gently. 'You're my sister, she's my mother – whether she wanted that or not – and this is my house. You and Mother were always friends – well, allies at least. What has gone wrong?'

Galatea sat with her lips bitten together, determined not to utter a syllable. Her hands were clutched together in her lap, her shoulders hunched to her ears.

'How long have you been travelling around like this?' Hippolyta persisted. 'Bath, Harrogate, Peterhead – how long has it been going on?'

Galatea flashed a look at her, but stayed silent.

'What does Mr. Milton think about it?' Galatea's husband had always been too much older than her for her to think of him as anything but Mr. Milton. Galatea's lips trembled, despite herself. She turned her face abruptly away, not meeting Hippolyta's eye.

'He doesn't like it, does he? And the children?'

'I miss them,' Galatea breathed. 'I want to go and see them.'

'And Mr. Milton?' Hippolyta asked, as softly as she could.

'I miss him, too.' The words came out twisted. Was Galatea going to cry? Hippolyta suppressed a squeak of shock. Galatea's shoulders slid down, easing out very slightly. 'We quarrelled.'

Hippolyta gave it a moment without speaking.

'What about?' she asked.

'He – turned down a case.'

Hippolyta waited.

'He keeps turning down things he doesn't like.' There was another pause. 'He turns down cases where he thinks the defendant is guilty.'

'So does Papa, for the most part,' Hippolyta could not help saying.

'I know! I know. But that's not the way to succeed in the lawcourts, is it? I believed he had other ideas. I thought ... I thought he would be successful.'

'You mean profitable,' said Hippolyta flatly. Galatea flashed her a look.

'I knew you wouldn't understand. But when you're older you'll know: you'll need to push Patrick too, no doubt, or he'll spend his days tending to poor people who'll never pay him, and wear himself out for nothing. And it takes a lot of work, making your husband do what he has to do ...' She let her head slump, staring at her fingers as they pressed one another white in her lap.

'You do not want for anything, do you?' Hippolyta asked, encouragingly.

'Not want, no.'

'And Mr. Milton is happier, I suppose, when he is doing what he feels is right?'

'Oh, he can be so foolish!'

'But more content?'

Galatea sniffed disparagingly.

'I suppose so.'

'Then why not let him be? Would you say the Pumptons were happy together?'

Galatea blinked at her.

'No, of course not. She trails him around the country spending his money while he wants to be at home with his business. You can't possibly compare us to the Pumptons.'

'No, but think about it. You're trying to push your husband

into a shape that doesn't fit him, just the same.'

'But if I don't tell him what to do ...'

'The world won't end.'

Galatea stared at her hands again. Hippolyta watched her, hoping something would work and make both her brother-in-law and her sister better pleased with each other. She had had no idea that her brother-in-law was so like her father: she had always assumed, because he was Galatea's husband, that he must be as ambitious and hard-working as she was. It would have been an interesting world if Galatea could have gone to work in the lawcourts instead, and Mr. Milton stay at home to bring up the children – perhaps they would have been better suited then.

'I still want to go home,' said Galatea, as close as Hippolyta was going to get to an admission that something had penetrated her armour.

'That's all right. I'll ask Patrick to go down and book you a seat on the coach. It doesn't leave until a quarter to three.'

'Oh. All right.'

'And I'll help you pack, if there's more to be done.' At least Mrs. Riach would be allowed a bit of peace, she thought. She laid a hand on Galatea's shoulder, was not rebuffed, and went to the kitchen to see how the housekeeper was, how the dog was, and whether or not Patrick would go and book the coach.

Galatea must have stayed up late, or risen early, for all her packing was done and she declared that she was going to lie down for the morning and rest before her journey. She had breakfasted and gone back upstairs before Mrs. Fettes appeared, looking even more aloof than usual.

'I intend to bathe this morning,' she announced.

'Of course, Mother,' said Hippolyta, standing attentively by the breakfast table.

'You will accompany me, I think. I was not at all pleased by your little dinner last night, Polly. You encouraged a level of disrespectful conversation which was not at all in keeping with your upbringing or what you owe to your better guests.'

'But Mother, the guests were principally your acquaintances, not mine!' Hippolyta could not help exclaiming.

'Nevertheless, they were allowed to behave badly. I trust you will not permit this again.'

'No, Mother,' said Hippolyta. Well, not while you're here, she added silently. 'But I really think that we need to know what Dr. Gilead was really like before we can understand why he was killed. After all –'

'And what business is it of yours to understand why he was killed?'

'It should be everyone's business, but –'

'What nonsense! I'll hear no more talk like that in this house.'

'This is my house, Mother,' cried Hippolyta desperately.

'I beg your pardon?'

'I'm sorry, but it's true. I apologise for any insult you feel you may have suffered here, but it is my house.'

'I will not be spoken to like this.'

'Of course not.' Hippolyta was shaking, and knew she was about to back down. She stabbed her palms with her fingernails, trying to control her voice. 'I am sorry, Mother.'

'Go and prepare yourself for bathing. I shall breakfast alone.'

'Yes, Mother.'

Hippolyta left the parlour, and went upstairs to her bedroom, and lay on the bed and cried like a child. Which perhaps, she thought, as she dabbed her eyes afterwards, proved her mother's point.

Mrs. Fettes had obviously expected Galatea to attend them as usual, but she made no comment when only Hippolyta appeared with her bonnet and gloves on, ready to go once again across the river to Pannanich. Hippolyta said little as they climbed the hill on the other side, even though her mother made regular comments on the people they passed or the view back down to the village. If bridge-building were required, Hippolyta thought sulkily, she did not have the heart for it.

It was a particularly fine day, and Mrs. Fettes chose first of all to sit by the lower spring and drink there. They gave their boots and stockings to an attendant and stepped on to the wet cobbles, forced to hold hands to steady each other as they turned and settled on the low stone seat, awkwardly keeping their skirts clear. The attendant scooped water for them from the stream as it tumbled out, handing them cups with a smile. Mrs. Fettes wiped the edge of hers before drinking. The water was never as cold as one expected, even here out in the fresh air, though anywhere it had touched quickly chilled.

A dark little figure emerged from the hotel and came to join them, handing slippers and stockings to the attendant and slipping nimbly over the stones. It was Mrs. Gilead.

'Good morning, Mrs. Gilead,' said Mrs. Fettes politely.

'Good morning, ma'am,' Mrs. Gilead nodded. 'I hope you are quite well this morning.'

'Very well, thank you.'

Mrs. Gilead swallowed the contents of her cup in one go, and shivered.

'I think I must leave this place,' she said after a moment. 'And yet it is very beautiful.'

'The view is delightful,' agreed Mrs. Fettes, gazing down over the valley from her seat.

'Just down there you can see the graveyard where they buried him,' said Mrs. Gilead softly.

'Oh! Ah, yes,' said Mrs. Fettes, taken aback. It was not quite the beautiful view she had been thinking about. 'Then it must produce very mixed sensations in your heart.'

'Yes. Yes, indeed.' She sighed. 'I shall go and visit it today.'

'That will no doubt be restorative, to an extent,' said Mrs. Fettes authoritatively.

The hotel keeper, Mr. Black, appeared in the courtyard, looking about him. He saw Mrs. Gilead, and scuttled over.

'A letter for you, Mrs. Gilead,' he said, with a little bow.

'Oh, yes? Thank you.' She took it, glanced at the address with what Hippolyta thought was surprise, and opened it without asking permission. Mindful of her anonymous letters, Hippolyta watched her as she read it. It only took a moment. Then she stood abruptly in shock, and raced back into the hotel without a backward glance – or even with her stockings and slippers.

'Good gracious,' said Mrs. Fettes. 'What singular behaviour. Shall we go and bathe now?'

Mrs. Fettes seemed to have forgiven the Pumptons and Nickells sufficiently for their lack of respect the previous night to settled down and take tea with them as usual after her bath. Mrs.

Gilead was not in evidence, and as usual Hippolyta was sent away to fetch some additional requirement from the recesses of the hotel. She took the opportunity to ask Mr. Black if Mr. Durris were still in residence.

'Yes, ma'am, he is. Shall I fetch him for you?'

'Thank you, yes.'

Durris appeared quickly enough, adjusting his glasses to fit the wary look in his eyes at her summons.

'Shall we walk outside?' he asked.

'As long as we're not in view of the parlour window!' said Hippolyta. 'Mother will wonder where I'm off to, when she only asked for more shortbread.'

'Who else is in there?'

'The Pumptons and the Nickells.'

'No Mr. Dewar? Or Mrs. Gilead?'

'No. Do you still have Peter Snark in the cell?'

'Yes, I do, though I don't yet know what to do with him.'

'Did Mrs. Gilead tell you she had received another strange letter?'

'No: has she?'

'I don't really know,' Hippolyta admitted. 'She certainly received something that she did not expect.' She told him about the scene at the well.

'You didn't see the cover?'

'No, I was at the wrong angle.'

'Well, it could have been anything, I suppose.' He pondered the matter for a moment, then asked, 'Well, how was your dinner?'

Hippolyta raised her eyebrows and shrugged.

'Not very comfortable, to tell you the truth. Mrs. Kynoch said how unhappy they all seemed.'

'That's true enough,' he agreed.

'There seemed to be a good deal of suspicion about the Dewars, though that perhaps was because they were not there to defend themselves. Nobody likes Peter Snark, but I think we knew that. Mr. Pumpton is worried about money and his business. Then Wullie – do you know Wullie? His brother works for Mr. Strachan, and Wullie's come to work for us, at least for now.'

'What about him?'

'He overheard a strange little conversation between Mr.

Pumpton and Mr. Nickell.' She outlined what Wullie had heard.

'How reliable is Wullie?'

'He seems bright enough. And he was a little reluctant to report something that might have been critical of a guest, so I think he at least is sure he heard it. Whether he has misunderstood something I don't know.'

'So he thought it sounded as if Mr. Nickell had killed Dr. Gilead, and was now planning to rob Mrs. Gilead.'

'That was his feeling, yes.'

'There's a thing,' said Durris thoughtfully. 'Dr. Napier will have told you I brought Peter Snark to his father's burial yesterday. He had a decent enough look to him on the way, wore the black neck cloth I'd brought for him and to judge by that face of his he was feeling some level of grief for his father. He was quiet, as he usually is, but more contemplative, perhaps. When he saw Mr. Nickell there, though, that smug smile came back to his face, the one that he uses when he wants to annoy most, it seems. It was there for a moment, then vanished.'

'Does he know something about Mr. Nickell, then?' Hippolyta asked. She wished she had seen it herself, not had to wait for the report the next day. It was hard to interpret looks one did not see.

'He seemed to – though whether it was that Mr. Nickell was the murderer would be a hard conclusion to reach from that. If he knows that, why doesn't he tell me, instead of waiting until he's on trial? Have they some plan together, that Mr. Nickell will flee the country before Peter Snark says anything?'

'He's showing no sign of fleeing the country. He has only mentioned perhaps returning to Yorkshire.'

'No, there seems no urgency at all about any of them. Yet I should like to see this matter solved as soon as possible.'

Hippolyta considered.

'Would you let me see him?'

Durris turned to stare at her.

'Would Dr. Napier allow it?'

'What if he came too?'

He turned away and stared out at the hills across the valley.

'If he came too, I suppose.'

'Today?' Hippolyta saw no need not to press the idea.

'Let me think.'

Hippolyta sighed.

'I'd better go back to my mother,' she said, glancing back at the hotel as if afraid her mother might emerge and summon her. 'Patrick is about, I believe, or he may be at the Lodge. If you see him you could ask him, couldn't you?'

'If I see him.' His face had set stubborn. 'I'll think about it.'

'Thank you, Mr. Durris,' she said humbly, and left him.

Patrick was just emerging from the driveway to the Lodge as Hippolyta and her mother eventually returned down the hill from the Wells. The Lodge was a substantial square building, originally built to take the overflow from the much smaller hotel and accommodate spa visitors, before the laird had arranged a bridge and planned Ballater village. The Lodge was well equipped for the sick and invalid, and at any one time Patrick usually had several patients there. He greeted them, looking tired, and as soon as he could speak quietly to Hippolyta without Mrs. Fettes overhearing he did so.

'Durris came to find me,' he said. 'He's gone on into town. What on earth are you up to?'

'I want to see Peter Snark. Well, I don't really, but it's very hard to understand him just from what Mr. Durris tells us, isn't it?'

'But to visit him in a cell! He could be a murderer, and even if he isn't, dearest, the circumstances!'

'Well, you wouldn't want me inviting him to dinner, would you?'

'Good heavens, no.' He thought for a moment, watching Mrs. Fettes' back as she interrogated one of the errand boys running up from the boat. 'I hope we're not going to find ourselves with another manservant. Would it not be enough if I went to see him on my own? I could say it was for some medical reason.'

'But don't you see, that would still leave me with a second hand account of him? I want to see him for myself.'

Patrick looked at her.

'You know you take much of your stubbornness from your mother, don't you?'

'Don't say that! Well,' Hippolyta qualified, 'perhaps determination is one of her better characteristics.'

'That's one way to put it.' Patrick tapped his foot on the rough road. 'Durris is dubious about it, as he might well be, but he says that if I come too he'll allow you to visit Snark this afternoon. He'll meet us there at three.'

'That's perfect: we can see Galatea off on the coach, then walk back up to the church!'

Patrick sighed.

'You need to be careful, dearest,' he said. 'One of these days your curiosity will bring you to some harm.'

Mrs. Fettes chose not to see Galatea off at the inn. It seemed to Hippolyta that she was sure Galatea was not really going to leave, particularly since it meant a journey alone back to Edinburgh, but if that were the case Mrs. Fettes was liable to be surprised. Galatea climbed into the coach with the happiest face Hippolyta had seen on her since she had arrived, and even promised to return for a longer visit with her husband and the children. Hippolyta managed to look delighted at the prospect. They waved the coach away, then Patrick turned to Hippolyta.

'Well, say good day to the pony: we'd better go and meet Durris.'

Durris, his face as expressionless as could be, was waiting for them by the church doorway. He nodded as they arrived, then led the way round the back of the building to a small door set into the granite rubble wall.

'The laird mustn't have expected much trouble in his village,' Patrick remarked.

'No,' said Durris shortly. 'It's not ideal.'

'Has Mrs. Gilead been to see him at all?' Hippolyta asked.

'No, not at all.'

'Not close, then: as we thought.'

Durris shook his head, and opened the door, showing them a tiny space inside with another door opposite. It had a grid in it, through which candlelight gleamed. Durris closed the outer door, leaving them reliant on that one candle until he lit another in a sconce on the wall.

'Mr. Snark, you have some visitors,' he said, and opened the cell door. Peter Snark was lounging on a plank bed at about knee level, and gazed up without much apparent interest at their arrival.

Seeing who it was, he allowed his eyebrows to rise just a little, and swung his legs off the plank slowly, rising to his feet in his own time.

'Mr. and Mrs. Napier!' he drawled. 'To what do I owe the pleasure?'

'I'm glad to see you well, Mr. Snark,' said Patrick briskly. 'Do you have any medical concerns? Mr. Durris is eager to see his prisoners well cared for.'

A thin smile crept over Snark's face.

'Oh, yes, you're some kind of doctor, aren't you?' He grinned. 'You'll understand I don't have a high opinion of doctors.'

'Well, we had to ask,' said Patrick, keeping his temper. Hippolyta took a deep breath.

'Mr. Snark,' she said, 'are you at all concerned at the prospect of being charged for your father's murder?'

He looked at her with amusement.

'No.'

'Why not?'

'Well, Mrs. Napier, for one thing I know I'm innocent.' He seemed delighted with his own cleverness.

'That's all very well, Mr. Snark, but you'll have to be able to prove that.'

'Oh, no, Mrs. Napier. The lawyers will have to prove that I'm guilty.' His smile broadened. Durris made a small noise, which might have been a note of cynicism.

'And you think they won't be able to do that?' Hippolyta did her best to look and sound impressed at his daring.

'They won't, because I'm not.'

'But if you can't show that you were somewhere else, at the very least …'

'But I can, Mrs. Napier.' He stepped very close to her, and she forced herself not to back off. 'I have a witness who knows I wasn't anywhere near that parlour when he died.'

'And who might that be?' Hippolyta kept very still. Would he want to show off enough to give her a name?

'That might be – that would be, Mrs. Napier,' he allowed his tongue to slip out and moisten his lips, then invested his next words with luxurious meaning, 'the lovely Mrs. Nickell. She was with me, outside the hotel, admiring the stars.'

Chapter Seventeen

'He's utterly vile!'

Hippolyta managed to wait until they were well out of earshot before she spat the words out: she had no wish for Mr. Snark to know how much he had upset her.

'I did have my reservations,' said Durris quietly.

'You were just right,' said Patrick, who was still quite pink. Hippolyta strode over the road and was halfway across the green before they managed to catch up with her. She was breathing quickly, and trying to overcome a desire to plunge her face and hands into the horse trough and wash off any remote taint lingering from her encounter with Snark.

'But it did work,' said Durris, presumably in an effort to console her. 'He was trying to impress you. It worked.'

She took a final deep breath, controlling herself.

'It did, didn't it?' She allowed herself a small, slightly hysterical laugh.

'I'll have to go and talk to her. If she confirms his story of course I'm going to have to let him go.'

'And then what?' Patrick asked. 'Do you have anything that points to anyone else?'

'In terms of motive, I have plenty pointing to several other people. In terms of trying to prove that any of them was anywhere useful at the right time, perhaps not.'

'Come in and have a cup of tea,' said Hippolyta. 'We can't talk here.'

Durris followed them willingly enough into the house, and Hippolyta rang for tea. Mrs. Fettes was in the parlour, and so they retreated to Patrick's study. Patrick checked under his desk for hens, and relaxed on the desk chair. Durris took the armchair next to the empty fireplace, and Hippolyta perched on a stool across the hearth. The tea arrived quickly: Mrs. Riach explained that Mrs. Fettes had just called for some, so everything had been to hand.

'Mrs. Milton gone, then?' she added, her face bland.

'Yes, we saw her on to the coach,' said Hippolyta, without emphasis. Mrs. Riach curtseyed very nicely, and left the room in a little cloud of satisfaction.

'I assume,' said Patrick, once she had closed the door, 'that you are concentrating on the Dewars, the Pumptons, the Gileads or Snarks, and the Nickells?'

'And Mother and Galatea,' added Hippolyta. 'All the people who knew him before he came.'

'That's right,' said Durris, giving her a thoughtful look. 'It makes sense.'

'Then do we know that any of them could not have done it?' Hippolyta asked. 'You said you were asking questions at the hotel. Mrs. Pumpton, by the way, thinks a professional rival did it, but she couldn't think of anyone here.'

'No, there's no sign of anyone like that about. As it happens there are no medical people staying either at the hotel or at the Lodge at present. Mrs. Pumpton was the easiest to eliminate, by the way: when she wasn't at the table by the bath house she was in the supper room, eating.'

'There's a surprise,' murmured Hippolyta. A smile twitched at the corner of Durris' mouth. 'Anyone else?'

'Mrs. Fettes was at the table almost all evening. She left it late on to go and sit by the fire in the supper room. Mrs. Milton, your sister, came with her but left her at the fireside, but Mrs. Pumpton was there with her.'

'I suppose that's something,' said Patrick, smiling at Hippolyta. She flashed him a relieved look.

'Mrs. Milton herself is not entirely accounted for, though,' Durris went on. 'She was with your mother, except when she was dancing, up to that point, and then she vanished.'

'She was talking to me for a bit, by the end of the dance floor,' said Hippolyta. 'But not for very long.'

'When was that?'

Hippolyta had to think quite hard.

'It was just before that woman sang 'Those Endearing Young

Charms', I think. Patrick, you and Mr. Dewar were talking together close by. I didn't see Galatea after that.'

'Perhaps I should have another word with her,' said Durris. Patrick and Hippolyta exchanged awkward glances.

'She's gone back to Edinburgh,' said Hippolyta, apologetically.

Durris looked at her.

'I see.'

Patrick cleared his throat.

'What about the Nickells, then, if Peter Snark is offering Mrs. Nickell as his witness?'

'Mr. Nickell was about from time to time,' said Durris, shifting in his seat. 'Various people saw him. The Strachans remember that he was eyeing up their daughters at one point. He left the ball room with his wife at the end of supper for a walk, but he was not seen with her after that. Then for a little while he was waiting to sing, arranging an accompanist and so on, and in the sight of a number of people. As for her, from when she left with her husband to when I believe you saw her return, Mrs. Napier, and said she chatted with you, we have no idea where she was and who she was with.'

'That was after I saw Galatea. Mr. Snark came back just before Mrs. Nickell did,' said Hippolyta suddenly. 'He didn't look like a man who had been enjoying himself: I remember thinking he seemed crosser than usual.'

'That must have been quite alarming!' said Patrick.

'She didn't stay long with me, and then she headed across to the hotel door – she was in a hurry to do something or other, she didn't say what so I assumed … well, I assumed she was going to find the privy. Well, anyway, Mr. Nickell was near the doorway and stopped her. How much one remembers when one tries!'

'He stopped her? Against her will, do you mean?'

'That's what it looked like. Then he practically marched her back to the table. Mrs. Gilead will have seen them: she was the only one there by then.'

'Ah, interesting: she did not mention that. Mr. Nickell, however, saw Mrs. Gilead earlier, when she was returning from her hunt for her husband outside.'

'It's all like one big eightsome reel, isn't it?' asked Hippolyta.

'Weaving and meeting and parting and weaving again.'

'I wish you had all stayed in the one place, certainly,' said Durris, without rancour. 'Then we have the Dewars.'

'Well, Mrs. Dewar managed a little supper, then went to lie down on her own. I mean, she said she didn't need any help from Mr. Dewar or from Dr. Gilead.' Hippolyta remembered that quite clearly. She could see Mrs. Dewar's lovely face, quite determined but with a gracious smile as she firmly rejected their offers of help.

'That's right. Several people noticed her going to the stairs, then no one saw her until Mrs. Pumpton found her at the head of the servants' stairs.'

'Inside the door or out?' Patrick asked with interest.

'Out, on the landing.'

'Ah, I did wonder what Mrs. Pumpton was doing on the back stairs. Well, from the moment of her collapse, whenever that was – and I have not questioned her on the subject yet – she would have been quite incapable of doing anything.'

'And was she attacked?'

'I still don't know. Her stomach was quite bruised, but whether that happened when she fell or whether someone – it would imply, though, that she was attacked by someone who knew what was wrong with her, and wanted to hit her where it would hurt most. I don't believe they could have been sure they would kill her – and of course, they did not. She has not been strong enough for any detailed questions, and most of the time I've used a fairly high dose of laudanum to help her with the pain so she has mostly been sleeping, anyway.'

'We'll have to talk to her soon.'

'I know. I'd like to be there.'

'Of course, Dr. Napier. Mr. Dewar, now, I haven't had much conversation with him, either, for obvious reasons. He's barely left the room. Now after his wife went upstairs he was around and about: at first he just seems to have been chatting – with you, for one, Dr. Napier?'

'That's right. He wanted to know what I thought of Gilead.'

'Hm. Then he disappeared – I think he may have gone upstairs to see if his wife was all right, for some time after that he reappeared, looking for her. She was presumably lying by the back stairs by that time, but he didn't see her there.'

'The passage is quite dark,' said Hippolyta.

'True. Like Mr. Nickell, he appears and disappears, asking people if they have seen her. I suppose that like Mrs. Gilead he went outside to look, too.'

'No,' said Hippolyta, 'for when he asked me if I had seen her, I suggested trying outside and he nearly devoured me. He said she thought the night air was harmful, or something. After that I tried to help him find her, and we discovered that the parlour door was locked.'

'And by then Dr. Gilead was dead,' said Durris, with an air of finality.

'So there's both Nickells – unless she agrees that she was with Peter Snark – Galatea, Mr. Dewar, and I suppose Mrs. Gilead, and possibly Mrs. Dewar,' Hippolyta counted on her fingers. 'Six possibilities. Oh, what about Mr. Pumpton?'

Durris looked up at her from his notebook.

'Oh, no one remembers seeing him at all.'

The Napiers nodded, accepting the likelihood of that. Durris cleared his throat.

'Mrs. Napier, tell me, if you will: how do you regard Mrs. Milton as a suspect? It must be extremely upsetting for you, forgive me.'

'Well ... yes and no,' admitted Hippolyta. Her mind had been skirting around the issue: there were so many mysteries at the moment surrounding her mother and sister that she had let slip the most important one. 'We have never been particularly close, but it is not a pleasant thought. But I can see clearly that it is one you have to consider, for she did nothing to hide her delight at the news of Dr. Gilead's death, she neither liked nor trusted him, and she – she and Mother have always been friends, and it seems to me that Dr. Gilead came between them, however he managed it.' She paused, not easy with talking openly about her family. 'She had had a quarrel with her husband, too, and was at last keen to resolve it, which is why she left, I believe. But as to whether or not she could have carried out such a murder ... I have to say that I think she probably could. And the use of the cordial balm would have appealed to her immensely: it would have seemed very fitting, in her eyes.'

Durris made one of his minute notes in his notebook.

Hippolyta's brow wrinkled anxiously: she had to tell the truth, but she was not happy with herself. Durris looked up at her and half-smiled.

'Let us hope we do not have to bring her back from Edinburgh, then,' he said. She felt very slightly reassured, but she was not sure why.

'I should say that the murderer had to be quite daring,' said Patrick, sensing it was time for a change of subject. 'To disappear into the parlour in full sight of everyone, lock the door, do what they wanted to do and then leave again – and lock the door behind them, in such a busy passage. What would have been their excuse if they had been caught?'

'Presumably they weren't, though,' said Durris. 'But I agree, they took several chances. I want to look at the parlour again this evening: I need to go and talk to Mrs. Nickell anyway when I go back up.'

'Will you take dinner with us first?' asked Hippolyta. 'It is almost time to change.'

'I have nothing to change into, Mrs. Napier.'

'That doesn't matter in the least,' said Hippolyta with a glance at Patrick.

'I can lend you a white neck cloth, and shaving things,' said Patrick willingly.

'And Mrs. Riach's mutton would revive an army,' added Hippolyta. 'You would work all evening on the strength of it.'

'I am very fond of mutton,' said Durris, in a moment of weakness. He smiled. 'If you are both sure it will not inconvenience you ...'

'By no means,' said Patrick.

'Then if you will allow it, before I make use of your shaving things, Dr. Napier, may I speak to your boy in the kitchen? The one who overheard Mr. Nickell and Mr. Pumpton.'

'Of course. Hippolyta will show you, if that's all right: I'll go and change, and then the way is clear for you.'

Wullie was a fine little witness, it turned out, and no particular respecter of persons: he eyed Mr. Durris up and down, came to a visible decision as to his trustworthiness, and told him precisely what he had told Hippolyta the previous night, with no wild embellishments and with the details matching. Hippolyta left Wullie to take Durris outside and show him the place where it happened, and incidentally the dog, which followed Durris with interest.

'Would we be able to give Mr. Durris dinner, too, Mrs. Riach?' she asked.

'Dod Durris? Aye, that'd be grand,' said Mrs. Riach, unexpectedly affable. Her familiarity with Mr. Durris made Hippolyta wonder again: he had seemed perfectly happy in the servants' quarters, easily entering the kitchen with a nod and a greeting. Was she making a mistake inviting him to dinner with her mother?

That certainly seemed to be Mrs. Fettes' thought when she came downstairs dressed for dinner and found Mr. Durris rising in the parlour to bow to her. The last time Hippolyta had seen a look like that on her mother's face had been when she found the kitchenmaid at home in Edinburgh in her brother's bedchamber, even though she had been alone and innocently looking for a missing saucer.

'Mr. Durris will be joining us for dinner at short notice,' said Hippolyta, trying to keep the hint of panic from her voice. 'He has had no opportunity to fetch his dinner things.'

'Clearly,' said Mrs. Fettes. 'Good evening, Mr. Durris.'

Durris made no overt attempt to impress Mrs. Fettes, but somehow by the end of dinner she had relaxed and was speaking quite as if she did not feel there was an intruder in the room. She even looked a little disappointed when he explained that he would have to excuse himself and return to Pannanich forthwith.

'I declare I am sorry you cannot stay longer, Mr. Durris,' she said unexpectedly, 'though I admit I am rather fatigued.'

'Patrick has to go up to see Mrs. Dewar, Mother,' Hippolyta put in. 'Why don't you have a peaceful little rest here alone, and I'll go with them for the exercise?'

'You must always be rushing back and forth, Poll. If this is the quiet country life then I think I am more peaceful in the city!' But she did not demur, and seemed happy enough when the Napiers set out with Durris for the boat.

'I'm not quite sure why you are accompanying us, Hippolyta,' said Patrick, as they disembarked on the Pannanich side of the river. 'Well, I know it is to satisfy the next wave of your curiosity, but I don't quite know what your excuse is.'

'You might want to have a woman nearby when you talk to Mrs. Nickell,' said Hippolyta artlessly. Patrick and Durris exchanged glances, which seemed each to be three parts resignation.

'Of course there are no other women at the hotel,' Patrick murmured.

'None as intelligent and informed,' said Hippolyta happily.

As it turned out, Mrs. Nickell was sitting on her own in the parlour when they arrived, staring out of the window miserably. She was still wearing black. She sniffed and turned when they addressed her, blinking in surprise.

'Mr. Durris? Again?'

'Some further information has appeared, Mrs. Nickell. May we sit down?'

She looked dubious, but did not protest as they arranged themselves near her. Hippolyta's presence seemed to puzzle her particularly, and Hippolyta gave her a bright smile. Durris leaned forward confidingly.

'You'll be aware, Mrs. Nickell, that I am currently holding Mr. Snark in custody in connexion with Dr. Gilead's murder?'

'Oh! Yes,' she agreed breathlessly. Her eyes were particularly prominent and shining, perhaps tearful at the memory of Dr. Gilead's death.

'He has offered us some evidence of his whereabouts at the vital time,' Durris went on, watching her closely.

'Yes?'

'To put it simply, he says he was with you outside the hotel.'

'Oh!' she squeaked.

'Was he? Were you together for part of that evening?'

'Oh, no! No, of course not! How could he say such a thing? Such a horrible man! Of course not!'

Her eyes darted from Durris' face to the parlour door and back. Hippolyta glanced around, but saw nothing.

'Are you quite sure, Mrs. Nickell?'

'Quite sure! Quite sure! Mrs. Nailor saw me come in on my

own, didn't you, Mrs. Nailor?'

'Mrs. Napier,' said Durris with the lightest emphasis, 'has indeed confirmed that you returned to the ball room alone, but Mr. Snark was only a little ahead of you.'

'Was he? I never saw him. Never at all!' Her eyes bulged, and she gripped the edge of the table until Hippolyta thought her gloves would burst from the strain. Her gaze flickered back to the parlour door again. 'I'd like you to leave me alone, please. I really cannot – I'm not well, you know. I need to be free from all anxieties. My heart!'

'Then please excuse us, Mrs. Nickell,' said Durris at once. He rose, and ushered the Napiers out of the room. They gathered outside in the courtyard, where they were less likely to be overheard.

'She's lying,' said Hippolyta at once.'

'I should say so,' Durris agreed. 'And she was expecting someone, or fearing the arrival of someone.'

'I wonder did Gilead tell her it was her heart?' Patrick added, pushing his glasses up his nose. 'It looks to me more like something to do with goitre – which of course causes a rapid heartbeat.' He looked thoughtful. 'You can probably cure it with cordial balm and infallible scarlet powders, though.'

'On which her husband feels he has spent a fortune,' said Durris. 'I wonder ... could we be looking for two people here?'

'Two? The Nickells?' Hippolyta asked.

'Or Nickell and Snark, as I suggested before?'

'Or Nickell and Mr. Pumpton? Could that be what they were out in the garden discussing?'

They fell silent, considering the possibilities. Dusk was descending, and tiny lights appeared here and there in the valley below them. There was a sound behind them at the door, and Black, the hotel keeper, appeared to light the lanterns in the cobbled yard. He nodded to them, working his way back and forth between hotel and bath house towards the wells. They called a greeting, and Patrick turned quietly back to Durris.

'I don't suppose you should be considering him? He knew where the keys were, after all.'

'But there was a key in the door anyway,' said Durris, then broke off as there was a cry from the wells. The hotel keeper's torch fell to the ground and fizzed out.

'What's the matter?' Durris strode into the darkness. Hippolyta hurried back to fetch a candle from the hall sconces, and followed Patrick after him.

Durris had the hotel keeper by the arm, at the edge of the stone circle at the well. Water, as usual, flowed generously from the wellhead, spilling about the steps and running down to the end of the bathhouse. It was hard to avoid it in the dark. Hippolyta clutched Patrick's arm, and held out her candle. The hotel keeper was gasping, too much to speak. Durris leaned forward to peer into the pool of light.

The leg was what they saw first, making sense of the dark clothing against the wet stone. Two legs, sprawled, a torso then arms, flailed to each side. Then the head, face down in the spring. Hippolyta gulped, and turned away. Her candle wobbled, and Durris seized her wrist, holding it steady while he took in the details. Patrick's arm was suddenly around her waist, and braced between them she was brave enough to look back again. The dark hair, whatever the damage to the skull, could be seen to be thin, the body long and skinny. She knew now who it was: Mr. Nickell was dead.

Three quarters of an hour later she was sitting with Mrs. Nickell in the parlour, still alone. The silence was eerie.

Dewar had brought the hotel keeper back to reason by speaking sternly of bringing lanterns and something for a stretcher. Patrick had given her a final squeeze then taken her candle to make a closer examination of the body. She had taken in the shape of it, the sprawling arms and legs, the great mess of the back of the head, the water trickling red still away from the corpse, then walked slowly and carefully back to the hotel and into the parlour, mind numb, fighting through the shock to try to find words for the new widow.

She had stopped Christy the maid in the hall.

'Can you bring brandy and tea into the parlour, please, for Mrs. Nickell and me? There's been an accident.'

'An accident!' cried the maid. 'I just kenned I was richt to leave the ferm!' and she sped off to the kitchen to fetch what was needed. Hippolyta went into the parlour, nodded to Mrs. Nickell and sat down near her without a word until the brandy and tea appeared. She took a strong sip of her tea, scalding her lips and wincing. Then she poured a cup for Mrs. Nickell, set it in front of her, and said,

'There's been another incident.'

'Another?' Mrs. Nickell's eyes flashed towards the parlour door and back, with a hunted look. 'Is it Mrs. Dewar?'

'No. I'm afraid it's someone much closer to you. Mrs. Nickell, I'm sorry to have to tell you that Mr. Nickell is dead.'

'Mr. Nickell? Jack?' She scrutinised Hippolyta's face, not understanding. 'My husband, you mean?'

'Yes, I'm afraid so.'

Her jaw dropped, eyes huge.

'You mean someone has killed him?' Hippolyta nodded. 'Why him?' Mrs. Nickell seemed genuinely baffled.

'Mrs. Nickell, you've had a bad shock. Take some tea.'

'Yes, yes, of course.' She took a sip, and set the cup and saucer down again. 'Where did it happen? Do they know who – who killed him?'

'I don't think so. It happened at the lower spring.'

'He was drowned? In the spring water?' Regrettably, Mrs. Nickell began to giggle. 'He hated that water!'

'Tea, Mrs. Nickell,' said Hippolyta, alarmed. 'And can I help you to a glass of brandy?'

Mrs. Nickell giggled helplessly, shaking her head.

'He really hated it!' she gasped.

Hippolyta glared at her.

'They'll bring him in shortly, no doubt. Then you can go and see him.'

'All wet!' cried Mrs. Nickell, still laughing. Hippolyta wondered if she should slap her: her mother certainly would. 'They'll have to dry him out! That was his good evening coat, you know: he won't want that all wet!'

Hippolyta stood, rounded the table, and smacked her across one bony cheek. Mrs. Nickell subsided with a squeak, and after a moment sulkily drank her tea, followed by her brandy. Hippolyta resumed her seat, and sipped her own tea.

'Thank you,' said Mrs. Nickell eventually. Hippolyta nodded, not looking at her. Mrs. Nickell cleared her throat, and took another glass of brandy, rather quickly.

'You've had a shock,' Hippolyta repeated, more kindly this time.

Mrs. Nickell nodded rapidly.

'I have. My husband, you know. You wouldn't like to lose yours, I think.'

'No, indeed.'

'That's why I lied to you earlier.'

'What?' Hippolyta turned to look at her. 'What was that?'

'Earlier. I said I wasn't with Mr. Snark – Peter – outside on the night of the ball. But I was. I was with him – for a while.'

'Then why did you say you weren't?'

'Jack asked me if I had been, and I denied it, of course. If Peter was telling everyone it was true, then Jack would have left me. And I'd have lost him.' She gave a little shiver, her scrawny shoulders hunched. 'I've lost him now anyway, haven't I? So I can tell the truth. I was with Peter Snark outside the hotel when Dr. Gilead was killed.'

Chapter Eighteen

'I gather the man Sim who normally checks the springs last thing at night didn't do it this evening,' said Durris. He looked tired, stretching his legs to the parlour fire. Mrs. Nickell had gone to bed, escorted only by the maid. Hippolyta and Patrick sat holding hands on the sofa, both weary.

'Why not? Where was he?' Hippolyta asked.

'On a bed in the kitchen with a broken ankle. He's the loon that fell off his ladder a few days ago.'

'Oh, him!' said Patrick. 'No, he wouldn't be up to checking springs just yet. Particularly the upper one.'

'Well, it wasn't him, and it wasn't Peter Snark,' said Hippolyta, 'and I don't believe it was Mrs. Nickell, either.'

'She could have done it and been back in the parlour before we arrived,' Durris pointed out.

'She could, but when she spoke to us she thought her husband was still alive. That's why she lied to us about being with Peter Snark on the night of the ball. I don't think she's clever enough to think that through and pretend.'

Durris and Patrick nodded, acknowledging the strength of her reasoning. Mrs. Nickell had a certain spirit to her, but did not seem particularly sharp. Durris sighed.

'Assuming,' he began cautiously, 'that Mrs. Milton has in fact gone to Edinburgh, she could not have done this, either.'

'She certainly seemed very happy to be on the coach,' said Hippolyta. 'Wouldn't it have looked a bit obvious if she stopped it halfway down the road to Aboyne, and asked to be let off?'

'And if she had wanted to be discreet about it,' Patrick added, 'and had taken the coach back when she reached Aberdeen, she wouldn't be here yet.'

'True … It seems unlikely, certainly,' said Durris. For some reason the words chilled Hippolyta more than anything else he had said about Galatea: it seemed that they brought home to her how much he had been prepared to accept Galatea as an ordinary suspect, just like the Pumptons or the Nickells. She watched him for a moment. Was he really as emotionless as he sometimes seemed? It would be useful in his job to appear to be, she supposed, but was it possible?

'Where are the Pumptons?' Patrick asked.

'They went up to their room after dinner, I'm told,' said Durris. 'No one has seen them since. I'll have to go and have a word with them.'

'With who?' demanded a voluminous voice from the doorway. Mrs. Pumpton sailed into the parlour like something with plenty of ballast. The men rose. Hippolyta smiled a greeting to Mr. Pumpton, bobbing in his wife's wake as usual.

'With you and Mr. Pumpton, madam, if I may,' said Durris, quite untroubled by her interruption. 'May I ask where you have both been since you left the dinner table?'

Mr. Pumpton glanced at his wife, but she paid him no attention.

'We were resting in our room, if it is any business of yours.'

'Both of you?'

'It is no scandal: we have been married for some time,' she said, with a slight shudder.

'Mr. Pumpton?'

'That's right,' said the little man. He had an honest face, Hippolyta thought, though she reminded herself that that was not always helpful. 'I wanted a word with my wife about the possibility of going home.'

'Yes, he did,' said Mrs. Pumpton with distaste. 'As if we could leave yet, with dear Dr. Gilead not even cold in his grave.'

'How can he not be cold?' murmured Mr. Pumpton. 'I've been cold since we left Edinburgh.'

'That's your own fault for neither eating enough nor taking the right medicines,' snapped Mrs. Pumpton. 'If you would take your scarlet powders as Dr. Gilead suggested, you'd be quite all right.'

'It's bad enough one of us taking them,' said Mr. Pumpton, whose courage seemed to be up this evening. 'If I started too we'd be bankrupted in half the time.'

'Oh, money, money, you're always thinking about money! You and Mr. Nickell: you're a pair of old women, always going on about expenses and business and money's worth. He's from Yorkshire, of course, but I don't know what excuse you've got, except you were just born mean!'

'Have you seen Mr. Nickell at all this evening?' asked Durris, breaking into this unedifying exchange.

'Mr. Nickell? Not since dinner. But I see Mrs. Nickell's not here either, so maybe they've taken their supper early and gone off to bed.' Mrs. Pumpton peered about the room, as though expecting to find the Nickells hiding behind the curtains, or under the table.

'Mrs. Nickell has indeed retired for the night,' said Durris with precision. 'Mr. Nickell, I'm afraid, has met with an accident.'

Accident, thought Hippolyta. Durris and Patrick had agreed he had been hit from behind, probably with a rock from around the spring, and left to drown with his face in the water. They were fairly sure it had not been an accident: the back of Mr. Nickell's clothes had been dry, so he had not fallen and struck the back of his head, then rolled over when he was unconscious.

'An accident?' snapped Mrs. Pumpton, echoing her thoughts. 'What kind of an accident?' Her eyes narrowed. 'Is this the kind of accident that you call it when someone's been murdered? Like Dr. Gilead?'

'It probably is, yes,' said Durris.

'Is it Mrs. Dewar?' demanded Mrs. Pumpton, with a distinct undertone of excitement. 'Because if it is, I hope you've arrested Mr. Dewar straightaway. He's killed both of them, his wife and dear Dr. Gilead, in a horrible jealous rage, and there's an end to his crimes: the man doesn't deserve to live.'

'It is not Mrs. Dewar,' Durris sighed. 'I said it had happened to Mr. Nickell.'

'Mr. Nickell? Why would anyone want to kill him?' she asked. It was a shadow of what Mrs. Nickell had said: it was almost as if, thought Hippolyta, the pair of them had made out a list of possible murder victims, and Mrs. Dewar had been at the top of it and Mr. Nickell had not been on it at all.

'You can't think of anyone who might have killed him, then?' asked Durris.

'Killed Mr. Nickell?' Mrs. Pumpton was still clearly having difficulty taking in the information. 'I have no idea. Why on earth would they? Are you sure it's him?'

'Yes, ma'am. We're quite sure.'

'Well. Well, I really don't know. Ring for supper there, would you?' she jerked her head at her husband.

'There was ...' Mr. Pumpton said slowly, then caught her eye and scuttled over to pull the bell.

'What was there, Mr. Pumpton?' Durris asked gently. Pumpton looked at him, alarmed.

'I don't know! He was very cross with Dr. Gilead and all the money he'd spent on him. That's all. Maybe he killed Dr. Gilead and then someone killed him, that's all. That's all. He said he'd done the job.'

'Done the job?'

'What?' shrieked Mrs. Pumpton. 'He killed dear Dr. Gilead? Mr. Nickell? If I'd known that, I'd have pushed his head into the well and held it there!'

'Good gracious!' exclaimed several people at once. She looked slightly shamefaced.

'Well, it does make me angry,' she said. 'All that talent – all that beauty, wasted by some violent fool.'

Durris took a deep breath. Mrs. Pumpton could not have carried out Dr. Gilead's murder, and from the abandoned way she had just threatened drowning, she had no idea how Mr. Nickell had died, which cleared her once again. Mr. Pumpton, however, was a different matter.

'When did he say he had done the job, Mr. Pumpton?' Durris asked.

'He told me last night. In – in your garden, when we took the dog out,' he said to Hippolyta. 'Lovely dinner, by the way,' he added politely.

'Ah, thank you,' said Hippolyta.

'He said the job was done.'

'Not that he had done it?'

Mr. Pumpton looked unsure of himself. He clearly had not realised that the serving boy who had appeared with the other dog might have heard and reported their conversation already.

'I'm not quite ... I thought he said, but you could be right.

Maybe it was just that he was really pleased that Dr. Gilead was dead.'

'The scoundrel! That alone ...' Mrs. Pumpton felt herself observed by the company, and tailed away with a snort.

'I'll take note of your idea, though, Mr. Pumpton, and of what you heard,' said Durris encouragingly. 'Very useful, thank you. Revenge for the first murder is a distinct possibility.'

'And quite justified,' added Mrs. Pumpton, daring anyone to disagree.

'Not in the eyes of the law, Mrs. Pumpton,' said Durris calmly. 'So neither of you heard anything unusual? Glanced out the window and saw anything odd? Bear in mind,' he added, 'that we do not at all know that it was revenge. The same killer could have carried out both murders, so it may well be that if we catch Mr. Nickell's killer we have Dr. Gilead's, too.'

Mrs. Pumpton gave him a sharp look, but she considered all the same.

'I never looked out of the window,' she said eventually. 'The shutters were closed when we went upstairs. And I think they block out most of the noise. Where did it happen?'

'At the lower spring.'

'At the spring!' You could see, Hippolyta thought, the realisation of what she had said a few minutes ago come back to her. 'He wasn't – he wasn't drowned, was he?'

Durris nodded slowly. Mrs. Pumpton went pale.

'I didn't – I didn't mean –'

'No, I don't think you did,' he said after a moment. She deflated like a hot air balloon.

'I think I need to go and lie down. Tell them to send our supper up to us, will you?'

She seized her husband's shoulder, and leaned on him as they left the parlour. He strained to take the weight, but bore up bravely, turning very slightly to nod farewell as they went.

'Their room is the right end of the building, now that they've swapped with the Dewars,' said Hippolyta thoughtfully.

'The shutters are quite thick, though,' said Patrick.

'I don't think she could possibly have done it. But could he?' Durris asked.

'Would she lie for him if he had slipped out to do it? They

said they were together all the time.' Hippolyta pointed out.

'I'm not sure. It seems unlikely,' Durris agreed.

'Well,' said Patrick, standing and stretching, 'do you want me to take another look at Mr. Nickell, now they've brought him inside? I have to go and see Mrs. Dewar, too.'

'I suppose we ought, before Martha comes up from the village to lay him out.' Durris rose stiffly from his armchair, and took reluctant leave of the fire. 'He's in the back parlour, where Dr. Gilead was.'

'There's going to be talk about that parlour,' Hippolyta warned them. 'In no time at all it will be haunted.'

'Yes. Stay here, please, dearest,' said Patrick. 'You manage all kinds of things, but I'm not going to let you in to see the examination of a dead body.'

A shame, thought Hippolyta as she sank against the back of the sofa. She was sure there were all kinds of things she would notice that Patrick and Mr. Durris would not. She let her mind drift. Was Galatea safely in Aberdeen? she wondered. Had their mother gone to bed yet? She had not looked quite as tired as usual: perhaps Galatea leaving had been a good thing. The tension between them had been very wearing.

There was a sound at the parlour door and she roused herself to find the maid there, curtseying.

'Ma'am, did you ring?'

'Oh! It was a little while ago. Mr. Pumpton rang for supper, but they have gone upstairs and would like it in their room.'

'Very good, ma'am.'

'Wait a second: Christy, isn't it?'

'Yes, ma'am.'

'You know what happened here this evening?'

'Yes, ma'am. There's no end of excitement working here, ma'am. My sister, she said don't go into service, stay on the farm, because service is dull. But there's always something here, ma'am. If it's no a ball it's a murder, and if it's no that it's loons falling down fae ladders! Every day is different,' she finished with the satisfaction of someone who feels it has all been done for their benefit.

'Well, I'm glad you're enjoying it so much,' said Hippolyta a little drily: she was sympathetic, though. 'Did you see anything strange this evening?'

'No, ma'am, I don't think so,' said Christy sadly.

'Who sat down to dinner?'

Christy gave it only a moment's thought.

'Mr. and Mrs. Nickell, ma'am, and Mrs. Gilead, and Mr. and Mrs. Pumpton, and Mr. Dewar came down for the first time since his wife was taken ill. My friend Gelis sat with her to let him come down the stairs. I think it did him good, you ken, ma'am, for he's no been out of that chaumer for days. He has no colour at all, ma'am. And he was a handsome gentleman when he arrived.'

'Did you help serve?'

'Aye, ma'am, what with Sim breaking his ankle an' all. Mr. Black says I'm gey swippert – ken, I have the dishes on and off the table when Sim would just be standing there thinking about it.'

'I'm sure you're very nimble,' Hippolyta agreed. 'And observant, too, I've no doubt. You'd have seen anything that was going on.'

'Oh, aye, I think so, ma'am.' Christy looked pleased at this recognition.

'And did you see anything that was going on? Mr. Nickell, for instance, the one who has died. How did he seem this evening?'

'He seemed happy enough, ma'am. Very happy, indeed: he was in a grand mood. He ordered a bottle of claret and shared it all around the table as if it was his birthday.'

'Did he say it was his birthday?'

'No, he didna. He was just like that. And then he said he was going to sing when he came back. He had a lovely voice, ma'am – did you hear him singing at the ball? A fine voice.'

'When he came back from where, though?'

'I dinna ken that. He went off out when everyone rose from the table.'

'The ladies didn't go out first?'

'Yes, of course they did. The ladies went to the littler parlour, the one that was the card room. The back parlour – well, nobody much wants to go into that now, and anyway Mr. Nickell's lying in there the now. But he wasna then, of course. The ladies went off into the little parlour, the men had their brandy in here, and then they went to tell the ladies they'd finished. I think Mr. Nickell hoped they'd all wait and hear him sing, but no: Mrs. Nickell came back into this parlour, then he went out, and everyone else went off upstairs.'

'You're sure?'

'Dead sure, ma'am: I stood at the bottom of the stair watching them, Mrs. Gilead, Mr. Dewar and the Pumptons, because I was thinking my friend Gelis would be down as soon as Mr. Dewar had settled himself with his wife again, and we would get our wee bit dinner.'

'But she would come down the back stairs, surely?' Hippolyta asked.

'Aye, ma'am, of course. I just minded what I was thinking as I stood there at the foot of the front stair.'

'And did she come down, then?'

'Aye, ma'am. She came down the back stair and we had our wee bit dinner in the kitchen. Now, that's funny,' she added.

'What is?'

'Well, there was no one left up the stair. I mean, Sim was in the kitchen, and the cook, and Mr. Black, and Gelis and me. But I heard someone come down the back stair. While we were eating.'

'Can you see the foot of the stairs from the kitchen?'

'No, it just goes out to the door at the front. Not the hotel door, the one at our end.'

'And you didn't look to see who it was?'

'I only half heard it,' Christy admitted. 'It's only now I'm thinking it was odd. There's people all over the place all day, ken, ma'am? You hardly take notice. It's only now I've remembered.'

'That's very helpful, Christy,' said Hippolyta, fishing in her reticule for a small monetary token of her appreciation.

'Was it the murderer?'

'I don't know yet, but it could well be someone who saw the murderer,' Hippolyta hedged.

'Michty me!' Christy exclaimed. 'I just love working here!'

'Someone on the stairs? The back stairs, where Mrs. Dewar was found?'

'That's right, and all the servants were downstairs,' Hippolyta confirmed. Mr. Durris looked pleased for once.

'And who was supposed to be upstairs at that point, then?' he asked, clarifying it to himself. 'The Dewars, of course.'

'And the Pumptons, and Mrs. Gilead.'

'And the dog?' suggested Hippolyta. Patrick grinned at her. 'Well, he was supposed to be looking after it: where was it?'

'It was back in the Gileads' room – I did ask,' said Durris with a wry look. 'Mrs. Nickell, was not upstairs, though: she was downstairs when the maid last saw her, and downstairs when we arrived. It would have made little sense, I think, for her to run upstairs just to come down the servants' stairs. Who sat with Mrs. Dewar while Mr. Dewar was at dinner?'

'One of the maids, Gelis.'

'Is it a coincidence, I wonder, that the first time Mr. Dewar leaves his wife for a week there is another murder?' Durris tapped his pencil thoughtfully on his notebook.

'Or is it too obvious?' countered Patrick. 'I have to go up and see them, anyway.'

'Was there anything interesting about the body?' Hippolyta asked, hoping that if she sounded matter-of-fact one of them would answer her without thinking about it. Patrick gave her a look that told her he knew what she was doing.

'No, there wasn't,' he said briefly. 'Head injury, and drowning.'

'Did someone deliberately leave him there to drown, or did they not realise they had not killed him outright?' asked Durris.

'Or were they interrupted?' asked Hippolyta, making a smug face at Patrick. 'It's not a very private spot.'

'There's only one window facing that way from the hotel,' said Durris, 'and it's upstairs.'

'That's Mr. Burns' room, and he's mostly bed-bound,' said Patrick. 'He has a servant, though.'

'But the shutters were already closed when we went out,' said Durris. 'I imagine Mr. Burns or his servant would have mentioned seeing a murder happening outside their window. I can't see that they're involved in this.'

'Probably not, no. I do need to see the Dewars,' said Patrick again.

'Very well: let's all go, and see if she's awake enough for questioning.'

'I'll put you outside the door if she isn't,' said Patrick firmly.

'Fair enough,' said Durris. Hippolyta thought he could try.

'Mrs. Napier, isn't it?' Mrs. Dewar, whose head was now propped on two pillows, put out a gracious hand to Hippolyta. Hippolyta took it at once, touched. 'My husband said you were nurse to dear Dr. Napier when he treated me. I cannot thank you enough!'

'It's thanks enough to see you with a better colour,' said Hippolyta sincerely. 'My husband says you are doing well, considering.'

'Thanks to him – to both of you,' said Mrs. Dewar. Even her voice sounded stronger. 'And do I see that I have another visitor?'

'A less comforting one, ma'am,' said Durris, coming forward. 'My name is Durris, and I am a sheriff's officer.'

'Good heavens!' said Mrs. Dewar wonderingly. 'Whatever's happened?'

Durris and Patrick exchanged looks.

'I'm not sure where to start,' Durris said, uncertain for once. 'A great deal has happened since the time of your collapse. I'm not sure what your husband might have told you.'

'He said,' she swallowed, looking down, 'he said that there had been an accident to Dr. Gilead, and that Dr. Gilead was dead.'

'That's right.' Durris glanced at Mr. Dewar. Mr. Dewar, who had been sitting by the bed, rose and walked across to the window, as if resigning his part in the conversation. 'Except – and I fear this may come as quite a shock, Mrs. Dewar – it was no accident. Dr. Gilead was murdered, and we do not yet know who murdered him.'

Mrs. Dewar gave a little gasp, and Patrick was instantly beside her, testing her pulse and temperature, reassuring her quietly. After a moment he nodded at Durris.

'I may as well tell you more,' said Durris. 'Peter Snark, Dr. Gilead's son, was for a time held in custody in connexion with the murder, but it seems now that he did not have the opportunity to do it, and he will be released shortly. We also know that Mrs. Pumpton and Mrs. Fettes did not commit the crime.'

'Women?' said Mrs. Dewar faintly. 'You cannot think –'

'Dr. Gilead was drugged with laudanum before being killed,' said Durris, 'so a woman could indeed have done it. He would not have struggled much.'

'Good heavens,' said Mrs. Dewar again. Her beautiful eyes were wide. 'You do not mention the Nickells, or Mr. Pumpton.'

'No: we are still considering them.'

'This is all very shocking!'

'I'm sorry: it is unfortunate that circumstances have dictated that you discover this all at once.'

Hippolyta looked back at Durris. It was hard to believe, when he said things like that, that this was the same man crouching to talk with Wullie in their servants' quarters that afternoon.

'Indeed. I sense there is more you have to say, Mr. Durris.'

'There is. This evening Mr. Nickell was himself found dead in the pool by the lower spring.'

Mr. Dewar spun round at the window.

'What?'

'Had you not heard? I thought perhaps one of the maids would have mentioned it, Mr. Dewar.'

'No! Was he murdered, too?'

'He was.'

'What kind of a place is this?' He pressed a hand over his face. 'I knew we should never have travelled away from Edinburgh again. I knew it.'

'I'm sorry, dear,' said Mrs. Dewar softly. 'I should have listened to you. You were quite right.'

He lunged back over to the bed and snatched her hand from Patrick, holding it close as he knelt by the bed. His face vanished into the sheets beside her.

'Now, Mrs. Dewar, that is the situation,' said Durris, not unkindly. 'You have been ill, and your husband Mr. Dewar has been very properly attentive to your needs, and it has not been appropriate to question either of you. Now, however, I'm afraid we have reached the point where we have to know what each of you knows.'

'I know nothing about Mr. Nickell's death, Mr. Durris!' Mrs. Dewar cried. 'I have not moved from this bed for a week!'

'Of course not, Mrs. Dewar,' he said calmly. 'We know that. But there may be other information you have – perhaps even without knowing it – that would be useful, vital even, in finding the person who has killed these two men. Or it may be more than one person,' he added, causing her eyebrows to rise even higher on her pale forehead.

'More than one person? This is indeed a terrible place.' She looked away for a moment, and released Hippolyta's hand to stroke her husband's thick hair softly. 'This is all very painful,' she said, eventually bringing her gaze back to meet Durris'. Patrick slipped towards her again, ready to be of succour, but she stilled him with a glance. 'I fear the pain that is mine here is of my own making, not the physical pain from my illness. The pain that is not mine ... I have also caused.' The white fingers rested on her husband's hair. He moved, looking up at her, his lips on her hand.

'There's no need,' he whispered. 'Please.'

'There is need,' she said clearly. 'This gentleman needs to know what was going on last Friday night – whatever the cost.'

Chapter Nineteen

They had to wait until Mr. Dewar had rearranged his wife's pillows and made her comfortable again. Patrick offered her more laudanum but she declined, even though Hippolyta could see the pain in her eyes when she moved. In Patrick's face she could read concern but also a little pride which was understandable: his patient was brave, and seemed to be, through his work, on the road to recovery. Hippolyta prayed that it was so, for all their sakes.

At last she was ready to speak: Mr. Dewar returned to his seat by the side of the bed and took her hand, and Hippolyta and Patrick perched near the end of the bed on either side, like nosy guardian angels, Hippolyta thought. Durris leaned against the wall nearby, where he could hear Mrs. Dewar even if her voice was not strong.

'I should say how all this started, I suppose,' Mrs. Dewar said with a smile. 'A little over a year ago I began to feel pains in my stomach and side. At first I was unconcerned, but eventually they grew quite bad and I consulted a doctor – in fact, several doctors, for they could not agree on what was the matter or what the right treatment should be. I grew more feeble and useless, and all this time my poor husband's business was growing very successful, and he had to spend so much time at his warehouse and with his customers, and I fear I must have been a worry and a distraction for him!'

Mr. Dewar murmured something, and she shook her head.

'No, I know it was unhelpful.' She smiled at him. 'He took me out to Pitkeathly to the spa there, for a rest cure. I'm not sure whether the waters did me any good or not: the bathing was certainly soothing. He had to go back to Edinburgh and leave me there. Then Dr. Gilead arrived.'

She stopped, uncertain how to go on just then. Mr. Dewar

offered her a sip of water, which she took.

'What can I say about Francis Gilead? I think he must have been some kind of wizard. He had an extraordinary effect on women, and he – I believe he very much enjoyed the effect he had.' She gave a little shiver. 'It was remarkable. Even sensible women swooned over him – Mrs. Fettes, if I may take her as an example, was as thrilled at his attentions as anyone, and yet she seems in all other respects a highly intelligent woman, to me.'

'She is,' Hippolyta agreed eagerly. 'I have never seen her like this.'

'She's not alone, if that is a consolation,' said Mrs. Dewar with a tiny breath of a laugh. 'He was magical. There was something in his eyes ... I had felt I was ill and fading and of no use or interest to my husband –'

'My dear, I am so sorry,' Mr. Dewar interrupted her. 'I should have done more ...'

'No, I won't have that, William. I take responsibility for this.' She shifted a little, easing her pain. 'I was flattered by Dr. Gilead. I knew he paid the same attention to every one of his woman patients – did he even have any men as his patients?'

'They just paid the bills,' muttered Mr. Dewar, and squeezed her hand.

'Indeed. But he had the women so entranced the men could do nothing but follow along. I saw all that, and yet I was still flattered. I still felt privilege when he took my hand or looked into my eyes – ridiculous, isn't it? Didn't you feel it, too?' she asked Hippolyta.

'No,' said Hippolyta honestly. 'I didn't like him at all. Nor did my sister.'

'That's true. Mrs. Milton was very resistant to his charms. Interesting ... but beside the point. Of course neither of you was his patient.'

'Maybe that was it: he didn't focus his charms on us.'

'Maybe.' She sighed. 'But then I realised that he was in fact singling me out for special attention. He begged me to meet him up here, knowing he was travelling up here from Peterhead. When I arrived – when we arrived – he asked me to run away with him.'

'In your condition of health?' Patrick was shocked.

'Strange, isn't it? But then, he thought his powders and balm were curing me, of course.'

'Did he really?' Patrick's tone was as angry as Hippolyta had heard it.

'He said the swelling was the poisons coming to the surface to be sweated out with the balm. I gather from what my husband tells me of your diagnosis that that was not the case.'

'Not remotely,' said Patrick. 'As far as I can gather, the man had no medical knowledge at all. He was simply lucky that for the most part the powders and balm he had concocted did no actual harm.'

'There are no tendrils in my stomach?'

'Absolutely not! Nor in anyone else's, unless they have eaten them!'

Mrs. Dewar gave a rueful smile.

'What we will believe when we want to ...'

Hippolyta admired her lack of bitterness. How much had she suffered unnecessarily from her tumour? Not to mention all that Mr. Dewar would have spent on the balm and powders that did no good at all.

'But did you agree to run away with him?' she asked, trying not to sound too eager to know.

Mrs. Dewar paused, then let out a long breath. Hippolyta could see that she was holding her husband's hand tightly.

'Yes. I did.'

'My dear,' said Mr. Dewar softly, 'there is no need ...'

'Yes, there is. I have to tell someone. And I owe these good people some explanation for my behaviour. Yes, I agreed at last, after he had asked and asked me. Even with his charms, I could see the hazards of such a venture. My life in Edinburgh, my family, my dear husband of course – all would be lost, and only Francis Gilead gained. Yet he seemed so sincere, so devoted ... I wonder now, now that I know how deceitful he was, how much he really meant it? Would I have been abandoned somewhere after he had tired of me? Yet at the time I trusted him with my life, my health, my whole person. I have been such a fool.'

'He was a very clever person, in that respect,' said Patrick. 'Whether he would have left you or not is another question. But you should not reproach yourself, for he seems to have been a very accomplished manipulator.'

'I wonder Mrs. Gilead could tolerate him at all.' She sighed.

'Well, he said we should leave during the ball, when everyone was busy and distracted. It seemed a sensible idea. We agreed to meet in the parlour at midnight – of course, it sounded more romantic than half-past eleven! He would slip in when it was empty, lock the door and wait for my knock. Then we would climb out through the window like a couple of young lovers and disappear down the hill and away before anyone realised we were gone.'

'And where then?' asked Durris, ever practical.

'I have no idea. For all I know he would have had me walking to Aberdeen through the night,' she laughed at herself. 'Then disillusion might have set in quickly enough! But he didn't tell me what was to happen after the first stages of the escape.'

Hippolyta and Patrick turned to meet Durris' eye. He was thoughtful, his notebook in his hand and his pencil poised.

'And how far did this go?' he asked.

'How far? Well, I had every intention that evening of going with him. After supper I said I needed to lie down for a little, so I went upstairs. In fact I really did want to lie down for half an hour or so: I felt very peculiar, dizzy and nauseous. I wondered if I had eaten something that had disagreed with me, and thought what unfortunate timing it was. I tried to pack a bag, but somehow nothing was making sense, and before I knew it it was time to go and meet him in the parlour. The bag seemed too complicated, and I abandoned it unpacked, and went out on to the landing. It was dark – it seemed darker than usual, and the walls were going around very briskly.' Her eyes widened at the memory. 'For some reason I could not find the head of the stairs. I stumbled along the landing until I reached the end of it, completely confused. I had no idea where I was. I remember trying to open a door, I think, but it seemed very tall and the handle was far above me. I must have fallen, of course, and I don't remember anything that happened after that with any clarity until I began to come round after your operation, Dr. Napier.'

'You don't think anyone attacked you that evening?' Durris asked, sounding as if it did not matter one way or the other. She blinked, surprised at the thought.

'I think I should have remembered something like that. I'm sure all I remember is feeling peculiar, then collapsing. I don't think there was anyone else around at all.' She frowned, and then her face cleared. 'Well, there mustn't have been, must there? Not until poor Mrs. Pumpton found me, or they would have fetched help.'

Well, maybe, thought Hippolyta. Unless it was someone who did not want to help.

'Thank you, Mrs. Dewar. Mr. Dewar, perhaps I could ask you for some account of your movements that evening, too?'

'You could ask,' said Mr. Dewar, his forehead wrinkled, 'but I'm not sure I remember much of it. I remember Susan saying she wanted to go and lie down, and that she didn't need any help from Gilead or me. Then I went outside for a little, perhaps ten minutes. I always try to take a walk after a heavy meal. Then presumably I came back in ... I remember talking to you, Dr. Napier, about what you thought of Gilead.'

'You did?' asked his wife. 'You had your doubts?'

'I always had my doubts, my dear, if nothing else because I saw the effect he had on you. And however much balm and powder you used, you never seemed any stronger or in any less pain.'

'My dear ...' She looked up at him intently. He kissed her forehead gently.

'I'm not sure what happened after that. I know at some stage – I don't know what time it was, though – I came up here, well, to our original room, to see if Susan needed anything. She wasn't there, and I began to look for her. I have to admit,' he said, 'that my first suspicion was that she was somewhere – that that man had led her away somewhere for some indiscretion. I am sorry, my dear.'

'But you were right! Or if you weren't actually right, then it was only because my silly health let me down. You were a far better judge of character than I.'

'Well. Anyway, I remember you offering to help, Mrs. Napier, and then we found the parlour door locked. I was convinced, somehow, that they were in there.'

'Again, your instincts are good, Mr. Dewar,' said Durris.

Dewar nodded wrily.

'Not that they've done me much good up to now.'

'When did you first know that Mrs. Dewar and Dr. Gilead planned to abscond?' Durris asked suddenly. Mr. Dewar blinked.

'When she told me – yesterday morning, I believe it was.'

'Not until then?'

'No. As I say, I had my suspicions, but there was nothing certain. I simply didn't trust the man. I didn't like the way he looked at Susan. It was as if he was lost.'

'My dear, I'm quite sure he wasn't,' said Mrs. Dewar. 'It was just another of his acts, and we both fell for it, in our different ways.'

'And were you near the parlour at any other time earlier in the evening?' Durris persisted.

'No, I wasn't. Well, you know, I walked past it a few times. No, wait: I tried the door earlier than the time I was with you, Mrs. Napier. It was closed … when would that have been?' He closed his eyes, rubbing his forehead with one hand. 'Do you know, if the hall clock there in the hotel is right it was a quarter before midnight! I remember: I thought to myself that Susan should really be in her bed and sleeping so late.'

'The clock keeps to time,' Durris told him. 'And was the door locked or not at that point?'

'It wasn't locked,' said Dewar definitely. 'I opened the door, and there was no one in there. I remember I glanced round and behind the door – that was odd, indeed. There's a shelf there, and it had a few tins of Gilead's damned balm on it. I remember glaring at it, as if that was going to help at all.' He scowled at himself. 'I wonder what that was doing there? He usually kept it locked away, so he could charge his three shillings a tin.'

Durris made one of his minuscule notes.

'Did you see anyone in particular near the parlour? Just outside in the passage, perhaps?'

Dewar thought, but shrugged.

'I was only looking for Susan, and possibly Gilead. I didn't notice anyone else, or if I did I don't remember.'

Durris observed him for a moment, then shifted position.

'Now, as to this evening,' he said. 'I gather you went down to dinner, sir?'

'I did. It's the first time I've done so since – since Susan's illness.'

'I told him he badly needed a change of society, or he ran the risk of becoming dull,' said Mrs. Dewar, with a little laugh. He smiled down at her.

'She did indeed! So I went down, but one of the maids, Gelis, came up to sit with her.'

'What did you do after dinner?' Durris asked calmly.

'Well, as usual I went out for a stroll – no, wait, do you mean straightaway? The ladies went into that little card room, the tiny one beyond the big parlour, and we took a very swift glass of brandy. Mr. Pumpton has never been much of a drinker, and Mr. Nickell seemed to have some plan, for he was twitching impatiently for us to be done. I wanted to see how Susan was doing, so we brought the ladies back to the parlour – there's not enough room in that wee card room for everyone, and then I think most of us went upstairs. Mrs. Gilead did, and the Pumptons, and I was last going up the stairs. The Nickells stayed downstairs, whatever they were up to. I came in here and saw that Susan was asleep, then made sure the maid was happy to wait a few minutes longer, then I went back downstairs for a quick breath of air.'

'Did you go down the main stairs or the servants' stairs?' asked Durris.

'The main stairs, of course! Why on earth would I go down the servants' stairs?'

'No particular reason,' said Durris. 'They would have been handier for you, though.'

'It never occurred to me. Where are they, then?'

'The door at the end of the passage,' said Durris.

'Are they? Well, I went down the main stairs. I was anxious about leaving Susan for too long, and I thought the maid wanted her dinner, so I stood at the main door and took my fresh air there, or maybe a pace or two outside.'

'Did you see anyone about?'

'I saw Mr. Nickell in the courtyard. He bade me good evening, and headed away towards the wells.'

'Anyone else?'

'No, no one that I can think of.'

'And upstairs, when you went up the first time or the second time, did you see anyone? Or hear anyone?'

'I heard Mrs. Pumpton,' said Mr. Dewar, with a hunted look. 'She was having a, well, a discussion with her husband in their room.'

'You heard him, too?'

'Well, no, not really. But I heard her quite clearly. She was telling him that they couldn't possibly go home yet, I think that was the gist of it.'

Another proof that Mrs. Pumpton was innocent, thought Hippolyta. She was safe, but what about her husband?

'So I came back here and the maid went off, and that was me until you came up to tell us the bad news.'

'Poor Mrs. Nickell,' said Mrs. Dewar. Her eyes were closing. 'To lose Dr. Gilead and now her husband: it is very sad indeed.'

'You need to rest, Mrs. Dewar,' said Patrick at once. 'Durris, are you finished for now?'

'I believe so.' Durris closed his notebook silently and pocketed it. Hippolyta slid off the bed and straightened her skirts. Patrick administered a little laudanum to Mrs. Dewar, and allowed Mr. Dewar to adjust her sheets and blankets softly over her. Durris bowed, and they left the Dewars alone in their room, a couple who had passed through a crisis and seemed the stronger for it, as far as Hippolyta could tell.

'We should go home now,' said Patrick when they were back downstairs. 'Mrs. Fettes might be growing anxious.'

'I want to go and make sure Gelis agrees with Mr. Dewar about his times this evening,' said Durris, 'but I've a feeling he's safe. So, again, is Mrs. Pumpton, who if she had been setting out to defend herself all evening, both evenings, could not have done better, I believe.'

'But we have made some progress, haven't we?' asked Hippolyta. 'All that about Mrs. Dewar meeting Dr. Gilead in the parlour at midnight, and the locked door. At least we know why he was there.'

'And that someone had planned it, for the tins of balm were already there,' added Durris, nodding.

'And that the door was not locked until after a quarter to midnight!' said Hippolyta. 'It's all coming together in one big picture!'

'Except for the identity of the murderer, of course,' said Durris. 'I did not ask her if the arrangements with Dr. Gilead were made in person or by letter.'

'Why should it make a difference?' asked Patrick.

'Well, anyone can write a letter!' said Hippolyta.

'Yes, indeed, Mrs. Napier: whereas an arrangement made in person could have been overheard, perhaps. It might indicate a particular direction.' He sighed. 'It's growing late. I'll talk to the maid and then try to sleep tonight. There's Martha.'

The woman from the village had popped her head out of the small parlour that was doubling as a dead room.

'Good evening to you, Mr. Durris,' she called across.

'Good evening, Martha. All well?'

'Aye, he's laid out and looking grand. No as handsome as that last yin you gave me to do, of course: he was a fine corpus, he was!'

'Good gracious, even after death Dr. Gilead casts his spells!' Hippolyta could not help it. Durris looked at her.

'Has Mrs. Nickell been down to see him?'

'I gather she's taken a sleeping draught of some kind,' said Martha, dismissing the widow as a weakling with one sniff. 'There's some canna take it, ken.'

'Have you been widowed, Martha?' Hippolyta asked, curious. Martha regarded her with one eyebrow raised.

'Aye, four times. Laid them out mysel' every time, an' all.' She let her gaze slide up and down Patrick, as though gauging him for a shroud too. Durris cleared his throat quickly.

'What about Mrs. Gilead? Did she help lay out her husband?'

'Aye, she did, an' all. Very nicely, too, though she kept greeting over the body and had to stop and wipe her eyes. But that happens, an' all,' she conceded, making generous allowance for a widow's grief. 'Onywyes, I suppose I'll have to sit with this one till she puts in an appearance.'

'I suppose so, Martha. Many thanks,' said Durris.

'Och, it's life, Mr. Durris,' she said with a shrug, and disappeared back into the parlour.

'I can't imagine Mother will be anxious,' Hippolyta remarked as she and Patrick climbed up from the shore of the river and into the village. 'Concerned that none of her attendants is around, perhaps.'

'That's a little ungenerous!' said Patrick. 'I'm sure she's

wondering where we are, if she's still up.'

'I still don't know why she and Galatea fell out,' Hippolyta complained. 'Neither of them will tell me anything: they think I'm still three years old, yet they bring all their arguments up here to our house. It's most provoking.'

'I admit it seems more peaceful now there is only one of them,' said Patrick. 'And of course it was fortuitous that Galatea left today, and could not be suspected of murdering Mr. Nickell.'

'Do you think a woman could have done it? Again?' Hippolyta asked.

'I see no reason why not. If a woman stood on one of the stone benches at the well, as they might well to keep their skirts from the water, they could easily have reached – or he could have been sitting down. The force was not particularly great, just enough to keep him unconscious while he drowned. Poor Hippolyta: I do give you too much information, don't I? The dangers of being a physician's wife!'

'You know I don't mind,' Hippolyta said seriously, squeezing his arm. 'Well, then, Mrs. Pumpton could not have done either murder. Mother is also free from suspicion in both cases, as is Mrs. Dewar. As I see it, we still have four suspects, with Galatea free as well: Mr. Dewar, Mrs. Gilead, Mrs. Nickell and Mr. Pumpton.'

'I don't see how Mr. Dewar could have killed Mr. Nickell,' said Patrick. 'Dr. Gilead, yes: he could have overheard his wife, or found Dr. Gilead's note, or even sent a fake one to each of them making the arrangement.'

'So why not Mr. Nickell?'

'Well, for one thing, why would he?'

'I was thinking about that,' said Hippolyta. They rounded the corner on the green, heading over towards their front gate. The village was quiet: it was late on Saturday night, and most respectable houses would be preparing for the Sabbath. 'Mr. Nickell said he was hoping to make back some of the money he had lost on all the cures. What if he knew who the murderer was, and was blackmailing them?'

'Or trying to, presumably,' said Patrick. He frowned. 'It makes sense: he threatens blackmail, or sends a note, perhaps, saying that he knows something incriminating, and arranges to meet the killer.'

'I don't think Mr. Nickell would ever imagine that the killer would get the better of him,' Hippolyta commented. 'He was very full of himself.'

'But they did: they didn't want the risk. Yes, it all fits.'

'You prefer that to Mrs. Pumpton's theory that Mr. Nickell killed Dr. Gilead and someone took their revenge?'

'I think so ... could Mr. Nickell have killed Dr. Gilead?'

He opened the front door and ushered her inside. The parlour and study were in darkness, though the candles were still lit in the hall: Mrs. Fettes must indeed have gone to bed.

'He was seen all over the place that evening, but I think he was just trying to keep an eye on his wife. He hardly seems to have had time to do anything major like murdering Dr. Gilead.'

'He did say the job was done, but I don't think that means he did it,' said Hippolyta thoughtfully. 'I think he was just happy it had happened. And I don't see how the money fits in if it isn't blackmail - or am I just too attached to my own brilliant idea?' she asked with a grin.

'It makes sense to me! So we're still stuck with Mr. Pumpton, Mrs. Gilead and Mrs. Nickell. Do you want to sit down for a little before we retire? A glass of wine, perhaps?'

'That sounds pleasant. There are no fires on, but the parlour is not chilly,' she said, opening the door. 'Well, not for me!'

'Ring for Mrs. Riach, then,' said Patrick, taking off his coat.

'No, I'll go and see who is up. If no one is still awake, I'm not going to bother waking them: I'll fetch the glasses and bottle myself.'

'All right, then.'

Hippolyta laid her cloak over the hall table and set her bonnet and gloves on top of it, then went to the door to the servants' quarters. The kitchen beyond was not quite in darkness: one candle still burned, and she found her way towards it quickly. She noticed in the light of it that the key was in the back door – odd, she thought. The door would usually be locked and the key hanging up if the servants had gone to bed. She had almost reached it to see if it was locked, when it opened in front of her and a figure almost knocked her over. She gave a little squeak of shock.

'What! Who's there!' said the figure. Pushing it away, Hippolyta whirled to the table and plucked up the candle. She turned to light the figure's face.

'What's happening?' called Patrick, appearing at the kitchen door in concern. 'Is everything – Mrs. Milton, what are you doing here?'

Chapter Twenty

'Well, that's a lovely welcome, I have to say,' said Galatea primly. 'I said I would come back, didn't I?'

'Well, yes,' Hippolyta admitted, 'but I wasn't expecting you to mean the same day. You can't have got very far!'

'Kincardine O'Neil,' said Galatea.

'And then what happened? Oh, the coach didn't crash, did it? Or tip over?'

'No, no. Everything was perfectly all right.'

'Then why did you come back?'

'I just thought perhaps I should,' she said, with an attempt at airiness that did not sit naturally with her.

'And how did you come back?' Hippolyta pressed on. 'There wasn't another coach due.'

'Does it matter?' asked Galatea. 'I'm back now.'

Hippolyta looked at Patrick. She hoped he was not thinking of holding her responsible for her sister. Or for her mother, for that matter.

'Well, you're back, and welcome,' he said, with remarkably good grace, considering. 'But what were you doing outside at this time of night?'

'Ah ...' Galatea's eyes wandered upwards, contemplating the ceiling. 'I wanted to make sure the hens were closed in for the night.'

'You did. The hens,' said Hippolyta, not sure she had heard correctly. 'You thought to check the hens.'

'Yes: I shouldn't be at all surprised, Hippolyta, but that housekeeper of yours is not to be trusted with valuable birds like those. She's completely –'

'Mrs. Milton,' said Patrick sharply, 'what is that in your hand,

239

may I ask?'

'Nothing.' Galatea, rather childishly, hid her hands in her cloak. Hippolyta stepped over to her.

'Show me, Galatea,' she said, automatically adopting her mother's tones. It worked again. Galatea drew out a small blue package, and showed it to them.

'That's from my dispensary!' said Patrick in disbelief. 'Have you been in my dispensary?'

'Oh, your dispensary, is it? A glorified medicine chest for a child to play in!'

'Galatea! How dare you be so rude!'

'Well, why not? You don't want me here any more than I want to be here. Why do I always have to be the grown-up responsible one? Why do I always have to help her? You got away, Poll, all the way up here, miles from Edinburgh: nobody cares what you do up here. You never have to take responsibility. What's this, you ask?' She waved the blue package at both of them in turn. 'It's headache powders. For Mother. While you two were out doing the Lord only knows what till this hour, she was in her bed with a sick headache and not a soul fit to tend to her. No wonder I had to come back! It's always my job. Even when I think I've got away, it's always my job.'

She sagged into a chair at the kitchen table, tossing the package to one side. Patrick discreetly picked it up, checked the contents and nodded at Hippolyta. It really was headache powders.

'Let me go and make up your bed, Galatea,' said Hippolyta, not unkindly. 'And I'll see how Mother is doing. Shall I take those?' Patrick handed them to her, meeting her eye. 'Will you find that wine, my dearest?' she added.

'Of course,' he said with feeling. Hippolyta wanted to hug him close: he was so proud of his dispensary, and now it had been assaulted in two ways at once.

Mrs. Fettes was sound asleep when she knocked gently and put her head around her mother's chamber door. She looked quite peaceful, and Hippolyta hurried back downstairs to find Patrick and Galatea seated in stony silence in the parlour, with a glass of wine each. As soon as Hippolyta came in, Galatea rose.

'I'll be off to bed, then,' she announced, as if defying them to applaud. 'I wish you a pleasant night.'

She paced out of the room. Hippolyta counted to ten, listening to her footsteps on the stairs, then shut the door and hurried over to Patrick.

'I'm so sorry! So sorry!'

He ran his arm around her waist.

'It's not your fault,' he said, hugging her.

'She just seems to be particularly horrible at the moment. Your dispensary! How could she?'

'That's what worries me,' he confessed. 'It's not all headache powders in there, as you know. There are lots of different drugs – including laudanum, of course, and other things which could perhaps induce confusion, dizziness, nausea … if applied cleverly.'

'Well, yes – wait, Patrick: what do you mean?'

'I mean –'

'That's how Mrs. Dewar said she felt on the evening of the ball!'

'Yes.'

Hippolyta sat down, and took a large mouthful of the wine Patrick had poured for her.

'You're suggesting that Galatea could have – what – found the laudanum here to drug Dr. Gilead and then killed him, but also drugged Mrs. Dewar? Why?'

'Perhaps to keep her out of the way while she killed Gilead? I don't know. I'm sorry, Hippolyta: I'm tired and I'm cross, and I had hoped that she had gone and that therefore not only did we have peace but also she was not going to cause you concern by being suspected of the murders. But now – well, we don't even know – what time did she return from Kincardine O'Neil, or wherever she was? Was she back in time to go and knock Mr. Nickell into the well? She doesn't look that pleased to be back, so why else might she be here?'

Hippolyta could not sleep for thinking about that.

Her best answer to it was that if Galatea had come back just to murder Mr. Nickell, why had she bothered returning to stay with them, when she so obviously did not want to be there? She could just have slipped away again as easily as she apparently came. But reason gave her a good explanation: Galatea might fear that she had been seen and recognised by someone, and what better excuse for being in Ballater but that she was visiting her sister again? Indeed, someone must have seen her coming back to Ballater, otherwise how on earth could she have returned, with all her luggage, too? Hippolyta devoutly wished she had not, but given that she had, she wished that Galatea would tell her a bit more, more of the how and why. To be kept at this level of ignorance by her own family was ridiculous: and now they would have to tell Mr. Durris that she was back, and she would have to answer to him. Hippolyta turned over again and tugged crossly at the sheets. Galatea, Mrs. Gilead, Mrs. Nickell, Mr. Pumpton. Maybe Mr. Dewar, whatever Patrick said. If Mr. Durris would hurry up and catch the right person, then Galatea would be proved innocent. What worried Hippolyta, though, was that it would take that now for her to believe that her sister was innocent.

In all the fuss they had forgotten to warn Galatea that there would be a visiting officiant for an Episcopalian service the next morning. Galatea stamped downstairs with her wrap over her gown to find the parlour transformed already into a worshipping space, and breakfast long gone. Mrs. Fettes was already seated in the front row, reading her Bible ostentatiously. Patrick was choosing hymns, while Hippolyta spread a clean white linen cloth over the hall table, brought in for the purpose.

'The servants are off to the kirk,' Hippolyta told her. 'If you want breakfast, it's in the kitchen.'

Muttering something about badly organised households, Galatea thumped away into the servants' quarters. Patrick felt on his watch chain without looking up: he had made sure the dispensary key was on his person today.

The congregation, starting to put on its summer numbers now that the visitors were increasing again, was already gathered and seated when the clergyman arrived in his usual haste.

'I have to go up to Pannanich Wells after the service,' he told Hippolyta briskly as he handed her a silver cross for the temporary Communion table. 'Apparently there was a murder there last night?'

'That's right, a Mr. Nickell.'

'I think that's the name, yes. An Englishman, anyway. Will there be people here who knew him?'

'Yes, indeed.'

'I'll bear it in mind. Well-liked, would you say?'

'Amiable enough, certainly. No one knows who killed him yet, but there was another death there last week. The minister did the funeral.'

'Oh, yes? So the situation is ... unusual?'

'Very much so.'

'I'll be discreet,' he said, with a nod. 'Anyway, I have to go up there later. Widow wants to talk about the funeral.'

'Then we won't keep you too long,' she said. 'Patrick has chosen some fairly short hymns, and we could always leave out a verse or two.' The thought would not please Patrick, but it would not surprise him, either: the clergy were always in a rush, with too many little congregations to visit too far apart.

'Splendid, splendid,' came the man's rich Oxford notes from within his crumpled surplice, and Hippolyta hurried off with the cross, placing it centrally and then stepping back to sit with her mother and Galatea at the front.

The clergyman and the Napiers were quite used to holding the service in the parlour now, though it had seemed strange at first. It took a little while to feel entirely at ease in the parlour again afterwards, they had found, but Patrick enjoyed playing the music for the hymns, canticles and psalms, and Hippolyta loved the way the raised voices seemed to make the room swell. She wondered if the Episcopalians of Deeside would ever have a chapel of their own, perhaps in Aboyne, and be able to worship in a normal fashion again – and how she would feel when they did. A little deprived, she thought to herself with a smile: it was rather pleasant to have church come to you, rather than to go to church, and it certainly made her feel important. Probably best if they built a church, then, before she grew too conceited.

When the clergyman had gone, and the congregation had helped themselves to a glass of negus against the chill spring air outside and drifted back to their homes or their lodgings, Hippolyta and Patrick chivvied the furniture back into place and sank with a sigh on to the sofa. Mrs. Fettes placed herself in an armchair and drank the tea Hippolyta had brought her: the servants were still at the kirk, where Mr. Douglas must have been giving them extra preaching for their time today. Galatea sulked at the table. Mrs.

Fettes had said nothing whatsoever in Hippolyta's hearing about Galatea's return, but she had a slightly more self-satisfied expression than usual.

'You were very late back last night,' she announced to Hippolyta, lightly adjusting her own scarf. Galatea scowled, but Hippolyta ignored her.

'Yes: I'm afraid there was an incident up at the Wells.'

'Poll has some great notion of investigating murders,' Mrs. Fettes commented to Galatea. 'That smart young man Mr. Durris seems quite capable of carrying out any investigations himself, and I suppose Patrick is competent on the medical side. Of course they have no need of Hippolyta trailing after them, getting in the way, no doubt.'

'We didn't ask last night, Galatea,' said Hippolyta, side-stepping the subject, 'but what time did you return to Ballater?'

'Time?' asked Galatea, as if she had never heard of such a concept. 'I have no idea. Dinner time?'

'We were here at dinner time,' said Patrick softly.

'Were you? Then a little later, perhaps.'

'What kind of incident?' asked Mrs. Fettes suddenly. 'Has Mr. Durris arrested poor Dr. Gilead's murderer?'

'No, Mother. Mr. Nickell was found dead.'

'Suicide?' asked Galatea, suddenly looking interested.

'No. Murder.' Patrick lent weight to the words, watching Galatea with care. Her eyes widened.

'Another one!'

'It may be revenge,' said Mrs. Fettes. 'Could Mr. Nickell have carried out the first dreadful murder?'

'It's a possibility,' said Patrick, 'or he may have been blackmailing the killer.'

'Not very successfully, then,' remarked Mrs. Fettes with a superior nod.

'No.'

'How did he die?' demanded Galatea. Her fingers, Hippolyta saw, were pressing down hard on the edge of the table, so that the knuckles were quite white.

'He was hit with a rock, and left for dead in the lower spring,' said Patrick clearly. 'He drowned.'

'Oh, dear me!' cried both Mrs. Fettes and Galatea. Hippolyta thought Galatea did truly look shocked – but what if she had hit his head and left him, not realising he might drown? That would be cause enough for shock, she thought. 'Even if it were revenge,' added Mrs. Fettes, 'that is a callous way to do it. Properly one should hand the man over to the authorities – your Mr. Durris, presumably – and let the law take its course.' She and Galatea were both married to advocates, after all: Hippolyta only wished her mother did not sound quite so much as if she had thought through the possibility of taking revenge, in some detail.

'Yet Mr. Durris has not arrested anyone yet?' Galatea asked, in a regrettable tone. The look she gave Hippolyta was sly.

'No. Some people have been eliminated from the list of subjects, though,' said Hippolyta triumphantly, and then wished she had not. 'Mother, for example, and Mrs. Pumpton,' she heard herself going on irresistibly.

'Oh, yes?' Mrs. Fettes looked satisfied, as well she might. 'And the Dewars?'

'Mrs. Dewar was not well, on both occasions,' said Patrick firmly. 'It would have killed her to rise and attack Mr. Nickell yesterday. I can vouch for that absolutely.'

Mrs. Fettes regarded him as if he were a pet dog that had suddenly shown some signs of having understood its training.

'And Peter Snark?' demanded Galatea.

'He is vouched for at the time of his father's death,' said Hippolyta, more carefully this time. 'And he was still locked up yesterday evening. I suppose he's locked up yet,' she added, without regret.

'Vouched for!' Galatea exclaimed, but did not challenge it. She had not asked about herself yet, Hippolyta noticed: what was she to make of that?

'Would anyone care for a stroll before dinner?' Patrick asked quickly. 'Hippolyta?'

'Oh, yes please! The weather seems to be holding fine.'

'Anyone else? Mrs. Fettes?'

'Not for me, thank you, Patrick. I was late to bed last night and early up this morning.'

As you always used to be, every day, thought Hippolyta. Was

she simply growing old? Even that did not seem to fit her mother.

'Mrs. Milton?'

'I'll come,' said Galatea unexpectedly. 'Too much sitting in coaches yesterday: makes my legs stiff.'

She strode out of the room straightaway to fetch her bonnet and tippet, and Patrick helped Hippolyta up from the sofa.

'We shouldn't be more than an hour,' he told Mrs. Fettes. 'We'll walk up towards Craigendarroch and back – does that sound all right, Hippolyta?'

'Yes, of course.'

'Very well,' said Mrs. Fettes. 'I'll make sure Mrs. Riach cooks when she gets back.'

'As if she wouldn't,' mumbled Hippolyta in the hall.

'Maybe we could train Wullie's dog to keep visitors out of the kitchen,' suggested Patrick.

'Or we could simply tell them that there's a dangerous dog in the kitchen. It would save the effort of the training,' said Hippolyta, grinning back at him.

'No, he needs at least to be taught to bark. No one seeing that dog would believe it to be dangerous, without some substantiation.'

'True.' Tam was unusually soft and fluffy-looking.

They set out into the trailing remnants of the kirk's congregation, dispersing to their homes in a cloud of sanctity and gossip. Hippolyta paused to talk to Mrs. Strachan and Mrs. Kynoch, but in truth almost everyone who saw them stopped to ask about the second murder, for they knew of Mrs. Fettes' connexion with the Wells and their visitors, and the Napiers' own links in Pannanich. Galatea rumbled along behind, forbidding any approach with her surly expression, though she glanced about her frequently enough as though she were expecting to see someone familiar – perhaps one of the visitors to the Wells, come down to the village for the service. Whoever it was, she seemed to have missed them, for she spoke to no one.

They strolled on up the gentle hill, past the shops, past the fine new house built by the Strachans as their family home, past the gateway to the grand but sombre Dinnet House, with the weighty mass of Craigendarroch at its back. The road grew rougher and the hedges more wild, full and noisy with nesting birds, while the crag above was smudged purple, bright green and grey with birch, bracken and bare rock in patches. Hippolyta regarded it with an artist's eye: she had painted it several times already in the last months, but each time she looked up at it she saw something different, a new colour or a sharp shadow or an angled sapling that caught her eye and made her want to paint it again. She had not painted the river since the flood: somehow she felt she did not know it yet, and often the memory of that awful night unnerved her. Soon, she thought, soon: before the new bridge is built, she would have to paint the bare expanse of it, perhaps with the little boat ploughing across the innocent-looking current.

'Haven't we gone far enough?' asked Galatea. 'There's hardly any road left.'

'This goes back round the crag to join the road to Braemar,' said Hippolyta, laughing a little at her sister's need for civilisation. 'We should take a trip there, if you both stay much longer.'

'Further into the wilds? I think not!' said Galatea flatly, and that was that.

By the time they returned to the village green, everyone from the kirk had gone home, and they headed straight for their cottage across from the church. Hippolyta called out as they entered the hall, and pushed the parlour door open, but it was empty except for a cat on the table, washing its face.

'She's probably changing,' said Galatea, and stamped up the stairs. In a moment she called over the banisters. 'She's not up here. Is she in the garden?'

Mrs. Riach had already appeared in the hall.

'Mrs. Fettes has gone out, ma'am,' she announced.

'Gone out? With whom?'

'With none but herself, so far as I know,' said Mrs. Riach self-righteously. 'A note came – one of the lads from the river said he bringed it fae the hotel. I took it in and she read it, then the next thing,' she went on, as if it had been a long series of unsettling events, 'she ups and says she's away out, and would I bring her a cloak and bonnet. Well, I did,' she conceded, 'and by the time I was back with them she had a note written for you. And here it is, ma'am.' She handed Hippolyta a small piece of paper, addressed to 'Poll'. Hippolyta bit her lip. She really hated that name.

Inside, there was only a short message:

'Note arrived from Mr. D. Gone to speak with him. Mother.'

'She's gone to meet Mr. Durris,' said Hippolyta. 'She doesn't say what Mr. Durris wanted to speak to her about.'

'He'll be up at the hotel. Why did she go on her own? She knew we would be back shortly,' said Patrick, a little anxious.

'She probably wanted to take charge of something or other,' said Hippolyta vaguely, staring at the note. 'I suppose we'd better go and see if she's all right.'

'I suppose so.' Patrick sighed. 'Mrs. Milton, do you want to come with us?'

'No,' said Galatea, 'I want my dinner.'

'Mrs. Riach, will that be all right? Mrs. Milton is hungry, but we want to wait till we come back with Mrs. Fettes, I think. She was tired, she shouldn't have chased off on her own like that.'

'She was gey thrawn,' said Mrs. Riach.

'She was what?' asked Galatea dangerously.

'Determined,' Hippolyta said quickly. 'Well, we know what she's like. She's maybe even turned back, though I doubt it. We'll go and catch her up, and see if we can bring her back. All right, Mrs. Riach?'

'Aye, I suppose.' Mrs. Riach gave Galatea a disgusted look, and curtseyed stiffly. Patrick caught Hippolyta's eye, and she shrugged. When Mrs. Riach's curtseys grew stiff, it was a bad sign for her mood.

Patrick and Hippolyta left the house again, and set out towards the street down to the river. As they approached it, though, a familiar figure appeared from the opposite direction, brushing down the front of his coat in a satisfied manner.

'Oh, no,' murmured Hippolyta. 'It's Peter Snark.'

She took a firmer grip of Patrick's arm, hoping that Peter Snark would perhaps be struck momentarily blind and not notice them, but alas, Heaven was not so generous.

'Good day to you, Mr. Napier. And Mrs. Napier,' he said, bowing and smiling his thin smile at the same time. They returned the greeting politely. 'You see me here a free man again!' he added. 'What a delight to walk your streets at liberty once more!'

'When were you fortunate enough to be released?' Patrick asked.

'Not fortunate, Mr. Napier, not fortunate. Clever, yes. Oh, Mr. Durris was very punctilious: almost looked me in the eye when he apologised for my improper imprisonment.' He pronounced the words with great clarity. 'He released me about an hour ago, Mr. Napier: I have to say I thought it an uncivil delay, waiting until this morning, but he explained that there had been some further tragedy up at the hotel. Mr. Nickell, I believe, has lost his life. A very sad loss,' he went on, though he did not even try to pretend that he meant it. 'I must go and er, console the grieving widow, I think. Mr. Durris allowed me the freedom of my cell to shave and make myself presentable, as you'll see, and gave me some fine broth and bread. I feel a new man!' He bowed again and was about to leave them, when a thought struck Hippolyta. Reluctantly she detained him.

'You say that Mr. Durris released you an hour ago? Has he returned to Pannanich, then?'

'I don't think so,' said Peter Snark, though he did not look as if he cared much.

'We'd better ask the boatman,' she said to Patrick. They walked a little apart from Mr. Snark down to the river, much to his amusement, and waited until he was securely in the boat. Then Patrick called out to the boatman.

'Have you taken Mr. Durris back across to Pannanich this afternoon?'

'The sheriff's man? He's hardly out ma boat these days. But no, I didna. Tell me, is this loon free again?' He jerked his chin at Peter Snark.

'He is, yes,' said Patrick.

'Aye, well. I thought to myself,' he said as he pushed off the bank, 'that yon one dying last evening was going to turn things tapsalteerie for Mr. Durris, aye.' Philosophically he set his oars, and took Peter Snark, scowling, back across the Dee.

'So where is he, then? She must have known where he was, or she wouldn't have gone after him, would she?' Hippolyta gazed back up into the village, as though Durris would appear instantly in the scene.

'Shall we start at the church? That's where we know he was last,' said Patrick. 'Maybe he has to clean out that unpleasant man's cell after him.'

'That's adding insult to injury,' said Hippolyta. 'I suppose we should look. Maybe the minister is there: he might have seen him.'

'The trouble is that everyone has gone home for their dinner,' said Patrick.

'So why has Mother gone out? It must have been urgent. Or at least seemed so to her.'

They walked quickly back up to the church, tried the door, and found the building empty. Back outside, they circumnavigated it, looking about them as well as ahead. When they reached the front again, unsuccessful, they met the minister, Mr. Douglas.

'I seen you wandering about,' he said amiably. 'Are you looking for something? Can I help?'

'We're looking for Mr. Durris, the sheriff's man,' Hippolyta explained. 'Have you seen him?'

'Not since the end of the service,' said Mr. Douglas. 'There hasna been another death, has there? Dear Lord, please no.'

'No, not since Mr. Nickell,' said Patrick quickly. 'So Durris was at the service? Then he must have gone to let Peter Snark out just after that.'

'Aye, that's what he said he was away to do. Did he no?'

'He did: we met Peter Snark on the hill. The cell door is locked again.'

'Och, I have the key to that,' said Mr. Douglas, and led them round the side of the church again. He drew a bunch of three or four keys from his pocket, and opened the outer door. Inside the candles had been extinguished: they peered into the darkness, called Durris' name, and Patrick felt around the floor of the outer room with his foot. He discovered by this method that the inner door of the cell stood open, so he repeated the exercise inside, touching the bed with his hands. It was bare, the blankets removed perhaps for washing: the cell was quite empty.

'Where on earth has he gone?'

'Oh, I let him out,' came a new voice at the door. They all turned abruptly. 'He'll be away back up to Pannanich, no doubt.'

'Mr. Durris!' cried Hippolyta. 'It's you we were seeking!'

They all emerged from the cell, breathing in the fresh air and blinking in the light. Mr. Douglas locked the outer door carefully and pocketed his keys.

'Why, what's happened?' asked Durris, concerned.

'Well, have you seen my mother?'

'No: should I have?'

'She went to meet you. You sent her that note, and she went out to meet you – somewhere.'

'Note? I sent Mrs. Fettes no note.'

'Then where has she gone?'

They all stared at one another in alarm. Then Hippolyta slapped her forehead in dismay.

'Mr. D! Not Mr. Durris – Mr. Dewar!'

Chapter Twenty-One

'I am such a fool!' moaned Hippolyta as they hurried back down towards the boat. 'I never even thought. I just assumed ...'

'To be fair, so did your mother,' said Patrick. 'She assumed you would know who she meant, that you would immediately conclude she meant Mr. Dewar, not Mr. Durris. And why on earth should Mr. Dewar be sending her notes, anyway?'

'Where's the boatman?' asked Durris suddenly. They had reached the end of the old bridge road. The usual boat was pulled up by the riverbank, well clear of the water, but regrettably on the other side of the river. The oars, they could see, were neatly laid along it, but the boatman by contrast was nowhere to be seen.

'Oh, for goodness' sake!' cried Hippolyta, bouncing with impatience, skirts swirling. 'Can you see any of the lads on the other side?'

'There's just the one, I think,' said Durris.

'He's asleep,' added Patrick. 'That's his foot sticking out from behind that wall.'

'I hope he is asleep, then,' said Durris suspiciously.

'Where does the boatman live? Does anyone know?' Hippolyta spun from side to side, trying within the restricted view of her bonnet to find someone who could help. In the end she marched up, Patrick following more slowly, to the inn, and found the innkeeper.

'Oh, aye, he come in here for his dinner a wee whiley ago,' the innkeeper remembered. 'He's away back across the water now, though.'

'Where's he gone? Do you know?'

'Oh, aye, he's away to see his aul mother. He always goes about this time on a Sunday, ken, for his passengers are at their dinner and he has no custom.'

'We're custom!' snapped Hippolyta, then at once regretted her impulsive manners. 'Oh, no, I'm sorry: it's not your fault. It's just – we need to get over to Pannanich quickly.'

The innkeeper sucked in her lower teeth thoughtfully, staring at the sky.

'There's no other boat here that could take you, not on the Sabbath, onywyes,' she concluded. 'But there's the wee ferry down the way, at Tullich.'

'Oh, yes: the wee ferry at Tullich.' Hippolyta turned to look at Patrick. He shrugged.

'It's a longish walk on this side, and a steep climb on the other. But we don't know when our boatman will be back.'

Durris appeared behind them.

'I think we should go to Tullich, Dr. Napier. I don't want to worry either of you at all, but I'm concerned at Mrs. Fettes going off on her own like that so suddenly. I take it she didn't leave the note she received?'

'Not that we saw,' said Hippolyta. 'Otherwise presumably we would have known she meant Mr. Dewar and not you.'

'Of course. Well, it's not getting any earlier,' said Durris philosophically. 'Shall we walk?'

'We could take the pony and cart,' suggested Hippolyta.

'We wouldn't be any faster, and we would have to wait for it to be harnessed,' Patrick objected. It was true: it could take quite some time on any given occasion for the pony to accept that it might make itself useful in any way. Hippolyta sighed, but nodded: Patrick and the pony had never really seen eye to eye. They thanked the innkeeper, Hippolyta patted the pony's nose, and they set off on the long straight road east towards Aberdeen.

At least the surface of the commutation road was smooth and easy for walking on, and they made good time over the mile and a half to the little settlement that was Tullich, with its ruined church and orderly graveyard around it. It was tending to dusk already, but she could easily see the reddish earth heaped over the newly cut grave of Dr. Francis Gilead. She wondered if his widow would put his real name on his headstone or only his professional one: in the dim evening light, too, she remembered all too clearly Mrs. Dewar's description of Dr. Gilead as magical, a wizard, someone who cast charms. Would he sleep easy here, with few to watch him? She had heard the locals tell stories of a wizard laird's grave somewhere in Aberdeenshire, where anyone who danced a hundred times around it on certain nights would be able to raise the wizard laird to return to his evil doings. She suppressed a panicky giggle: would Dr. Gilead return to try to sell his ghostly balms and powders to unsuspecting patients?

She glanced up across the river valley: already the lights were being lit at Pannanich Hotel, up on the hillside. She shivered, feeling the place watching over the valley – or not the place, for it had always been friendly enough, but whoever it was that had killed Dr. Gilead and Mr. Nickell. Were they watching now? Or were they contemplating another death, waiting for Hippolyta's mother to come up to the wells in answer to their summons?

The note might not even have been from Mr. Dewar at all, she thought: if the murderer had faked a note to bring Dr. Gilead to the parlour, then they could have faked one to bring Mrs. Fettes out of the safety of her son-in-law's house. But no: did that work at all? If the notes had been faked, then why had the murderer wanted to bring Mrs. Dewar into the parlour as well, since that would have meant trying to kill both of them at once or have a witness? She shook her head hard. She was growing fanciful and confused: it was best for now just to concentrate on crossing the river and finding her mother, and bringing her home safely.

They stood by the side of the road and strained to see the ferryman's hut in the darkness, but the ferryman must have noticed the dying of the light too and suddenly a flare of flame appeared, settling to a single tiny candle point. Patrick found the break in the wall and they scrambled along a flat, rough path between pastures, stumbling over half-seen rocks and tufts of grass, and clutching at each other for support. At last they reached the hut, taking the ferryman by surprise even with the noise they must have been making.

'Can you take us across to Pannanich, please?' asked Durris, pulling out some coins. The ferryman eyed them, not unfriendly, but he did not budge from his tiny creepy stool. Durris waited a moment, then tried again. 'We need to cross the river, please.'

'Fit's a'?' The man stared up at them, wide empty eyes shining in the lantern light, then he finally took in the quality of their clothing and rose slowly to his feet.

'We need to cross the river,' Durris repeated, more slowly and clearly.

'The river? Aye, aye.' He hesitated. 'All of yiz?'

'All of us, yes.' Durris nodded hard. The man looked Hippolyta up and down with blatant curiosity.

'The quinie an' all?'

'Yes.'

'Fit's a'?'

'Yes! The lady is coming too.'

'Michty me!' remarked the ferryman, shaking his head. After another pause a thought occurred to him. It seemed to be a novelty. 'An' is it the nicht yer wantin' to gae?'

'What? Yes, yes please. We want to go now.'

The man tutted at such urgency, making Hippolyta's feet dance with impatience. This was worse than having a boat and no boatman: they should have taken their chances back in Ballater. Patrick put a restraining hand on her arm.

'Would that be possible?' he asked the ferryman. The man was startled at a new voice in the conversation, and turned to stare at him before replying.

'Ah've never had so many all at once! I dinna ken that I can do it, see, not wi' so many. My wee boatie's only wee,' he explained.

Durris and Patrick exchanged looks. Hippolyta ground her teeth, and tried not to.

'Then could you take two of us, and then come back for the other one?' Durris asked.

'Fit's a'?'

'Could you take two people – could you take these two,' Durris pointed at Patrick and Hippolyta, 'and then come back for me?'

The ferryman considered, eyeing up the Napiers and perhaps assessing their combined volume and weight.

'Aye, aye, I could do that, right enough. Or I think I could, likely enough. It'll tak a wee whiley, mind!' He smiled genially, enjoying the conversation.

'Then perhaps we could make a start?'

'Fit's a'?'

'Can we start?' Durris' voice was just short of a shout: his patience was admirable, Hippolyta thought, but perhaps not useful.

'Oh, aye, aye!' said the ferryman, and lifting the lantern he squeezed past them at last to lead them down to the edge of the river. Even in the lantern light the boat did not inspire confidence. The oars were distinctly mismatched, and the gunwales looked as if something large had been chewing them. There are no kelpies around here, Hippolyta told herself sternly – but weren't those teeth marks?

The ferryman made a meal out of pushing the boat into the river, even helped by Durris, and Patrick handed Hippolyta aboard. The boat sank alarmingly, but steadied, and with a look of anxious alertness Patrick followed her in. The ferryman fiddled with ropes and oars for what seemed an eternity, but eventually he gave the boat a final feeble shove and scrambled damply into it, flailing the oars into position.

'Good luck,' came Durris' voice from the dusky shore.

'You, too!' Patrick called back, and they were off.

The boatman at Ballater was across the stream in a matter of minutes. This ferryman seemed to feel they needed to appreciate the full width of the river in three times the time: Hippolyta was overcome by the urge to jump out and swim across, sure it would be faster, even encumbered by skirts. At last they grounded sharply on a little rocky beach and clambered out. Patrick turned to push the boat off again, but the ferryman sat motionless for a moment, luminous in the lantern light, bobbing on the current as if he had forgotten what to do next. In a moment he would be carried down the stream and away.

'Can you fetch our friend across now?' Patrick shouted, and the ferryman began rowing with a sudden jerk, disappearing into the darkness across the river with his pool of light. Hippolyta and Patrick hugged one another close in the darkness, keeping warm, and after nearly half an hour the boat returned with Durris leaping to the shore before ever it had reached it. He solemnly paid the ferryman, who saluted and rowed slowly away.

'I like dry land,' Durris remarked after a moment, watching him vanish. 'I was not sure I was going to touch it again.'

'Perhaps we'll go home the other way,' suggested Patrick, and they all nodded.

'We should have offered to buy his lantern from him, though,' said Hippolyta as they tried to make out their path up the steep hillside to the hotel. 'Where on earth do we put our feet?'

'At least there are trees to hold on to,' said Patrick, as a branch broke loudly in his hands. 'Perhaps not that one, though. Give me your hand, Hippolyta.'

Slowly they dragged themselves and each other up through the birch and rowan trees, slipping and slithering back towards the lurking river every few steps. Hippolyta was heartily relieved to see the wall of the stables almost opposite the hotel looming above her, and to achieve the level of its cobbled yard. She stood and tried to bring her breathing back to normal as the others brushed leaves and mud from their trousers: she had no idea what her skirt looked like but she was sure it would not be accepted in an Edinburgh salon.

The hotel and bath house glowed with welcoming lights off to their left, and they took the last few steep steps up to the road and across to climb again to the hotel's front door. The hotel keeper, Black, greeted them with surprise, taking in their bedraggled appearance in one professional glance of shock and sympathy.

'An accident?' he murmured.

'We took the wrong ferry,' said Durris shortly. 'Has Mrs. Fettes been here this evening?'

'Mrs. Fettes? No, I don't believe so.'

'Where are the other guests?' Hippolyta had already glanced into the parlour, laid out as it was for dinner. Dinner appeared to be over, and the maid Christy was clearing the last of the dishes from the room. Hippolyta slumped on to a chair in the hall. What had her mother done now? She was so sure, she had convinced herself so firmly that they would find her mother here in the hotel – perhaps in some odd meeting or awkward situation, or perhaps not pleased to see them, but safe, nevertheless. What now?

'Let me think, ma'am,' said Black, watching Christy absently. 'Mr. and Mrs. Pumpton are in the card room: the ladies had gone in there while the gentlemen had their brandy, but it was only the Pumptons and Mr. Dewar and Mrs. Gilead this evening. And Mr. Snark's back, a' course.' He sighed sharply. 'I dinna think Mrs. Pumpton is finding the company yonder very entertaining. Mrs. Nickell is sitting with her husband's body in the small parlour.

Mrs. Dewar is of course still upstairs, as you'll no doubt know, Dr. Napier. The maid Gelis is sitting with her again. Mr. Dewar ... has he gone into the card room, too, or is he back up to sit with his wife? Nae doubt Gelis'll be down just now and tell us he's up there.'

Christy turned with a tray full of glasses and a look that anticipated more excitement.

'Please, ma'am, Mr. Dewar stepped outside not ten minutes ago for his after dinner walk, he said.' She curtseyed with the faintest of clatters from her tray. Black sucked in a breath, waiting for the crash of broken glass.

'Did you see which way he went, Christy?' asked Hippolyta. Durris and Patrick were already moving towards the door.

'I think he headed off that way, ma'am. Towards the wells,' she said, indicating as best she could with the tray in her hands.

'Thank you, Christy!' She hurried after the men, and caught up with them in the courtyard. 'Towards the wells,' she said.

'But ten minutes ago: that's time enough to move some way away. Has he lingered at the wells, or gone on down on to the road? Or into the woods?' asked Durris,

'We need a lantern,' said Patrick, taking half a step back towards the hotel door. Through the nearest window they could see the Pumptons seated silent in the card room, Mrs. Gilead facing them, the ladies picking at a little embroidery and the gentleman behind a newspaper slightly larger than he was. Conversation looked far from lively. She wondered where Peter Snark had gone.

'No, not yet,' said Hippolyta, a hand on his arm. 'I'm not sure we want him to know we're following, do we? Not until we know where Mother is.'

'Can you move quietly in that – thing?' Durris asked suddenly, waving at her skirts. She shrugged.

'I can try.' Her walking dress was soft gros de Naples and her petticoats were practical flannel: at least they would not slither and scrape. Fortunately her outfit was also warm: the night air was very chilly.

'Then let us see what we can find,' said Durris softly.

Silent, he led the way along the cobbled courtyard to the end of the hotel building, moving slowly enough to survey the area in front of them as best they could. The courtyard was deserted, the door to the bath house firmly closed. Away from the hotel's lighted windows, it was just possible to make out shapes and movements, and to see that the stone bench to either side of the lower spring was empty, as was the raised circle before it where they had found Mr. Nickell sprawled the previous evening. Behind them was the end of the bath house, in darkness now, and beyond that a set of shallow rough steps led down to the road, the black hulk of the stables they had passed earlier lying low on the other side. From where they stood they peered up the grassy hill to the little upper spring, but could see it quite clearly in the starlight, with no one obscuring it. The narrow stone steps to the upper spring were a dim path tucked into the dip of the grassy slope, near the hotel's end wall, but no one could have hidden there. Beyond the wells and their tended ground, the woods began, birch and rowan, light and airy in the day time but at this time of night an almost impenetrable darkness. They stopped and listened: the only sounds were the soft soughing of the wind in the tree tops, and beneath it the steady trickle of the water from both wells running down towards the bath house. Hippolyta looked up at the gable end wall of the hotel beside them. There was only the one window, at the front on the upper floor: Patrick's patient Mr. Burns had already had his shutters closed for the night. Though the hotel was busy and well lit, out here it seemed suddenly very lonely: Hippolyta would have sworn there was no living creature within twenty yards. Where had Mr. Dewar gone? Surely he would not have set off into the woods at this time of night: perhaps he had walked down to the road and towards Ballater, or had turned back along the road to return to the hotel from the other direction, to the east. She was on the point of suggesting it, peering down the road for any sign of him there, when she jumped. There was a figure, slipping across the road from the shadow of the stables and up into the woods on their side of the road. She tapped Patrick and pointed quickly. He nodded, and at the same moment Durris half-turned, pointing in the same direction.

'Only one thing,' Hippolyta breathed into Patrick's ear, 'it looked like a woman.'

'Your mother?' he mouthed back. She shrugged slowly. What would her mother be doing running around like that? But if it were not her mother, where was she?

They strained to see into the woods where she was likely to reappear, and almost at once Hippolyta caught sight of the pale shape of a skirt amongst the birches. She moved softly towards the woods: the figure was not hurrying, but stopping and starting, seeming to find it a difficult path between the trees, turning from side to side. Even stepping carefully it was easy to draw a little closer: Durris was clearly in no hurry to approach her directly, and Hippolyta knew he wanted to wait and see what she would do, first. But if it were her mother, and she met Mr. Dewar, and he were to be the murderer ... were they close enough to catch him, and save her?

'What's that?' whispered Patrick, snatching at both their arms. He was pointing down ahead and to their right, where the road was now beneath them. Another figure was just leaving the road, scrambling across the ditch and up into the trees, leaving the comparative light of the roadway for the darkness of the trees.

'Too fat for Dewar,' said Durris softly. 'What could be going on here?'

He slid away from Patrick's hand and on into the wood, after the pale skirted woman and the large man following her. In the middle distance, Hippolyta's strained senses picked up other noises, suddenly stilled: snuffling, like a badger – or perhaps a dog? – and maybe even something larger. Durris paid them no attention.

They had only made a few more awkward, angled paces between the trees, trying not to catch their feet in the low-lying blaeberries, when Durris put out an arm to stop them. He jerked his head forward, and they peered ahead.

The fat man had stopped behind a tree, too slim a trunk to hide him. He was visible to them but not immediately apparent to the woman he seemed to be watching. Beyond him, the woman had also tucked herself low down amongst the blaeberries, her skirt sprawled pale behind her, intent on something further on. What was she watching?

Ahead of her, as they focussed on a lighter clearing amongst the trees, was a third tall figure, a man by its clothing, standing still in the faint starlight. As far as Hippolyta could see, by contrast to the rest of them, there was very little tension about him: the impression he gave was of a gentleman pausing on his country ramble to admire the view. He was not completely still, shifting his feet a little, making no effort to keep silent. Was he waiting for someone? Or simply out to stretch his legs? She tried to judge whether or not it was likely to be Mr. Dewar: everything she could see fitted her recollections of him.

She was just wondering how long they would all stand there, half a dozen fools scattered about a wood by night, when the woman moved.

She stepped out into the clearing with an authority that Hippolyta recognised instantly, even if it had not been followed almost immediately by that voice.

'Sir, I accuse you -'

The challenge was broken off at once. The man in the clearing spun round to her, struck out at her face with extraordinary speed, and fled.

'Mother!' cried Hippolyta, but already the second man was running through the wood heavily, careless of noise, towards the fallen figure. Durris pushed past Hippolyta, rushing towards the fleeing man, then Patrick seized her hand and hauled her after him to where her mother lay in the clearing. The large man was down by her side.

'Leave her alone!' screamed Hippolyta. She was free of Patrick's hand and launching herself at the stranger in a second, beating his broad back with her fists. His hat fell off and he lurched, trying to twist away from her, while Patrick ran to Mrs. Fettes' other side and used leverage to shove him back off his balance. Hippolyta wound her arms around his neck and pulled at his throat. The stranger, gasping, over-balanced and as she whirled free, he sat with a grunt on the soft earth of the clearing, and Hippolyta flung herself down beside her mother.

'Is she all right?' she demanded at once. Patrick brushed upset hair back from Mrs. Fettes' face just as her eyes snapped open. She struggled to sit up, against Patrick's instructions.

'Let me catch him!' Mrs. Fettes hissed urgently.

'Who? Mr. Dewar? Or this man?' Hippolyta spun back to the stranger, but her gesture stopped even as her hand went out to him. 'Papa?'

'Hippolyta, dear,' said her father, plump and bewildered on the woodland floor, 'who taught you to fight like that?'

Chapter Twenty-Two

Patrick helped Mrs. Fettes back through the rustling night woodland to the hotel, though she leaned on him as though he were as lifeless and unfeeling as a walking stick. Mr. Fettes followed behind, watching her every step, and Hippolyta brought his hat, which he seemed to have forgotten in the confusion. There was no sign of Durris or Mr. Dewar, even as they stepped out of the concealing woods and passed the lower spring once again, into the secure embrace of the hotel and bath house buildings with the hotel's friendly lights shining out expectantly on them. Patrick guided Mrs. Fettes in through the hotel's front door, and Mr. Fettes and Hippolyta followed them into the main parlour and to a sofa by the fire. The Fetteses sat on the sofa, she straight and forward-facing, her bonnet somehow exactly in place despite the blow to her cheek; he was turned towards her, his hat and gloves abandoned on his lap, and Patrick pulled chairs over for himself and Hippolyta, so that the four of them could speak quietly together.

'Mrs. Fettes,' he began, 'I think you should probably go and lie down for a little. You've had a knock on the head, and that's always an unchancy thing.'

'Yes, yes, Patrick, I'll lie down when I'm ready to lie down. Be quiet.'

Patrick raised his eyebrows, but said nothing further. Hippolyta, insulted on his behalf, was still more concerned for her father's health. He looked fit and well as ever, now she could see him in the candlelight, plump and rosy, but older, perhaps, and worried.

'Papa, are you all right?'

'My dear?' He turned to her, puzzled, then tried to make light of the occasion. 'It was only a little walk through the woods!'

'I mean are you in good health? You are not ill, at all, are you?'

'Me? No! Not at all. If I look tired it is because the journey from Edinburgh was a long one.'

'Thank Heavens!' cried Hippolyta. 'Not the journey, I mean. But Mother – in that case, will you please, please tell me what is going on?'

'You mean you don't know either?' Mr. Fettes asked in surprise. 'I thought I was the last to know.'

Mrs. Fettes sighed sharply, and turned to Hippolyta.

'I have no idea what you think your father's health has to do with it,' she said. 'You always were fanciful, Poll.'

'Don't call her that, dear, you know she hates it,' said Mr. Fettes. His wife cast him a glance, but otherwise ignored him.

'And I have told you before that whatever Galatea and I might be doing here is none of your business, Poll. You –'

'I hear he's dead.'

Her jaw dropped. Clearly Mrs. Fettes was not used to her husband interrupting her.

'Wh – who is dead?'

'Your pet quack. The Gilead fellow.' Mr. Fettes nodded at her.

'How did you hear that?' Mrs. Fettes was shaken. Her hand went to her throat.

'I met Galatea,' said Mr. Fettes simply.

'But she – she didn't have time to get back to Edinburgh. She said she had turned about in Aboyne or Kincardine or some such.'

'She turned round when she happened to meet me coming in the opposite direction,' said Mr. Fettes coolly. 'She's not at all pleased with you either, you know.'

'But how – what were you doing coming here?' asked Mrs. Fettes. 'We didn't tell you …'

'No, you didn't tell me,' agreed Mr. Fettes. 'Left with the thinnest of notes, poor John Milton as much bewildered as I was and the children packed off to their aunt with scarcely a goodbye. I didn't know if you had gone to Bath or Brighton or Samarkand, until I saw a notice in the paper that Dr. Francis Gilead – or is it Snark? – was to be found holding court in the northern spa of Pannanich Wells. Then of course I realised where you had gone.

Have you no pride? To be following that mountebank about the country like that?'

He clearly intended to sound severe, but the hurt was like a bass note through his words, and in his eyes. Mrs. Fettes for once looked a little shamefaced.

'But why?' Hippolyta could not help asking. 'Why did you even consult him in the first place?'

Her mother looked across at her, and drew breath to speak, but at that moment there was a commotion at the door of the hotel. A man burst in, fell against the wall, and cried out:

'Help! Murder! Help!'

It was Mr. Dewar. The hotel keeper appeared at once, and Hippolyta sprang up to see what was going on. Patrick followed, as the door of the card room along the passage opened and Mrs Pumpton emerged with more speed than one would have thought either possible or wise.

'What is going on? Mr. Dewar, is it your wife?'

'No, no! Outside in the woods! Attacked, attacked! I fought back, and ran!' He sagged against the wall. The door of the smaller parlour opened and Mrs. Nickell, framed in black bombazine, peeked out in shock.

'Murder? Another one? Are we all to be killed, and my husband not even in his grave?'

The hotel keeper, who had momentarily vanished, reappeared with brandy and a tray of glasses, which he distributed liberally, knocking one back himself when everyone was served. He still jumped and spilled spirit from the bottle as the front door crashed open again, and Durris threw himself into the hall.

'Mr. Dewar!' he gasped. 'Would you mind explaining your behaviour just now?'

'My behaviour?' Dewar sagged on to a chair, eyes wide. 'I have been attacked and pursued through the woods! I thought I would be lost forever, murdered in some lonely spot and left for the wolves to devour! It was pure chance I found I had run in a circle, and tumbled down a precipice on to the road further along from the hotel here. I could hear my pursuer thundering after me, crying out most terribly! But I reached the safety of this place, and here I am, the Lord be praised!'

Durris had been staring at him through this speech, and at the end of it seized one of the glasses from Black and filled it full of brandy. He took a long, sustaining sip.

'Mr. Dewar,' he said gently. 'I was the person pursuing you through the woods. Would you like to meet your attacker?' He waved Dewar up from his chair, and guided him to the door of the parlour. 'See? Mrs. Fettes was the one who approached you in the wood. Mrs. Fettes was the one you punched – though I believe in genuine panic.'

'That's him!' Mrs. Fettes glanced at the doorway, and instantly leapt from her seat, pointing decisively. 'That's the murderer!'

Mrs. Pumpton shrieked, and her husband, Mrs. Gilead and Peter Snark, previously resistant to the goings-on in the hallway, emerged from the card room.

'What is it, dear?' asked Mr. Pumpton, eyes half-closed as if in self-defence. The shrieking was certainly an assault on the ears.

'Mrs. Fettes has declared Mr. Dewar the murderer! And he has not denied it!' she added, changing pitch with deep significance.

'Madam,' said Durris through the confusion, 'he has scarcely had a chance. Mrs. Fettes, I hear what you say: could we perhaps retire in here to the parlour and have a little privacy?' This was addressed without emphasis, and for a moment it seemed that Mrs. Pumpton would insist on being present at any interview in the parlour, but just then Mrs. Nickell had the decency to faint in the doorway of the little parlour. Torn between two dramas, Mrs. Pumpton opted for the one she could more easily involve herself in, and sank down beside her friend in a balloon of black satin. The hotel keeper discreetly emptied another glass of brandy, and went to call a maid. Durris pushed Dewar firmly into the parlour, waved Mrs. Fettes back into her seat, and closed the door.

'Now, then,' he said, leaning against the parlour table. 'I think there has been some misunderstanding here, and it would be best if it were all sorted out as quickly as possible.'

'I'm not sure …' said Mr. Fettes, looking about him.

'Father, may I present Mr. Durris, sheriff's officer? He has been investigating Dr. Gilead's death – and Mr. Nickell's. Oh, and I don't know if you have met Mr. Dewar? He's from Edinburgh, too.'

'Well, nearby,' said Mr. Dewar with a bow. 'Mr. Fettes, a

pleasure, sir.'

'Mr. Fettes?' said Durris. He pulled out his notebook and made a small mark in it. 'I understand from Mrs. Napier that you are an advocate, sir.'

'That is true,' said Mr. Fettes, a concerned look on his face. 'You're a sheriff's officer, eh? Interesting.'

Hippolyta could see on her father's face the usual confusion people seemed to feel when they met Durris. Where did he fit in? Below stairs or above?

'I'm honoured to make your acquaintance, sir,' Durris added with a bow. 'I only wish the circumstances were more favourable. Now, as to this evening,' he continued in a business-like fashion. 'Mrs. Fettes, I believe you received a note this afternoon.'

She eyed him, perhaps still trying to balance the dinner guest against the officer.

'I did.'

'From whom did you receive it?'

'The housekeeper brought it in,' said Mrs. Fettes. 'Poll, that woman has the most dissatisfied expression it has ever been my misfortune to observe on a servant's face. It borders on insolence.'

'Really, Mother?' Hippolyta tried for a tone that would not encourage her mother to digress: besides, she could only agree about Mrs. Riach.

'The note, Mrs. Fettes,' said Durris.

'The note was from Mr. Dewar.' Her lips closed tightly together, as if she felt she had said enough.

'Mr. Dewar, did you send a note to Mrs. Fettes today?' Durris asked.

'I did not,' said Dewar. He drew himself up in his chair, blinking in alarm. 'I believe I could truthfully say I have never sent a note to Mrs. Fettes in my life.'

'Yet a note was received. Did you send a note to anyone today, Mr. Dewar?'

'Yes,' said Mr. Dewar. 'I sent a note to Dr. Napier here.'

'To me?' Patrick was surprised to be involved. 'Is Mrs. Dewar all right? I hope the note was not urgent, for if it was it has miscarried.'

'No, no, the note did not concern my wife,' said Mr. Dewar, a little red in the face. 'It was really, I suppose, for you, Mr. Durris, only that I did not know how to address it, and I was sure that the servant would be able to find the doctor's house. A real doctor,' he added with unnecessary feeling.

'And what did the note say, then?' asked Durris. 'If it was intended for me, I think I have the right to enquire.'

'Of course, of course! It was that I remembered something I had seen last night. I had said there was no one in the courtyard when I stepped out for my very short walk, and then I remembered I had indeed seen someone.'

'Was this the note you saw, Mrs. Fettes?' asked Durris, without accusation.

'It – it may have been,' said Mrs. Fettes, not quite looking at him.

'Was it addressed to you, Mother, or to Patrick?' Hippolyta asked suddenly.

'I don't know,' said Mrs. Fettes defiantly. 'I scarcely looked.'

'You don't know? You are in someone else's house and you don't check to see to whom a note is addressed before you open it? Mother! Is that something you would forgive in me? Or in Galatea?'

'I don't know what you're talking about, Poll.'

'It could have been information from a patient! Private information!' Hippolyta was furious. 'Mother, how dare you!'

'Well, someone needs to take responsibility,' said Mrs. Fettes, judging, as usual, that attack was her best form of defence. 'Would you have realised the significance of that note? Of course not: you're both just sitting there now while that man makes excuses. It was obvious to me from the moment I opened it. He was only writing to you with some distraction because he's the killer. He murdered dear – ' she had the grace to glance at her husband and swallow that word, 'Dr. Gilead and then he killed Mr. Nickell last night. It's quite clear: he was jealous over his wife. Why doesn't anyone else see what is laid out so plain for you? That man is a murderer!'

'Mother! That is no excuse. If you thought that –'

'Mrs. Napier, please,' said Durris quietly. When she looked up at him, reproached, he softened the words with a slight smile. 'What were you doing, if you believed Mr. Dewar to be a murderer, coming up to the hotel and concealing yourself across the road at the stables, Mrs. Fettes?'

'Mr. Dewar always takes a walk after his dinner. I wanted to catch him on his own and accuse him of the murders.'

'What!' Hippolyta could not help herself.

'Mrs. Fettes, that was most unwise. Did it not occur to you that if you were correct in your assumptions, he might attack and kill you, too?'

'Don't be ridiculous: he wouldn't dare,' said Mrs. Fettes calmly. 'It's obvious he tricks his victims and traps them: look at how he must have lured dear – lured Dr. Gilead into the parlour and drugged him. I had the advantage over him because I had planned the meeting, and I knew what he was.'

'Yet he hit you and knocked you out,' put in Mr. Fettes mildly. 'If we had not been there he could easily have killed you, my dear.'

'He – ' But it seemed that in fact Mrs. Fettes had no answer to that. She touched her fingers to the reddening bruise across the side of her face. 'He attacked me,' she said eventually. 'That shows he's guilty, doesn't it?'

Mr. Dewar, though, was even more confused.

'Just a moment,' he said, finally working out some of what had happened, 'are you saying that I hit you? I didn't hit anyone! Except when the killer attacked me in the woods!'

'That's the point, Mr. Dewar,' said Durris patiently. 'We were watching Mrs. Fettes. Mrs. Fettes was following you, and then approached you apparently about to accuse you of being the killer. You, I believe, were taken by surprise and lashed out at the person approaching you, and ran. I, not sure who had done what, followed you – in a great circle up the hill above the hotel. The Napiers stayed with Mrs. Fettes and brought her back here before we returned. As to where Mr. Fettes comes into this, I am not sure: was there a reason for you to be following Mrs. Fettes through the woods without her knowledge, sir? When did you arrive in Ballater?'

'I came yesterday,' said Mr. Fettes, solemn, but with the least smile in his eyes. 'I was trying to find my wife and thought I had seen her slip into the woods here, so I followed, concerned for her safety.'

'What time did you arrive yesterday, if I might ask?'

'Around dinner time. They can tell you at the inn: I'm lodging there. I like your wee ferry boat at the river: very efficient!'

'The bridge was better,' murmured Hippolyta.

'Then this was all clearly a misunderstanding,' said Durris. 'Mrs. Fettes, please do not chase anyone alone into the woods in these dangerous times, whether you believe them to be a murderer or not. Mr. Dewar, no doubt you will be wanting to return to Mrs. Dewar. I assume you are heading back down to the village now, Dr. Napier?'

'That would be delightful,' said Patrick fervently, 'if I can just quickly see my patients,' he added to Hippolyta. She smiled.

'Of course. But don't be long, dearest!'

Patrick bowed to the Fetteses and headed for the door, intending to take Dewar with him. Mrs. Fettes' authoritative tones rang out again.

'Are you not arresting that man, Mr. Durris?'

'I'm not, Mrs. Fettes: offering information is not proof of guilt.' He sighed, and Hippolyta thought she could see why: if he did suspect Mr. Dewar, Mrs. Fettes' accusation without proof had not made his life any easier. Or it might just be that he had had enough for now of her family inveigling their way into his work.

'Mr. Dewar,' he said, turning as Dewar rose from his seat. Mrs. Fettes' face filled with stern anticipation. 'You still haven't told us. Who did you see last night?'

Mr. Dewar's expression grew self-important.

'Well, I couldn't say exactly who it was, but it was someone over at the well, just standing there, waiting. Only when I looked down that way, they pulled back into the shadows.'

'Did they, indeed? And this was as you were standing at the door?'

'That's right. I was no more than a couple of steps from the hotel door.'

'Well, it was quite a distance, I suppose, at that time of night. Still, a pity you could tell nothing about them.'

'Except that it was a woman, no,' said Mr. Dewar with a sigh.

'A woman?' Durris looked sharply at him. 'Are you sure?'

'Or a man in a skirt. Didn't I mention it? I'm quite sure it was a woman.'

Hippolyta's mind refused to work any more that night. They made their way down the hill to the boat almost in silence, Hippolyta arm in arm with Patrick, and her parents, also arms linked, ahead of them.

'Patients all well?' she asked him automatically.

'Yes, yes.' He touched her arm with his free hand, reassuring. 'Mrs. Dewar is doing splendidly. The loon with the leg is enjoying being served hand and foot in the nice warm kitchen by Gelis and Christy: he may take longer to recover.'

She grinned.

'I'm glad to see your father,' he went on in a lower voice.

'Yes, and well. Thank goodness,' she murmured back. He squeezed her arm.

'I hope the boatman is there. I'm not tramping back up to the hotel to slide down that hill and try to attract that old fellow's attention at this time of night.'

'The boatman's boat was this side. If he's not there,' said Hippolyta, 'let's steal it.'

'I agree.'

Fortunately, however, for their mutual reputation the boatman was dozing in the boat under a plaid when they found him.

'Aye, more of the family! That's grand,' he remarked, taking them across the water at a speed the ferryman at Tullich would have found terrifying. They were out and up on to the road in no time at all.

'Papa, will you come home with us for some supper?' Hippolyta said when she realised her father was heading for the inn.

'May I? I should love to!' he exclaimed. 'I have to say I was half-dreading going back to the inn just yet. There's a pony stabled in the yard there has already nipped me twice. Why are you laughing, Hippolyta?'

'Oh, Papa, it is lovely to see you!' They embraced in the middle of the road with enthusiasm. 'But if you need your coat to be mended after that pony has been at it, I fear the responsibility is mine.'

'Oh, Hippolyta: it is not another of your animal cases, is it?' Mr. Fettes sighed, and gave her his arm. 'Now, let me guess: your house will be the one brim full of dogs, cats, pigs and donkeys!'

'Not quite,' she said. 'Cats and hens, perhaps. And oh! Yes, there is a dog: though Mother brought that one in.'

'Surely not!' Mrs. Fettes looked sternly at her. Patrick offered her his arm.

'The dog came with the boy,' he explained.

'Oh, the boy,' said Mrs. Fettes. 'Yes, I meant to mention him.'

'Well, he has mentioned himself, and the dog, too,' Hippolyta called back to her. 'He has been in residence for a week, and proving himself quite useful!'

'Well, there you are, then,' said Mrs. Fettes, almost cheerfully. 'Something achieved.'

'I wonder where Galatea is?' said Patrick, poking his head into an empty parlour. 'I trust she has not chased off after receiving a note.'

'Someone else's note,' added Hippolyta darkly, but her mother had gone upstairs to change. 'Come in, Papa: the fire is lit, anyway.'

'What a lovely house!' said Mr. Fettes, settling down on the sofa and taking a cat on to his generous lap. 'I fancy I recognise a few things here! But they sit admirably well in their new home – as do you, my dear!'

'I'm very happy, Papa – all the more now you are here to visit, too! But I had better see Mrs. Riach about the supper: she'll have to be soothed about dinner, too, no doubt.' She exchanged a wary look with Patrick, and headed for the kitchen.

'Mrs. Riach, please forgive us for spoiling your dinner plans,' she began as she entered the kitchen. Mrs. Riach again had her feet up and the dog Tam on her lap: Ishbel was mending something and Wullie was nowhere to be seen. 'We were very anxious that my mother had met with the murderer up at Pannanich, but I'm pleased to say that she is back safely.'

'Oh, aye?' Mrs. Riach did not look quite so delighted at the news.

'And my father has arrived from Edinburgh. He is staying at the inn for now: I should not ask you to make up another bed this late except in an emergency,' she added, and even then she would be lucky, she thought. 'But if we could all have some supper now, that would be very welcome. We have had a trying afternoon.'

'Naebody else killt?' Mrs. Riach asked sarcastically.

'Nobody, thank goodness.'

'Well, I'll see fit I can find tae fling on to the table,' Mrs. Riach sighed, and set the dog carefully on to the floor by her feet before hauling herself out of the armchair.

'Where's Wullie?'

'At hame wi' his folks again. It's the Sabbath,' she added, in a voice that implied no end of ungodliness in this household. Hippolyta nodded, then thought of her other missing person.

'Oh, and have you seen Mrs. Milton at all?'

'Aye, she's out the back.'

'Is she, indeed?'

Galatea could not be seeing to the hens at this time of night. Anxious, Hippolyta went to find Patrick, who was playing the violin to an appreciative Mr. Fettes.

'A moment, please, Patrick,' she said, and he laid the instrument down at once, following her into the hall. 'Galatea has gone out into the garden again,' she said in a low voice. Patrick immediately patted his watch chain.

'I have the dispensary key,' he said. 'What could she be doing out there?'

'This time, let's take a lantern,' said Hippolyta firmly. They fetched one on their way through the servants' quarters, and slipped out of the back door. Cats slithered around them, pale shadows in the dark. Hippolyta led the way to the hen house, but there was no sound from it except contented murmurs from the hens within. All was locked securely. Patrick held the lantern high and looked about the garden from side to side.

'There's no sign of her,' he sighed. 'Could she have gone back into the house without Mrs. Riach noticing?'

'I suppose it's possible,' Hippolyta said, though she was not at all sure. 'Is there no other key to your dispensary?'

'There's a spare one in one of the presses where the linen is,' said Patrick. 'I'm sure she would never have looked there.'

'Oh, are you?' Hippolyta remembered very distinctly finding Galatea checking over her linen presses. She marched back up the path, leaving Patrick to follow with the lantern. She listened for a moment at the dispensary door, then tried the handle.

'Locked?' said Patrick. But the door opened. Inside, well lit by Patrick's best candles and working on something reddish at Patrick's workbench, was Galatea. She turned, mouth open, at their entrance.

'Leave me alone!' she cried.

Chapter Twenty-Three

'Galatea!'

She jumped, and dropped a tin on the floor. She took some time to pick it up.

'Mrs. Milton, I asked you not to come in here,' said Patrick, with what Hippolyta felt was remarkable restraint. 'If you needed something, like your headache powders, then you had only to ask. And if it is headache powders, and you need more than you had last night, I have to wonder if you are taking too many.'

'It's not headache powders,' said Galatea.

'Then what is the matter?' Patrick asked. 'What can I do for you?'

'You? You're hardly out of school,' said Galatea dismissively.

'I know you have had some considerable experience in helping with medical cases, Mrs. Milton,' said Patrick, diplomatically. 'But even if you wish to mix your own cures, please ask me first. There are substances in here that could be very dangerous.'

'Then you should label them better.'

Patrick took a deep breath. Something suddenly struck Hippolyta: her older sister, the grown-up, was acting like a sulky child. She decided to take advantage of the fact.

'Galatea, our parents are in the parlour. I'm going to tell Papa what you've been doing.'

Galatea's jaw dropped. Hippolyta turned on her heel and darted back into the house, knowing that Galatea would follow at once to make sure her side of the story was heard.

In the parlour, Mrs. Fettes had joined her husband on the sofa, and was even scratching the cat's head. Hippolyta skidded to a halt in front of them.

'Papa! Galatea's been in Patrick's drug dispensary again, and he specifically told her not to!'

Galatea was indeed just behind her.

'I was only mixing up some stuff,' she said defensively. 'I wasn't doing anything wrong.'

'She shouldn't have been in there! There are poisons and everything!'

Hippolyta wondered if she had overdone her childishness, but Galatea had her hands folded tight in front of her and her head low, while both parents looked stern. She decided to be quiet, if she could, and see what happened.

'Is this true, Galatea?' asked their father. It was not quite what they called his court room voice, but it was close. 'Have you been meddling with drugs in Patrick's business rooms?'

'Yes, Papa.' It came out as a reluctant confession.

'With poisons?'

'No, Papa!'

'But you know which the poisons are?'

'Of course.' Her head came up at that, proud. 'I do learn things when I help Mother with her charities, you know.'

'Galatea! You are becoming very ill-mannered,' said her mother, and no court room voice was necessary. Both daughters felt their spines tighten in reaction.

'I understand that Mr. Gilead –'

'Dr. Gilead,' Mrs. Fettes corrected automatically, then blushed, waving her husband on.

'He was poisoned, from what I understand.'

Hippolyta opened her mouth to explain the niceties of Dr. Gilead's death, then closed it again in silence. There was no need to go into detail, when the bald statement was more likely to draw information from Galatea.

'I had nothing to do with that!'

'You were pleased enough to see him dead!' her mother objected. 'The glee in your face was indecent!'

'Well, I was pleased he was gone,' Galatea admitted. 'That's true enough. Gone to where he could do no more damage, with his stupid cures.'

'They're not stupid,' said Mrs. Fettes at once. 'No more than he was. He was a great physician, and if I'm alive now it's because of his knowledge and skill.'

Hippolyta tried not to look at her. She still could not afford to interrupt at this stage.

'No, you're not, Mother.' Galatea drew in a long breath and blew out sharply, as if bracing herself for something. 'You haven't even been using his stupid cures for the last week and a half.'

'Yes, I have,' objected Mrs. Fettes. 'The packets and tins are upstairs, and I've been taking the powders and using the balm just as usual.'

'No, you haven't.' Galatea blew out again. Hippolyta had glimpsed a street fight once, set up for bets, in a pend near the lawcourts in Edinburgh. In her artist's eye she could still picture one of the fighters, pausing while his opponent readied himself, the same focus in his eyes, the same quick, controlled breaths. She felt a chill across her back. 'Since we came here,' said Galatea with unnatural steadiness, 'and I had access to Patrick's dispensary, I have been making the powders and the balm you've been using.'

'What?' Mrs. Fettes went white. Her hand moved to her throat, as if she was unaware of it.

'I've been making the powders and the balm,' Galatea repeated. She straightened her shoulders. 'I did it first of all because I thought if you had another source, some other way of getting the cures you needed, then you wouldn't have to follow that – follow Dr. Gilead around the country any more. Do you know how foolish you look?' But rather than accusatory, Galatea's voice was anguished. 'I've always admired and respected you, Mother – in fact I have been proud of you, and all that you do, your energy and your intelligence. But in the last months it was as if you had lost your judgement with your energy. I know you've been worried,' her voice softened. 'Frightened, even. But to follow Dr. Gilead like – like a maenad dancing after Bacchus –' Hippolyta met Patrick's look and their eyes widened at the extraordinary image. 'It was shameful. And the money you've spent!'

'But how did you know how to make it?' Mr. Fettes asked. Hippolyta thought there was a hint of approval in his voice.

'Well,' said Galatea, 'you could tell it had mint in it, and hot peppers. Then I saw a bill that Mrs. Gilead left on the table one day – she snatched it back as soon as she saw it was there, but I don't think she knew I had seen it – and that had some other bits and pieces on it. She's the one who makes up the medicines, you know, Mother, not Gilead. She's the brains in the whole business. Gilead was just the shop window, the salesman, the one all the ladies fell for,' she added bitterly. 'I don't know what she'll do without him now, the little mouse.'

'So you made up the recipe as best you could,' Mr. Fettes brought her back to her own account. 'And filled your mother's tins and packets with it?'

'The first time, yes,' said Galatea. 'Then it occurred to me: if I could prove to you, Mother, that his cures had done you no good, then perhaps I could break you from him altogether. I could change the ingredients so that the things in the balm and the powders were completely useless, wait for you not to notice, and then tell you that you had been thoroughly tricked.' She broke off. To Hippolyta's astonishment, she was sobbing.

'And you were not tempted to remove Dr. Gilead entirely from this performance?' asked Mr. Fettes.

'Tempted, yes,' Galatea admitted, digging for her handkerchief. 'Oh, I was tempted! But no, I could not do such a thing. And anyway, I think I knew that killing Dr. Gilead without any other action would only elevate him to the position of saint and martyr in Mother's eyes. I want her to see, to understand completely, what an utter fraud he was. Mother, there was nothing in that balm but hot peppers, mint and chalk, and nothing in the powders but red dye, soda and salt. Yet you noticed no decline, did you? No advance in your – in your disease?'

Hippolyta's heart was beating so hard she was sure everyone could hear it. What disease? Mrs. Fettes was staring across the room at nothing, though her hand was unconsciously at her throat again. She swallowed hard, wincing.

'No,' she said at last. 'I noticed no difference at all.'

Hippolyta could bear it no longer. She flung herself down on her knees between her parents.

'Please, Mother, what disease? What is wrong with you?'

Mrs. Fettes looked down at her distantly.

'I have a cancer of the throat,' she said, with uncharacteristic gentleness. 'Dr. Gilead –he said it would kill me, very soon, if I did not take the powders and apply the balm every day, the powders for the inside of the throat, the balm to reduce the swelling in the glands outside.'

She tugged the scarf she had been wearing around her neck. Her glands did look swollen, as if her throat was sore. Hippolyta had never seen her look so helpless, so afraid.

Patrick, who had been standing in silence near the door, cleared his throat.

'Mrs. Fettes, would you mind if I examined you?'

Mrs. Fettes glanced up at him dubiously. Her husband laid a hand on his arm.

'You've been ready to believe a charlatan with, I suspect, not a medical qualification to his name. Why not try listening to someone who has actually passed his examinations?'

Mrs. Fettes gazed at him, then looked up at Patrick. At last she nodded.

'Very well.'

Patrick stepped forward at once.

'Hippolyta, will you bring that candle over and hold it where I can see into Mrs. Fettes' mouth? Thank you.' He touched Mrs. Fettes' throat, gently pressing on her thick glands, then touched her chin and asked her to open her mouth wide. He peered in, moving his head a little from side to side to see every angle. Then he stood back, and considered for a moment.

'I think I may be able to help,' he said diffidently. 'Will you permit a small operation?'

'An operation! But Dr. Gilead said such a thing would not be advisable!' cried Mrs. Fettes.

'I don't think Dr. Gilead, ah, knew enough to risk any kind of operation,' said Patrick. 'I assure you, this will be painless and should take a matter of seconds.'

Mrs. Fettes still looked dubious, but Patrick was more confident in his actions. He slipped out of the parlour and returned in a few minutes with a box of medical instruments and a glass of something cloudy. He handed the glass to Mr. Fettes.

'Would you mind holding that, sir?'

'What's in it?' Galatea asked, whose interest in drugs was clear.

'Lemon juice and water,' said Patrick, opening his polished wooden box on the table. He drew out one long, slim blade, and examined it in the candlelight. 'You feel pain when you're eating, don't you?' he asked. Mrs. Fettes nodded. 'And a sharp pain sometimes afterwards? Difficulty in swallowing?' She nodded again, her eyes nervous. 'Mrs. Milton, could I ask you to come and stand behind Mrs. Fettes and hold her head? It's just a matter of keeping it steady: you've always struck me as quite strong enough to nurse,' he added, without emphasis. Hippolyta contained a smile. 'Hippolyta, you need to hold the candle just there,' he moved her wrist. 'Mrs. Fettes, lie back, please, so that your head is against the back of the sofa. It's very important that you don't move in the least. Mrs. Milton, a hand each side, please, and brace yourself on the back of the sofa so you don't move either. Mr. Fettes, sir, just stay still – or if you feel you might not be able to, could you leave the sofa now, please, before we start?'

'I'll stay,' said Mr. Fettes, taking his wife's hand. 'If there's pain, my dear, just squeeze me hard.'

'There shouldn't be,' said Patrick. 'Now, is everyone ready? Open your mouth, please, Mrs. Fettes.'

She was a brave woman: there was not the least tremble in her jaw even as Patrick leaned over and inserted the long, thin blade into her mouth. She did not even close her eyes, watching his every move as best she could. The blade slipped down to the back of the throat, and there were a few little cutting motions, almost imperceptible to anyone watching. Patrick withdrew the blade carefully and moved Hippolyta's hand again to light up what he had done. He inserted the blade once again, shifted it slightly, then pulled it clear, peering in again and then nodding in satisfaction.

'Please sit up, Mrs. Fettes. Mr. Fettes, the lemon juice, please. Mrs. Fettes, drink this down.'

She took the glass, eyes wide, and swallowed the cloudy mixture, blinking. When it was finished, she swallowed several times more, her hand to her throat.

'It's … it feels odd, but I believe it has gone!'

'Is that how a cancer is removed?' Galatea asked with interest.

'No! Not at all,' said Patrick with a laugh. 'But it wasn't a cancer: it was a large salivary calculus. I don't know that I have ever seen or read of one so large: no wonder it was uncomfortable! Now that it is gone, your glands should go down again in a day or two: you could try cold compresses to help that, if you wish. For now, more lemon juice until the discomfort diminishes, and then in a little while perhaps a nice cup of tea.'

Eyes still wide, Mrs. Fettes was swallowing experimentally. Hippolyta ran to the kitchen to fetch more lemons and a jug of water. When she returned, her parents were embracing, and Patrick was wiping his blade with a clean cloth.

'Will it recur?' asked Galatea. 'What might have caused it?'

'We don't really know,' Patrick admitted, 'but it's not likely to come back. It's quite rare.' He suddenly looked tired.

'I'll ring for tea now, I think,' said Hippolyta, immensely proud of him. 'Then I think it may finally be time to retire for the night.'

'May I stay, Hippolyta?' asked her father. 'I know the inn is not far, but it seems so just at present.'

'Of course, Father!' How pleasant it was to have a guest who did not treat the house as their own, she thought. Wullie could run to the inn for his night things, and they would all be together at last. As to the question of who had murdered Dr. Gilead and Mr. Nickell, for tonight she did not care. Her father was well, her mother was cured, and Galatea was happy, and Patrick, her lovely Patrick, was the hero of the hour.

The next morning, the feeling of familial bonhomie continued: Galatea came out into the garden to keep Hippolyta company as she fed the hens, but said nothing about servants or linen. Instead she asked friendly questions about Patrick's practice and dispensing: she certainly seemed well informed on the subject of medicine. Mr. and Mrs. Fettes came down to breakfast much restored to their former selves, and if in Mrs. Fettes' case this still meant a rather distant and stern affection, at least it was familiar. Dr. Gilead was not mentioned, though Mr. Fettes still expressed an interest in seeing the Wells properly in daylight and sampling the water as a local point of interest, rather than as an addition to Dr. Gilead's infallible cures.

'The country around here is very fine,' he remarked, 'and the views are delightful. I do not wonder at anyone settling happily here, never mind a young doctor with an eye to a good and prosperous practice. Well done, Patrick: you and Hippolyta seem to have found an ideal spot.'

'Thank you, sir,' said Patrick with a grin. 'Hippolyta has made a study of some of the best views – you must see her paintings.'

'I look forward to it!'

'I don't know that they are very good,' said Hippolyta, 'but I must find something to do while he is off attending to his patients! And there we are,' she added with a knowing look as they heard the front door risp rattling. 'The first summons of the morning.'

She smiled at Patrick as they listened to Ishbel padding along the hall to answer the door. A familiar voice murmured something, then the front door closed again and Ishbel opened the parlour door. Patrick and Hippolyta were already turning in their seats to greet their visitor.

'Mr. Durris! Will you join us for breakfast?' asked Hippolyta. Mr. Durris bowed to the company, noting Mr. Fettes' presence.

'I apologise for my intrusion, Mrs. Napier,' he said, 'Mrs. Fettes, Mrs. Milton, good day to you. I had no thought of interrupting your breakfast.'

'Sit and take a cup of tea at least,' Patrick urged him, making room at the table. Durris sat and accepted a cup, sipping it with apparent satisfaction. 'Are you just down from Pannanich?'

'I spent the night in the village,' Durris explained, 'for I wanted to make sure I caught the post this morning. And I was pleased enough, I confess, to be away from the hotel for a night.'

'I can imagine,' said Mrs. Fettes. 'It must be a strain at present.'

'But I must go up there as soon as possible this morning,' said Durris, nodding to her. 'I have received a message from Mrs. Nickell: she has something to tell me, and obviously cannot leave her husband's corpse to come down here. I wondered if you would care to accompany me, Dr. Napier? And the invitation includes Mrs. Napier, if you are coming, Doctor.'

'What business is it of Hippolyta's, Mr. Durris?' Galatea asked, though with less hostility than she would have done the day before.

'Mrs. Napier has proved herself very observant in the past,' said Durris blandly. 'And when a man questions a woman, there are often finer points he misses. Of course she will be in no danger, and Dr. Napier will no doubt be present at all times.'

Mr. Fettes nodded slowly, eyeing Hippolyta with some curiosity. Mrs. Fettes looked uncharacteristically proud of her youngest daughter, though she said nothing. Hippolyta was quite sure that in the same place, her mother would be in the midst of any investigation, and probably telling Mr. Durris how to proceed.

The boatman saw the six of them approaching half an hour later, with a look of satisfaction on his face.

'That'll be the twa boat loads, Mr. Durris,' he said. 'Has there been another murder?'

'Not that I'm aware of,' said Durris.

'Aye, well. I dinna ken that murders are very good for the hotel yonder, but I'd have to say they're affa good for my business.' He settled the Napiers and Mr. Durris into the boat and set off, turning efficiently at the opposite bank to fetch the Fetteses and Mrs. Milton while the lads roused themselves to see if there was anything in it for them. Patrick gave his medical bag to the middle-sized boy whose turn it was, and when they were all assembled they headed once more up the hill. Mr. Fettes breathed the fine air in deeply, and gazed appreciatively about at the pale birch woods with their purple clouds of young branches, the hulk of Craigendarroch down behind them, a token of more distant and greater hills to the west with peaks where the snows still lingered, the river winding below them, wrinkled like an overwashed silk ribbon laid along the green valley. The morning was clear and bright, the sun in their eyes when the woods allowed it, and Mrs. Fettes strode out as if the very air was a tonic, her strength already returning after her first hearty breakfast for months.

The hotel had a subdued air, even on this fine morning, which was not to be wondered at, with one funeral done and another corpse waiting. The hotel keeper, wearily, met them at the door with a welcoming smile that was more automatic than heartfelt, but he agreed to send an attendant along to the wells so that Mr. Fettes could try the waters. Mrs. Fettes and Galatea went with him, leaving the Napiers and Durris to ask if Mrs. Nickell was watching over her husband's body or resting. The hotel keeper rubbed his forehead and thought for a moment, then nodded.

'Aye, she's back in there. She come out for a wee bittie but I think she's away back in again. She sent a note down the hill to you, did you get it, Mr. Durris?'

'That's why we're here,' said Durris.

'She's no ill, is she?' asked Black, frowning at Patrick.

'I don't think so,' said Patrick, reassuringly. 'But I'll pop up to see Mrs. Dewar and your man in the kitchen later.'

'Aye, aye, grand.' The hotel keeper rubbed his forehead again, nodded, and disappeared into the kitchen quarters.

'He could do with a rest after all this,' Hippolyta remarked, and they went over to the door of the small parlour where Mr. Nickell's body was still laid. Durris knocked gently on the door, and they were bidden to enter.

Mrs. Nickell and Martha, from the village, were sitting in silence near the fireplace, which was cold and empty. Mr. Nickell lay on a table which had been covered with a dark cloth, with a sheet shrouding him up to his neck. One hand lay outside the sheet, and the three visitors politely touched the hand before turning to Mrs. Nickell.

'Martha, if you want to go and eat something,' Mrs. Nickell said without looking at her. Martha neatly packed up a stocking she was knitting, curtseyed in the general direction of Durris and the Napiers, and left the room, closing the door behind her. Mrs. Nickell was pale and tired looking, unsurprisingly, but there was anxiety there, too, in her eyes. Presumably she was keen to find out who had killed her husband.

'Mrs. Nickell, you wanted to see me,' said Durris, after waiting for her to speak. She glanced at him, and then looked over at her husband.

'Yes, I did.' She stopped again.

'Can I help at all?'

She sighed.

'Look, I made a mistake, all right?'

'A mistake? What kind of mistake?' Durris looked calm: Hippolyta was not. Was Mrs. Napier about to confess to something? She looked as if some terrible information was on the tip of her tongue. If the female figure Mr. Dewar said he had seen on the night of Mr. Nickell's death was not Galatea, then who was it? Though of course, Mrs. Nickell had admitted to being with Peter Snark at the time of his father's death. Her mind, after a night's rest, was flinging itself back into the mystery. What was Mrs. Nickell going to say?

'I was mistaken about Mr. Snark. I wasn't with him that night.

I saw him when I was outside with my husband, that's all. Briefly.'

'You weren't with Peter Snark at all?'

'No. I was with my husband the whole time.'

She would not raise her gaze. It was so obviously a lie, Hippolyta thought: she herself had seen Mrs. Nickell come in from outside while Mr. Nickell was inside, at the hotel entrance. Of course that was no proof that she had been with Peter Snark, but why was she trying now, now that her husband was dead anyway, to establish that she had been with him all along? She did not even look as if she expected them to believe her. Hippolyta sat suddenly in the chair beside her where Martha had been, and reached out for her hand. Mrs. Nickell let her have it in surprise: a tear trickled down her bony cheek.

'Mrs. Nickell, has anyone tried to make you tell us this?' Hippolyta asked. Mrs. Nickell turned to her, shocked, her mouth open. Then she shook her head vigorously.

'No, no, not ever. Why would anybody do that?' The tears suddenly flowed faster. 'Dear Dr. Gilead – and now my poor Jack! Who will protect me, Mrs. Nailor? What shall I do now?' She bent over with all the grace of a painter's easel folding, and heaved great sobs into her lap. Hippolyta laid a soothing hand gently on her thin back, but looked up at Mr. Durris and Patrick. Why had Mrs. Nickell brought them up here to tell them such an obvious lie?

Chapter Twenty-Four

It was clear they all felt uneasy about Mrs. Nickell's story. Hippolyta patted her back and rose eventually, stepping over to the window to think. Patrick and Mr. Durris stayed by the fireside with Mrs. Nickell, whose sobs were beginning to ease. Hippolyta gazed out absently. The view from the parlour was not inspiring: it faced the back of the building, and the hillside along which the hotel and the bath house below it had been built rose steeply behind it. While the bath house was arranged on a single floor on the upper side, with an additional floor below on the road, or lower side, the hotel's rear elevation was two storeys high, but this meant there was only a narrow path outside the window between the hotel's wall and the grassy slope behind. As the servants' wing faced the front of the hotel, this path was evidently little used: it was mossy and damp and not worn. Hippolyta put a hand to the window frame to open it and look further along the back of the building, but her gloved fingers slipped a little as if the frame were greasy. She glanced down at her right glove. It was marked with some pale substance across the dark blue leather. She sniffed. It was unmistakably Dr. Gilead's cordial balm.

'Mrs. Nickell, have you opened this window at all?' she asked. Mrs. Nickell looked blankly at her.

'Why should I do that? It's cold enough in here,' she complained, clearly baffled. Durris stepped over to see what she had seen and she showed him her glove. His eyebrows rose.

'Well, Mrs. Nickell,' he said, 'if you are sure of your memory now – that you did not spend any significant time away from your husband and with Peter Snark on the night of the ball – then I thank you. We should leave you to your grief,' he added compassionately.

When they had left the little parlour, with Mrs. Nickell and her husband's body within, Hippolyta rang for Martha to come back and keep the widow company. It did not seem wise to leave her alone, but they needed to talk. The main parlour across the passage was empty, and they moved into it quickly, making sure no one else was about.

'Do you believe her?' Hippolyta asked at once.

'I don't,' said Durris.

'It seems so unlikely,' Patrick agreed. 'After all, she denied it at first, when her husband was alive, then as soon as she knew her husband was dead and presumably would not be angry with her, she admitted what we thought was the truth, the story that Peter Snark had already given us, that the two of them were together.'

'She looked so frightened,' said Hippolyta. 'This time, I mean, just now.'

'Yet she denies being pushed into this story,' said Durris, lifting his hands in bewilderment. 'And who would push her? The person most likely to push around here seems to me to be Peter Snark, yet what would he gain from it? He would lose the only witness who was able to substantiate his innocence. His alibi,' he added, giving it the professional term. Hippolyta nodded knowledgeably: there were advantages to having an advocate as a father.

'Well, who else would try to push her? Let's think,' she said. 'Mrs. Pumpton can be frightening, but what would she do it for? She has alibis for both murders – unless she simply wants to incriminate Peter Snark.'

'Mr. Pumpton does not look frightening,' said Patrick, 'and Mrs. Dewar is not in a position to threaten her at present. Mr. Dewar?'

'In order to incriminate Mrs. Nickell, perhaps?' suggested Durris. 'After all, he's the one who says he saw a woman walk along to the wells the night Mr. Nickell was killed.'

'But he doesn't seem very threatening – unless he's trying to protect himself. He was the last person to see Mr. Nickell alive, I suppose, apart from the murderer, and unless he is the murderer.'

'He certainly has a strong motive.' Durris walked over to the window, and looked out at the courtyard.

'But all she would have to do, if Mr. Dewar frightened her into saying she was with Mr. Nickell, is to go back to Peter Snark,' said Hippolyta. 'He wouldn't let her go that easily, surely.'

'Mrs. Napier found some of Dr. Gilead's balm on the window frame in there,' Durris said to Patrick, nodding back across the passage. 'We didn't look at the window at all, did we?'

'No: do you think the murderer climbed out, with balm still on his hands?'

'That's my thought. And it would make sense: we've already said what a risk he would have taken, first going into the parlour in the crowd, and then being seen to come out and lock the door. The key was in the porter's little cupboard, but there's no reason why it could not have been put back there.'

'Yet I still find it difficult to believe that Dewar left Nickell for dead, and calmly climbed back upstairs to sit with his wife,' said Patrick. 'I've spent a good deal of time with him this past week, and he has never struck me as having that kind of nerve. Look how he ran when he thought your mother had attacked him,' he said to Hippolyta. She smiled at the memory.

'Yes, he is more of a silly coward than a calculating killer, I think,' she said. 'Why don't we go and ask Peter Snark?'

'Do you think he'll simply admit to bullying Mrs. Nickell?' Patrick asked.

'Maybe not, but at least we can see whether or not he agrees with her new story, or even knew she had changed it.'

'A very good point,' agreed Durris, and Hippolyta tried not to look too superior. 'I wonder where he is at the moment?'

He rang for information. Hippolyta wished she could ask for tea and shortbread, too: it was just long enough since breakfast, but she felt that Durris would not approve of such weakness when there were people to be interviewed, so she made herself think of other things. She wondered if her parents and Galatea were still paddling at the lower spring.

Christy appeared, thrilled to see them.

'Is something exciting happening?' she demanded immediately.

'Christy, dear!' exclaimed Hippolyta, managing to stifle a laugh.

'We'd like to know where Mr. Snark is,' Durris explained.

Christy's nose wrinkled as if someone had pulled a string from the tip to her forehead.

'He's in the card room taking waters. His mother's there an' all.'

'Thank you, Christy,' said Durris.

'Why don't you like him, Christy?' Hippolyta asked.

'He's just no very nice, ma'am. I dinna like the way he looks at you, as if he kens all about you and he thinks it's funny.'

'Nothing more than that?' asked Durris mildly.

'No, sir.' Christy curtseyed and left the parlour.

'I know what she means,' said Hippolyta with a shiver. 'Oh, if only he didn't have an alibi! He's a horrible man: he really ought to be a murderer.'

'Well, I'd better go and see him, nevertheless. Would you rather stay here?' Durris asked. Hippolyta seriously considered the suggestion for a moment. Then curiosity overcame her.

'No, I have to go, or he'll have won. Horrid creature!'

'The card room it is, then.'

Durris led the way back down the passage to the room where Hippolyta had seen, through the window, the Pumptons and Mrs. Gilead sitting just before they followed Mr. Dewar into the woods last night. Where had Peter Snark been then, she wondered: it had not occurred to her at the time, so used was she to his being locked up. Then she remembered the dog in the woods, the one she was sure she had heard. Had Peter Snark been watching them as they followed each other through the woods? Watching as if he kenned all about them and thought it was funny? She shivered again.

The little card room was warm by contrast to the small parlour where Mrs. Nickell had been sitting: without the worry of a dead body to keep chill, the fire was lit and cheerful, and the window was sunny. Mrs. Gilead in stiff black was sewing something in an upright chair at the window: the cloth and thread were also black, presumably parts of extra mourning clothes. Peter Snark was by the fire with last week's paper, reading parts aloud to his mother: he would have been locked up when it came out from Aberdeen, and Durris probably did not provide newspapers to his prisoners. Snark slid unctuously to his feet when he saw them enter the room, and bowed, with that sly look in his eye that Hippolyta – and

Christy – hated so much. Mrs. Gilead looked over with a more welcoming expression, though it was hardly a smile.

'Mrs. Napier, gentlemen: good day to you. I trust Mrs. Fettes and Mrs. Milton are well, Mrs. Napier: I saw them go past the window a little while ago. Have they gone to the wells?'

'I believe so, Mrs. Gilead. They are quite well, thank you.' She did not add that her mother was recovering splendidly from the ill effects of Mrs. Gilead's husband's misdiagnosis: it might not have been Mrs. Gilead's fault if Dr. Gilead was imaginative in his analyses.

'I believe the wells are very effective,' agreed Mrs. Gilead, 'particularly the lower spring. Peter is taking some now to counteract the strain of spending several days locked away, aren't you, dear?'

Peter Snark waved a large glass in their direction. From the smell, he took his waters in some brandy.

'I don't like that metal taste,' he said, with a conspiratorial smile. 'Do you, Mrs. Napier?'

'It seems fine to me,' she said without looking at him. 'Very refreshing.'

'It's about you being locked away that I've come to see you,' said Durris. 'I'm afraid I have no other news just yet.'

'What about it?' asked Peter. 'Have you come to apologise?'

'Now, now, Peter,' said his mother firmly. 'As I understand it, Mr. Durris, Peter misled you about his movements on the night – the night when my husband was murdered.' She spoke clearly, though with a slight quaver in her voice.

'He was initially reluctant to tell us the name of a witness who could vouch for his whereabouts at the relevant time, yes,' said Durris mildly. Snark smiled at him, and took another long draught of the healing waters. The smell of brandy was strong: the man must have a head of iron, Hippolyta thought.

'As a matter of fact I've been meaning to speak to you about that,' Snark said, still smiling. 'I might have misremembered. It was a very confusing evening, you must agree, and of course I was suffering the effects of a terrible shock. It's not every day your father gets murdered, is it?' He drank again.

'You mean you didn't spend all that time outside the hotel with Mrs. Nickell?' Durris asked, as if mildly surprised. Snark laughed.

'Ah, no. I was mistaken.'

'You mean it was a different lady you were idling with? Mr. Snark, you need to be more careful of a lady's reputation – besides that it can hardly be flattering to discover that the gentleman who has spent time with you cannot distinguish you from some other female.'

'Well, no,' said Snark, 'the thing is, I must have spent some time with Mrs. Nickell on some other evening, and confused the two. She's a charming lady, you know, very, ah, entertaining.' His smirk almost drove Hippolyta to slap him on its own. 'But on the evening of my father's death, I was in fact more usefully employed, helping my mother to look for my father. She was quite naturally anxious that he might be dallying with a certain lady patient, as I'm sure you know. No doubt her husband has told you all about it. I cannot imagine that he was pleased at being cuckolded, can you?' He paused to drink deeply again. 'It seems pretty clear to me where you should be looking for your murderer, Mr. Durris. I wonder that you have not arrested him already.' Was it wishful thinking, Hippolyta wondered, or could she hear him start to slur his words?

'Be careful, Peter,' said his mother. 'You do not want to make accusations where you are not sure. Mr. Dewar may be perfectly innocent. I'm sorry, Mr. Durris,' she added. 'As my son says, we have been under a great strain this last week, and while I know you cannot rush such things – well, I should imagine not, for it is the first time I have known such events – I shall be very grateful when someone is finally found guilty of my husband's death. But not the wrong person,' she added primly. 'That would be very short sighted, to wish for just any conviction.'

'Indeed. Did you spend much of the evening with your son, Mrs. Gilead?'

'Only after supper, as he says, when we were looking for my husband. Not every moment, either,' she clarified precisely, 'for now and again we would go our separate ways to check two different places at once, and then meet again, but we would only have been apart a matter of minutes each time.'

'This question only follows on an idle thought, Mrs. Gilead, so do not read too much into it, but can you think of any reason why

Mrs. Nickell might have wanted to kill your husband?'

'Mrs. Nickell?' Mrs. Gilead looked incredulous. 'I cannot think why she should. Unless she was jealous of his affection for Mrs. Dewar, but she seemed too attached to my husband ever to do him harm. So many of his patients grew very attached to Francis, you know, Mr. Durris.'

'Did that bother you at all, Mrs. Gilead?'

She laughed.

'No, no! They might have been devoted to him, but he stayed with me. Didn't he, Peter?'

'What's that?' Peter Snark looked round in surprise: he seemed to have been off in a dream.

'Oh, Peter! You have taken too much brandy with your water again! Here,' she said, and for the first time Hippolyta noticed that the white terrier was in the room, cowed behind a chair, 'take the dog out for a walk, would you, and clear your head? The waters will do you no good that way!' Smiling, she handed him a lead, and he bent unsteadily to try to attach it to the dog's collar. 'I'm sorry, Mr. Durris: he does like his brandy, and he doesn't like the water!' She shrugged fondly. 'I think I'll go and have a little lie down, if you'll excuse me.'

Durris bowed and gestured to the Napiers: there was nothing more to be achieved here for now. They left the card room with its cosy fire, and returned to the main parlour, but by now a couple of visitors to the wells had appeared to take some tea. There was no privacy, and they retreated to the courtyard, on the way nodding to Mrs. Gilead who was climbing the stairs to her room.

'I'd say it was Peter Snark who pushed Mrs. Nickell, wouldn't you?' asked Hippolyta as soon as they were clear. 'What a smug, self-satisfied, odious man!'

'A smug, self-satisfied, odious drunkard just at the moment,' Patrick remarked, watching Peter Snark emerge from the front door of the hotel. He lurched against the door frame, tugging back suddenly on the terrier's lead, and then walked with the concentration and speed of the nicely overdone, towards the wells. They waited until he was well clear of them before going on with their discussion.

'But why did he deprive himself of his alibi?'

'He didn't: he just changed it,' said Durris. 'He's deprived

Mrs. Nickell of hers, though.'

'And given his mother one, or a more solid one, in the process,' agreed Patrick.

'Now why would he suddenly think it was necessary to do that?' asked Hippolyta.

'Because he thinks she needs it?' suggested Durris.

'Because she does need it?' countered Hippolyta.

'That brandy was very strong,' said Patrick, squinting down the courtyard after Peter Snark and the terrier. They were out of sight already.

'You think he was pretending to be drunk?' asked Durris, looking the same way.

'No ... it certainly smelled strong enough to have that effect on him,' said Patrick, still staring down the courtyard thoughtfully. 'I just wonder if there was a reason for its strength.'

'What reason could there be? Except that he didn't want to taste the chalybeate waters.'

'Or someone else did not want him to taste something else,' said Patrick.

'What are you talking about, dearest?' asked Hippolyta. He turned back to her.

'Remember the smell around Dr. Gilead?

'The balm? Yes.'

'No, not just the balm. Remember? To make him easier to suffocate, he had been drugged with laudanum, probably in a glass of that extraordinary punch they were serving.'

'Brandy ... you think someone has tried to drug Peter Snark? But why?' she asked.

'For the same reason!' said Durris suddenly. 'To make him easier to kill!'

'We need to find him,' snapped Patrick, and all three spun towards the wells.

Mr. and Mrs. Fettes and Galatea were still seated on the little half-circular seat, paddling their feet in the water.

'This is so refreshing, Hippolyta!' her father called. 'Won't you join us?'

'Not just now, Papa,' she panted. 'Did Peter Snark come past here?'

'He did,' said Galatea, 'surly creature. He didn't even say

good morning.'

'I think he was drunk,' said Mrs. Fettes disapprovingly.

'Drugged, I thought,' said Galatea with a frown. She looked up quickly at Patrick.

'Which way did he go?' Hippolyta interrupted.

'Oh, into the woods. He looked down the path to the road, but he went up into the woods,' said Galatea. 'With that little white terrier.'

'Thank you!' called Durris, and the three of them hurried on, waving conciliatory farewells as they went.

The woods were much easier to negotiate in daylight. They scrambled along the side of the hill, pausing now and again to listen. The ever present breeze hustled the tops of the birch trees, teasing them with almost-noises on the ground below. Then something stopped Durris: he put up a hand for stillness and silence, and waited. Then he dropped down to the ground, and inched forward. Patrick and Hippolyta, less used to such activity, followed cautiously, Hippolyta irritably hampered by her gown. Durris reached a hand back to them, signalling them to stop once more – then he pointed ahead.

In a clearing, perhaps the same one where Mrs. Fettes had staged her attack on Mr. Dewar, Peter Snark stook facing half away from them, arms dangling by his sides, shoulders slumped. He seemed on the point of collapse. The dog was nowhere to be seen.

Then, just as Hippolyta was about to whisper something to Durris, a suggestion for tackling him, she saw another movement between the trees. Mrs. Gilead stepped forward into the clearing, one hand out to her son, the other tucked into her skirts. She walked slowly, a bright smile on her face.

'Peter, dear, are you quite well?' she asked, reaching him. She took him by the arm. 'Here, you had better sit down. You're sleepy: you need a rest.'

He sat easily enough on the ground, with a bit of a bump: he was taller than she, and she brought him down a little awkwardly. She sat behind him, in an island of her black skirts, cradling his head on her bosom. He seemed three-quarters asleep, unresisting, sagging against her.

'I've lost the dog,' he mumbled, sounding cross and defensive at the same time.

'That's all right: don't worry about him. No doubt he'll make his own way back to the hotel,' she said. She spoke softly, but the wind carried her words easily over to where they lay. Fortunately the sound did not travel the other way, for when they saw what she brought out from the folds of her skirts, Hippolyta gasped. It was a large knife.

She recognised it as the one they had found in Mrs. Gilead's room, the one she had presumably used for cutting up herbs for her cures – the cures sold under her husband's fake name. Why did she have it here? Hippolyta felt she was being very stupid, feeling her way slowly through the mystery as though through tangled embroidery silks in a basket. But there was no time to wonder, for Mrs. Gilead had lifted the knife, and laid it across her son's thick throat. She drew a deep breath, and her arm jerked – but no blood flowed.

Hippolyta blinked.

Mrs. Gilead tried again, but again she stopped at the last moment. She sighed, letting her knife arm drop a little.

'I can't do it,' she murmured. 'I was afraid of that. Oh, why did you have to go and change your story, Peter? It was only then that I realised you knew. Up till then I thought you and that silly woman had been off enjoying yourselves and no harm done, but then you had to go and change your story, you stupid boy. What better to bring Mr. Durris asking questions? You should have kept your mouth shut!' For a moment she was angry, then she looked down at him again. The knife angled away, she stroked his rough hair, and kissed his head. Peter snored unattractively, and she smiled. 'Was it when you found the stuff all over your gloves? Was that what made you realise?' Alone like this with her son, her London accent was stronger, tinny, quite distinct.

'I just couldn't take it, Peter: you know that. All those silly patients, silly women, over the years, eating their chopped hay, thinking he was so wonderful, so clever! He was my puppet, and he knew it. Oh, I know you didn't approve, but you liked the money, same as he did. But then that Covent Garden abbess comes along – oh, granted, she seemed all decency and modesty! But she was after him, nonetheless. I'd have done her, too, if I'd had the chance, but she didn't come ... I needed him more than she did.

Who would buy cures from someone like me? It was my skills and his sales, that's what kept us going against the rest.'

She fell silent a little, just stroking Peter's hair and face, while he snored steadily. She stared into the woods. Hippolyta wondered why Durris did not just jump up and seize her, but he was a man of seemingly infinite patience, solemnly watching.

'Then that greedy Jack Nickell,' the murmuring began again, 'thinking himself so clever: it didn't half turn my stomach when that anonymous letter arrived, seeing I had written the first ones! I thought I'd frighten him off his jade, thought the whiff of scandal would put him off, but no ... And Jack Nickell said he wanted some of his money back, that he'd seen me coming back into the ball room and he realised later I could have climbed out of the parlour window and come round the building. Too clever for his own good, he was: you'd have thought he was standing there watching me.' Was he? Hippolyta thought. Was that how Mrs. Nickell had known that the balm had been stuffed into Dr. Gilead's mouth? Jack had told her? 'But he also thought I would just hand over the money like a good little woman. Ha! No, I wasn't going to stand for that. And you couldn't have done me any good then, could you, my poor love? You were in jail, no use to me at all. So I had to do what had to be done. Same as I have to now ...'

She straightened the knife again, and seemed to brace herself, still cradling Peter's head against her heart. She laid it steadily against the grey flesh of his throat, and took a deep breath.

'Mrs. Gilead!'

Durris was somehow on his feet. He strode into the clearing, a hand out authoritatively for the knife. Mrs. Gilead half-spun on her knees, looking up in alarm at the intruder. She gave a great cry, and with a wild, determined flail of her arm, buried the knife to its hilt in her son's chest.

Chapter Twenty-Five

'All right, what's left?' Patrick asked, as they sat in the main parlour of the hotel once again. Hippolyta, who had successfully neither fainted nor been sick, was nevertheless hugging herself as close to the newly-lit fire as she could go, and seemed to find it hard to shut her eyes. The Fetteses were on the sofa again, Galatea held Hippolyta protectively, and Durris sat at the table, rubbing his face as if exhausted. They had explained as much as they could to Hippolyta's family: had to, really, as they had staggered back out of the woods almost on to their laps at the lower spring, white-faced and with the struggling, spitting figure of Mrs. Gilead on their hands.

'I've sent a couple of men into the woods to fetch – Mr. Snark,' said Durris.

'He's definitely dead,' Patrick confirmed. 'She's a surprisingly competent woman, for all she appears such a little mouse.'

'She ran the whole thing,' said Hippolyta with a shiver. 'She made the cures, ran the business, arranged the accommodation – and pretty much told Francis Snark, as he was, what to do, making full use of his charm and handsome looks to sell her products.'

'But she didn't think she could do it without him,' said Patrick.

'He was her product, too: she didn't want to lose him to someone else.'

Mrs. Fettes had been unusually quiet throughout their explanation, and had her hand looped around her husband's arm, gazing across the room at nothing in particular – or into her memories. The hotel keeper, Black, arrived with brandy and with Christy, who brought a tea tray. Her eyes were glowing with excitement.

'Is it true Mrs. Gilead's locked up in the bath house?' she asked.

'Christy!' Black was not pleased.

'She is, Christy: don't let her out,' said Durris. 'She's already killed three people.'

'There's another one dead?' Christy's eyes were like pewter plates.

'Peter Snark.'

'Oh. That's one I won't miss,' said Christy, and bobbed something like a curtsey before disappearing out of the parlour.

'I'm sorry, Mrs. Fettes. She's altogether too pert, that one,' said Black helplessly. 'Mr. Durris, are you going to want a room for Mr. Snark as well? Only, it's getting to be I near have more corpuses in this hotel than living guests.'

'I've sent word to the minister: we'll take him to the church,' said Durris.

'Thank you, Mr. Durris.'

'Only it might take a while: the boatman was not that keen to take Dr. Gilead's coffin across, and since he'll have to take Mr. Nickell, too … I might have to take Mr. Snark round some other way.'

'I'll help you find a cart,' said Black quickly. 'Is it true Mrs. Gilead climbed out the windae?'

'Apparently so.'

'My! I'd never have thought she was up to that!' said Black, almost admiring. 'But thank the Lord she's soon away. It'll be a long time before I'll have a doctor stay here again. Saving yourself, Dr. Napier, of course.'

'Thank you, Black,' said Patrick with a grin. The hotel keeper retreated, off to find a cart for Snark's body as quickly as he could.

'Poll –' said Mrs. Fettes, but winced as her husband dug her in the ribs. 'Hippolyta, I mean: we hope to go home to Edinburgh tomorrow. Father has his carriage at the inn: we don't need to wait for the coach.'

'I understand.'

'I have a great deal of work to catch up on, you know.'

'And I still want to see the children. And John,' said Galatea fervently.

'It's been a short stay for me this time, my dear,' said her father, 'but I hope you'll allow me to come and visit you again soon?'

'Of course, Papa! You are welcome any time.' And she almost included her mother and sister in the sentiment, too.

The following day they walked down to the inn around midday, determined that the travellers should get away before the coach and not be held up behind it on the road. Galatea's luggage was packed once again along with her parents' on to the pony cart at the front gate, and grinning at her father's wry look Hippolyta led the irritable pony down the street to the inn where the bridge had been, where the road to Aberdeen began.

'The roads are excellent from Banchory onwards,' Mr. Fettes reassured his wife, 'and there's only the crossing of the great Firths to delay us. And they are very scenic.'

'The boat is faster,' Galatea said for around the fifth time that morning.

'The time will pass quickly enough,' said Mr. Fettes reassuringly. 'You can entertain your mother and me with all your knowledge of medical concoctions.'

Galatea scowled at him, but she was grinning, too. Then she frowned again.

'Is that not your boy Wullie?'

Hippolyta kept a secure hand on the reins as she turned round. Wullie was following them, and Tam was following Wullie. Once again Hippolyta felt she had joined a travelling fair.

'Wullie, what are you doing out here? Has Mrs. Riach sent you out for something?'

'No, ma'am, I wanted to thank Mrs. Fettes for giving me my job, before she gangs hame.' He pulled himself straight and pushed his hair back from his face. 'Mrs. Fettes, ma'am, thank you for giving me my job.'

Mrs. Fettes looked at Hippolyta.

'Dr. and Mrs. Napier have given you your job, Wullie. But I'm glad you are enjoying it.'

'Oh aye, ma'am. And Al canna beat me up.'

'A distinct advantage. Now, run along back to the house, Wullie, before Mrs. Riach misses you. And Tam.'

Wullie bowed, and skipped off, Tam following importantly. Galatea shook her head.

'You really have no idea how to run a household, Poll, have you?'

'Hippolyta,' said Hippolyta.

'Hippolyta, then, but you really don't!'

'Then Mrs. Riach and I will have to work it out between us, to everyone's satisfaction.'

'I'm already quite satisfied,' said Patrick, 'if I have a say in the matter.'

'A say in the matter and a hen under your desk,' Hippolyta said, and squeezed his hand, as her family bundled themselves into the coach to prepare for the long drive to Edinburgh.

About the Author

Lexie Conyngham is a historian living in the shadow of the Highlands. Her Murray of Letho and Hippolyta Napier novels are born of a life amidst Scotland's old cities, ancient universities and hidden-away aristocratic estates, but she has written since the day she found out that people were allowed to do such a thing. Beyond teaching and research, her days are spent with wool, wild allotments and a wee bit of whisky.

Follow her professional procrastination at www.murrayofletho.blogspot.com, or email contact@kellascatpress.co.uk to join our minimalist mailing list. Lexie also has pages on Facebook, Pinterest and Goodreads.

The Hippolyta Napier series:
A Knife in Darkness
Death of a False Physician

The Murray of Letho series:

Death in a Scarlet Gown
Knowledge of Sins Past
Service of the Heir
An Abandoned Woman
Fellowship with Demons
The Tender Herb: A Murder in Mughal India
Death of an Officer's Lady
Out of a Dark Reflection
Slow Death by Quicksilver

Stand-alone books:
Windhorse Burning
The War, The Bones and Dr. Cowie
Thrawn Thoughts and Blithe Bits (short stories)